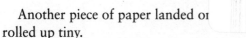

Another piece of paper landed on rolled up tiny.

This time, there was only a phone number.

Hunter felt like someone had punched him in the stomach and he couldn't remember how to breathe.

Then he pulled out his cell phone and typed under the desk.

Come here often?

Her response appeared almost immediately.

First timer.

Beamis was facing the classroom now, so Hunter kept his gaze up until it was safe. When he looked back, Kate had written again.

I bet I could strip naked and this guy wouldn't even notice.

Hunter's pulse jumped. But this was easier, looking at the phone instead of into her eyes.

I would notice.

There was a long pause, during which he wondered if he'd said the wrong thing. Then a new text appeared.

I have a theory about boys who picture you naked before sharing their name.

He smiled.

My name is Hunter.

Have you read all the Elemental books?

Elemental

Storm

Fearless

Spark

SPIRIT ✳ *The Elemental Series*

BRIGID KEMMERER

KENSINGTON PUBLISHING CORP.
www.kensingtonbooks.com

KTEEN BOOKS are published by

Kensington Publishing Corp.
119 West 40th Street
New York, NY 10018

ISBN-13: 978-0-7582-7283-6
ISBN-10: 0-7582-7283-9

First KTeen trade paperback printing: June 2013

10 9 8 7 6 5 4 3 2 1

Printed in the United States of America

First electronic edition: June 2013

ISBN-13: 978-0-7582-8916-2
ISBN-10: 0-7582-8916-2

For Bobbie—
You're my hero

ACKNOWLEDGMENTS

I always start with my mother, and this time is no exception: without my mom's encouragement, support, and constant guidance throughout my life, I would not be where I am today, and this book wouldn't be in your hands. Mom, you're a constant inspiration. Thank you for everything.

Mandy Hubbard is my amazingly talented agent and the only person to know about the unicorn I have chained under my desk. (Oh, crap. Now you all know, too. Shh, 'kay?) Mandy, thank you for everything. I'm so excited to be on this journey with you.

Alicia Condon is one badass editor, and it's very possible I do a little happy dance every time my phone lights up with an e-mail from her. Alicia and the rest of the team at Kensington have been nothing short of amazing, and I'm grateful for all of their hard work on my behalf. I would be remiss in not extending special gratitude to my fabulous publicist, Vida Engstrand, for all her help whenever I need it.

I wrote my acknowledgments for *Storm* and *Spark* before I knew how awesome the team at Allen & Unwin (my Australia/New Zealand publisher) would prove to be, so I need to say it three times here: thank you, thank you, *thank you*. Eva, Jodie, Lara, and the rest of the "Onions," you are beyond compare. Thank you for everything you've done to make the Elemental books a success.

Many, many people helped make *Spirit* come together. Bobbie Goettler and Alison Kemper Beard have been my faithful friends and critique partners since the very beginning, and without their help, this book wouldn't be what it is. Ladies, as always, you're amazing mothers, amazing writers, and amazing friends, and I wouldn't be here without you.

Readers! Book bloggers! Librarians! Teachers! You are all amazing. I have met so many amazing people since beginning this publication journey, and it would be impossible to name you all, but please know you have all touched me deeply. I love (and try to respond to) every e-mail/Twitter/Facebook/Goodreads/carrier pigeon/etc. message I receive. Thank you all for your support.

I do owe special thanks to a few amazing bloggers and friends, who took a chance on a debut author and independently put together an amazing blog tour last April: Sarah from Saz101, Brodie from Eleusinian Mysteries, Badass Bookie Lisa, Braiden from Book Probe Reviews, Kai from Amaterasu Reads, Lisa from Read Me Bookmark Me Love Me, Shirley from Shirley's Bookshelf, Celine from Forget-Me-Not, and Becca from Reading Wishes. (If I'm leaving someone out, please, please, please forgive me. You are no less amazing.) Thank you all for your efforts and enthusiasm. I cannot adequately express how much that meant to me.

A tremendous thank you to Wes Parker, who singlehandedly mans the Elementalists fan page on Facebook. Your Photoshop skills never cease to amaze me. You've believed in me since before my book hit shelves, and I hope I one day get to buy you a cup of coffee (or heck, a whole frigging dinner) so that I can meet you and say thank you.

Additionally, many people read an early draft of *Spirit* and offered their thoughts: Sarah Gonder, Wes Parker, Tom Berry, Nicole Kalinosky, and Sarah Fine, you guys are awesome and amazing. Please don't tell anyone what those original drafts looked like, okay?

Finally, to my Kemmerer boys, Jonathan, Nick, and Baby Sam: you remind me every day of how lucky I am. But extra-special thanks to my amazing husband, Michael: my best friend, my personal cheering section, the man I'm lucky I married. Thank you, honey, for everything.

CHAPTER 1

Hunter Garrity awoke to the click of a gun.

His grandparents kept a night-light in the utility room, but either it wasn't working or someone had killed it—his basement bedroom was pitch-black. His breathing was a shallow whisper in the darkness. For an instant, he wondered if he'd dreamed the sound.

Then steel touched his jaw.

He stopped breathing.

A voice: soft, female, vaguely mocking. "I think you dropped this."

He recognized her voice, and it wasn't a relief. His arms were partially trapped by the sheet and the comforter; he couldn't even consider disarming her from this angle.

"Calla," he murmured, keeping his voice low so as not to spook her. He had no idea how much experience she had with guns, and this didn't seem like the right time for trial and error.

"Hunter." The barrel pressed harder into the soft flesh under his chin.

He needed her to move, to shift her weight. Right now, she was just a voice and a weapon in the darkness.

He let out a long breath. "How did you get in here?"

"I drugged your dog and picked the lock."

It took great effort to keep still. He had a knife under his pillow, but going for it would take about three hours in comparison to the amount of time it would take her to pull the trigger. "You *drugged* my *dog*?"

"Benadryl in a New York strip." Her voice turned disdainful. "You don't even walk your dog on a leash."

He never walked Casper on a leash. His grandparents lived on an old farm. Like he should have considered that psycho teenage girls might be leaving tainted steaks for his dog to find. "If you hurt him, I'll kill you."

"You know," she said, ignoring him, "I thought about just burning this place down. Kerosene, match, whoosh."

"What stopped you?" He slid his hand beneath the blanket, just a few inches to see if she would notice.

She didn't. "Nothing. There's still time."

"I don't believe you," he said. "If you wanted to start a fire, you wouldn't be here right now."

"We want you to get a message to the other Guides."

"I don't *know* any other Guides," he hissed.

Well, he knew one, but Becca's father was just as far off the grid as Hunter was.

His hand slid another few inches, clearing the blanket.

"Come on, Hunter," she said sweetly. "Aren't you your father's son?"

Her voice had grown closer. She was leaning in. The gun moved a fraction of an inch.

All he needed was a fraction.

He swung for her wrist, going for deflection, ducking under the movement. His other hand was free, flinging the blankets at her while he slid to the ground. He threw a punch where her knee should be, but she was gone already, somewhere back in the darkness.

He tried to slow his breathing, his heart, trying to convince his body that he needed to *hear*.

"Nice try," she said.

He focused on the air in the room, asking the element to reveal her location more precisely, but it was never something he could force. He had to wait.

And the air wasn't talking.

At least the darkness was working to his advantage. If he couldn't see her, she sure couldn't see him.

He slid a hand under his pillow, and the knife found his fingers, the hilt a reassuring feel in his palm. He'd never cut anyone with it, but he knew how to throw.

Then he heard her breath—or maybe he felt it. Close, too close. He lifted a hand to throw.

Something hard cracked him across the side of the head—a board, a book, *something*. He went sprawling, and for a painful moment, he didn't even know if he was lying faceup. Now the room was full of light: stars danced in his field of vision.

She kicked him, rolling him onto his back. "Idiot," she said. "You think I'd come alone?"

Rolling sent the back of his head into the carpet. It hurt. A lot. His knife was gone.

"I should shoot you right now," she said. "But we *need* you."

"Go to hell." He could taste blood when he talked. He slid his hand against the carpet, looking for his knife, but a booted foot stomped down on his fingers.

God, how could they *see* him?

The gun went against his forehead. "A message," said Calla. "Are you listening?"

"Yeah," he ground out. He still had a free hand, but he had no idea whether her "helper" had an extra weapon.

"We're going to keep burning houses," she said. "Until the Guides come."

She was nuts. "They'll destroy you," he said.

"I don't think so," she said. "Tell them to come and see."

"You'll kill ordinary people—"

"No. Until they come, that's on *you*." She shifted the gun. "You like piercings, right?" The hard steel pressed into his bare shoulder. "How about a little bullet hole to convince you?"

Hunter whipped his free hand out to deflect again, this time rolling into the motion and trying to break her wrist.

She shrieked and dropped the gun.

He didn't let it distract him—he kept moving and drove his fist into the leg of whoever pinned his other hand.

This time, he connected. He heard a male grunt of pain. His other hand was free. Movement filled the darkness around him, and he knew they were getting ready to retaliate.

And then Hunter found the gun.

He didn't wait.

He pointed at motion, then pulled the trigger.

Kate Sullivan awoke to the click of a gun.

Irritated, she rolled over. She should have closed the door before going to bed. Silver was checking his weapons again. He did this several times a day.

She'd known him for seventy-two hours, and it was already making her nuts.

She glanced at the clock and called out. "You know it's not even five in the morning."

"I have the capacity to tell time, my dear."

She slid out of bed and went to the doorway. He had a British accent completely at odds with his olive complexion, slightly slanted blue eyes, and sun-streaked blond hair. She'd asked him about his heritage, and he'd told her he was poured straight from the melting pot.

Apparently that pot poured into one hell of a mold, because Silver was hotter than the day was long.

The name almost didn't fit him. His skin and hair were sun-kissed, as if he spent an insane amount of time outside. He'd be right at home on a beach, with a surfboard staked in the sand beside him. His hair was short, but just this side of too long to be called military style. She'd been tempted to call him Iceman, after the bad-boy hottie in *Top Gun*—eighties' movies were kind of her thing. But then she'd gotten a good look in his eyes, which were a cold blue that made her shiver.

She glanced through the opposite door bedroom he'd claimed—though *claimed* overstatement. They'd walked into the furn terday, and he'd said, "Sleep wherever." Ju were flat and perfect, almost military styl slept or he'd made the bed like he was in bo

"You should be sleeping," she said.

He clicked the magazine into a semi-auton ....ugun and slid it into a holster. "But we must play the proverbial early bird today."

She leaned her forehead against the doorjamb. "I don't want to go to high school."

"You are, in fact, a teenager. Isn't this some kind of rite of passage? Couldn't you find some time to *rah* with the cheer girls while killing rogue Elementals?"

"I think you've been watching too many shows on the CW."

He didn't answer, and she peeked through the spill of blond hair that fell across her cheek. He'd moved on to other weapons, knives this time. He slid each out of its sheath and checked the edge of the blade.

Kate sighed. He practically had an arsenal in the truck, more deadly toys than she would know what to do with. More guns, of course. Knives of varying length. An honest-to-god bow with a quiver of arrows.

She'd mocked him about those. "Oh, good! Are those for when we fight the elves?"

An arrow had just *appeared* in his hand, the point pressed into her throat hard enough to draw blood. "No, they're for when my trainee gets mouthy."

The accent, the danger, the weapon in his hand—it all combined to make him immeasurably sexy and terrifying at the same time. Kate had no idea how old he was, but he couldn't be *much* older. His features were smooth and unlined, his body lithe and muscled. She wouldn't put him past the age of an average college student, but he probably couldn't pass for high school.

s why *she* was here. To infiltrate the local high school, to rmine who the true Elementals were, and whether they were s powerful as rumor said.

Silver was here to kill them.

Kate hadn't expected an assignment at her age—she'd only been in training to be a Guide for about six months before the call came.

It was an honor to be picked, even if her ancillary role had been emphasized to the point of irritation. Silver was in charge of this mission. She was the apprentice. The student.

Her mother would be so proud.

Kate dropped into a chair at the table with him. A gun sat there, a Glock 9mm, and she ran a finger across the barrel.

He watched her but didn't say anything.

"Have you ever killed any of them?" she asked.

Silver nodded. "Of course." He didn't have to ask whom she meant. There was only one *them*. The pure Elementals. The ones with enough power to level cities.

Everyone on earth had some connection to an element—but only a select few were *pure* Elementals. Kate imagined it like a circle with a five-pointed star inside. Four points of the star represented each of the classical elements of Earth, Air, Fire, and Water. If everyone alive was put inside the circle, some would fall between branches and some would fall on a point.

The closer you fell to a point, the greater your affinity to that element.

If you fell directly on a point, you could harness that element's power and bend it to your will.

Kate was a pure Elemental, too, but she fell on the fifth point, which represented the Spirit. Once she fully grew into her abilities as a Fifth, she'd be able to control all four elements. Beyond that, her connection to the human spirit meant she had a greater connection to the people around her.

Years ago, the pure Elementals used to wreak havoc: mass destruction spanning centuries. The great Chicago fire. Earthquakes. Tsunamis. The Fifths, connected to human suffering by their very abilities, banded together to destroy pure Elementals and stop the destruction.

Now Fifths were selected to become Guides, and trained to kill pure Elementals before they could come into their full power.

Kate's connection to her element should have made it hard for her to kill anyone.

But when it came right down to pulling a trigger, it wasn't hard at all.

Her mother always used to say it was *for the greater good.* Kate wondered what she'd say about that now, after everything that had happened.

She watched Silver's fidgeting for another moment. "Do you expect them to be hard to kill?"

His eyes left the gun to flick up and meet hers. "Nervous?"

She matched his tone. "Of course not."

He smiled, but there wasn't anything amiable about it. "You have some familiarity with weapons, yes?"

Kate picked up the Glock and took it apart in four seconds. The bullets plinked out of the magazine onto the table. "A little."

"A bullet to the head is one of the few sure ways to kill them."

"I have some familiarity with killing, too."

"So I've heard." He ignored her attitude and started putting the stripped gun back together. "I've seen an Air Elemental take four shots to the chest and still come up fighting."

"An adult, right? I thought we were killing teenagers."

"We are." He paused. "And how does that make you feel, Kathryn?"

She looked up in surprise. "Fine. Why?"

"Honestly, when they told me you were my 'trainee,' I was surprised."

"Why?" she asked.

"Because I don't know what you're doing here."

It shouldn't have hurt—but it did, like getting a pinch in the arm from a vicious child. She'd earned her spot here. "I was assigned to help you."

"You seem eager."

"I've proven myself. I'm ready to *do* something." She needed to succeed here. If she couldn't, it meant her mother's death was for nothing.

His hands stilled on the firearm, and he looked over. "You must have done something already, to be assigned with *me*."

"Why, you think you're such a badass?"

"I don't need to think that, Kathryn."

"Stop calling me that. Only my mother called me Kathryn."

He looked back at the gun, checking the sight this time. "I heard a rumor about your mother."

"She was very good at what she did." Kate kept any thread of emotion out of her voice. "I'm better."

"I should hope so. Obviously your mother wasn't good *enough*."

Kate wanted to punch him, but it probably wouldn't end well. "I took care of it."

"I heard a rumor about that, too."

"What did you hear?"

"That your mother was assigned to destroy a Water Elemental but failed." He paused. "That you went after the Water Elemental yourself and succeeded."

"My mother made a mistake."

"A mistake the size of the Gulf of Mexico, I heard. Stupid, to go after one of them in the middle of the water."

Silver was baiting her. Kate knew it.

It was almost working.

"My mother knew what she was doing. She used to say, no matter how good you are, there's always someone better."

"And clearly she learned that lesson the hard way."

"I think it's time to stop talking about my mother."

He smiled. "Can you get close to these Merrick boys?"

"Yes."

"Without them knowing what you are?"

"*Yes*."

"And if they display the traits of a full Elemental, what will you do?"

She licked her lips. "Kill them."

His hands went still. "Wrong answer."

She flung herself back in her chair and rolled her eyes. "Report back to you."

"Good girl." He snapped the magazine into the gun and slid it across the table to her. "Now get dressed. We have work to do."

CHAPTER 2

The gun clicked empty, and Hunter swore.

A laugh in the darkness, somewhere ahead of him. "You thought I'd take a chance with it loaded?"

Then his bedroom door slammed and footsteps were pounding up the steps to the main level.

His mother was upstairs. His grandparents.

Kerosene. Match. Whoosh.

Hunter didn't have the power to stop a fire by himself—and he'd done a pretty good job killing any sort of friendship with the one guy he knew who *could*.

He flung the door wide and sprinted up the stairs.

And there was Casper, his German shepherd, flopped out in the front hall, snoring loudly.

Hunter couldn't really blame him. He'd been fooled by Calla once, too.

Glass was breaking in the kitchen, then something heavy crashed to the floor. Hunter darted through the foyer as more glass broke. What were they *doing*? Flinging dishes at the floor?

Yes, that's exactly what they were doing. Calla was sweeping her hand along the counter as she headed for the door, sending ceramic canisters and the glass cutting board onto the floor. A guy Hunter didn't recognize shoved the baker's rack away from the wall, sending pots crashing to the ground. The table was overturned already, and shattered glasses and plates littered the floor.

Hunter wasn't sure what to do. The gun was still downstairs— not like it mattered. It was empty, and besides, he couldn't exactly shoot them for breaking dishes.

At least she wasn't starting a fire.

Calla pulled a knife from the wooden block on the counter then flung the block at the floor. Half the steak knives skittered free and landed among the rest of the mess. She dragged the blade along the wallpaper by the door. "Need more convincing?"

God, his head hurt, and the whack to his skull downstairs was only part of it. "Get out of here, Calla."

"Or what? You can't do anything to me, Hunter. I'm not working alone, you know. I'm not the only one who can start fires."

Hunter glanced at her friend by the door. Dark hair, pale skin, a little on the skinny side. Close to their age, if not a little younger. Totally not familiar, but Hunter had only been in school here for a few weeks, so that didn't mean anything.

The guy noticed Hunter's scrutiny and grinned, though it looked a little crazed. He flipped hair out of his eyes. "Maybe we should start a little one, let you know we're serious." Then he shoved the microwave off the counter. It hung from its cord for a long moment, then jerked free and crashed to the floor.

Hunter heard a muffled curse from upstairs, then the floorboards creaked.

His grandfather.

Hunter felt pretty sure an adult wouldn't help this situation.

He so didn't want to deal with this. He sighed and picked up the cordless phone from the holder on the wall.

"Who you calling?" said Calla. "You think the Merricks can help you?"

The Merricks were probably the last people who would offer to help him, but Calla didn't need to know that. "No," Hunter said. "I'm doing what you're supposed to do when people break into your house." When she raised her eyebrows, he added, "I'm calling nine-one-one."

Her smile wilted around the edges. "Liar."

He spoke into the phone. "I'd like to report a break-in at one-eleven North Shore Road—"

"Calla!" said the guy by the door.

"Hang up that phone!" she hissed.

"They're still here," Hunter said into the receiver. "They're armed."

Calla dropped the knife. "I'll kill you, Hunter," she seethed. "You know I can—"

"Please hurry," said Hunter. "They're threatening to kill me."

A siren started wailing somewhere in the distance. The dark-haired guy grabbed Calla's wrist and yanked. They bolted through the door.

Hunter set the phone back on the receiver. He'd never dialed at all.

That siren had been sheer luck.

What a mess. Hunter ran his hands through his hair. The length of it still shocked him every time. He hadn't cut it in months.

The floorboards in the hallway creaked, and Hunter swore under his breath. He had no idea how to explain this. If he said someone had broken in, his grandfather really *would* call the cops.

After he'd been arrested for his involvement in the fire in the school library last week—a fire *Calla* had started—Hunter didn't need any more interaction with cops.

Thank god the gun was still downstairs.

His grandfather stopped short when he saw the mess. It was too dark to make out his expression—not that Hunter wanted to try. The man was tall but lean and muscled from years of farm labor, with short gray hair and a permanent look of displeasure. He hit the switch on the wall, and the light made things look a hundred times worse. His eyes narrowed at his grandson. "You'd better have a good explanation."

Like Hunter had woken up in the middle of the night and started trashing the kitchen.

But really, this was exactly how every conversation with his grandfather went.

"I didn't do this," he said. His father had never had much tolerance for attitude, so Hunter was well practiced in keeping it out of his tone. It had just never been this much of a challenge with his dad.

"Who did?"

"Kids from school. A prank." He paused. "I'll clean it up."

"And you'll pay for it."

Hunter set his jaw, but didn't say anything.

When he and his mother had first pulled up the driveway six weeks ago, his grandfather had watched Hunter climb out of the car, then said, "We're not going to have any of your nonsense *here*, you understand me, boy?"

Hunter had turned to his mother, looking for . . . something. Direction, maybe. A cue for how to respond.

But his mother had already been crying on his grandmother's shoulder. If she'd heard the comment, she didn't acknowledge it. And then she'd allowed herself to be hustled into the house, to be comforted over tea.

While Hunter had been left to unload the car under his grandfather's glaring eyes.

He'd learned pretty quickly to make himself scarce.

Even now, he probably had about three minutes before he'd hear a lecture about his piercings, about how he needed a haircut, about how if he was his *grandfather's* son, he'd clean up his act or he'd be sleeping on the porch.

At first, Hunter had tried being perfect. He'd done chores without being asked. Taking out the trash, mowing the lawn, doing all his own laundry. He'd fixed the two loose boards on the porch, then repaired a shutter that was hanging crooked on the front of the house—things his father would have expected him to do. No backtalk, just respect for his elders.

His mom was no help. She was so lost in her own sorrow that even *talking* to her about his grandfather seemed petty and insignificant.

So he'd tried to get along. He'd tried hard.

"It's drugs, isn't it?" said his grandfather.

Hunter sighed and carefully stepped around broken glass to right the baker's rack. "No. I don't do drugs." He barely ate processed food, and this guy thought he'd put *drugs* in his body?

Sometimes this whole arrangement just felt like a big cosmic joke. Where was the grandfather who'd take him fishing and put an arm around his shoulders and ask if he was sweet on anyone at school? Why did he get saddled with the guy who didn't seem to give a shit that Hunter had lost the two people he felt closest to, less than six months ago? That he was starting at a new high school in his junior year? That he'd spent his life training for something he'd never get to do, because his father's and uncle's deaths had left him with no path to follow?

Hunter began stacking pots on the shelves of the baker's rack. For an instant, he envied Calla.

He wished he could throw a few things himself. But he was a Fifth—his father had drilled endless lessons of self-control into Hunter's head. He'd been trained well, and he wouldn't let that training fail him now. Not over this.

His grandfather was still standing there, watching him.

Hunter wanted to punch him. Instead, he gently eased the Crock-Pot back onto the lowest shelf.

"Let me know how much everything costs," he said. "I'll figure out a way to pay you back." He wasn't entirely sure how. He didn't have a job here, and while he had some money in an envelope in his dresser, it was slowly creeping toward zero each time he had to fill his jeep with gas.

Definitely not enough to replace everything that was lying in a shattered mess on the floor.

Maybe in between trying to stop a psychotic pyromaniac, he could find a job flipping burgers at McDonald's.

It would be hilarious if it weren't so sad.

Sometimes he wished he could just tell his grandfather about what he was, what he could do. How his military training would put Navy SEALs to shame. How he could sense the electricity in the walls, or the humidity in the air, or the anger in his grandfather's head.

Then again, that talk would probably lend credence to this new drug theory.

"I'm done with this attitude, boy."

Hunter looked up. "I'm not giving you any attitude. I said I would pay for everything."

"It's no wonder your mother can't get it together, with all the trouble you give her."

Hunter stiffened, but he didn't say anything. He had no idea why his mother couldn't get it together. He didn't *think* it had anything to do with him, but maybe it did. The last time he'd gone up to her bedroom, her eyes had filled with tears. She'd put a hand against his cheek and said, "I wish you'd cut your hair again, Hunter. You used to look just like your father."

He'd pushed her hand away. *What are you so sad for?* he'd wanted to ask. *Dad was just using you.*

His grandmother was no help, either. She didn't rag on him like his grandfather did, but she'd watch him with pursed lips, and he could feel disapproval radiate through the room until he wanted to grab her by the shoulders and rattle her body and shout in her face.

"What?" he'd yell in this imaginary scenario. "Not *good enough* for you?"

And then he'd shake her so hard that her dentures would fall out, and she wouldn't be able to make that expression with her mouth anymore.

Hunter almost smiled, but he only let himself enjoy it for half a second.

His grandmother didn't even *wear* dentures.

A hand closed on Hunter's arm, hauling him to his feet. "You think this is funny?" his grandfather demanded, his voice rising in pitch as well as volume. "Your friends destroy hundreds of dollars' worth of our property, and you think this is *funny?*"

It took every ounce of self-control not to jerk free and drop his grandfather on his ass.

But Hunter met the man's eyes. "Let me go."

His grandfather's grip tightened, his thumb pressing into the muscle behind Hunter's elbow. It hurt, but Hunter wouldn't let it show.

He knew some of this was his ability. His talents drew people to him—and that usually meant pulling their attention in whatever way they were wired to give it. Sometimes it was nice—like with Becca, his almost-could've-been girlfriend.

Sometimes it was not.

Like now.

"I should have left you in jail last Monday," his grandfather said. "Let the justice system scare some sense into you."

Like his grandfather had done anything more than pick him up at the police station. The cops hadn't even pressed charges. No evidence—because he hadn't started that fire. "Let me go."

"You're going to straighten up, or you're going to be sleeping on the porch. You understand me?"

Hunter wouldn't even consider that a punishment. He loved being outside.

Then again, it was getting into the thirties some nights, and all his camping gear was still in storage from the move.

"I understand," he said. God, his head hurt. "Let me go."

His grandfather let him go, adding a little shove. "Get this cleaned up before school. And I expect you back here right after, too."

"Yes, sir," said Hunter.

"And cut the sarcasm."

Fuck you.

But Hunter didn't say it. He wouldn't give his grandfather the satisfaction.

Instead, he held on to his temper and cleaned up the mess on the floor.

If only the mess in his life would be so easy.

CHAPTER 3

School had been closed for a week, but that didn't mean Hunter felt any eagerness about returning. He sat in his jeep in the parking lot and watched students stream through the doors.

He didn't want to go inside.

He shared American Lit with Calla. How was he supposed to sit there in class with her and pretend nothing was going on?

Calla had been using Ryan Stacey to start fires in an effort to bring the Guides to town. She'd been drawing pentagrams in lighter fluid inside each of the houses they burned—a mocking call to the Guides, who painted pentagrams on houses where they suspected pure Elementals lived.

Now Ryan Stacey was in jail, and Calla had renewed her threat. She and that mystery boy would start burning down houses until he brought Guides here. How the hell was he supposed to do that?

And even if he could, was that any better? Luring people into a death trap?

He pulled out his cell phone, scrolling through his contacts until he found *Bill Chandler*.

They hadn't spoken in days, but Becca's father answered almost immediately. No preamble, just: "Hunter?"

"Calla Dean broke into my house this morning."

"What did she want?"

Hunter couldn't get a read off his voice. No curiosity, no anger, no boredom or exasperation. Hunter never had any idea where he stood with Becca's father—which was reassuring in a way because he'd never had any idea where he stood with his own, either.

"She wants me to bring the Guides here."

A pause. "This isn't news."

"She said she's going to keep burning down houses until they come."

"If these arson attacks continue, she'll bring the Guides here on her own, eventually. She doesn't need you."

That wasn't the answer Hunter was looking for. "Do you have any idea who she could be working with?"

"No, and I don't care."

Hunter blinked. "You don't . . . care?"

"No. The Guides will come and eradicate the problem. If I get involved, it puts Becca at risk."

"Calla will kill people. She's not making little fires. She—"

"She's alive because you missed an opportunity, Hunter."

Shock trapped the words right in Hunter's throat, lodging there until he could barely breathe around it.

"I told you to make sure Gabriel Merrick didn't cause trouble. Instead, you helped him find it. *You shouldn't be involved.*"

Hunter gritted his teeth. Yeah, Bill had asked him to keep an eye on Gabriel Merrick, a Fire Elemental with a temper to match. But Gabriel had been using his abilities to rescue people from the mysterious fires popping up all over town.

Hunter had helped him.

But when Ryan Stacey had set the library on fire, Calla had revealed herself to be the Elemental behind the arson attacks.

She'd also taunted him, claiming to be responsible for his father's death. Hunter had drawn his gun.

And then he'd been unable to pull the trigger.

Hunter squeezed his eyes shut. "People would have died—"

"They didn't. You saved them. But you allowed Calla Dean

to get away, and now she has leverage." He paused, a weighted silence full of judgment. "You made your bed, kid. Now you lie in it."

The phone clicked off.

The shock settled into something like fury—at himself. Twice before, he'd had the opportunity to fix a problem, and he'd hesitated before employing lethal force.

And then he'd stood in the library, surrounded by fire, listening as Calla recounted her crimes.

All that training, and he couldn't pull a trigger.

Now he'd have to confront her. Here, at school, where she couldn't cause a scene.

The school hallways were crowded: the main corridors that led past the library were blocked with yellow caution tape, forcing people to go through the basement locker areas just to cross from one side of the school to the other. Hunter was bumped at least three times while he was trying to get his books together for morning classes.

Then a hand came out of nowhere and shoved the books straight out of his arms, sending them skidding across the tiled floor. "Welcome back, jackass."

Gabriel Merrick.

The gesture had been casual. The venom in his voice had not.

Hunter stared after him, wondering if he should retaliate—or if he should swallow his pride and take it.

Because he kind of deserved it.

"Hey," he called.

Gabriel flipped him off and disappeared around the corner.

Hunter figured he was lucky Gabriel hadn't set his books on fire.

In homeroom, he ignored the morning announcements and tried to think of a plan. He shared fourth period with Chris and Becca. Maybe he could start there. If they knew what Calla was up to, they'd want to help.

Or they'd tell him to screw off.

He needed a backup plan. He couldn't stop Calla by himself.

Someone cleared her throat, and Hunter blinked, realizing that the room had gone silent. Everyone in class was staring at him, including the elderly teacher who only monitored homeroom and study hall.

He'd missed something important.

"Hunter?" Mrs. Goodchild said. "Did you hear the intercom, dear? You're wanted in the guidance office."

Hunter sighed and grabbed his things. This would be the third time he'd been called to the office since school started. It seemed like every week they needed a new form signed by his mother. Maybe they needed another backup-backup emergency form filled out in triplicate. The headache from this morning was back, like a ball-peen hammer at the back of his eyeballs.

The main office was crowded: kids clamoring for late slips, a guy on crutches with medical forms in one hand, two men in suits who looked like salesmen but were probably college recruiters, and the hottest girl Hunter had ever seen.

For half a second, he could barely think to put one foot in front of the other.

She was standing by the main secretary's desk, a messenger bag slung over one shoulder. Her hair was thick and blond and chin length, and a few strands fell across her face, framing green eyes. Striking eyes, full of intelligence instead of boredom. Her lips were pink and full and almost pouting. Her clothes were fitted and current and expensive-looking: a short brown leather jacket that flared from her waist, jeans that clung to the slight curve of her hips, and knee-high boots with just enough buckles and zippers to be intriguing.

But it wasn't just her looks that held him spellbound. It was the energy in the air around her, as if the light and the air flared with tiny sparks.

Her eyes flicked sideways and she caught him looking.

Now his pulse tripped, but at least she couldn't see that. He needed to shut this down. Girls were a complication he didn't need right now. He shifted his bag higher on his shoulder and didn't flinch from her look.

Her eyes narrowed and she tossed the hair off her face. Her

lips parted, as if she were about to speak—but the secretary hung up the phone and held out a packet of papers to the girl. "Miss Sullivan, here's your locker combination and some emergency forms for your parents to fill out. First period is about to start, so . . ."

She was a new student. Maybe fate was repaying him for that crap with Calla this morning. Maybe he'd been called down here to escort her around school. Maybe—

"Alice?" A voice called from the guidance counselor's office. "When Hunter Garrity gets here, can you please send him in?"

Damn it.

He sighed and headed toward Ms. Vickers's door.

As he moved past the new girl, he caught her scent, something sweet with a spicy kick to it, cinnamon over apples.

She was still watching him. "Like what you see?"

She said it boldly, but not cattily. Like a genuine question—without any doubt of the answer.

It embarrassed him anyway. He shouldn't have been staring.

He opened his mouth to answer, not even knowing what to say. An apology? Something cocky, like *Yeah, I do?*

But one of the guys in the late line said, "I like what I see, baby!" And the guy next to him gave him a high five and said, "Why don't you show us a little more—"

"Leave her alone," Hunter snapped. He took a step toward them, and they mocked him, pretending to be afraid.

"Boys!" said the secretary.

The girl rolled her eyes, shoved the papers in her messenger bag, and turned for the door.

So that was that.

Like it mattered. He turned back for Vickers's office. The door was half open, and he pushed it wide, wondering why on earth he'd been called down here.

And then he saw the student in the chair, the girl with a tear-streaked face who was cradling her wrist, and his heart just about stopped.

Calla Dean.

* * *

Kate stood in the empty hallway and checked her phone. Already, a message from Silver.

Honestly. She'd been here fifteen minutes.

Surveillance only. Do not engage.

As if he hadn't told her that enough times this morning. Like she was stupid enough to engage with a bunch of rogue Elementals right here in the middle of school. The caution tape lining some of the hallways was proof enough of their propensity for destruction.

What did Silver think she was going to do? Start a fight in the cafeteria?

Her phone buzzed, the silent feature loud in the empty hallway.

Meet anyone interesting yet?

She snorted at the phone. The secretary had been interesting because she'd misspelled Kate's name twice—and how hard was it to spell Kate Sullivan? The boys in the office had been interesting because they lived up to every promise about high school, leering at her like she was a pinup poster instead of a real live girl.

Except that boy with the piercings and the white streak in his hair.

He'd been interesting because of the way the air hung quiet around him, as if he walked in a sphere of his own control.

The phone buzzed again.

Status?

God! She was tempted to take a picture of her middle finger and send it back. Her fingers flew across the screen.

Heading to first period. Maybe you can do something more useful than texting me.

As soon as she pressed SEND, she regretted it. Silver stood between her and more missions like this. She started to type a new message that would take the sarcasm out of the first, when one of the classroom doors flew open.

A middle-aged teacher in a tweed sport coat and wire-rimmed glasses stood there. Students in his classroom, seated by twos at lab tables, peered out curiously.

The teacher didn't look so curious. He gave her a knowing look. "Don't you have somewhere to be, Miss?"

Kate slid the phone into her bag and flipped blond hair out of her eyes. She could charm anyone. She had a bedroom answer ready, but the way this guy was looking at her told her it wouldn't be appreciated. She slapped a distressed look on her face and yanked at one of the sheets the secretary had given her.

"It's my first day," she said, making her voice plaintive. "The secretary said she'd have someone escort me to my first class, but then she got busy . . ."

The teacher nodded and snapped his fingers at a student in the front row of the classroom. "Nick. Show her where she needs to go, and come right back."

Kate slid the map back into her bag and laced her words with sugar, touching the teacher on the arm. "Thank you so much. I've been so lost."

He hmphed and stepped back into the room, ignoring her.

Wow. So much for charm.

"Hey. I'm Nick. Where do you need to go?"

She blinked up at the boy who'd appeared in the doorway—and almost dropped her bag.

Not just because he was a looker—though that was part of it. Dark hair, blue eyes, a few freckles across his cheekbones. Taller than she'd expected.

Because she'd seen his picture before. It was in a file on her phone, right now, in fact. She almost wanted to yank it out of her bag to double-check. Nick. Nick Merrick.

Kate locked down any trace of her abilities, though it was a challenge. She wanted to touch him, to see if she could sense his power right here in the hallway.

He sure didn't look like part of a band of marauding killers.

She'd expected to hate him on sight. She knew what these full Elementals could do—those lessons had been drilled into her head since day one. Hell, she had firsthand evidence: her mother had lost her life trying to destroy one of them.

Right in front of Kate.

But this guy standing in front of her seemed so . . . *normal* that she was having a hard time dredging up a powerful emotion like hate. He had an easy, engaging smile that made her want to smile back.

But she'd seen the news footage of the recent tornado damage in town. She'd seen photos of the bridge that had been destroyed in an earthquake and the resulting flood.

She'd seen newspaper articles showing the victims of the recent arson attacks—all caused by these Elementals.

She had to stop staring at this guy. She dug through her bag for the blue sheet of paper that had her class schedule.

The teacher cleared his throat. "Is there a problem?"

Kate shook herself. She was better than this. "No. Sorry." She found the paper and yanked it free triumphantly.

Nick pulled the classroom door shut and took a glance. "This is on the other side of the school. We have to go under the library. I'll show you."

She should thank him. Flirt. Try to get close.

She just couldn't get past the fact that she'd pretty much walked in here and he'd fallen into her lap.

Kate just nodded and walked alongside him. Her nerves were screaming at her.

This boy is a killer! Do something!

Don't engage don't engage don't engage.

"I didn't get your name," Nick said.

"Kate." Finally, her brain decided to work. "Is that guy always such a tool?"

Nick shrugged. "Dr. Cutter? Nah, he's all right. Anytime someone interrupts a lecture on inclined planes, he gets all flustered." He caught the door at the top of the stairwell and held it for her.

Holding the door! A gentleman, too!

"Where are you from?" he said.

"Here," she said. "I just transferred from St. Mary's in Annapolis." A complete lie, but Silver had told her that someone from out of town might arouse suspicion—and they couldn't afford suspicion right now. She'd spent hours in the truck learning landmarks and popular hangouts just so she could pass for a local.

She could almost feel Nick's power in the air around them, and it took everything she had not to let her guard down.

"Sucks to move in the middle of high school," he said.

"Not for me. I couldn't stand those stuffy old nuns."

He smiled and glanced at her schedule again. "My brother's a junior, too. Chris."

God, her brain wasn't working. She almost said *I know.* "Nice," she choked.

"I think he has fourth-period History. If you're still lost by then, he'd help you out."

"Thanks," she said. "I'll look for him."

Chris Merrick. Fourth period. Check.

Seriously, this was like shooting fish in a barrel. Silver was going to be *stoked.*

Nick looked over. "Juniors and seniors have lunch at the same time, so if you need somewhere to sit, feel free to look for me. I could introduce you around."

And then Nick went and said something like *that.*

It threw her off balance for a minute.

Then Nick gave her a slightly wicked smile. "Though I don't think you'll have any trouble making friends."

Aha! So there was a little tarnish on his gentlemanly armor. It helped her dial back the bit of conscience niggling at her. She shook hair out of her eyes and looked up at him. "I never do." She paused. "But I think I'll take you up on lunch. If you don't mind."

"I wouldn't have offered if I did." He gave her a breathtaking smile. Nice *and* handsome.

She almost hated to kill him.

Almost.

CHAPTER 4

Calla was sitting in the cushioned chair in the guidance office, sniffling, cradling her arm. She wouldn't look at Hunter.

He glared at her and tried to hang on to his temper as the guidance counselor droned on.

"I asked you a question, Hunter," said Ms. Vickers. "Did you leave those bruises on Calla's wrist?"

Right this second, he wanted to leave a lot more than bruises. Calla had pretty much just guaranteed he'd have to leave her alone—in school and out. He gritted his teeth and lied right through them. "No."

Calla sniffed again. "Ms. Vickers, I really don't feel comfortable being in the room with him."

"Hunter, we had a talk on your first day here. I said that we wouldn't be tolerant of any physical altercations with other students. Do you remember this conversation?"

"Yeah," he said, his voice tight.

"And while I understand that the police found you unarmed during last week's fire, I do not like the rumors that you have access to a gun."

"He does," Calla whispered with a catch in her voice. "He showed it to me. When we were fighting, he said if I didn't go out with him, he'd—"

"Cut the act," he snapped.

Calla flinched. She deserved an Academy Award.

Hunter kept his voice even. "I have *never* threatened you."

She looked up. There were tears in her eyes. "I liked you, Hunter. I really did. But—"

"Stop it." He wanted to list everything she'd done. The fires, the break-in, her mission to kill people. But he'd sound like a raving lunatic.

When *she* was the one who was nuts.

Ms. Vickers rocked back in her chair. She had to be in her forties, with that many gray streaks in her brown hair. Her eyes were tired over sagging cheeks, but she still had a steely gaze. "I've asked Calla to come see me every morning," she said. "I'm going to ask you to give her some space, Hunter."

"Gladly."

"We take harassment very seriously."

"Fine. Whatever. I won't harass her. I won't even talk to her. Can I go?"

"No. I'd like Calla to go. I think you and I should talk for a few minutes."

Calla sniffed a final time and picked up her backpack, grabbing a few tissues from the box on Ms. Vickers's desk.

Hunter couldn't look at her when she edged past him. The door closed behind her with a soft click.

He didn't want to look at Vickers, either.

"Do you want to tell me your side of the story?" she asked.

"There is no story."

Vickers didn't say anything.

Hunter could feel her waiting, and he finally looked up. "There's no story," he emphasized. "I will completely avoid her."

"You sound like you feel you're being victimized."

Victimized. There was no safe answer to that, so Hunter just looked away again.

"How would your mother feel," said Vickers, "if she knew why I called you down here today?"

He snorted. "She'd say, 'Hunter who?'"

Ms. Vickers seemed to freeze, and he realized it was the wrong thing to say.

"Should we talk about your mother?" she said quietly.

This was just great. "What, you think I'm not getting attention at home, so I'm roughing up girls?"

"Are you?" said Vickers.

"No. God. *No.*" Hunter leaned forward and put his hand on the edge of the desk. "I don't want to have this conversation." He grabbed his bag and stood to leave.

"Hunter," she called after him.

He paused in the doorway.

"I want you to steer clear of Calla Dean, do you understand me?"

"Yes." He grabbed the doorknob.

"No contact."

"Got it."

"And I'd like to have a conversation in a few days to see how things are going."

He rolled his eyes. "Can't wait."

As he stepped out of the main office, he considered that there'd once been a time when he wouldn't even have *thought of* walking out on a teacher—much less acting like that in her presence. Then again, there'd once been a time when he'd had expectations to live up to.

He wondered if Becca would talk to him. He'd sent her a text during the week school had been closed, and he'd been surprised to get an immediate response.

Then he'd read it: *No offense, but no one trusts you, Hunter.*

But here, at school, she might be more receptive. Especially if he told her what Calla had said.

In fourth-period World History, Becca was sitting with Chris, as usual, her dark hair hanging down over one shoulder. She looked up as soon as Hunter walked into the room, and the intensity in her gray eyes almost pinned him against the doorjamb.

When he'd first moved here, he'd sensed that Becca was a Fifth, like he was, but he'd known right away that she wasn't a Guide. Becca was too trusting. Too kind. He'd liked her right away—but he'd come here to finish his father's task of destroying the Merricks, and she was an easy link through her friendship with Chris. So Hunter had used her.

And he'd lost any chance he'd had with her.

She stared at him for a long moment, then turned her head to whisper something to Chris.

Hunter felt a flicker of . . . something. Not quite regret—and not quite longing, either. He begged the air to carry her words to him, but it refused.

Maddening, especially when Chris laughed under his breath and gave Hunter a *look*.

Hunter wanted to stride across the room and hit Chris Merrick in the face. He pictured it happening, aiming his punch *through* his target like his father had taught him, imagining the way bones would give way under his hand.

"Excuse me."

He was blocking the door. Hunter shifted to the side to let the girl pass. He forced his hand to unclench.

Then he caught the aroma of cinnamon and apples, the sheen of light on blond hair. The new girl from this morning was frowning at a blue paper. "Is this World History?"

"Yes." He racked his brain for something intelligent to say, but then her eyes lifted from the paper and stole every coherent thought from his head.

Like what you see?

Inexplicably, he wanted to touch her, to feel her heartbeat under his fingertips, to catch some of that scent on his palm.

Now he was glad he couldn't speak. He'd probably sound like a psycho.

She shifted the bag higher on her shoulder. "You're big on staring, huh?"

He jerked his eyes away, feeling heat course up his neck. "Sorry."

"Don't apologize. Just don't blame me for staring back."

He swung his gaze back. Again, he had no idea whether she was flirting. Her tone was so . . . *direct*.

"I have a theory about piercings," she said.

"I'd like to hear it." He could be direct back.

Mr. Beamis, the ancient History teacher, cleared his throat behind them. "Perhaps we could all take our seats?"

The girl didn't move, so Hunter didn't, either.

Three empty seats were available in the classroom. One immediately to their left, the desk almost touching the teacher's. One at the back, directly behind Becca. And one in the third row, two seats over from Hunter.

"Where do you sit?" the girl said.

He nodded toward his seat in the third row. The desks were arranged two-by-two, and he'd been paired with Monica Lawrence for the semester project.

Monica appeared to be examining her hair for split ends.

And a few rows past that, Becca was watching his interaction with the new girl a little too carefully.

Mr. Beamis cleared his throat again, a bit more emphatically. "Sometime today, if you don't mind."

The girl turned and surveyed the room as if the teacher's impatience didn't matter one bit. Then, without another glance at Hunter, she slipped between the desks and dropped into the chair two rows over.

He made his way into his own seat and refused to look her way.

Beamis turned toward the board and immediately started droning. Hunter could totally sleep through this class—he'd taken World History last year, at his old school, and even though he'd told them that at registration, they'd still dumped him in here. Monica wasn't the type to care whether he paid attention or not, so he usually used this class to catch up on homework from his other teachers.

Today, he was keenly aware of the new girl sitting a few rows over.

He should be plotting a way to stop Calla. He should be figuring the best angle to approach the Merricks to get their help.

He just couldn't think past cinnamon and apples and blond hair.

Then he slammed a door on those thoughts. He'd been burned twice now—once by Clare, a girl who'd been using him for his father's weapons. And once by Calla, a girl who was using him for his father's connections.

Before their final trip, Hunter's father had imparted one last lesson, and death had made it stick: *Use them before they use you.*

He pulled out his essay for Honors French and pretended the new girl didn't exist.

A folded triangle of paper landed in the center of his notebook.

Normally he'd unfold it discreetly, but Beamis was so clueless that the note could have hit *him* in the head and he wouldn't notice.

Loopy script in purple pen. The paper smelled like her.

What's your #?

Wow.
Hunter clicked his pen and wrote below her words.

I have a theory about girls who ask for your number before asking for your name.

Then he folded it up and flicked it back.
It took every ounce of self-control to not watch her unfold it.
The paper landed back on his desk in record time.

I have a theory about boys who prefer writing to texting.

He put his pen against the paper.

I have a theory about girls with theories.

Then he waited, not looking, fighting the small smile that wanted to play on his lips.
The paper didn't reappear.
After a minute, he sighed and went back to his French essay.

When the folded triangle smacked him in the temple, he jumped a mile. His chair scraped the floor, and Beamis paused in his lecture, turning from the board. "Is there a problem?"

"No." Hunter coughed, covering the note with his hand. "Sorry."

When the coast was clear, he unfolded the triangle.

It was a new piece of paper.

My name is Kate.

Kate. Hunter almost said the name out loud.

What was *wrong* with him?

It fit her perfectly, though. Short and blunt and somehow indescribably hot.

Another piece of paper landed on his notebook, a small strip rolled up tiny.

This time, there was only a phone number.

Hunter felt like someone had punched him in the stomach and he couldn't remember how to breathe.

Then he pulled out his cell phone and typed under the desk.

Come here often?

Her response appeared almost immediately.

First timer.

Beamis was facing the classroom now, so Hunter kept his gaze up until it was safe. When he looked back, Kate had written again.

I bet I could strip naked and this guy wouldn't even notice.

Hunter's pulse jumped. But this was easier, looking at the phone instead of into her eyes.

I would notice.

There was a long pause, during which he wondered if he'd said the wrong thing. Then a new text appeared.

I have a theory about boys who picture you naked before sharing their name.

He smiled.

My name is Hunter. Where you from?

This time, her response appeared immediately.

Just transferred from St. Mary's in Annapolis.

Now he was imagining her in a little plaid skirt and knee-high socks.
Another text appeared.

Stop imagining me in the outfit.

He grinned.

How did you know?
You're a boy.
I'm still waiting to hear your theory on piercings.
Right. IMO, you have to be crazy hot to pull off either piercings or tattoos. Otherwise you're just enhancing the ugly.

Hunter stared at the phone, wondering if she was hitting on him—or insulting him. Before he could figure it out, another message appeared.

What does the tattoo on your arm say?

He slid his fingers across the keys.

It says "ask me about this tattoo."

Liar.

Mission accomplished, I'd say.

He heard a small sound from her direction and peeked over. She was still staring at her phone, but she had a smile on her face, like she was trying to stifle a giggle.

Mission accomplished, he'd say.

CHAPTER 5

A million and one worries should have been clouding Hunter's brain.

Instead, he spent all of fourth period texting with Kate.

And most of fifth period, too.

After World History, he'd been ready to finish their conversation live—but she slipped out the door without even looking at him. He'd stood in the hallway and watched her cut through the crowds of students, somewhat dumbfounded. Had he misread all those text messages? Maybe she hadn't been flirting at all. Had she just been killing time?

Then his phone had buzzed in his hand.

Again with the staring?

He'd never met a girl who could send his heart tripping with a few words on a screen.

Now he was headed for the cafeteria with a shadow of a smile on his lips—and a shadow of doubt coiled in his chest. He'd sent her a text:

Want to stare at each other over a table at lunch?

But she hadn't responded.

Maybe it was better if she didn't want to sit with him. He could confront Becca or the Merricks and get them to carry some of the weight of Calla's threats.

He checked his phone while he waited to grab a tray for the line.

Blank.

Hunter sighed and slid it into his pocket, taking an apple, a plate of grilled chicken and greens, and a bowl of vegetable soup. He didn't have to wait for any of it—there was never a line for this stuff. But over by the tater tots, you'd think they were giving food away.

When he turned away from the register, Calla was suddenly there, in front of him. She had a soda in one hand and a wicked look in her eye.

He scowled and moved to step past her.

But she ran her shoulder into his and shrieked, stumbling back and dropping her soda. "Don't *threaten me,* Hunter!"

One of the assistant football coaches was on cafeteria duty and headed their way. "What's going on?"

Hunter gritted his teeth and backed away from her. "Nothing."

"He shoved me!"

"I didn't *touch* her!"

The coach put a restraining hand on Hunter's shoulder—even though he hadn't moved an inch. "Just keep walking. Cool off."

Calla dissolved into tears. People were staring. Another girl from the volleyball team came up and pulled Calla away, whispering reassurances while throwing a murderous glance at Hunter.

It had taken Calla less than three seconds to completely derail his day. Again.

Hunter sighed through clenched teeth and turned to head for the back of the cafeteria.

Only to meet Kate's eyes from twenty feet away.

One look at her expression said she'd seen the whole thing.

Well, definitely not the *whole* thing. Just enough to leave her staring with judgment on her face.

There went that.

At least she'd found a cure for his staring. He couldn't meet her eyes knowing she thought he was a guy like . . . like *that*. He faced forward and kept walking, his hands gripping his tray so hard the surface of the soup was trembling.

His insides felt like a coiled spring, one rotation away from snapping. He kept his movement measured and even, but in his brain, every step was a prelude to a lethal strike. He'd never been one of those guys to hit the gym in the middle of the day, but right now he'd kill for a pair of wraps and a heavy bag.

He forced himself to take a long breath, letting it out slowly, forcing his hands to relax while he walked.

"Hey, Jackass. Hungry?" A hand hit the edge of the tray and flipped it up.

Hunter jerked back. The chicken and salad missed him.

The soup didn't. Hot liquid hit him square in the chest.

That spring snapped. Hunter whirled and threw a fist.

Gabriel Merrick hit him back.

Hunter stepped into the punch, using his opponent's momentum to trap his arm and send a knee into his gut.

Then they were being dragged apart. Too soon. Hunter tasted blood on his lip—but he let himself be dragged.

That assistant football coach got between them, and he was talking, though Hunter wasn't really listening. Something about fighting and the guidance office and . . . Hunter didn't give a crap.

His eyes were on Kate, standing there among the gathered crowd, next to Nick Merrick, Gabriel's twin.

Nick was talking, his tone full of an almost resigned exasperation. "So now you've met my other brother, Gabriel . . ."

Hunter wasn't listening to him, either.

He was staring at Kate. Or more precisely, her hand.

And the way it was resting on Nick Merrick's arm.

Hunter slouched in the chair in the guidance office and stared at the corner of Vickers's desk. His shirt was wet and tacky from the soup, and somehow it had turned ice cold on the walk down here. He didn't want to give Gabriel the satisfaction of hearing him complain about it.

Kate and Nick. How had that happened? Wasn't Nick dating Becca's friend, Quinn?

The air felt tight and scratchy against his skin, like a wool sweater that didn't fit right.

Ms. Vickers was tapping her pen against her desk blotter. "Twice in one day, Hunter."

He wanted to ask if she could just give him detention or whatever so he could get the hell out of this room.

But he bit back the words. Becca's father's parting comment kept ricocheting around his brain, adding to the headache. *You made your bed, kid. Now you lie in it.*

It sounded so much like something his father would have said.

Ms. Vickers shifted in her chair. The fluorescent light in the ceiling was buzzing with a tiny flicker. "And Gabriel Merrick. I'd hoped your recent brush with the law would keep you out of my office for a while."

"I'm happy to leave."

She didn't crack a smile. "You know we don't take physical altercations lightly here. Who wants to tell me what happened?"

Hunter didn't lift his eyes from the corner of her desk, waiting for Gabriel to sell him out.

But Gabriel didn't say anything, either.

Ms. Vickers sighed. "All right, Hunter, what happened with Calla Dean? Coach Taylor says you had a run-in in the lunch line."

Hunter felt his hands form fists. "I didn't do anything."

"She says—"

"She's lying. *I didn't touch her.*"

Ms. Vickers pursed her lips. "I asked you to stay away from her entirely. If I don't think you can do that, you're going to force me to suspend you."

This was ridiculous. "I'm trying!"

"You didn't make it through lunch. I'm not sure that qualifies as trying very hard."

Hunter almost came out of his chair. His hands were ready to snap the plastic armrests clean off. "I didn't—"

"Hey." Gabriel's voice was sharp.

Hunter rounded on him, ready to finish what he'd started in the cafeteria. "What?"

Gabriel didn't flinch from his look. "Dial it back a notch." He glanced up.

And then Hunter realized that the overhead light was buzzing more frantically, making loud clicks within the tube. The air in the room had to have dropped ten degrees.

He'd always been able to sense the elements, and *control* was a newer talent, but he'd never affected anything to this extent.

Hunter closed his eyes and took a slow breath. In through his nose, out through his mouth. Then another. His hands unclenched, and he dropped back into the chair.

"Very zen," said Gabriel. "Should I light a candle?"

Hunter's eyes snapped open. "Fuck you."

"*Gentlemen,*" said Vickers.

Damn. Everyone was managing to burrow under his skin today.

"I'm sorry," Hunter bit out. "I'll stay away from Calla."

"Three strikes and you're out, Hunter." She shivered and pulled a cardigan off the back of her chair, then forced her arms into the sleeves. "If we have this conversation again, you'll be looking at a three-day suspension. Do you understand?"

"Yes."

Her eyes shifted to Gabriel. "The same goes for you, Mr. Merrick."

"Roger." He mock-saluted her.

"Can the two of you make it to next period without fighting? Or should someone stay with me?"

Hunter shot out of his chair. "I'm good."

Gabriel followed him into the hall. Hunter ignored him, though he wanted to slam him into the bank of lockers. The bell hadn't rung yet, and the halls were still empty.

"Nice shirt," said Gabriel.

"Go away."

"What, you're not still tracking me so you can report back to your keeper?"

Hunter ignored him and kept walking.

Gabriel kept after him. "Don't like being called a traitor?"

"I'm not a traitor."

"Did you turn on your dad, too? Is that what you feel so guilty ab—"

Hunter spun. Gabriel caught his wrist before he could throw a punch.

"Don't be an idiot," he snapped. "Do you *want* to get suspended?"

Hunter jerked free. "I want you to leave me alone."

"Oh, it's okay for you to follow *me* around—"

"I wasn't following you around!" God, Hunter would pay good money for a handful of ibuprofen. "And you know what? Why don't you cut the martyr act?"

Gabriel looked incredulous. "Me. The martyr act."

"Yeah. You." Hunter glared at him. "Like I screwed *you* over. You didn't even give me a chance to explain—"

"All right." Gabriel stopped walking. "Explain."

Hunter took a breath—and had nothing to say.

"Yeah, whatever." Gabriel moved away.

"Can you blame him?" called Hunter.

Gabriel hesitated, but didn't turn. "Blame who?"

"Bill. Becca's dad. Can you blame him for thinking you'd cause trouble? I didn't drag you to that first fire."

Gabriel laughed low, under his breath, but not like it was really funny. He turned and walked back to Hunter. "No, jackass. I blame you. Where'd you learn how to be a friend, anyway?"

Hunter stared at him. "What does that mean?"

"It means you need to pick a fucking side."

Then the bell rang and people flooded the hallway, separating them until Hunter lost Gabriel in the sea of students.

CHAPTER 6

At the end of the school day, Kate burst into the afternoon sunlight with the other students.

Then she got a glimpse of the roadway in front of the school and sighed.

Silver was waiting for her, leaning up against his truck, one hand hooked into a pocket. The sun caught the lighter strands in his hair and turned them gold, and the black T-shirt he wore didn't leave a whole lot to the imagination.

She wasn't the only one appreciating it, if the number of giggling girls passing close to the truck were any indication. But Silver was only looking at Kate.

She sighed and pulled her sunglasses from her bag, slipping them onto her face along with a bored expression, before looking both ways to cross the street.

For a moment, she wished she'd asked Nick Merrick for a ride home, just to get under Silver's skin, but at lunch she'd met Quinn.

"Nick's *girlfriend*," the other girl had emphasized, her voice full of steel daggers.

Kate had picked up one of Nick's fries—he'd offered—and smiled back sweetly. "Sounds like paradise."

Then Nick had smiled that wicked way and said, "See? I knew you'd have no trouble making friends."

Kate crossed the street with a bored expression on her face. "Haven't you ever seen *Sixteen Candles*?"

That threw him. Silver tilted his head to the side. "I'm sorry?"

"It's a classic. All you need is the red sports car. Come on, *Jake*, I'm hungry."

But as she moved to walk past him, he caught her around the waist and drew her into his body. She gasped, and he caught her breath, pressing his lips against hers. Despite the shock, he was one *hell* of a good kisser. She made a small sound, her body softening against his automatically, enjoying the feel of his hands sliding under her leather jacket to warm the skin at her waist.

Her power sparked with his, pulling heat from the sunlight and kicking the air into little whirlwinds around them.

Silver pulled back, lifting a hand to push her sunglasses up onto her forehead.

She stared up at him, feeling a bit dazed, though she didn't want him to know that. "Missed me, did you?" she said, mocking his accent.

"Not at all." He kissed the end of her nose. "Just setting a story so we have a reason to be seen together. Get in the car."

Then he smacked her on the ass and stepped back.

Kate's hand formed a fist, but before she could get past her shock and *move*, Silver glanced over. "Hit me and I'll hit you back."

He was smiling, but the glint of danger in his eyes said he wasn't kidding. She couldn't let him see that he'd gotten to her. She pulled her sunglasses back into place and drew a slim tube of lip gloss from her bag, deliberately moving slowly though her fingers were shaky with adrenaline. "Is that a promise or a threat?"

"Both. Did you mention you were hungry?"

Silver took her to the Pizza Hut near the school, a place with sticky tables, a sticky floor, and sticky toddlers screaming over the ancient jukebox in the corner.

It probably had sticky buttons. She didn't want to find out.

Kate raised her eyebrows at him when the waitress brought

thick plastic cups of soda. "Really. I say I'm hungry and this is where you take me."

He ignored her. "What did you learn today?"

She took a sip of her soda and cast a glance around the room. Harried mothers, tired servers, bored busboys. Silver looked completely out of place in the red vinyl booth. But then, she probably did, too.

She shrugged and swirled the straw in her glass. "They're boys. One of them got in a fight right in front of me and was stopped by a teacher." She rolled her eyes. "We could probably go back and take them out right now."

"If we take out one, we have to take out all. We can't risk collateral damage."

"Say 'collateral damage' again. That sounded sexy."

He didn't smile. "Are you not taking this seriously, Kathryn?"

His voice was low and dangerous, but she was still smarting from his treatment in the parking lot. It made her long for the easy banter of the text messages she'd exchanged with that boy with the piercings and tattoos. *Hunter.* How quickly he'd defended her this morning, standing up to those idiots in the school office.

She wondered what kind of kisser *he* was.

Then she squashed the thought. She had a purpose here. She couldn't let Silver catch her being distracted.

And that boy, Hunter, had shoved a girl in the cafeteria. He'd picked a fight with Gabriel Merrick. He'd seemed so collected, so controlled.

Then she'd seen it all go to hell in less than a minute.

She pushed Hunter and his text messages out of her mind. "I don't understand all this caution. They're not organized. There are only four of them."

"Every Guide who has come to destroy them has disappeared. That begs caution. Don't let your age make you impetuous."

"My age." She glared at him. "You're not that much older than me. How did *you* get assigned to this?"

"I'm twenty-one. And I followed orders."

"You followed orders."

He didn't say anything. Just looked at her.

She narrowed her eyes. "Well, that's not too impressive."

"Perhaps not." He leaned in. "But I do it well."

His voice was full of the promise of danger, lending more weight to the words than they'd carry on their own. She quickly took a sip of soda and glanced away.

Time to change the topic.

"I sat with Nick and Chris at lunch today. They were nice."

"Nice?"

It was the wrong thing to say. She could hear the judgment in his voice. What the hell had made her say *that*?

They were *nice*? The people they were here to *kill*?

Was she insane?

She quickly added, "They bought my story. I should be able to work an invite back to their house by the weekend."

She'd thought Silver would be pleased, but his expression darkened. "I don't like you going there alone."

"Jealous?"

"It's a risk." A little part of her wondered at the thought of him worrying about her—but then he crushed it. "Surrounded by all of them, you may give yourself away. And if they kill off my decoy, I'll have to start from square one."

"Stop it. You're getting me all hot and bothered."

"You may be talented, but you aren't strong enough to take all of them by yourself, Kathryn."

Just like before, it was an insult and a compliment all rolled into one. She took another sip of her soda. "I can take care of myself."

Silver regarded her silently for a moment. "Find another way to spend time around them. We'll figure out a way I can monitor the situation."

He was making her feel like she was about twelve years old. "What did *you* learn today?"

"I sat outside the school and read police reports on the recent arson cases."

"You sat in the truck *all day*? Why?"

"I didn't just sit in the truck." He hadn't touched his soda, but now he ran a finger around the rim of the glass. "And I wasn't sure whether you'd need help."

"They have laws against stalking high school students."

"No one saw me." He paused. "They arrested a boy for these arson attacks, and the fires have stopped. But from what I can see, this Ryan Stacey has no connection to Elementals. The police are chalking up the pentagram patterns at the arson locations to simple cult obsession."

Kate snorted and took another sip of her soda. "Idiots."

"According to the police reports, Gabriel Merrick was arrested and released. He was never charged with the crimes. In one article, it's claimed that he and another boy—" Silver checked his phone. "—a Hunter Garrity, rescued students from the fire in the school library—"

Kate choked on her soda.

Silver raised his eyebrows. "Problems?"

"I met him. Today. Hunter Garrity. He's the one who fought with Gabriel Merrick in the cafeteria."

"The plot thickens."

Kate wiped at her mouth with the napkin. "It does? Why?"

"One of the first Guides sent to take care of our friends the Merricks was named John Garrity. He never made it. While I believe in coincidence, that strikes a bit too close to home, does it not?"

Kate froze. She remembered the way the air went still around Hunter in the school office.

"Can you get close to him?" said Silver.

She nodded, thinking of those text messages.

"Find out what really happened to his father."

"What else?"

"Find out whether he had something to do with it. It concerns me," said Silver, leaning in, "that there may be more Elementals at play here than we realize."

"More than you can handle?" said Kate.

"Never." He laughed, low, under his breath. "I'm worried, my dear, that they're more than *you* can handle."

"I can do this," she said, losing any trace of humor. "I can."

"Good," he said. "Then prove it."

Hunter found his mother and his grandparents sitting in silence when he walked in.

Then he stopped short.

His gun was on the kitchen table between them. His two knives were laid out beside it. And the spare magazine, plus the box of bullets.

They'd searched his room.

Casper nosed at his hands, begging to be petted, but for the first time, Hunter couldn't even acknowledge his dog. His emotions were wildly vacillating between fury and fear, and they couldn't decide where to settle. His heart felt like it was beating a path out of his chest.

His mother looked like she'd been crying—but that seemed to be a daily occurrence, so Hunter didn't read too much into it. His grandmother looked disappointed, as usual.

And his grandfather looked like he wanted to load the gun and use it.

Hunter was tempted to go for it first.

He cleared his throat, and his voice didn't want to work. "What's going on?"

His mother opened her mouth, but his grandmother put a hand over hers and squeezed—hard, it looked like.

His grandfather's eyes were like steel, solid and unwavering. "You tell us," he said.

Hunter bristled. "No, you tell *me*. You searched my room?"

"A good thing, too, considering what we found."

Hunter glanced at his mother. She wasn't looking at him now. "Those are Dad's," he said, his voice low. "You knew I had them."

She didn't answer. His grandfather did: "I don't care whose they were. Look at me."

Hunter dragged his eyes back to his grandfather.

The man gestured to the table. "You think it's appropriate for a fifteen-year-old boy to have access to these kinds of weapons?"

"I'm sixteen."

"Don't get smart with me, kid."

Hunter gritted his teeth. "I'm not getting smart. I *drove* here, for god's sake—"

"Cut the attitude." His grandfather was suddenly on his feet. "You're *this close* to being on the street."

Hunter was so sick of the empty threats. Especially today. He moved to brush past him, to go to his room, to burrow under the covers until he had to wake up and start another day.

His grandfather grabbed his arm. "Don't you walk out of here. You've got friends breaking in here at all hours of the night, you're in trouble at school for roughing up your girlfriend, and now we find weapons in your bedroom."

So Vickers had called the house. Great.

Hunter kept his voice even. "Let me go."

"You're not walking out of here until you apologize to your mother."

Hunter looked at his mom again, wondering how she'd turned into this unraveled mess of a woman who had to be held together by her parents.

He didn't even know what he was supposed to be apologizing for, but she was looking at him for the first time in days, and the disappointment there was more painful than anything his grandfather could say.

"I'm sorry," he said.

Her eyes filled and she swiped at them quickly.

Hunter swallowed—but then his grandfather shook him. "You're selfish, putting her through this stress when she's already going through a difficult time."

Hunter felt guilty and resentful all at once. He couldn't look at his mother anymore, but he didn't want to look at his grandfather, either. "Just let me go."

"You're not staying under this roof until you tell us what you're going to change."

"Fine. I'll sleep in the car."

His grandfather let him go with enough of a shove to make Hunter fall back a step. "Good," he said. "You're already packed."

Whoa.

Wait.

"What are you talking about?"

His grandfather pointed. "Come back with a new attitude."

Hunter looked. Two duffel bags—*his* duffel bags—were by the baker's rack, stuffed full of what looked like clothes.

He couldn't breathe. It felt like he'd swallowed hot tar.

He glanced at his mother. She wouldn't look at him now.

"You're throwing me out?" His voice almost cracked and he didn't care.

"You're not going to break the law and live here," said his grandfather.

"I'm not breaking the law!"

"*Something* is going on with you, boy, and I'm sick of it. Do you understand me? I don't know how your father raised you—"

"Don't." Hunter had to take a deep breath, and it shook. "Don't you talk about my father."

"What do you think he'd say about you hitting women?"

"It's not like that."

"What's it like, then?"

Hunter almost couldn't speak through the tightness in his chest. "It's—it's a misunderstanding."

"Is *this* a misunderstanding?" His grandfather hit him.

The blow snapped Hunter's head to the side. He'd seen it coming, but his brain couldn't quite believe it, so he didn't make a move to defend himself.

It hurt.

He'd been hit before, but there was something different about it coming from his grandfather, as if their history—not all of it bad—was loaded into that backhand slap.

Hunter sucked in a breath through his teeth. His mother's hand was over her mouth, but she hadn't said a word.

"You want to hit someone," said his grandfather, "you pick on someone your own size." His grandfather hit him again, an open hand slap this time. "How's this feel?"

Hunter forced his hands to stay at his sides, but he couldn't keep them from curling into fists. "Stop it."

"Stop it? Can't take it? Did she ask you to stop?"

Casper barked.

"It wasn't—I didn't—" Another hit, and Hunter flung up an arm to protect his face, but it didn't help. His grandfather wasn't being gentle. These were full hits with strength behind them.

An adult had never come after him this way. His eyes were burning, more fury than tears. Anger lay coiled in his chest, ready to spring free and slam his grandfather to the ground, but Hunter was having trouble fighting through this layer of bewilderment and disbelief.

His grandfather was hitting him. *Hitting him.*

And his mother was *letting it happen.*

Then his grandfather caught him on the cheek, a sharp hit that stung. Hunter shoved him back. His breathing was loud in the sudden silence.

He had to get out of here. Hunter turned, hunching his shoulders, keeping his hands tight at his sides.

His grandfather grabbed his arm, and it was like pulling a trigger. Hunter whirled and struck.

The man wasn't ready for it—or maybe he just didn't expect Hunter to hit back. His grandfather hit the counter and fell.

His grandmother cried out. Casper was barking, bouncing on his hind legs, waiting for Hunter to give some direction.

His mother was crying again. "Hunter, *stop.*"

As if he'd started this.

You made your bed, kid. Now you lie in it.

Maybe he *had* started this. His breathing was too fast.

His grandfather was struggling to his feet. There was blood and a murderous expression on his face.

Hunter had no idea how to fix this. And all he could think about was his father's final lesson, how he'd had the opportunity to employ lethal force, and he'd *failed.*

Just like he'd failed with Calla.

His thoughts were spinning in a dangerous direction, and he couldn't rein them in. He needed to get out of here, before he did something he couldn't undo.

You already did something you can't undo.

Then his grandfather was coming after him again.

Hunter ran. He was through the front door before registering that he'd grabbed one of the bags by the door, and then his jeep tires were spinning gravel from the driveway. Casper was in the back, his head hanging between the seats, his tongue rasping against Hunter's cheek.

Hunter brushed him away and yanked the wheel to pull onto the main roadway. His heartbeat was a roar in his ears, his lungs grabbing for breath. He needed to slow down. He needed to get hold of himself.

He drove to Quiet Waters, the only county park he knew. He'd come here once before, with Becca. It felt like a lifetime ago.

Kids were attacking the playground equipment, so he drove to the other side of the grounds, stopping his jeep by the pond. The sunlight was dying in the west, but there was still enough to warm his face.

His cheek felt hot and sore where his grandfather had hit him.

Hunter killed the engine and focused on breathing.

In. Out.

His mother had let him go. She'd let her father throw Hunter out of the house.

She'd let his grandfather *hit him*. He and his own father had scuffled, sure. But his dad had never hauled off and decked him.

But his mother thought he'd hit Calla. She thought he was involved in illegal activities. She hadn't even asked for his side of things, hadn't waited for an explanation.

He'd barely been able to get eye contact out of her in *months*, and now she thought he was—

Stop.

More breaths. He could do this. He could figure it out.

He picked up his cell phone. No messages. His mother hadn't tried to call. Should he call her?

She'd stood there and watched his grandfather belt him, then told *Hunter* to stop.

More breaths. He needed to slow down. He rubbed at his eyes.

Finally, he opened the door to let Casper out of the car. He pulled the duffel bag onto the front seat and unzipped it. Clothes, all clothes. Not a lot, but enough for a few days. The only shoes he had were the ones on his feet. It had been windy today so he was still wearing a hoodie under a denim jacket, along with the jeans he'd worn to school. No soap, no razor, but it wasn't like he had access to anywhere to use those things. He could go to school early and shower there. Maybe things would look different in the morning.

He checked his wallet. Seventeen dollars. He had half a tank of gas in the jeep. He hadn't eaten dinner, but the rest of his money was in an envelope in the top drawer of his dresser—if his grandfather hadn't already confiscated it during the "search." Seventeen dollars wouldn't last very long, especially if he burned through the rest of his fuel.

All he had to feed Casper was a baggie of milk bones in the glove box.

Suddenly it seemed cruel to have brought the dog.

Hunter swallowed. Wind whipped across the pond to lace through his hair and make him shiver.

"Yeah, yeah," he said.

He looked at his phone again, wanting to call . . . someone. He just couldn't think of anyone who wouldn't hang up on him. Explaining what had just happened—he couldn't take it. He already felt guilty enough. He didn't need someone else to add to it. No way he could ring up Becca or the Merricks and say he'd been thrown out of his house.

Gabriel would probably laugh in his face.

It would be dark soon. He could go one night without eating. Hunter fished the milk bones out of the glove box, divided them in half, and tossed them in the grass for Casper.

Then he lay back in the grass and stared at the darkening sky, attempting nothing more challenging than filling his lungs with air, until a park ranger came around and told him to leave.

After writing him a citation for his dog being loose.

Hunter shoved the citation in the glove box and started the

ignition. His fingers felt like icicles, and his empty stomach was starting to protest this whole not eating thing.

The headache was back, clawing at his temples.

Hunter didn't want to drive far, because he didn't know how long he'd need to make his fuel last. He settled on the parking lot behind the twenty-four-hour Target on Ritchie Highway, parking in a row of other cars that probably belonged to employees. He blasted the heat as high as he could tolerate, until his breath fogged the windshield and even Casper was panting. Then he pulled an extra pair of sweatpants over his jeans and climbed into the backseat, cramming his legs into the small space and resting his head on the duffel bag.

Casper crammed himself onto the bench seat, too, pressing his back against Hunter's chest and his nose into the space under Hunter's chin.

He'd be covered in dog hair in the morning, but Hunter didn't care. Casper would keep him warm.

He checked his phone again. Nothing.

His throat felt tight.

He told himself to knock it off.

He wished he knew how to fix this. All of it.

His breath was catching. Casper lifted his head and licked Hunter's cheek.

There was no one here to see, but *he'd* know, and he wouldn't let himself lose it. Not when he'd been the one to cause this.

But his breath wouldn't stop hitching, and he buried his face in the scruff of Casper's neck.

He missed his father so much.

He thought of where he was right now, and how he'd gotten here, and knew exactly how disappointed his father would be.

He'd fix it. Somehow. He'd fix this.

His phone chimed, and Hunter swiped at his eyes. His heart flew with hope. Maybe his mother had reconsidered? Maybe she'd give him a chance to explain?

But it wasn't his mother's number on the face of the phone.

What do you stare at when you're not in school?

Kate.

Hunter lifted his head. For an instant, he thought about turning the phone off and burying it in his pocket—but really, what else did he have to do?

Obviously I stare at text messages from girls with theories.

Her response was lightning quick.

Slow night, huh?

He smiled.

Long night would be more accurate.

A long pause, then:

What's with you and the girl from the caf?

Hunter frowned. She meant Calla. He remembered the look on Kate's face when she'd watched, standing there with her hand on Nick's arm.

Wasn't it obvious?

No. And don't get all >:O at me.

How did you know I was >:O?

Please. Your text style screams >:O.

Hunter smiled again, but only briefly.

It's complicated.

I have a theory about complicated boys.

He smiled. Before he could type anything else, another message appeared.

BTW that was a pretty sweet spinning backfist you used on the guy who flipped your tray. Where did you learn to fight like that?

His smile vanished altogether.
Another sentence appeared before he could say anything.

Though you're out of practice. You were lucky that teacher stopped him. Your timing needs work.

He stared at the phone, wondering if he should be impressed or insulted. Then he typed.

This is me right now. :-O

I prefer you like this: :-)

He smiled. Another message from Kate appeared.

Seriously. Where'd you learn to fight like that?

Ninja school.

Funny. Why are you having a long night?

He paused, studying the phone. He didn't know her at all. But somehow this was easier, sending text messages into the ether.

Family stuff.

Mom or dad?

Grandfather and mom. My dad died at the beginning of the summer.

After he hit SEND, he stared at the words. It wasn't the first time he'd said them, but it was the first time he'd typed them into a text message, and now they were burning themselves into his brain, like they held more power in writing.

He typed something else quickly, just to make the screen scroll.

We live with my grandparents now.

Her message appeared almost instantly.

I'm sorry about your dad.

A long pause, and then another message from Kate.

My mom is dead, too.

Her words held weight, too, as if the screen knew their power. He typed automatically.

I'm sorry.

Then he added,

Don't you hate when people say that?

Yes. I'm sorry I said it.

Me, too.

This time the pause was really long, as he fought for something to say after *that*. He wondered if she'd given up on the texting, when a new one appeared.

How did your dad die?

Normally the question would piss him off. But it was different in a text message, from someone else who'd lost a parent.

In a car accident. I was with him. My uncle died, too.

My mom drowned last year.

Hunter flinched. Somehow it seemed worse—but what was the difference?

Another message popped up on the screen.

It wasn't supposed to happen that way.

It should have seemed like a weird statement—but he got it.

I know exactly what you mean.

Were you and your dad close?

The words hit him like a bullet. *Close.*

He and his father hadn't always gotten along, but Hunter had always felt like his father *understood* him.

He slid his fingers across the screen.

Yeah. Sort of. Sometimes not at all. Bizarre, right?

We're all pretty bizarre. Some of us are just better at hiding it, that's all.

He smiled.

Was that a quote from The Breakfast Club?

O_O Most people don't get that one.

My uncle loved eighties movies. I've seen them all.

Nobody puts Baby in the corner.

Wax on, wax off.

I can't believe I gave my panties to a geek.

He froze. That one sent his thoughts in a dangerous direction. His phone buzzed.

STOP THINKING ABOUT MY PANTIES.

He grinned.

Can't help it now.

Stare at me tomorrow?

Sure. I'll be in the caf early.

And that was it. She didn't respond.
But that was okay. For five minutes, he didn't feel so alone.
Hunter put his head down against the duffel bag, closed his
eyes, and smiled.

CHAPTER 7

K ate sat in the cafeteria and sucked on the end of a Twizzler.
She should have been looking for the Merrick brothers.

Instead, she was waiting for Hunter. Her heart was buzzing, and she told it to knock it off. She was here on assignment. She had a *task*.

And she remembered the way he had gone from total control to utter disaster with the flip of a switch, like watching an intricate glass sculpture shatter into a thousand pieces—only to pull together again until you could barely see the seams. Something about that was intriguing, like the guileless way he responded to her text messages.

Silver didn't know anything about that.

She had no intention of telling him.

Her cell phone chimed.

I can't come sit with you.

She didn't bother looking around. She just texted back.

Why not?

Complicated.

Kate shoved the bag of Twizzlers into the front of her back-pack.

I'll come to you. Where are you?

He didn't respond, so she sent another text.

Don't tell me. You're sitting by the pool on the roof.

That got a response.

Please tell me you didn't fall for that one.

Kate smiled. Like she'd fall for a freshman prank.

I almost fell for the one about the bomb shelter under the school. Then I realized it was probably just a euphemism. Where are you really?

I'm headed back to my car. You're sitting near someone I'm not allowed to be around.

She frowned and looked up. She didn't see the Merricks, so this wasn't about the one he'd fought with yesterday. But there, at the next table, was the girl with punk hair and flame tattoos along her wrists. The one he'd shoved.

It seemed so incongruous with the way he'd defended her in the office.

Kate gathered her things and started for the parking lot. She had no idea what kind of car he drove, and it wouldn't be easy to find him—the lot was packed with arriving students. Wind whistled across the pavement to sneak under the lapels of her leather jacket and make her shiver. She wanted to beg the sunlight for warmth, to ask the air to ratchet back a few degrees, but there were too many Elementals at play in this town, and she kept her guard up.

Her phone chimed.

You didn't have to come looking for me.

She held the Twizzler between her teeth and wrote back.

I thought we had a staring date. Vehicle?

A long pause. She shivered again and wished she'd worn something heavier under her coat.

Finally, her phone chimed again.

White jeep. 20 yards to your right.

She spotted his car at the end of the row, under an oak tree with sagging branches. The engine wasn't running, but at least she'd be out of this wind. She didn't even hesitate; just climbed right in and flung her bag on the floorboards.

Hunter glanced over, but it was quick. "Hey."

She opened her mouth to respond, but a German shepherd stuck his head between the seats and gave a low *woof* of greeting.

Kate grinned and rubbed the dog's ears. "You have a dog!"

Hunter nodded, his eyes on the windshield. "His name is Casper."

His voice was easy enough but carried an undercurrent of strain, which made Kate stop playing with the dog and really look at him. The ends of his hair hung across his face, still damp, from a shower probably, and he hadn't bothered to use a razor this morning. His eyes looked vaguely shadowed, as if he'd been up half the night.

This was a very different boy from the one she'd met yesterday.

She wondered what had happened. The fight with Gabriel Merrick? The girl with the tats? The family issues he'd mentioned last night?

She should drop her guard and touch him, to let the elements feed her information, so she could report back to Silver.

Kate immediately called bullshit on her subconscious.

She wanted to touch him because Hunter looked like he needed someone to be gentle with him for five minutes.

She softened her voice. "You want to talk about it?"

"I'm just tired."

"This looks like more than just tired."

He laughed briefly, without much humor to it. "You don't know me at all."

She pulled her cell phone out of her pocket and whipped her thumb across the keys.

You want to text about it?

His phone chimed almost instantly. Hunter glanced at it and gave a ghost of a smile.

Then his fingers slid across the face of his phone quickly. He didn't look at her.

Her phone buzzed in her hand after a moment.

My grandfather threw me out of the house last night. The school counselor called and told him I was hitting Calla, the girl you saw in the caf. So he punched me and told me to get out.

She snapped her head up. Her mouth opened, but he held up a hand, his eyes still on the windshield.

"Don't," he said.

No wonder he was barely holding it together.

In a flash, she remembered the first time her mother had brought her to that tiny farm somewhere in southern Virginia, saying they were going to the "training compound," which turned out to be a dark barn that reeked of alfalfa hay and blood. She hadn't wanted to go inside, and then a massive man had walked out of the darkness.

When his hand came out, she'd thought he was going to introduce himself.

She'd never been hit in the face before that moment.

She remembered rolling in the dust and scattered straw, wondering when the world would right itself, hoping her mother would intercede.

Instead, she'd said, "Stop disappointing me, Kathryn."

Kate typed quickly on her phone.

Are you OK?

When his phone chimed, he glanced down. Then he looked back at the windshield.

And shook his head.

She knew that feeling, when your life felt so out of control that you had to do something to get it back on a track, any track, just so you didn't explode with tension from staying in one spot.

She was supposed to be doing some kind of reconnaissance, but she couldn't disregard the brittle state of the boy sitting beside her.

"Was Calla your girlfriend?" she asked softly.

He hesitated. "No. I thought—I don't know."

"What did you think?"

His eyes were locked on the steering wheel. "She found me at a party a few weeks ago. Her dad is in the Marines—mine was, too. I just thought she needed someone to talk to. I didn't realize—"

Kate waited, but he stopped there.

"You didn't realize what?" she said.

Hunter took a deep breath—but then he didn't let it out, and the tension rolled around in the car with them. "You should get out and go inside. I think I'm going to cut, and you'll be late for first period."

"I'll cut with you."

He shook his head. "No—I mean, I've got things I have to do."

Things? What kinds of things?

Her phone buzzed in her hand, and she was so surprised that she almost dropped it.

Silver.

What are you doing?

She hit a button to clear the screen. Her pulse jumped.
It buzzed again.

Is that our mysterious Hunter Garrity?

Did that mean Silver was watching them *right now*? She
cleared the screen again and shoved the phone into her pocket,
where it vibrated a third time.

"Someone wants your attention," said Hunter.

"He's like a toddler," she agreed.

Hunter's eyebrows raised just the tiniest bit. "He?"

"No one important," she said. But her phone buzzed again.

The emotion in Hunter's eyes was walled up now, and she
could see the tightness in his jaw. He looked so tightly wound
that she was almost afraid to leave him alone. "Where do you
want to go?" she said. "I'll go with you."

He didn't look over.

She put a hand on his arm. "Come on. Maybe you can show
me around—"

He caught her wrist. Not hard, but fast enough that it made
her gasp.

"I don't want to be a jerk," he said, his eyes shifting to meet
hers. "But I can't do this."

She didn't understand. "This?"

His eyes were tired and wary—but also sharp and intelligent.
"Yeah. This."

Kate stared across at him. "What just happened?"

He glanced at her phone. "Boyfriend?"

"What? No." Then she remembered Silver's cover story. If
she denied it now, would it screw things up later? "It's not like
that."

But she'd fumbled her words, and she knew exactly what it

looked like. Hunter leaned across her body to pull at the handle to release the door. Cool air streamed into the car.

He was throwing her out?

His expression said he was.

"You're getting this all wrong," she said.

"I don't think I am."

She slid out of the car. Before closing the door, she said, "I just thought we could get to know each other."

He finally looked at her fully, and he laughed shortly. "If you're lonely, why don't you text Nick Merrick? He seemed perfectly willing to stare at you."

Then, without waiting for an answer, he reached out and grabbed the door, pulling it shut and leaving her out in the cold.

Hunter waited until he couldn't ignore the hunger clawing at his stomach, then bought two breakfast sandwiches at Dunkin Donuts. He was hungry enough to inhale both, but he'd fed Casper the last of the milk bones this morning, and the dog was staring at him desperately. So he set the second sandwich on the wrapper on the ground.

Eleven dollars left, and a third of a tank of gasoline.

His cell phone remained blank. At least he had a car charger for that.

He'd been so stupid, entertaining the thought of . . . of *anything* with Kate. Like his life wasn't complicated enough right now. She'd climbed into his car, he'd almost broken down, and then she'd started texting with some other guy.

God, he'd looked like such an *idiot*.

Really, it shouldn't have been a surprise that she'd pick him to screw with. His abilities drew people to him. He was just used to the heckling, fist-swinging type of attention. He'd been dumb enough to think this would turn out differently.

Besides, he had other things to worry about.

Like finding a way to earn money. It would cost a fortune to fill his gas tank, and if he had no transportation, he was sunk.

His mom hadn't even called to see if he was okay.

He felt like he shouldn't care—she'd let his grandfather throw him out—but he did.

A lot.

Stop. Focus.

He could fill out applications. How hard would it be to find a job?

Three strip malls later, he knew the answer: hard.

He wrote his personal information so many times that he started to bore himself. At first he was meticulous, knowing that he only had one opportunity to make a first impression. He knew to make eye contact, to shake hands, to speak confidently.

Regardless, it was like a fist to the gut when bored workers would take his completed application and fling it in a box.

It was a slap in the face when he was told he *couldn't* complete an application because of how he looked.

This was at a little café on Ritchie Highway. The hostess had frowned when he asked for an application—reminding him of his grandmother's constant look of disapproval—and said, "No piercings, no long hair, no tattoos."

He'd nodded and thanked her, figuring it was just a fluke. An old people's place.

Then two more stores said the same thing.

Like what he looked like would matter if he was washing dishes or stocking boxes in the back.

By three o'clock, he was bitter and jaded and starving again.

And exhausted. He'd slept in the car all night, but he hadn't really *slept*.

His phone chimed, and Hunter immediately thought of Kate. No. Becca.

You ok? Why aren't you in school?

His thumb hesitated over the screen—but then he remembered her brush-off, the way she'd whispered about him with Chris. The way she didn't trust him anymore.

His car was down to a quarter of a tank of gas. He spent a

dollar fifty on a bottle of water and told himself it would have to suffice until dinner.

Less than ten bucks left. And he was starting to run out of options.

Home Depot sat with two other big box stores off the main road, but they had a NOW HIRING sign out front.

The man behind the service desk was counting cash in a drawer. He didn't glance up when Hunter asked for an application.

"You've gotta be eighteen, kid."

Hunter had heard this one before. "I am eighteen."

The guy's eyes flicked up and his hands went still on the money in his hands. "Sure. Prove it."

Okay, he hadn't heard that yet.

The man laughed and went back to counting cash.

"All right, look." Hunter felt like he'd reached the end of his rope and found it a frayed, tangled mess. "I need a job. You've got a sign out front. I can work hard. I don't understand why everyone has to act like I'm some—"

"You look." The man flung the stack of cash into the drawer. "Forgetting the fact that you're underage, I've got guys coming in here with families to feed. You want me to turn them down because some kid wants money to take his girlfriend to the prom?"

Hunter glared at him. "I need a job."

"Join the club." Then the phone beside the register rang, and the man turned away to answer it.

Hunter stood there, feeling the air bite at his cheeks. The fluorescent lights in the warehouse ceiling seemed to be buzzing more loudly than normal, but maybe it was just his shot nerves.

At this rate, he'd have to drop some of his remaining cash on a bottle of Motrin.

Then he realized that the man had left the cash drawer open, and he was now facing away, flipping through a binder full of laminated pages.

Hunter stared at the cash. He'd watched the man count it—a

big stack of twenties. There had to be several hundred dollars there.

The store wasn't even that crowded. He could grab a twenty and run.

He'd never stolen anything in his life.

The lights buzzed more loudly. Hunter wanted to rub at his head, but he was afraid if he lifted a hand, it would grab the cash almost against his will.

"Hunter?"

He turned his head, feeling like he'd lost a minute of time.

Michael Merrick stood there, two rolls of something green hooked under one arm. A red shirt with the Merrick landscaping logo stretched across his chest, already sporting a fine layer of dust, and a stain near the hem. He had a couple inches on Hunter, but that might have just been the work boots on his feet. It was the first time Hunter had ever seen Michael clean shaven.

Hunter had no idea what Michael thought of him, but considering the way his younger brothers were treating him, it probably wasn't good.

Then again, Michael wasn't swinging a fist or openly mocking him, so maybe this was better.

Michael said, "Why aren't you in school?"

Hunter froze. He'd been ready for that question all day—but Michael was the first one to ask, and probably the only one who wouldn't buy a line of bullshit.

Then Michael glanced at his watch. "Jesus, is it after three already?" He shifted the rolls under his arm and looked at Hunter a little more critically. "You all right?"

The question took him by surprise. "Yeah. Fine."

The cash drawer slammed behind him, and Hunter jumped.

Well, there went an opportunity. Hunter scowled and wondered if he should be relieved or pissed.

The service manager cleared his throat. "I can take those for you here, if you're ready."

"Sure." Michael put the stuff on the counter. Then he pulled out his wallet. Hunter could see cash trapped in the folds.

The service manager was watching him. "You need something else, kid?"

He needed to stop staring and get the hell out of here.

Before he did something he'd regret.

"No. Forget it." Hunter unclenched his fists and turned away.

"Hey," called Michael. "Hunter."

Hunter whirled, ready to be hassled. "What?"

Michael was swiping a credit card through the machine. "The guys are all busy this evening, and I'm already behind. Feel like helping me build a retaining wall?"

Hunter stared at him for a second. Lack of sleep and food was making him stupid. "I don't—what?"

Michael looked up. "It's easy work, it just takes a long time, and I don't want to lose the light." He paused. "If you've got somewhere else to be, don't sweat it."

Hunter stared at him, waiting for the other shoe to drop. There had to be a trick here. Had to be. "You want *me* to help you?"

"Sure. I mean, I'll pay you. Fifty bucks fair?"

Hunter almost choked on air. Fifty bucks? That would probably carry him into the weekend. If Michael wanted him to cut grass by pulling up individual strands, he'd do it.

But then he remembered Casper. "My dog is in the car."

Michael slid the credit card back into his wallet. "Bring him. As long as he doesn't dig up the landscaping, he won't bother me. Meet me at the truck."

CHAPTER 8

Michael made for quiet company. Aside from giving Hunter a ball cap with their company logo on it and saying, "This way you'll look official," he didn't say anything. Hunter curled the hat in his hands and wondered if this was a mistake—but they were already driving, and he'd feel like an idiot backing out now. The truck windows were down, air streaming through the cab. Casper sat in the backseat but hung his head over Hunter's shoulder to let the air blow his ears.

Hunter's cell phone was in his pocket. No new messages.

"I don't have any idea how to build a retaining wall," he finally said.

"Then you'd better get out of the truck right now."

Hunter figured he was kidding, but Michael's voice was so flat he wasn't sure.

Michael glanced over. "Can you keep your mouth shut and do what I tell you?"

"Yeah."

"Then you're an expert at building retaining walls." Michael hit the turn signal. They were pulling into a Wendy's parking lot. "Hungry? Tell me what you want."

Hunter hesitated. The thought of food was almost making him dizzy—but he didn't want to spend his last nine dollars until he was sure Michael would be good for the fifty he'd promised.

But watching someone else eat would be the worst form of torture. Hunter reached into his pocket for his wallet.

"It's on me," said Michael. "Since you're doing me a favor."

"Whatever you're having, then."

It wasn't until ten minutes later, when he had half a grilled chicken sandwich left in his hands, that his suspicion fully kicked in. "Why are you being nice to me?"

Michael pulled a handful of fries from the bag but didn't glance away from the road. "Nice?"

"I thought you were all pissed at me because of what happened with Bill Chandler."

Michael shrugged.

And then he didn't say anything.

Hunter scowled at the windshield. Pride was pricking under his skin, trying to convince him to climb out of the car at the next stop light.

The promise of fifty bucks was keeping his ass right here in the passenger seat.

But really . . . the atmosphere in the car wasn't tense. He had a task, something to take his mind off his mother and his grandfather and the mess of a situation he was in.

Michael hit the turn signal and eased the truck onto a gravel driveway that led back to a sprawling ranch-style house on the water. "Look," he said. "I'm not upset about the Bill Chandler thing. I get where he was coming from, asking you to watch Gabriel."

"I wasn't—it just—" Hunter stopped himself and sighed. "It wasn't like that."

Michael stopped at a curve in the driveway and threw the truck into park. "Put the hat on and grab those rolls of landscape fabric."

So they weren't going to talk about it. Fine.

Hunter slid out of the cab. He pushed his hair back from his face and tucked it under the cap, breathing in the air off the water. The house sat alone on a few acres of land, and even here, in the driveway, they were a good hundred feet away from the front door. He felt better now that they were outside, with the sun on his skin. Casper bounded out of the truck to sniff at pallets set off to the side of the driveway, stacked with cut stone and sacks of soil and mulch.

Despite the breeze and the water, the whole place had a quiet stillness. It felt nice against his senses.

"Is anyone home?" said Hunter.

"Nah. They don't need to be." Michael pointed inside the curve of the driveway where the manicured lawn was broken by an eroded slope. "We'll build a wall to match the curve today, then I'll come back next week to plant stuff on top. Here. I have a sketch." He reached inside the truck to grab a clipboard.

Hunter took a glance at the rough drawing. It was probably a good thing Michael was paid for landscaping instead of art-work. "Got it. What's first?"

Michael was looking at him a little too closely. "Did you get in a fight at school?"

"What? No."

"Then what's with the bruise?"

Hunter wanted to pull the hat off and let his hair fall across his face again. He hadn't noticed a mark this morning, but then he'd been hustling to get out of the locker room before the first bell since he wasn't sticking around for classes. "It's nothing."

For a second, he thought Michael was going to push. Hunter didn't look away, but inside his head, his brain was spinning out trying to think of some excuse to give.

But Michael just gave half a shrug and turned, gesturing to the grassy slope again.

The work was harder than Hunter expected. He kept his mouth shut and did as he was told, digging and laying stone dust and staking rebar. It felt good to work, to put his hands in the earth and let the sun draw sweat from his back. The cut stone was heavy, and he was really feeling it in his shoulders before they had a third of the wall built.

He straightened and stretched his back.

And from the corner of his eye, he saw a flash of movement between some trees by the road.

Hunter froze. He watched for a moment.

Nothing.

Stupid. This house was way back off the main road. It could have been a deer, or a tree branch moving in the wind. All he could hear was his breathing and the water hitting rocky breakers. He dropped his guard and let the elements speak to him— but whatever it was, the elements didn't mind its being here.

But something about it had bothered him, caught his attention and held it.

He kept thinking of Calla in his bedroom, sneaking in to hold a gun against his cheek.

He wished he had a weapon. He wished he had a weapon *right now.*

"What's up?" said Michael.

"Nothing," said Hunter. "I thought I saw something."

He was ready for scoffing, because there was absolutely nothing around, but Michael put a hand to the ground and tilted his head. "I don't feel anything malicious." He paused. "But I'll pay attention."

Hunter kept his senses wide open now, laying stones as Michael directed, but focusing most of his attention on the road.

Michael glanced over. "Does this have something to do with the fight you didn't have?"

Hunter didn't look at him. "No." He shrugged. "I'm just on edge."

Another stone went on the wall. Michael wiped his forehead against his sleeve. "Does this have something to do with why you were ready to level the Home Depot?"

Hunter's hands went still on the rock in front of him.

Michael didn't say anything else, just laid another one without stopping. He flung the stones like they weighed nothing, and they slid into place perfectly. Hunter would have called him a perfectionist, but he'd bet Michael did it without thinking.

Another stone hit the wall, and Michael glanced over. "Think and work at the same time."

Hunter grabbed a stone, letting a slow breath out. "I wasn't going to level the Home Depot."

"Maybe not intentionally."

Hunter ran through the last twenty-four hours. Calla. School. Kate. His grandfather. Spending the night in his car.

Jesus, his throat felt tight again. He slammed the stone into place, feeling the impact all the way up to his shoulders.

Michael flung a stone next to his and remained silent.

And after a minute, Hunter realized he was going to stay that way. Michael wasn't going to push. Hunter relaxed into the rhythm of the work again.

Then he felt . . . *something* brush his senses. His head snapped up.

Just as Casper growled from the grass nearby.

Wind came off the water to blow across the lawn, toward the road. The air carried no power, no direction. No help there. The sun had dropped behind distant trees and houses, leaving long shadows tracing across the grounds. Michael had a hand against the dirt, his eyes trained on the clusters of trees now.

Hunter thought of Calla again and wondered if she'd been following him, whether she'd choose *this* house to set on fire, just to screw with him.

But she would have had to follow him all day, right?

Casper growled again.

There! Movement. Definitely someone in the trees.

Hunter didn't realize he'd started forward until Michael grabbed his arm. "Wait," he said.

Hunter waited.

"Grab your dog," said Michael.

He didn't have to grab him, but Hunter issued the command for Casper to stay, wondering if the dog also had trouble hearing over a suddenly thundering heartbeat.

No further motion from the tree line.

Michael stood and brushed his hands against his knees. "Come on. I'll finish in the morning. I'll tell them I lost the light."

"You just—you want to leave?"

"It's probably nothing, but we're out in the middle of nowhere. I'd rather be safe than sorry."

When they were in the truck, Michael fed Casper old fries from the Wendy's bag. He kept the windows closed, but Hunter peered out at the trees as they passed.

Nothing.

Michael glanced over. "Any problems at home?"

Hunter almost choked on his breath. "What do you mean? Why?"

"No pentagrams or anything?"

Oh. Those.

"No," he said, speaking around the sudden gravel in his throat. "No pentagrams."

And again, he waited for Michael to push, but they just drove in silence back to the parking lot at Home Depot. It wasn't that late, but it was a weeknight, and the lot was mostly empty.

Hunter slid the cap off his head and ran a hand through his hair, letting it fall across his face. His muscles were starting to knot together with tension and exhaustion, and he couldn't stop thinking about Calla's threat to burn more houses.

Even if she hadn't been stalking them at the landscaping job—and he still couldn't make that work out in his head—she could be planning something tonight.

And he had no way to stop her.

"Thanks," said Michael, pulling twenties from his wallet and holding them out.

Sixty bucks. Hunter looked up. "I don't have enough change."

"Don't worry about it."

Hunter wanted to take two twenties and leave the third— but who knew when he'd be able to get his hands on cash again. He closed his fingers around the bills and shoved them into his pocket.

The night had turned pitch-black so quickly. The halogen lights in the parking lot blazed like suns against the darkness.

Hunter put his hand on the door handle, ready to burst into the cold air.

Into the promise of another night alone.

Hunter checked his phone. No messages.

His throat felt tight again.

He needed to get the hell out of the truck before Michael called him on being a freak.

Then Michael said, "You want to talk about it?"

For some reason, the words were a relief and an assault simultaneously.

Hunter couldn't even get it together to answer him. He kept his eyes on the strip of metal where the truck door met the window. It must have been colder than he thought; his breath began to fog in the air.

Michael flipped on the heat in the cab. "Nick does that, too."

That pulled Hunter's gaze off the window. "Does what?"

"Drops the temperature when he's stressed. I'd bitch about it, but I can just turn the heat on. If you set the truck on fire, I don't have as many options."

Hunter held his breath, but there was no judgment in Michael's tone, and no urgency or impatience, either. "I've never lost control like this before."

"You're sixteen, right? It'll get worse before it gets better."

Hunter scowled. "Great."

Silence streamed through the truck again, accented by the hiss of air through the vehicle's vents.

Just as Hunter was ready to climb out of the cab again, Michael said, "Why do you need money so badly?"

Hunter looked over at him, feeling his eyes narrow. Michael must have heard the conversation with the store manager. "So this was a pity job?" He thrust a hand into his pocket for the cash, ready to fling it back. "You thought—"

"Chill out. Pity would have been if I'd handed you the cash. You earned it. What's going on?"

"Nothing."

"That's bullshit, Hunter, and you know it."

"What the hell do you care?" Hunter threw the door open. "I'm not one of your brothers." He waited for Casper to scramble out beside him, then slammed the door, stalking toward the jeep.

Michael shifted the truck into gear and accelerated out of the parking place.

Good. He could take all that stupid concern back home. Hunter shoved his key into the door of his jeep.

Just as Michael pulled his pickup directly behind it, effectively blocking Hunter's vehicle in the spot, along with the Honda Civic parked beside it.

When Michael got out, Hunter glared at him. "Now I *want* to set your truck on fire."

Michael came close enough to speak low. "Look, if you think I'm letting you get behind the wheel when you're ready to make it snow in October, you're out of your mind."

"Move your truck."

"No. I'll drive you home so you can chill out."

Hunter was going to hit him in a second. *"Move your damn truck."*

Michael didn't even blink. "Save it. Get in. I'll take you home."

Hunter felt his hands curl into fists. He could lay this guy flat and move the truck himself.

But all of a sudden, it felt like too much. His head was pounding again, and the air was freezing. It took forever to find his voice.

"You can't," he said.

Michael's voice was impassive. "I can't what?"

"You can't take me home. My grandfather—" His voice *almost* broke, so Hunter just stopped talking. His keys were cutting into his palm, and Casper nosed at his free hand.

Michael waited for a moment, then said, "Get in. You can come home with me."

God, that would be *worse*. "No way."

"Look, just take a few hours to get it together, and I'll bring you back for the jeep."

Hunter just stared at him.

Michael opened the cab of the truck and whistled through his teeth. "Come on, doggie."

Hunter expected Casper to stay at his side, like always.

But his dog leapt into the truck and lay down on the rear bench, his tongue lolling out. He looked at Hunter as if to say, *Stop being such a baby.*

So Hunter sighed and climbed in after him.

CHAPTER 9

"So let me get this straight," said Michael. "Calla trashed your place and said she's going to burn houses down until you bring Guides here."

"Yeah."

"And then she told Vickers that you roughed her up."

Hunter set his jaw. "Yeah."

"Well, there haven't been any more fires—yet. Gabriel downloaded a police scanner app or something and he's been keeping tabs on it. The fire marshal thinks the real arsonist is behind bars, so they're not expecting more. But I've got a bigger question. Why you?"

Hunter looked at him. He hadn't said anything else about his grandfather, and he was glad Michael was focusing on Calla's role in this mess. "Why me?"

"Yeah." Michael shrugged. "Why you? If she wants Guides here, they'll come eventually, right?"

"That's what Bill said, too."

"You told Bill? What did he say to do?"

Hunter snorted. "He said I made my bed, so I should lie in it."

Michael made a disgusted noise. "What a dick. I don't even know what that means, but it pisses me off."

Hunter blinked, surprised at the vehemence—and a little shocked that Michael would take his side. "He said I should have killed Calla when I had the chance."

"What a coward. *He* didn't help pull those kids out of the library fire. You and Gabriel did. He's the frigging Guide. If he wanted her dead, he should have gone and taken care of the problem himself." Michael hit the turn signal a lot harder than was necessary. "So frigging typical, setting someone else up to do his job. Is that what this is about? The hell with him, Hunter. Seriously. *Fuck him.*"

It had been so long since someone had taken his side that Hunter had forgotten what it felt like. Some of the tension that was coiled around his chest slipped free.

"But he's right," he said. "I should have just shot her."

"You're a kid. You shouldn't have been there at all, and you definitely shouldn't be expected to kill someone. Jesus, I want to drive over there and shake some sense into that guy."

Hunter didn't know what to say to any of that, so he just looked out the window again.

After a moment, he said, "Thanks."

"Sure."

Then he added, "I did shoot someone once."

Michael glanced over, but he didn't say anything.

Hunter realigned the rocks strung along his wrist. "The father of a girl I went to school with. Her name was Clare. He was beating up her and her mom. I hit him in the shoulder." He paused. "My dad—he was disappointed I didn't kill the guy."

"Your dad was *disappointed* that you hadn't killed someone?"

"Maybe disappointed isn't the right word. He used to say that being a Fifth means it's too easy to want to help people— even people who aren't doing the right thing. He'd tell me that to become a Guide, I'd have to learn to overcome that."

"No offense, Hunter, but I'm glad you didn't."

Hunter gave him half a smile, but it was grim. "Because otherwise I'd have shot you in the face when I came here to kill you all?"

Michael didn't smile back. "No, because that sounds a whole lot like turning off your conscience. Who gets to decide *right* and *wrong*? You?"

"It's not turning off your conscience."

"Why not?"

"It's just *not*." Hunter made a frustrated sound and glared out the window again. "You don't understand."

"I'm not judging you." Michael paused. "You're talking about life and death here, Hunter. One of those, you can't undo."

As if he hadn't been thinking of his father and uncle all day. Hunter didn't say anything.

All of a sudden, he wanted to get out of the truck at the next stop light.

Especially when Michael said, "What happened with your grandfather?"

They were on the 50-mph stretch of Ritchie Highway, so Hunter just shrugged and said, "It was a misunderstanding."

"About what?"

Hunter hesitated. The worst part was that he was *embarrassed* to say what had happened. "Vickers called the house and told him what had happened with Calla."

Michael let that sit out there for a long moment. "And?"

"And he believed her."

Another long pause. "You're going to have to throw me a bone here, Hunter, because I don't know what that means."

Hunter swung his head around. "He *believed* her, okay? So did my mom." His voice was shaky with fury, and he couldn't stop it. "So they packed up my stuff, and they told me to get out, and when I tried to explain that it was a misunderstanding, he—he just—"

Hunter stopped, feeling his hands curl into fists. His breath was fogging in the air again, and Michael reached over to kick up the heat.

"It doesn't matter," Hunter finished. "I took my stuff and left."

"Was this today?" said Michael. "Is that why you were so keyed up at Home Depot?"

Hunter shook his head. "Yesterday."

"*Yesterday?*" Michael glanced over. "Where did you go last night?"

"I slept in the jeep." His voice was small. "Behind Target."

To his surprise, Michael reached over and smacked him on the back of the head. "Are you insane? Jesus, Hunter, you should have called the house."

"Why?" he snapped. "So your brothers can keep giving me shit?" They were rolling to a stop at the end of Old Mill Road, just one turn away from the Merrick house. Hunter grabbed the door handle. "I don't need this."

Michael grabbed his arm. "Stop." He didn't let go, and turned the truck one-handed. "They might be giving you shit at school, but if you'd called and said you had nowhere to go . . ."

Hunter jerked free. "I can take care of myself."

"Oh, really? Is that why I'm blasting the heat right now?" They were pulling up the driveway. Michael threw the truck in park in front of the garage. "Come inside and get something to eat. Your dog could probably use some water, too."

It was the mention of Casper that made Hunter pause. His dog's head was hanging over the seat back, his tongue lolling out from the heat blasting in the cab.

"Fine," said Hunter. "But you can't blame me if I end up punching Gabriel in the face."

"Don't worry," said Michael. "He usually deserves it."

Silver was fiddling with his weapons again, laying them out on the table.

He'd been pissed off all evening.

Finally, Kate couldn't take it anymore. "What's your problem?"

His eyes flicked up. "You very nearly gave us away."

"I told you it was a bad idea to follow them."

"I wouldn't have *had* to follow them if you'd been able to get more information from Hunter Garrity."

She scowled. "I'm trying. He made me get out of his car. What do you want me to do, throw myself at him?"

"I have doubts whether you can do even that effectively."

"Shut up." But she kind of agreed with him.

Silver gave her a look that stopped her heart in her chest and made her very aware that he was holding a loaded weapon. "Let's remember our roles here."

She held his gaze and didn't apologize—but she didn't say anything else, either. Her heart had restarted and was kicking up a rapid pace.

She had to clear her throat to speak around the thunderous rush of blood in her ears. "What should we do next?"

"The more I consider it, I rather like your idea of spending time around all of them," said Silver.

She snorted. "I almost had an invite back to their house today, but Nick Merrick's girlfriend is a *bitch*."

"Not their house. I'm thinking somewhere more public. Somewhere with the chance to see if they take the bait to cause a little damage."

She fought the urge to sulk. "Somewhere you can watch me?"

"You should not be so dismissive of my protection."

"Fine. Whatever. What did you have in mind?"

His eyebrows lifted, and his hands went still on the weapon. "A little less attitude, perhaps."

She raised her own eyebrows and stared at him, waiting.

Silver pulled a folded piece of paper out of his pocket. "You'll go to this."

Kate took it. She'd seen and ignored the posters around school. "A school carnival? Seriously?"

"Seriously. It's public, they'll likely all attend, and I can observe without being noticed. It's also tomorrow night."

"And what should I do while I'm there?"

"You'll make sure you haven't blown our cover."

A new edge had found its way into his voice, matching the darkness in his expression. Kate looked at her nails and did her best to ignore it. She'd barely spent any time with the Merricks—she couldn't imagine she'd blown their cover.

But she kept thinking about Hunter, and the way he'd thrown her out of the car.

She'd touched him, and he'd caught her arm. Had he figured it out somehow?

She glanced up at Silver, but he was looking back at his laptop. "And if I have?"

"You'd do well to run."

"From them?"

He met her eyes. "From me."

CHAPTER 10

Gabriel and Nick Merrick were sitting at the kitchen table when Hunter followed Michael into the house. They were identical twins, but Hunter had never had a moment's trouble telling them apart. Their powers were so different that they registered differently against his senses. When he'd first met them, he hadn't known what that meant—he'd never spent any time around full Elementals. But once he knew their abilities—Nick's affinity for air, and Gabriel's for fire—he wondered how he'd ever missed it.

Nick had a thick textbook open on the table in front of him, with a notebook beside it. He looked irritated, and he was watching Gabriel break Oreos into a bowl of milk.

"You know," Nick was saying, "you could actually make dinner for a change."

"I am making dinner."

They hadn't spotted him yet.

Hunter didn't exactly want to remedy that.

But Casper didn't care, he just followed Michael into the kitchen, his tail waving like a banner behind him.

Hunter watched their expressions change, saw their eyes follow Casper as his nails clicked across the ceramic tile, then watched them swing their gazes around to the kitchen doorway.

The silence lasted about three seconds.

Then Gabriel's expression sharpened, and he said, "Look, Michael brought home a dog and a—"

"Gabriel. Leave him alone." Michael grabbed a bowl from a cabinet and filled it with water.

Hunter had no idea how this was going to go, and he didn't really want to be standing here, waiting around to find out. He could sit on the front porch while Casper got a drink.

Before he could move to take a step, Nick cleared his throat. "You help Mike with a job or something?"

"Yeah."

"Want something to drink?"

Hunter hesitated, like this could be a trap. But Nick was just looking at him, waiting for an answer.

So Hunter shrugged. "Sure."

Then he tensed, realizing he'd probably walked right into it, that Nick would say something shitty like, "Too bad," or he'd throw a glass of water in his face, or—

Or he'd just walk to the fridge, fetch a bottle of Gatorade, and toss it.

Hunter snatched it out of the air but hesitated before unscrewing the cap. "Thanks."

"No problem."

Gabriel watched this whole exchange. "What the hell are you doing here?"

There was something reassuring about the hostility. This, Hunter could deal with. He took a sip and made Gabriel wait for the answer. "Your brother blocked my car and forced me into his truck at Home Depot."

Nick's eyebrows went up. He looked at his older brother, who was dropping into a chair at the end of the table. "Really."

Michael shrugged but didn't say anything. He reached for the package of Oreos.

"Gee, Mike," said Gabriel. "I'm sure that didn't look sketchy *at all*."

Michael didn't answer him; he just looked up at Hunter. "What are you going to do tonight?"

Hunter shrugged and leaned against the doorjamb, swirling the Gatorade in the bottle. "I'll be all right."

"What's tonight?" said Nick.

Then the front door slammed, and a pair of feet came down the hallway. Hunter moved to the side, and Chris appeared in the doorway, his eyes narrowed. "You're *here*." He tossed car keys on the counter. "Well, that was a wasted trip."

Hunter raised his eyebrows. "Meaning?"

"Becca made me swing by your house before I dropped her off." Chris made it sound like Becca had asked him to swing by the county dump. "You weren't in school and then you didn't return her texts. She was worried."

Becca was worried. Hunter was oddly touched.

Then Chris said, "Your grandfather said you left."

Hunter's chest tightened until it was hard to breathe again. His grandfather said he'd *left*? Like he'd just walked out?

"I figured you'd skipped town," said Chris. He dropped into the chair next to Nick. "Guess we're not that lucky."

"Guess not," said Hunter. His hand gripped the Gatorade bottle so tightly the plastic crackled. His thoughts were spiraling like a tornado, and he couldn't make them settle. His mother had watched—his grandfather had—his mother—his—

"Casper," he called. *"Hierr."* The dog shot to his side and nosed at his hands. Hunter glanced at Michael. "Will you drive me back now?"

"Why don't you wait," said Michael. "Have some dinner."

Hunter glanced at the bowl of crushed cookies in milk. "Thanks, I'll pass."

"You going to sleep in your car and skip school again?" said Michael.

Well, that changed the tenor of the room. Hunter couldn't look at any of them now. He could feel them staring, and that was bad enough.

"Forget it," he said. "I'll walk."

The night air stung his face when he stepped out of the house, and Hunter pulled the hood of his sweatshirt higher against his neck. No one followed him.

Good.

He was dirty from helping Michael, and a hot shower would have helped ease the soreness across his shoulders, but that would have to wait until tomorrow morning. He wasn't sure how long he could keep using the school gym showers without someone noticing he wasn't going to class, but he'd do it as long as he could keep it up.

Your grandfather said you left.

Hunter swallowed. Stupid old man. Like he wanted to be there anyway.

He thought of the Merricks, sitting around the kitchen table, a room full of aggression and old wounds—but full of camaraderie and solidarity, too. The brothers didn't always get along, but they *knew* each other.

His grandfather didn't even know that Hunter would *never* have hit a girl.

His grandfather hadn't even hesitated before hitting *him*.

Hunter had to swallow again.

God, stop being such a wuss.

His father would be so disappointed.

Hunter rubbed at his eyes.

His cell phone chimed, and he yanked it out of his pocket, stupidly hoping it would be his mother.

It wasn't.

Bueller . . . Bueller . . . Bueller.

Kate. Hunter smiled and wanted to kick himself. He stared at the text and wondered how to respond.

He felt a flicker of guilt at the way he'd thrown her out of his jeep.

Sneakers ground on pavement behind him, and Hunter whirled, hands up. Then the air sparked with Gabriel's presence.

He shoved the phone in his pocket and kept walking.

Gabriel fell into step beside him.

Hunter didn't even glance over. "Leave me alone."

"Having a good cry?"

He wasn't, but Hunter set his jaw anyway. "Go to hell."

"So yesterday," said Gabriel. "Remember when I flipped your tray?"

"No. I forgot all about it."

"Totally didn't know you'd have soup on there. Jesus, I didn't even know the cafeteria *sold*—"

Hunter stopped on the street and looked at him. "What do you want, Gabriel? What?"

"I want to know why you pretended to be my friend."

Hunter started walking again.

Gabriel kept after him. "Michael said your grandfather threw you out because of what happened with Calla."

"So what?"

"Does *anyone* trust you? Or do you just feed everyone a line of crap until it catches up with you?"

Hunter couldn't look at him now. "You don't know what you're talking about."

"Remember that day we went running? Remember how you sat on the side of the trail and cried about your father? Was that real? Or just one more act? Something to get me to talk, so you could report back to Bill?" His voice turned into a breathy lisping mockery of Hunter's. " 'Guess what I learned today. Gabriel Merrick misses his mommy.' "

"Fuck you."

"No, fuck *you*, Hunter." Gabriel got in his face and shoved him, true anger behind the motion. "You know why you slept alone in your jeep last night? Because you've screwed over anyone who might help you."

Hunter shoved past him and kept walking. He remembered that day, jogging on the trail, racing Gabriel for fun until they ran out of energy and adrenaline and collapsed in the grass. The air had been crisp and clean with the sun beating down—and memories of his father had clouded Hunter's brain until he couldn't help but talk about it. Emotion was tightening his chest again, just thinking about it.

A car rolled down the road, swirling dead leaves from the roadside in its wake. Night wind snuck into the space between Hunter's collar and his neck. He begged the air for warmth, but it was merely content to nip at his skin and make him shiver.

"What I don't get," said Gabriel from behind him, "is how you could trust that asshole."

Hunter didn't say anything.

"I mean," Gabriel continued, "you know he abandoned his own daughter. You know he trapped Chris and Nick and used them as bait. Hell, you saw the news footage of the bridge when he tried to blow up Becca's *car*. Some fucking father."

Hunter just kept walking.

"And if you want to pick Bill's side, then why did you help Michael tonight?"

"I needed money."

Gabriel caught his arm and spun him around. "Bullshit."

"It's not bullshit. I did need money." Hunter jerked free.

Gabriel shoved him in the chest. "Lying to yourself, too?"

Hunter gritted his teeth. "Go away."

"Why can't you even answer a straight question?" Another shove. "I've seen you drop Mike on his ass one-handed, so I don't buy this crap about him forcing you into the truck."

Gabriel shoved him again, a fierce motion that drove Hunter back a step. He didn't want to fight. He didn't want to *be here*.

"Are you messing with my family again, Hunter?"

"Stop it."

"If you wanted to finish what your father started, then you should have shot us on the soccer field." Another push, another step. "Quit screwing around so I can decide whether to help you or kick your ass."

Hunter moved to shove him—and when Gabriel shifted to brace and strike back, Hunter stepped into the motion, hooked an ankle, and spun. The back of his fist caught Gabriel in the face, and the other boy went down. Hard.

Hunter glared down at him, fists clenched and ready for retaliation. "You could *not* kick my ass."

Gabriel winced and touched the back of his head. "Dude, this is concrete."

"Good."

"Jesus." He winced again and sat up on the curb. "One of these days you'll have to show me how you do that."

Hunter stared down at him, feeling his breathing settle and his hands loosen. He sighed and dropped to sit on the curb. Casper came and pressed against his knees, and Hunter buried his fingers in the scruff of fur at the dog's neck.

"I'm sorry," he said. "I should have told you. About Bill."

Gabriel didn't say anything, so Hunter kept his eyes on his dog. "When I followed you to the first fire—I wasn't even going to let you know I was there. But then I could tell someone was trapped, and I couldn't *not*—well, you know."

"I remember."

"I never told Bill anything. He asked, but I didn't tell him any of it. Not about the fires, or about the—the other stuff. About my dad, and your mom—"

"I get it."

"Sometimes . . ." Hunter hesitated. "Sometimes I don't know what's *right*, you know?"

"Yeah, man. You do."

Did he? It made Hunter think about Michael's comments in the car, about turning off his conscience. Who decided what was right?

Gabriel stood and held out a hand. "Come on. You can crash in Nick's room."

Hunter peered up at him. "What? Why?"

"Because he's got more floor space for an air mattress."

"What about all this crap about not trusting me?" Hunter took the hand and pulled himself to his feet.

"Keep your enemies closer, right?" said Gabriel.

But the tension, the challenge and aggression, was gone from his voice.

"Thanks," Hunter said. "Maybe just one night."

"Stay as long as you need to."

Hunter was surprised by the sudden lump of emotion in his throat. He couldn't say anything.

But then Gabriel smiled. "Besides. If you fuck with me or my brothers again, I'll just let Nicky suffocate you in your sleep."

CHAPTER 11

Hunter stared at the ceiling and waited for sleep to find him, but it didn't seem to be looking too hard. Casper was a heavy weight at his side, his muzzle tucked under a paw. Nick's breathing was slow and even, a solid indicator of sleep.

Hunter pulled the phone out of his pocket and scrolled through the menu until he found Kate's last text.

Bueller . . . Bueller . . . Bueller.

He'd never responded.

He should have just deleted it, but his message from this morning, the one about his grandfather, sat there right above it.

He'd been such an *idiot*. Why had he told her about it? God, he'd been ready to completely unravel in front of her, and then she'd started texting some other guy.

The phone suddenly vibrated in his hand, and he almost dropped it.

I am going to stare at you until you respond. O_O

It made him smile.
He told himself to knock it off.
His phone vibrated again.

O_O

And again.

O_O

Hunter slid his thumb across the keys.

Careful. Your eyes will dry out.

As always, her response appeared almost instantly.

I knew the staring would get you.

He didn't know what to say to that. A pause, and then another message appeared.

What are you still doing up?

I couldn't sleep while someone was staring at me.

Why did you throw me out of your car this morning?

Hunter had no idea how to respond. *I didn't want to get played* seemed like the wrong thing to say.

He already felt like a loser for almost breaking down in front of her. No sense adding more weight to that.

Then again, she'd lost her mother. Maybe he'd misread this morning entirely.

Nick's breathing changed, and he shifted on the bed, running a hand across his face before looking down at Hunter. "What are you doing?" He glanced at the clock on his nightstand. "It's two a.m."

"Sorry. Can't sleep." Hunter clicked the phone off and shoved it under the blanket.

"Who are you texting?"

"Nobody."

A pause. A long one.

A weighted one.

Then Nick's voice gained an edge as he said, "Is this some elaborate trick to get in our house? Are you reporting back to Bill about us—"

"I'm not." Hunter paused. "It's just a girl."

"Prove it."

Hunter's pride wanted him to refuse—but he really couldn't blame Nick for not trusting him. He pulled the phone out from under the blanket, unlocked the screen until Kate's texts were visible, and tossed it.

Nick took a quick glance, then tossed it back. The edge was gone from his voice. "Kate? The one who just transferred?"

Hunter looked up in surprise—though her name was clearly at the top of the screen. "How did you know?"

"She asked me about you today."

"She did?" That statement was full of highs and lows. She'd asked about him—but she'd asked *Nick*. Had she sat with Nick again?

He didn't care. He didn't.

Yeah, he did.

God, he needed to stop being such an *idiot*.

But he couldn't stop thinking about her. "What'd she say?"

"She asked if I knew why you were ditching school."

His heart felt like it was beating faster. No, it felt like it wanted a break from being inside his rib cage. His phone was a warm weight in his hand, and he wanted to pull it out from under the blanket to see if she'd written again. "And what did you say?"

"Ah . . . I said *no*."

Right.

Hunter rolled back to look at the ceiling.

Nick said, "Do you know her?"

Hunter shook his head.

"Interested?"

Yes. Immensely. "Not really." Hunter looked down at Casper, who was blowing puffs of warm breath against his arm. "She seemed into you, though."

Nick snorted. "Yeah, in a way that made Quinn want to pull her hair out by the roots. I think she's just friendly." He paused. "You don't have to worry about me being interested."

Well, at least that was something. "You and Quinn getting serious?"

"Something like that."

"I think Kate's a player."

"Yeah?"

Hunter pushed the hair back from his face and sighed. "She climbed in my car this morning, but then started texting some other guy."

"Quinn saw her get into a truck with someone yesterday."

Well, there went that. Hunter let go of his phone. It fell off the air mattress and onto the carpet.

Nick continued, "To hear Quinn tell it, he was—well, I'm not going to repeat her phrase, but let's just say Kate seemed into him."

Hunter didn't say anything.

His subconscious was screaming at him. *DUDE. You are an IDIOT.*

She was probably laughing about him with this other guy.

The room was so silent that Hunter was sure Nick had fallen back to sleep. Tension still had him by the throat, but he started to doze himself.

Nick's voice caught him. "Hey." His voice was rough with almost sleep. "I didn't mean to see the text about what happened with your grandfather. You didn't say that earlier."

Now Hunter was fully awake again. "It's fine."

"I won't tell—"

"I said it's fine," he snapped. This whole situation was just one big reminder of all his failures. Besides, Hunter didn't want to think about his *home stuff*, not now, in the dark, lying on the floor of someone else's room.

Then he realized that he probably shouldn't be a total shit in someone else's room, either.

"Sorry," he said. "Long day. I really . . . I just don't want to talk about it."

"I get it." Another pause. "Gabriel can come on like a freight train, but he doesn't hate you."

Hunter wasn't too sure about that.

"Chris, either."

"Really? So Chris turning the water ice cold while I was in the shower was friendly?"

"Gabriel paid him twenty bucks to do that."

Hunter smiled.

Nick added, "And then he felt like a *moron* when I told him he could have just turned off the hot water in the basement . . ."

Hunter laughed softly.

And all of a sudden it nailed home how lonely he'd been. The Merricks had each other. He had no one.

He lost the smile. The air in the room suddenly felt heavy. Hunter looked back at the ceiling.

Nick sighed, then rolled up on one arm. "Do you want some space? I can go crash with Gabriel."

Hunter had no idea what the right answer to that was.

"Seriously, man," said Nick. "I can feel your tension in the air."

That made Hunter look over. "Really?"

"It woke me up."

Hunter looked back at the ceiling. "Sorry." He paused. "My dad always used to say that Air Elementals were the ones you really had to watch out for."

Nothing but silence for a moment. Then, "I think it's a breathing thing. People breathe differently when they're stressed." Another pause. "It's new. I've only recently been able to sense emotion that way."

Hunter remembered a day when Nick had gotten into a fight with Gabriel and made him stop breathing, and Hunter thought maybe his father had been right. "My dad told me about this one guy who always knew if someone was lying, using that same thing, I think. He said he was the strongest Air Elemental he'd ever seen. The guy could jump across buildings, like in Spider-Man, you know?"

"Now *that* would be useful." Nick sounded intrigued, but then he hesitated. "What happened to him?"

His father had never said specifically—but if he had *known* the guy, he hadn't known him long. Hunter looked away. "I don't know."

"Yeah, you do."

Hunter gave him a sharp look. "Then so do you. You know what my father was."

Nick didn't back down, but he didn't say anything, either. That weighted silence again.

Then he said, "Why aren't you like *that*? Aren't you supposed to be in some training program or something? Isn't that what happens with you Fifths?"

Nick's tone almost mirrored the way Hunter's father used to talk about pure Elementals. "I would have. This fall. I wanted to go when I was younger—when I first *knew*, you know? But my dad wanted to wait, to make sure I was strong enough."

And he hadn't been strong enough. He'd thought he was: he'd begged his father and uncle to take him along on their last assignment. Uncle Jay had argued on his behalf, claiming it was just supposed to be surveillance—only his dad had put his foot down.

But his dad changed his mind. They came back for Hunter.

And then one of the numerous rock walls along the Pennsylvania Turnpike had come loose, and the car had been crushed.

Calla claimed responsibility. But Hunter knew it was his own fault.

He shouldn't have been in the car with his dad and his uncle when it crashed. He shouldn't have been along at all, because they shouldn't have turned back for him.

If he hadn't pitched such a fit, the car wouldn't have gotten trapped in that rock slide. Calla and her friends would have been too late.

"Do you know other Guides?" said Nick.

Hunter shook his head. "Calla thinks I do, though."

"Would you bring them if you could?"

"I don't know."

"She's going to kill people."

Hunter looked over. "She's going to kill people either way. If I convince a bunch of Guides to come here, is that better?"

"Michael says they'll come anyway, if she keeps this up."

"He's right."

"So I've got a question."

"Yeah?"

"When they do, whose side are you on?"

Hunter didn't move. He couldn't. He'd never nailed it down to such a fine point.

But Nick was right. If the Guides came, they wouldn't stop with Calla and her crew. They'd take out the Merricks, too.

Hunter had no idea where that left him.

Nick rolled out of bed, dragging his pillow and his comforter with him.

Hunter sat up. "What are you doing?"

"I'm going to crash on the floor in Gabriel's room."

Hunter didn't know whether to apologize—and before he could figure it out, Nick was through the door.

He probably should have offered to go downstairs himself.

Nick stuck his head back in the door. "We're not trying to screw with you, man. None of us are. We're trying to *help* you."

Hunter didn't look at him.

Nick snorted before pulling the door closed. "Maybe doing the same for us wouldn't be out of line."

CHAPTER 12

Living in the Merrick house was both complicated—and not. Hunter hadn't thought it would be possible to feel so isolated in the middle of so much . . . *energy.* Gabriel woke him up at the crack of dawn with a cup of water to the face and a kick in the ribs.

"Get up, slacker. Don't you have a marathon to run at the end of the month?"

Hunter tried to jerk free of the sleeping bag. It wasn't even four thirty in the morning—and he hadn't drifted off until after two. "God, are you insane?"

Gabriel was already heading out the door. "Be grateful I didn't light you on fire."

"I'm going to break your ankles."

"Have to catch me first, jackass."

But the run felt good, getting out of the house and feeling the fresh air on his face.

Even if Gabriel didn't talk much.

It made Hunter wonder how much of his conversation with Nick had been repeated.

Probably all of it.

There'd been breakfast, a selection of cereals like Lucky Charms and Cookie Crisp. When he'd asked for fruit or eggs, they all looked at him like he'd grown a second head.

They weren't mean. They weren't indifferent.

They were just guarded.

It was exhausting.

By the time school started, he was ready to focus his attention on something else, no matter how mundane the subject.

But then he found Calla Dean by her locker—looking innocent as ever, applying lip gloss. As usual, she looked like a punk sex goddess, tight jeans, an almost see-through shirt, and black rubber bracelets lining her arms, crisscrossing over the flame tattoos. Feather earrings, a bright yellow streak in her hair.

His fists were tight at his sides, but he couldn't approach her.

He'd gotten a lecture from Michael this morning. *If you're staying here, you go to school, and you stay out of trouble. We don't need attention right now. Understand?*

"Hunter."

He turned at the soft voice and found Becca standing there, a spill of dark hair hanging over one shoulder. For the first time in a long while, her voice was gentle, and her eyes were intent on his.

She'd been the first girl he noticed in this school, the first one who didn't look at him like something to eat—or something to despise. He hadn't been able to parcel out the Merrick brothers' powers at first, but hers—hers, he'd sensed from the beginning.

"Hey," he said.

"Are you okay?"

He glanced past her. "I've been better."

"Chris told me about your grandfather."

Hunter gritted his teeth. "Yeah, well. I've got bigger things to worry about."

Calla had put her lip gloss away and was staring at them now. She tapped her wrist and mouthed, "Tick tock."

Hunter sighed. "Come on. Before Calla causes a scene."

Becca followed him, and her voice was low. "Chris said she's threatening to start more fires?"

"Yeah."

Becca's eyes hardened. "And we can't just take her out ourselves?"

Of course Becca would immediately want to challenge her. "We need to find out who she's working with. She had someone with her when she trashed my house. I've never seen him before."

"Another teenager?"

"I think so, but I've been watching for him around school and I haven't seen him." He couldn't figure that out, either. Calla's friends looked at him like they genuinely believed he was roughing her up. They weren't like Calla, calculating and manipulative, whispering taunts at every turn.

Who was the missing kid? And who else was she working with?

Becca was staring back at Calla now. "Can't we just ask her?"

"She's told half the school that I smack her around. I can't even get close to her."

"Can *I* ask her?"

Hunter shook his head. "Your dad would lose it if I dragged you into this."

"All the more reason to help." She turned on her heel as if ready to confront Calla right there in the hallway.

Hunter grabbed her backpack and hauled her back around. He smiled in spite of himself. "Easy, tiger. Let's not get crazy."

"Fine. Give me your gun. Let's just shoot her."

He didn't bother getting shocked over her reaction—he thought about the same thing at least once a day. "My grandfather confiscated it. And you can't just *shoot* someone."

"People died in those fires," Becca whispered fiercely. "Fires that *she* started. Ryan Stacey might have been involved, but she—"

"Yeah, I know." Hunter held her eyes for a minute, then let go of her backpack. It was only eight a.m., but he was already exhausted. "I don't want her to start any more fires, either. I'm just trying to figure out how to stop her."

Becca stared up at him.

And then, to his surprise, she threw her arms around his neck.

Hunter caught her automatically. Her body was warm, and her closeness reminded him of the night she'd slept pressed against him. He'd never had a girl want to be so close to him, and for her to trust him enough to fall asleep in his arms that night—well, he hadn't wanted to fall asleep himself, just so he wouldn't miss a minute of it.

He'd wanted to tell her, then. About himself, about who his father was, about his reasons for being in town. He'd told her half-truths, about the accident and about his mom.

He would have told her the rest.

But then Chris Merrick had shown up to drive her to school.

Hunter's cell phone chimed, snapping him back to the present. He ignored it. Being held felt so good that he didn't want to let go for anything.

But she pulled back, and he had to release her. "What was that for?" he asked.

"You looked like no one had given you one for a while."

Hunter stared at her, unsure of what to say. It reminded him of Nick's comments last night, just in an entirely different way.

She tucked her hair behind her ear. "I'm around if you need to talk."

"Oh, yeah? Is Chris okay with that?"

"This isn't about Chris."

Hunter snorted. His brain felt like it was misfiring about *everything*.

Becca looked at him sternly. "Don't. Whatever you're about to say, don't. You build everyone up to be your enemy, and they're *not*. Chris and his brothers are trying to help you."

He took a breath and stared across the hallway at the lockers there. "I know."

"So am I." The bell rang and she turned away. "Remember that."

He watched her walk down the hall, wondering, not for the first time, what would have happened if he'd been honest with her from the start.

Before that thought could go too far, his phone chimed again.

Two texts. Both from Kate.

The first was the one he'd missed while he was hugging Becca.

So are you the pot and I'm the kettle?

Hunter looked up, scanning the hallway, which was quickly emptying of students. If Kate had been watching them, she wasn't around now.

He looked back at his phone and scrolled to the next message.

Who's the brunette?

Wow. His fingers flew across the screen.

She's just a friend.

Her reply popped up in a heartbeat.

She looked very friendly.

He frowned at the phone and typed furiously.

I heard you were pretty friendly with some guy with a pickup truck.

A long pause. Hunter felt his heartbeat slamming against his rib cage.

It felt fantastic to push against someone, to have the upper hand about something.

But it also felt like crap.

You build everyone up to be your enemy.

Did he really do that?

The phone chimed.

I don't understand what happened.

He frowned at the phone. Then typed.

Me, either.

And he waited, but she didn't write back.

All day.

At the end of the day, Hunter drove to the Merrick house, but he sat in the jeep with the engine running.

It felt ridiculous, but he wasn't entirely sure if he was welcome for another night. He hadn't gone to the cafeteria at lunch, because he'd been making up a quiz he'd missed while job hunting, and it wasn't like he and Chris ever said a word to each other in World History.

Really, if Casper weren't locked in the house, he might have gone back to the Target parking lot again.

His breath was fogging in the confines of the car, and he swore. He wasn't used to being so off balance.

Finally, he threw himself out of the car, setting his shoulders and shoving his hands into the pockets of his hoodie. If they didn't want him here, he'd just grab his dog and leave.

The front door was unlocked, but Casper wasn't inside the house. No one was.

For an instant, Hunter wondered if this was some big trick, if they were all screwing with him.

Then he heard a dog bark from the backyard.

He strode through the kitchen and slid the glass door open. The sky was a gradually darkening gray, and the chill in the air had been biting through his clothes all afternoon. Michael was out in the grass, throwing a tennis ball while Casper went tearing after it.

Michael noticed him and looked up. "Hey. How was school?"

"I didn't get hassled by Vickers or Calla." He paused. His dog was trotting back to Michael with the ball half hanging out of his mouth. The only acknowledgment he gave Hunter was a quick *woof* muffled by the ball. Hunter smiled. "Thanks for letting Casper out."

"He's been out all day."

"He has?"

"Yeah. When I walked out the door this morning, he bolted past me and jumped in the bed of the truck. I tried to get him back in the house, but he wouldn't go. So I just took him with me."

Casper dropped the ball at Michael's feet and barked.

"Traitor," Hunter called.

Michael picked up the ball and beaned it into the woods. He had one hell of an arm—the ball was *gone*. Casper took off like a shot.

"Where's everyone else?" Hunter said.

"I didn't have an evening job, so they all made plans. I think they're hitting the school carnival later. Aren't you?"

A carnival. Like he could possibly go to something like that while Calla was probably sitting at home figuring out which house she was going to torch first.

"Nah," he said.

"So I called your mom today," said Michael.

Hunter snapped his head up. Michael had asked for his mom's phone number last night—under the pretense of needing it in case of an emergency. "You *what*?"

"She needed to know where you were."

"She has my cell number," he snapped. "She could have found me if she wanted." Hunter felt like he couldn't catch his breath. Emotions ricocheted around in his head.

She'd watched him walk out. He shouldn't give a crap what she thought.

But he did. A lot.

He didn't want to ask what she'd said. His fingernails were digging rivets into the porch railing.

Casper was back, dropping the ball at Michael's feet and nosing it forward when it wasn't thrown immediately.

Michael obliged him, flinging it into the woods again. It cracked against a tree somewhere out of sight. Casper was off.

Michael glanced up at the porch. "She said she'd put the rest of your things together, if you want to come get them."

Those words hit hard. Michael could have thrown the ball at *him* and the impact would have hurt less. Hunter couldn't even speak. His voice would break and he'd look like a total wuss.

She hadn't said, "Tell Hunter to come home."

She'd said she'd pack up his stuff.

Splinters from the railing were beginning to drive up under his fingernails, but the pain was keeping him grounded.

"You doing anything right now? Have any plans?" said Michael.

Hunter swallowed and told himself to knock it off. "Nothing."

"Good. Come on, I'll drive you over."

"I don't—that's—" He had to slow his thoughts down or they'd never make it out of his mouth coherently. "I don't want to go over there."

"Why?"

Because I don't want to see her.

Because I don't want to see him.

Because if I pick up my stuff, that means I really don't have anywhere to live.

Hunter set his jaw. "What am I going to do, dump it in your basement? Keep sleeping on Nick's floor?" His voice was hard, but inside, his heart was a frigging *wreck*. "Casper," he called. *"Hierr."* The dog bolted to his side, but Hunter was already off the porch and heading for the front of the house.

For his car.

"Hey," Michael called after him.

Hunter didn't stop.

But Michael was faster than Hunter gave him credit for, and he caught up before Hunter could close the door to his jeep.

Hunter slammed the door back at him, making Michael fall back a step. He followed it up with a solid shove. "Leave me *alone*," he shouted. "Just leave me—"

Then his voice broke and he was crying.

This was horrible and humiliating and he wanted to throw the jeep into neutral and just let it roll over himself.

Michael didn't touch him. Good thing, because Hunter would have punched him.

He imagined it, the motion, the impact, exactly how much force it would take, what a *release* it would be.

It didn't help. If anything, he felt coiled more tightly.

He slammed the door and dropped onto the pavement of the

driveway, leaning back against his car and pressing the heels of his hands into his eyes.

"Go away," Hunter said, hating that his voice was thick and made him sound like a sniveling six-year-old. Casper jumped out of the jeep and lay down beside him.

Michael sat down on the other side.

"That is the opposite of going away," said Hunter.

"Look," Michael offered. "Your mom was worried about you."

"I don't want to talk about her."

Michael didn't say anything to that. He didn't say anything for so long that Hunter swiped a sleeve across his face, then turned to look at him. "I'm not one of your brothers. Stop sitting here. *Go. Away.*"

"I don't think," Michael began slowly, "that your mom offered to pack up your stuff because she didn't want you to come back."

Hunter wanted to hit something. Unfortunately, the people who *really* deserved it weren't available. "How the hell do you know?"

Michael looked out at the trees lining the driveway. "I don't. Not really, I guess." He paused. "You know, there's not a manual to the whole parent thing."

"What is that supposed to mean?"

"It means . . . I think your mom feels badly about what happened, and she's not sure how to fix it." Another pause. "I think . . . by offering to pack up your things, she might think she's helping."

Hunter rested his arms on his knees and didn't respond.

Michael sighed. "I remember when I was eighteen, it was a total shock to realize my parents had been winging it the whole time. Like, there was this one time that Chris—"

"Save it," said Hunter. "I don't need any Merrick family anecdotes."

"Fine," said Michael equably. "How about a Garrity family anecdote?"

"What?"

"You tell me, Hunter, because we—you and me—don't have a history here beyond you trying to kill me, and me finding you ready to flatten the Home Depot. You're not this mad at your mom just for letting your grandfather throw you out. What else is there?"

Hunter gritted his teeth and stared at the trees. The air was crisp and cold, biting through his clothes as easily as the chill in the pavement was biting through his jeans. But being outside helped settle his nerves.

And Michael just waited.

Hunter realized he was holding on to everything so tightly that it was all going to snap and come apart if he wasn't careful. Like with Gabriel in the cafeteria.

Like with Kate in the car.

And just like that, he found himself talking.

"My parents were a bizarre couple," he said. "I mean, I never really thought about it, but everybody said so. My dad was in the Marines for a long time. He went through special forces, the whole deal. Even when he got out, he worked private jobs—the dangerous kind. It went right along with being a Guide. I don't even know all the jobs he took. A lot of them were classified—and now . . . well, now they're going to be classified forever, I guess."

He paused, rubbing at the scruff of Casper's neck.

Michael waited.

"Mom was . . . unique. She had a new age store in the town where we lived, and she played up the part. She did tarot readings, crystal healings, stuff like that. She gave me the stones. I didn't realize until I started getting powers that they'd start to feel like a part of me . . ." Hunter paused and lined them up along his wrist. "She didn't know what my dad was—like the Guide stuff—but she always used to dote on him and say he had a special connection to the world around him." Now, knowing what he knew about his mother and father, Hunter wondered if his dad had laughed about that behind her back.

"Have you ever wanted to tell her?" said Michael. "About what your dad was?"

Hunter shook his head. "No. When I was younger, it was something between me and him. Not like a secret, but more like he *got* me—" He made a dismissive noise. "This is stupid."

"It's not. I get it."

Hunter glanced over, and Michael shrugged. He was still looking at the trees, which made this whole conversation easier.

"My dad was an Earth Elemental, too." Michael paused, and it was weighted with feeling. "We didn't always get along, but— well, you know."

Hunter nodded and looked back at the trees himself. "People always ask if my dad was strict, and he was—but he wasn't. I never—I didn't—"

He had to stop.

His dad would have shit a brick if he'd known Hunter was sitting here *crying*.

"Was he proud of you?" said Michael.

Hunter snorted. "I never knew where I stood with him." He had to swallow. *God, suck it up.* "I never will."

"I'm sure you have *some* idea."

"I don't. The day before he died, he told me that the only reason he was with my mother was because he was *using* her. Their whole relationship was based on that. And she has no idea."

"Wow." A pause. "What do you think that means about your relationship with him?"

"He said I needed to learn to use people, that it would keep me safe because of what I am."

"Well, that explains a lot."

Hunter snapped his head around.

Michael put a hand up before he could say anything. "Take it easy. You don't have to be on such a hair trigger, kid." A pause. "But if you don't mind me sharing one thing I learned when I was eighteen, something that's bothered me since my parents struck that messed-up deal with the other Elementals in town . . ."

"What?"

"Sometimes parents are *wrong*."

The words hit him hard again, and Hunter flinched.

"Come on," said Michael. He clapped Hunter on the shoulder. "Let's go get your stuff."

"I don't want—"

"Come *on*," Michael said. "Let her be wrong for once. It'll be good for you both."

CHAPTER 13

No one was home.

Or at least, neither his mother's nor his grandparents' cars were in the driveway.

"Well, this is anticlimactic," said Hunter. He hadn't even killed the engine in the jeep.

Michael glanced over. "You have a key?"

"Sure."

But he didn't want to go inside. This felt like a free pass, and he was tempted to peel out of here, spraying gravel behind him.

"If your stuff is packed up," said Michael, "we can just grab it and go, right?"

Point.

The house felt the same as he remembered, some lingering scent from his grandmother's chili—which she made every weekend—combined with the faint whiff of the potpourri sitting out in the living room. Cool and quiet and still.

Nothing was in the front hallway, but maybe she'd left his stuff downstairs.

Or maybe she hadn't packed it up at all.

Hunter couldn't decide which option he was hoping for.

He felt jittery now, not knowing where everyone was or when they'd be home. He was just standing there between the dining room and the living room, keys jingling nervously in his hand.

"So . . . ," started Michael. "Upstairs?"

"No. Down. Follow me."

The basement was ten degrees colder than the rest of the house, something he'd never really noticed until today. He hit the switches to light up the space.

She'd packed. Two plastic storage boxes plus a duffel bag were laid out on his bed.

His *old* bed. His quilt was gone, either packed away or folded in one of these boxes. His Xbox and alarm clock were gone. His books, his old school notebooks—everything. The room looked like it was waiting for the next tenant.

He snapped the lid off one of the boxes. Mostly electronics and notebooks, though two framed pictures lay right on top.

Michael picked up one. "Your dad and uncle?"

For some reason, Hunter wanted to snatch it away from him.

"Yeah." He held out a hand. "Don't say I look exactly like my dad. I get that all the time."

Michael glanced up. He handed back the frame. "Hunter, there is nothing about you that would make me say you look exactly like this guy."

Hunter stared back at him in surprise.

"Look in a mirror sometime," said Michael.

Hunter glanced at the picture again. He was trying to decide whether or not that was an insult when the front door of the house slammed.

It might as well have been a gunshot right into his heart. His pulse rate tripled.

"Relax," said Michael. "Your mom said you could come get your stuff." He put the plastic lid back on the box Hunter had opened—leaving the frame clutched between Hunter's hands. Then he jerked his head at the other one. "Grab that, huh?"

It spurred him into motion. Hunter slung the duffel bag over a shoulder, grabbed the box, and headed for the stairs, Michael following.

He didn't really want to see any of them, but he hoped it was his mom. She seemed like the lesser of two evils.

But of course it was his grandfather who appeared at the top of the stairs.

Hunter stopped short and stared up at him.

He knew about thirty ways to disarm someone bare-handed, but just now he wanted to duck behind Michael.

That realization shocked him into movement again. "I'm just getting my stuff," he said. "Mom said I could."

His grandfather didn't move from the top of the steps, and Hunter stopped there on the second to last step, the plastic box a barrier between them.

The man was glaring. Hunter glared back.

He wanted to shove him with the box. Hard.

"Who's your friend?" said his grandfather. "One of the ones who trashed the kitchen?"

"No," said Michael. "One of the ones offering Hunter a place to live."

When no one said anything and no one moved, Michael added, "Could you please step aside so we can take these out to the car?"

To Hunter's surprise, his grandfather actually stepped back— but he didn't look happy about it.

"Just keep walking," Michael said quietly.

Good advice. Hunter broke the staring match and started walking.

Unfortunately, his grandfather seemed to think he'd won some battle. He grabbed Hunter's arm before he could go past. "Maybe I should check those. Make sure you aren't taking anything that's not yours."

Hunter gritted his teeth. "Mom packed them."

"You still owe me for the mess in the kitchen. Maybe I should take that GameBox thing—"

"Fine," snapped Hunter. "Take it. I don't give a—"

"Whoa." Michael caught Hunter's arm.

Hunter realized he'd slammed his own box onto the ground, and it seemed like he'd been ready to swing a fist.

He took a breath. It felt like the first breath of winter, a stinging cold that sliced into his lungs.

He was better than this. He took another breath and tried to get it together.

"How much does he owe you?" said Michael.

His grandfather looked like he was hoping Hunter would try to take a swing again. "It was a lot of damage, so—"

"How much?"

"Three hundred."

The number might as well have been three million. "Fine," said Hunter. He jerked away from Michael. "Keep my stuff. I don't—"

"He'll pay you," said Michael. "In two weeks. Fair?"

"Two weeks. I'll believe that when I see it."

Michael looked at Hunter. "Can you work six nights for me in the next two weeks?"

Hunter stared back at him until Michael raised his eyebrows in a *Dude, wtf?* expression. Hunter shook himself. "Yeah. Sure."

"Done." Michael picked up his box. "Let's go."

"And just who are you? What kind of *work* is this?"

Like the eldest Merrick brother was going to have him selling weapons to foreigners or dancing naked on tables. Michael shifted the box to one hip and pulled a business card out of his pocket. "I'm Michael Merrick. I do landscaping. Feel free to call me if you want those mums out front to stop dying."

Then he left the card on the corner of the dining room table and headed toward the door.

Hunter knew when to make an exit. He hustled to catch up.

His grandmother was sitting in the kitchen, that same sourpuss look of disapproval on her face.

"Hi, Grandma," Hunter called cheerfully, knowing it would irritate her even more than if he'd flipped her off.

Then he was in the jeep and they were driving away, his hands almost shaking on the steering wheel.

Michael hadn't said a word. Hunter wasn't entirely sure what to say, either.

Finally, he said, "Those mums weren't dying."

"They'll look like it."

Hunter smiled. Then laughed. "Thanks."

"Sure." He glanced in the back. "You can throw those in the basement until you figure out what you want to do."

Hunter lost the smile. He wondered if there was a time limit attached to the offer—and because he was scared of the answer, he didn't want to ask. "Okay."

"Gabriel's been trying to catch up in math and some other classes, because he wants to qualify for an EMT course in the spring. He usually helps on Tuesdays and Fridays. Want to take his nights for the next two weeks? Maybe some weekend time?"

So Gabriel was going to take the firefighter thing seriously. Hunter was envious for a moment, that his frenemy had figured out a path in life, when it felt like his own life map had been put through a shredder. "Sure." He paused. "You don't have to do that—I can sell some of my stuff—"

"If your whole life is in those boxes, Hunter, I want you to hold on to all of it."

Well then.

They pulled into the Merrick driveway, and nothing had changed—Michael's brothers were still out.

Michael hesitated before getting out of the jeep. "I'm picking up Hannah in an hour. She wants to take James to the carnival, too. No one will be at the house tonight."

Hunter had no idea who Hannah and James were. He glanced over at Michael and wondered what he was implying. "Do you not want me to be here by myself?"

Michael sighed. "Jesus, Hunter, take a breather. I want you to go be a teenager. You've got a car, there's fun to be had. Go. Find it."

CHAPTER 14

Kate didn't see how this carnival was supposed to make money for the senior class. The field was packed with rides and food kiosks, then lined with silly game stands. The lights and noise were overwhelming, a mash-up of neon and carnival music and the smell of popcorn and funnel cake.

Her senses couldn't make heads or tails of anything.

Frustrating on a good day, but doubly so today.

Silver would be watching her every move tonight.

So she'd done a quick lap of the grounds and found the Merricks.

Nick was playing skeeball with that bitchy blond cheerleader.

Gabriel was with a dark-haired girl and a younger boy, throwing darts at balloons way at the end of the row of game stands.

Chris was sitting on a bench with the brunette who'd clung to Hunter in the hallway, and they were sharing a box of popcorn.

The crowds were giving her a headache, and she clung to the shadows between two tents, wondering which Merrick brother she should attach herself to.

"Looking for your friend?"

Kate turned. Hunter had found *her*.

And his eyes were full of suspicion.

Was Silver right? Did Hunter suspect what she was?

What *they* were?

But there was also a spark of challenge in his eye. If he knew they were Guides, wouldn't he be doing something about it?

"What's your problem?" she said. She slid a tube of gloss from her bag and ran it across her lips.

"Can't figure out your angle."

"My angle?"

"What's with the little texts? Old boyfriend not doing it for you?"

She wanted to kill Silver for making it look like they were a couple. "Maybe I just like you."

"Maybe I just like you back."

His voice was quiet and intense, more sure than she was ready for. She turned away, suddenly flustered, heading into the darkness behind the tents. Even Silver couldn't see in the dark.

"I don't think that's all," Hunter said, following her. "I think you're playing me for something."

She hesitated. Suddenly he was closer.

"The problem is," he said, "I just can't figure out what."

And then, before she had an answer, he was moving away.

God, he was making her insane.

She went after him. "Are you always this direct?"

"Saves time."

She felt breathless, like he'd snatched control of this little interlude and was now playing keep-away with it. "I can't even figure out whether you're mad at me."

She'd thrown a little plea into her voice, but he didn't turn. "You're not fooling me," he said.

"I'm not trying to fool you."

"Trust me, Kate, I know a lot about using people."

What did that mean? She stared after him for a moment, watching him walk. He moved like a jungle cat, all purposeful, calculated motion—wrapped up in fluid grace.

She chased after him again. "I don't get you," she said. "Are you interested or not?"

"Not." He kept walking.

"Liar."

He lifted a hand in a halfhearted wave—but didn't even look back.

"Running from a girl?" she called.

He ignored her. So she went after him *for real*, grabbing his arm from behind and trying to spin him.

Even though she'd seen him fight before, his speed was a surprise. He used her spin to grab her arm. Her defense training kicked in, letting her drop enough to twist free and send an elbow into his gut.

Or it would have been, if he hadn't deflected her arm. He blocked her next strike and caught her wrist, twisting it to pin it behind her back and pull her close.

Then he didn't strike back. His eyes were dark, and he held her against his chest.

She stared up at him, feeling his chest rise and fall against hers. His fingers were gentle on her arms, sending little bolts of electricity along her skin. She'd only ever felt strength like this with pain behind it.

Gentleness was new.

"You've got some nice moves," he said.

"Thanks. I was going easy."

He smiled, but instead of humor it was a little sad.

"Let me go," she said. "I'll prove it."

He let her go. "I really don't want to play, Kate."

But she swung a fist anyway, throwing real strength into it. He blocked and trapped her arm, but she twisted free to aim a high kick into his ribs.

She wasn't ready for him to catch her ankle and take her to the ground.

He pinned her there, but he was smiling. "Still going easy?"

Her breathing was too quick. She almost wished he wouldn't let her go.

But he did. The smile slid off his face, and he backed up to stand.

She launched herself off the ground to punch him in the

stomach, using all of her momentum. Then a leg sweep. He went down.

She was straddling his chest before he could move.

"I can throw you off," he said.

"But you won't." She felt breathless and exhilarated and wished he would. She loved the feel of his hands, the way his power sparked against her skin, the way she felt him in her space.

Hunter smiled. His eyes studied her face, and she knew she was flushed. Her heart was almost louder than the music from the carnival.

Crap. The carnival. She glanced around. Silver was probably watching.

Hunter felt the change. Kate watched his smile fade. "Get up, Kate. I wasn't kidding. I don't want to play."

The Merricks could wait for fifteen minutes.

She put her hands on his shoulders and looked down at him, feeling her hair fall along her face. "Where'd you really learn to fight like that?"

"My father. Where did you learn?"

"My mother took me to some guy who lived in a barn and slaughtered animals to make cured beef. He taught me."

"Now that's a touching story."

She wondered what he'd say if she told him the whole story, how every night Roland had come after her with the same knives he used on the beef.

She wondered why Hunter didn't *know* who Roland was. She'd been told that every Guide went to Roland first.

If Roland broke you, you were out.

Hunter was still looking at her. Either he was the greatest frigging actor in the world, or he didn't know what he was.

Or what *she* was.

She smiled. "He taught me enough to bring *you* down, didn't he?"

Hunter gave her a look, like he was merely tolerating her weight on his chest. "What did your dad think of the slaughter-house treatment?"

"He didn't think much about it at all." She paused and shrugged. "I never knew my father."

"Divorce?"

"Nope, my mom said she got what she needed out of him." She raised a suggestive eyebrow. "Get it?"

He frowned and reached up a hand to push a strand of hair out of her eyes.

Such a simple touch, but her breath caught.

She knocked his hand away. She couldn't take simple touches right now—this was throwing her all off balance. Was she really talking about her *mother*?

Kate leaned closer to Hunter. "How about a ride?" she whispered.

Hunter's eyebrows went way up.

She pointed at where lights rose high above the ground, blues and yellows and reds. "Ferris wheel?"

He looked like he was going to refuse.

"Come on," she said. "Don't make me kick your ass again."

He pushed the hair back off his face and sighed.

She put her forehead down to his, until she could feel the rings in his eyebrows, until his breath was warm on her lips. "Don't make me stare at you."

He smiled—but pushed her shoulders back until she was sitting upright.

"You're dangerous," he said.

She smiled and rolled off of him. "You have no idea."

Hunter pulled the door closed and latched it with the little chain. The air whispered to him about the oil of the machinery, the sweat of the college kid checking the latch, and the apple and cinnamon spice of Kate's lotion or shampoo or whatever.

He didn't want to admit how much he'd liked their scuffle behind the booths.

It was such a contradiction to the argument with Michael, or the confrontation with his grandfather.

She'd said she was going easy, but she'd aimed hard. He'd had to use true effort to deflect without hurting her, nothing like when he practiced with Becca, or fought with Gabriel. Finding a perfect balance took mental energy and forced clarity, and it was nice to put his worry aside for one minute of the night.

He shouldn't even be at this stupid carnival. None of them should. But what was the alternative? Sitting around the Merrick house listening to Gabriel's scanner app? Waiting for Guides to come to town again?

Everyone else had a girlfriend. Hunter had clung to the shadows, looking for Calla. She hadn't made good on her promise yet—but it was only a matter of time.

And then he'd seen Kate.

He shouldn't have said a word to her.

But every time she crossed his path, he couldn't stop thinking of those flirting texts, the way she'd been in class that first day.

Here he was trying to protect the whole county from a psychotic pyromaniac, and he couldn't stop thinking about one random girl.

"You okay?"

He glanced over. Kate was curled onto the bench, her bright hair flashing with the colored lights on the Ferris wheel supports. She looked so perfect, like an angel trapped in this steel car with him, her trendy clothes so at odds with his piercings and rough-cut hair.

It reminded him of Michael's comment about the picture.

"I'm fine," he said.

"You were glaring at that bar like you wanted to snap it." She gestured out at the night sky, where stars hung high above, bright in the crisp air. "It's a beautiful night."

"I have a lot on my mind."

"I know." She paused. "Want to spill?"

He sighed. For a split-second, he was tempted.

Then Kate shifted closer. "Why don't you tell me about Calla Dean?"

His head snapped around.

Kate shrugged. "I heard you had a bad relationship with her."

His jaw tightened. "You heard wrong."

"Why would she say it?"

"Because she's—" He stopped himself.

"Because she's what? A bitch?"

"No. Because she's nuts." He made a circular motion at his temple, feeling the pulsing pain of a headache there. "Certifiable."

"She seemed pretty lucid to me."

"I guess sometimes you just don't know about people." He looked away.

Silence hung in the car for a while, and he looked out at the other students milling around the carnival grounds. Chris and Gabriel were shooting hoops now at a booth, Layne and Becca laughing with them. He didn't see Nick and Quinn anywhere.

Then he spotted Layne's little brother, Simon, at the balloon popping booth, tossing darts with a girl who looked like a freshman. Hunter smiled.

Then some guys he didn't recognize walked over and got in Simon's face.

"Jesus," Hunter muttered.

"You know them?" said Kate.

"Yeah. Hold on." He fished out his phone and shot off a text to Gabriel.

Help Simon at the balloon booth. I'm stuck on the wheel.

He watched to make sure Gabriel received the text, then relaxed when he saw all four of them head off to help Simon.

"He's deaf," Hunter explained to Kate. "He gets a lot of crap for it."

She was watching him with a bemused expression on her face. "That's nice of you." She paused. "I didn't think you liked that Gabriel guy."

"Yeah, well . . ." He paused. "It's a long story." Then he realized something. "You can tell him apart from his brother?"

She looked startled for the barest second. "Well—his brother's dating the blonde, right?"

The Ferris wheel stopped to let more people on, and they hung suspended at the three o'clock position.

"Yeah," he said.

"So . . ." Kate started. "You're in a love-hate bromance with Gabriel Merrick, you've got mixed feelings about this Calla chick—"

"Why don't we talk about something else?"

She leaned back against the wall of the car. "Like what?"

"You."

"Me?"

"Yeah. You said no games. Who's the guy in the pickup truck?"

"His name is Silver." She paused. "He's a friend."

Like he would buy that now, after hearing about Quinn's comments. "Do you make out with all your friends?"

"Only the hot ones."

He snorted again and looked away.

"Why?" she said. "Interested?"

His pulse jumped, but he had no tolerance for bluffing. He met her gaze head on. "Sure."

And then she was straddling his lap. The car rocked forcefully, and he swore and caught her automatically, one arm going around her waist, one arm catching the bar for support.

Her fingers tangled in his hair and she didn't let him go, laughing a little as she pressed her lips to his.

He sucked in a breath and pulled away.

She took it in stride and kissed the spot just below his ear. "Startled you, did I?"

He was very aware of her body and the way she still pressed against him. This was very different from the fight behind the tents. He wanted to move, to push her away, but he was pretty sure his hands would betray him and go the other direction.

Her fingers were still in his hair, her breath against his earlobe, and it was making it hard to think straight.

He closed his eyes. *Focus.* "I thought you were bluffing."

She caught his earlobe with her lips, then her teeth, sucking it into her mouth.

He felt it all the way through his body. He gasped and had to catch her waist with both hands, still unsure whether he wanted to push her away—or pull her closer.

One of her hands sneaked under his jacket, stroking across his chest with her fingertips. Her lips moved to his neck, and she caught the skin there with her teeth.

He wasn't going to be able to talk in a second. "Kate," he said. "Kate—"

She arched into his hands, grabbing one of his wrists and forcing his hand higher on her body, until his palm was over her breast and his thumb was brushing intimate things through the fabric of her shirt.

Hunter hissed a breath through his teeth and had to shift on the bench. It felt like the Ferris wheel was spinning fiercely yet simultaneously standing still. He could only see lights and stars and the glowing halo of her hair.

This time when her mouth fell on his, he didn't pull away at all. Her tongue slipped between his teeth, teasing at his until he sat up straighter, his free hand at the small of her back, just inside the waistband of her jeans, pulling her closer. He felt silk and lace and skin under his fingertips. All at once, clothes were an irritation, and he moaned into her mouth, drawing at her tongue until she was panting against him.

He was dangerously close to the farthest he'd ever gone with a girl, and here he barely knew her. Instead of that being a deterrent, he never wanted it to stop. The hell with the fires, the hell with his living situation—if he could spend the rest of his life in this Ferris wheel car, doing this exact thing, it would *totally be fine.*

And then she caught his wrist again, making his hand go still against her. "Easy," she breathed.

He froze and moved his other hand to safer ground, too. "Sorry," he said, his voice a whispered rasp of sound. God, he wanted to crack his head on the metal wall of this car. Five minutes ago he'd been pissed at her, and now he didn't want to stop touching her. How had he lost control like that?

But her eyes were so close, sparking with light. "Are you imagining me naked again?"

"Ah . . . only in the most respectful way."

She smiled. Beyond her, the stars were still. They'd come to a stop at the top of the Ferris wheel.

She leaned in close, until her breasts were against his chest and her breath was warm against his ear. Her hands went under his jacket again, sliding over his shoulders, and he wished that one of his abilities could make clothes disappear.

Then she spoke against his ear. "Touch me again."

He hesitated, unsure. But then she kissed him again, thrusting her tongue into his mouth. When his palm slid up her side, she grabbed his hand and slid it under the low neckline of her shirt, until his fingers were inside her bra.

He almost came undone right there. His senses were firing like crazy, and all he could think about was apples and cinnamon and the wet addictive pull of her mouth and the softness of the skin under his fingertips.

Suddenly he was powerfully aware of the elements surrounding them. The sharp bite in the air, the electricity firing in the bulbs of the Ferris wheel, the sweat on her skin. A breeze swirled through the car, making her shiver and break the kiss. The lights on the fairgrounds blazed brighter.

Hunter shrugged out of his jacket and wrapped it around her shoulders. They were moving again, so she tucked in close to him and breathed against his neck.

He ducked his head and brushed a kiss against her temple, wondering how the night had conspired to put him in this position. Kate was a warm weight against him, thrilling and provocative and challenging—yet someone he wanted to wrap up in his arms and protect.

When she turned her head, he met her lips, kissing her slowly, without the fierce aggression that had gotten out of control so quickly. And even slow, kissing her was like setting a pot to simmer. All sizzle on the surface, searing heat on the inside.

Maybe Becca and the Merrick brothers had been right: maybe he just needed to relax and stop worrying about everyone's angle.

Her phone buzzed, and he was so close that he felt the vibration through her body.

Ignore it, he thought. *Ignore ignore ignore—*

She sat up, straightened her shirt, and reached into her pocket, not meeting his eyes.

She sat back on his knees and kept the phone out of view.

Hunter looked past her, out at the night. He'd completely forgotten about "her friend." All it took was a little skin, and he'd turned into the world's biggest moron. God, he'd been such an *idiot*.

He didn't know how to undo this. He felt hurt, but that was stupid. What did he expect? They'd just been talking about the other guy! How had he let it go so far? Thank god he hadn't said anything about wanting to hold her forever or any of that other crap.

Now he wanted to bang his head against the wall of this car for an entirely different reason.

Kate was shoving the phone back into her jeans. Hunter didn't even want to look at her.

She put her hands against his chest, but she must have felt the stiffness in his body.

He expected her to climb off his lap, but she didn't. "Jealous of a text message? Already?"

"Don't play with me."

"You weren't fighting me off a minute ago."

"Now I wish I had." He had things to do here. He needed to find his focus before he forgot all that.

He quickly scanned the grounds. No problems that he could see.

Kate was watching him, and the wicked look was off her face. "I didn't mean to hurt you."

That surprised him, and he met her eyes. "You don't even know me."

"I'd like to."

He couldn't think with her saying things like that while straddling him. He grabbed her waist and lifted her, setting her beside him on the bench. Then he ran his hands back through his hair.

"I don't know what's real. I don't know if you're screwing with me, or if you really want to know me. You know what? Play it straight for a minute. Because I can't do this."

Her breathing was quick, and she looked troubled and doubtful.

He was glad, because that was exactly how he felt, too.

"I can't tell you," she whispered.

"Why?" he demanded.

Her lips parted.

And then, across the fairgrounds, generators started exploding.

CHAPTER 15

Hunter stood and grabbed at the bars of the car, feeling it rock with his motion. Two generators had exploded, and flames blazed against the sky. On the ground, people were screaming, forming panicked swarms moving in every direction.

He had a perfect view from up here, though the wheel was still turning on its axle, as if the fires were just another spectacle to see from up high.

Another generator exploded, off to his left.

More people screamed. The swarms shifted, moving in a new direction.

Kate was beside him, leaning out as well.

Then her phone chimed, and she looked at it.

What was *up* with her and this other guy?

Hunter leaned over the side, yelling for the ride operator to let them out—or at least to make the ride stop. He almost couldn't hear himself over the pandemonium below, so he wasn't surprised when the guy didn't look up.

People from other cars were leaning out and screaming, too.

The panic in the air was almost enough to choke him.

Another generator exploded.

The kid running the Ferris wheel yanked a lever in his booth and bolted.

The ride lurched to a stop, so suddenly that Hunter lost his balance and clutched at the bar. The car swung wildly, stuck in the two o'clock position.

Fire was spreading now, leaping from one tent to the next, sending black smoke billowing into the air.

Another generator exploded, also off to his left. The entire carnival was surrounded by fire.

Five generators in a circle. Didn't get much clearer than that.

Hunter looked for Gabriel, for any of the Merricks. The chaos on the ground was insane: he couldn't recognize anyone, and the smoke was getting thicker. Several people lay crumpled on the ground, but he couldn't make out any of them. Sirens screamed somewhere in the distance.

The rage in this fire was familiar: he'd felt it a week ago, during the inferno in the library.

Calla.

He'd been so stupid. He'd expected her to take out a house. *One* house.

There had to be hundreds of people here. He could feel the fire spreading, forming a true circle, preventing escape. She was going to kill them all.

And here he sat, fifty feet above the ground, unable to do a damn thing.

"We're trapped," said Kate.

Hunter looked at her. His head was clouded with too many complicated emotions, and he had to shut them down.

He studied the multicolored lights along the Ferris wheel supports. The whole thing was really just a big complicated wheel held together by steel bars and high tension wire.

The nearest support was in front of him, but lower, about ten feet away.

No, seven. Seven sounded better.

If he thought about this too long, he'd chicken out.

He climbed onto the safety bar, grabbing the steel frame and holding on.

"Holy crap," Kate cried. "Are you insane?"

His hands were going to be making an impression in the steel in a second. He could feel sweat beginning to collect under his fingertips. "Don't rock the car!" he shouted.

She went completely still.

Air whipped around him, excited by the frenzy of activity. He had nowhere near enough control to ask it to help him make this jump, but he tried anyway.

"You're crazy," said Kate.

"Thanks for the vote of confidence," he said.

And then he jumped.

He hit the supports hard. The entire frame rattled. The metal rails were narrower than he'd expected, wet and hard to grip. Blood streaked the white paint, and he realized the rusted metal had sliced into his hands.

It didn't hurt yet.

That meant it would hurt *a lot* later.

He swung his legs until he found purchase, then looped an arm around the support to take the pressure off his palms.

He took a glance. His hands were a mess.

Then he heard another scream and realized there were a lot of people a lot worse off than he was.

Hunter started to climb. It was like this stupid Ferris wheel had been built precisely to frustrate him, because each support was about a foot too far from the next for him to reach. He had to climb *in*, toward the center, before he could start climbing down.

His hands were still bleeding. They kept slipping.

Something hit the Ferris wheel and sent a shudder through the frame. He swore and had to loop an arm to stay upright. Had some idiot tried to follow him?

Yes. Kate.

She'd taken the impact better than he had—or maybe she'd just learned from watching him. She'd caught the bars with her arms, and now sat braced in the corner where two supports met. Hunter felt a moment of panic, wondering if he should climb up to help her—or continue climbing down.

But then she started to move, and he realized he should be following her lead.

Kate moved like a frigging *acrobat*. She twisted between the supports as if they'd been assembled specifically for her use. She'd almost caught up to him in a quarter of the time it had taken him to cross the same distance.

She looked like she belonged in a movie, her blond hair and fair skin striking against the backdrop of the Ferris wheel lightbulbs and the smoky blaze behind her.

"Seriously," she called. "The staring?"

He shook himself and kept climbing. His palms burned but he ignored it.

The ride had stopped between passengers, so no car sat by the booth. The wheel stopped about ten feet above the platform—which was a six-foot square with a tiny operator booth, sitting about ten feet above the ground.

If he missed this jump, it would almost be worse than the first one. The first would have killed him.

This one would just hurt like a bitch.

He let go and dropped.

It hurt anyway. He felt the impact through his ankles and into his knees.

But he was down, and he was alive. Kate landed beside him, absorbing the jump like a cat.

They stared at each other for a moment. People were still screaming overhead, begging for someone to get them down.

He could still feel their panic.

He could also feel Kate's hesitation.

If she wasn't going to take action, he needed to. He gave her a quick shove toward the controls. "Get them down!" he said. "Before this generator goes."

Then he didn't look back. He leapt off the platform and went after Calla.

Fire was everywhere. Flames had jumped from the exterior booths to the food stands, and lightbulbs were popping left and right. The heat was intense, and people were running in panicked circles.

He couldn't even *help* them—there was no way out until the fire was stopped.

Hunter felt for the cord of power holding this inferno together.

Then he followed it.

At the center, of course. He should have known.

Calla stood amidst the flames, her expression one of glee. The fire was hottest here, and bodies littered the ground around her. He didn't want to know which ones were dead, but his senses told him.

More dead than alive. And the living ones were in pain. So much pain that it singed his senses, weighing him down.

All these people. He'd failed them all.

And he couldn't stop her now. He didn't even have a gun anymore. He didn't know where the Merricks were, didn't even know if he could control a fire of this magnitude if they *were* here.

"I told you," she said, her voice high above the roar of the flames. Wind swirled through the fairgrounds, whipping the flames higher. "I told you what we would do."

This was more power than she could generate on her own—and it was wild, almost uncontrollable. He wondered again who else was working with her.

How could they do this? Who could want a war so badly that they would kill innocent people?

"I'll bring them," Hunter said. He could feel the anguish and suffering in the space around him, and it made his voice break. "I'll bring the Guides, Calla. Just stop this."

"You had your chance. You knew what we would do. We want a war."

"Please," he said. "Please, stop this. I'll bring them."

"No, you won't. You're afraid of them. I know what you are, Hunter. I know what your father did."

Of course she did—wasn't that the whole problem? "I don't—what are you—"

"I don't think you understand how serious we are. They're killing people, Hunter. Good people. Hypocrites."

"*You're* killing people, Calla."

"For the greater good, right? Isn't that what the Guides say?"
Her eyes flashed in the darkness. The smoke in the air was hard
to breathe through, but she smiled. "They need to take me seriously. Why should *you* get to live, when the rest of us don't?"

"I don't understand," he said. His voice broke again. "Please."

Her mouth opened, but before any sound could come out,
her body jerked.

Twice.

At first he didn't get it. But then she crumpled.

And then Hunter saw the man with the gun.

Oh. Oh, *shit*.

He ran like hell.

He made it about fifty feet before someone called his name.

Someone. Kate.

Her voice drew his attention, made him almost turn.

And then something hit him in the shoulder. He stumbled and
saw stars. His forearms were suddenly in the dirt. For a horrifying moment he thought he was going to be sick on himself.

Run, he told himself. *Run, you wuss.*

He forced himself back to his feet. One foot in front of the
other.

This didn't feel like running.

He stumbled again. The ground came up and hit him in the
face. His arm wouldn't work.

Then he *was* sick and he hated that they were going to find
him dead, lying in his own puke.

His dad would be so disappointed.

"Hunter." Someone was shaking him. Rolling him. "Hunter."

He opened his eyes. It felt like he'd been sleeping for hours,
but fire still filled the air. He could feel it everywhere, burning
against his senses.

Gabriel was there, backed by fire, looking down at him.
"Can you hear me?"

"Guide," said Hunter. His voice sounded funny, distant and
somewhat tinny. "You have to run."

"I saw," said Gabriel. "Don't worry, we'll—"

Hunter didn't worry. The flaming sky went black.

Chapter 16

Kate made it to Silver's side just in time to see him pull the trigger again.

Too much was going on for her to examine the sudden wrench in her chest. "Stop!" she cried. "He's not the one who started this!"

"I know." Silver's ice-blue eyes flicked her way.

"Then why are you shooting him?"

"Because he was negotiating with the one who did. You were with him. Why didn't you detain him?"

"I was getting the people off the Ferris wheel."

Wind was snapping at her hair, throwing smoke in her eyes and inciting the flames higher. Silver, by comparison, seemed to stand outside the maelstrom, as if it didn't dare ruffle him.

"That is not your task here, Kathryn."

"Isn't our task to protect people?"

"Have you never heard the saying, the end justifies the means?"

He glanced at the sky, and Kate followed his gaze. The flames were over ten feet high now. At first she'd thought smoke obscured the stars above, but now she realized those were clouds moving in.

Heavy clouds, flickering with lightning. Thunder cracked overhead, and she watched Gabriel Merrick crouch over a very still Hunter.

Silver raised the gun again.

Kate didn't know if he was pointing at Gabriel or Hunter. Her heart was beating a path into her throat.

She had to think. *Think think think.*

Silver cocked the gun.

"Kill them now and you'll send the rest to ground," she said.

She kept her voice even, a mere observation in the middle of an inferno fed by a windstorm. Sweat rolled down her back, tracing a line between her shoulder blades, and she ignored it.

Silver hesitated.

Kate shrugged like she didn't care. "They've already outsmarted . . . how many Guides did you say?"

He released the hammer and lowered the weapon.

"Don't you have a body to get rid of anyway?" Kate asked, thinking of Hunter's issues with Calla—and wondering how this all fit together.

He'd been *negotiating* with her?

"I'll make sure the fire takes care of it," said Silver.

Thunder cracked overhead again. A bolt of lightning struck the carousel. Sparks shot into the air. Kate jumped a mile. She could feel cool air swirl through the grounds, tickling her cheeks despite the fires.

Hunter and Gabriel were gone.

Silver had his gun up again, and he was headed for where they'd been. "I will not stand by while they cause more harm."

Another bolt of lightning blasted into the dirt ten feet behind them, and this time even Silver jumped, whirling with the gun in hand.

The power stroked along her skin, so she knew Silver had to be feeling it. Part of her wanted to drop her guard and ride the streamers of energy.

She shut down the thought almost before it could form. That would make her like *them.*

If Hunter's father had been a Guide—what was he doing with the Merricks?

How did they fit with that Calla girl?

The sirens were close now. The wind picked up more fully,

swirling sparks and debris from the ground, lashing at her face. The power in the fire pulsed against her skin. It had to have spread farther with the wind—she couldn't see an end to the flames. For a while she'd felt nothing but pain and suffering, but now she felt nothing.

Had she made a mistake, stopping Silver when he could have stopped the Merricks? Were they working with Calla? Did that explain Hunter's fight with Gabriel in the cafeteria?

Were they spreading the fire even now?

She had more questions than answers.

"We must find them," said Silver. "They're spreading the fire. They've already taken enough lives—"

"Wait." She held out her arm. A drop of water clung to her wrist, but it quickly evaporated.

Another appeared.

And another.

Then rain was pouring down, a full deluge, the kind you usually saw in late summer. Lightning crackled in the clouds overhead, but the rain was heavy, wet, and constant.

And it put out every single lick of flame.

Hunter was drowning in darkness, every now and again breaking the surface of awareness.

The first time, his eyes were pried open, and the light was blinding. He flinched away. He wondered if he'd fallen in among the flames, because his entire body felt like it was burning and freezing at the same time.

A woman's voice was speaking. "He's lost a lot of blood. He's going to need—" But just as he was about to make out the rest of her words, everything went black again.

The second time, he opened his eyes to fire and darkness, and he felt sure they'd left him. He sucked in a huge choking breath, breathing more smoke than oxygen. A hand squeezed his, hard, sending sparks of pain shooting through his shoulder. Gabriel Merrick's voice. "Come on, Hunter." Then the sparks took over, and he was out again.

The third time, Hunter woke to whispers.

At first, the sounds were nonsensical, and he couldn't puzzle them out through the haze in his brain. His eyes didn't want to open yet. He didn't sense fire or danger, but rain rattled against windows.

Windows. He was inside.

He just didn't know *where*.

Now he kept his eyes closed on purpose, trying to assess more before revealing that he was awake, and alert.

Think.

Carnival. Ferris wheel. Fire.

Calla.

The way her body jerked.

The way he'd run. The way he'd hit the ground.

He wanted it to be a dream, but the pulsing ache in his shoulder convinced him it wasn't. None of it was.

Hunter fought to keep his breathing even.

The whispers drew close, but he still couldn't make sense of the words. Breath brushed his cheek, then a finger stroked across his eyebrow.

Hunter flung out a hand and seized a wrist. He jerked upright and looked at his captive.

A boy, looking just as shocked as Hunter felt. Young and blond and wide-eyed, he couldn't have been more than five or six. His expression was frozen in that state where crying was a possibility.

Hunter let him go.

Then he winced, as the adrenaline wore off and his body suggested that sudden movement hadn't been a bright idea.

The little boy hadn't moved, but at least he didn't look like he was going to cry anymore. He'd leaned forward. "Why do you have earrings in your *face*?"

What the hell? Hunter rubbed his eyes. He was sitting on a couch, a comforter thrown over him. The room was dim, pale light breaking through the rain, meaning either early morning or early evening. His shirt was gone, but he still had on his jeans. His shoulder hurt like hell. One of his hands was bandaged across the palm.

Hunter's brain couldn't piece it all together.

Wait. He knew this room.

The Merrick house.

But then who was this kid, peering at him curiously, reaching out a hand to touch the piercings in his eyebrow?

Hunter caught his wrist again, but more gently. "Where is everyone?"

"Mommy is working." His voice dropped to a hushed whisper. "I'm supposed to be sleeping, but I wasn't tired anymore."

The house was a well of quiet, insulated by the rain smacking the glass outside. At least that meant it was probably morning.

The boy stretched for a remote control on the coffee table, ignoring Hunter's hold on his wrist. "Can I turn on cartoons?"

This was . . . surreal. Hunter let him go again. "Sure." He paused. "Do you know where everyone else is?"

"They're sleeping." The boy climbed up on the couch next to him as if he'd known Hunter all his life. Then he clicked on the television.

Hunter sat there for a full minute and wondered what to do.

Unfortunately his brain kept replaying the previous night.

Fire.

Gunshot.

Calla.

The music from the cartoons was like water torture. Hunter rubbed at his eyes again, suddenly worried he was going to be sick.

He needed to find out what had happened, whether they were still in danger.

He stumbled off the couch, leaving the boy there. The front door was locked, but he threw the bolt and stepped onto the porch.

Rain coursed down from the dark gray sky, slapping against the siding and running in rivers down the driveway. It had to be very early, because he didn't sense motion from any of the houses on the street.

Wait—maybe he still had his phone.

No, his pockets were empty. But blood stained the waistband of his jeans and streaked down one leg.

Hunter stepped onto the front walk, letting the rain hit him. He put a hand out. No power in the drops; just a normal storm.

"I thought the only person crazy enough to stand out in the rain was Chris."

Hunter turned. Gabriel stood in the doorway, wearing sweatpants and an old T-shirt. His hair was rumpled from sleep. He didn't look panicked, but he looked tired.

About thirty questions came to mind, but Hunter said, "Who's the little kid?"

"James. Hannah's son."

That meant nothing to Hunter. "Who's Hannah?"

"Mike's girlfriend. You've seen her; she was one of the firefighters at the police station last week. She stayed at the carnival to help, so Mike brought him here." Gabriel paused. "You want to come in out of the rain or what?"

Hunter realized he'd just been standing there, feeling rain trail through his hair and run in rivulets down his chest.

But the rain felt good on his shoulder, so he didn't move. "What happened? How did I get here?"

"Do you remember the carnival?"

"Yeah."

"Do you remember the fires?"

Was Gabriel kidding? They were permanently etched on the insides of Hunter's eyelids. "I remember the generators. I had to climb down from the Ferris wheel."

Gabriel glanced back in the house, then pulled the door shut. "That kid hears everything." He leaned back against the doorjamb. "Do you remember getting shot?"

Hunter froze. "I got shot?"

"Yeah. In the shoulder." Gabriel looked out at the gray sky. "And no offense, dude, but you weigh a fucking ton."

That left Hunter with more questions than answers. His shoulder hurt, but he sure hadn't missed a bullet hole.

That meant one of them had used power to heal him.

"Go clean up," said Gabriel. "I'll make coffee. School's closed for the day, so . . ."

"Are we in danger?"

Gabriel snorted. "When are we not in danger?" He paused. "I have no idea. Nothing has happened since the fires."

Hunter snuck into Nick's room to find clean jeans from his bag, trying to be as silent as possible. He probably didn't need to bother. Nick was practically unconscious, an arm hanging down over the side of the bed. The entire second floor felt thick with sleep. A quick glance at the clock revealed it wasn't even six in the morning.

The shower felt even better than the rain had, but questions were burning the inside of his brain, so he rushed.

James was eating Cookie Crisp straight from the box when Hunter walked past the family room. He'd wrapped himself in the comforter.

Hunter wondered what it would be like to feel so comfortable in his surroundings. He couldn't remember *ever* feeling that way, even around his own family.

He heard hushed voices from the kitchen, and that didn't mean anything until Michael's words registered.

"This is the first time I've considered leaving town."

Leaving town. Hunter hesitated in the hallway.

Gabriel said something in response, but Hunter couldn't catch the words.

Then Michael said, "I don't know. What do you think?"

Hunter could feel Gabriel's surprise from here. Hunter strained to hear him. "I think this is the first time we all have a reason to stay." He paused. "You're dating a girl who left her kid with you, Michael."

"Exactly. I'm putting them at risk."

"There's no pentagram on the door."

"Yet."

Gabriel paused. "You sound like you've been thinking about this for a while."

"Only all night." A tapping sound that Hunter couldn't make

sense of. Then a heavy sigh. "Money would be tight for a while, but we could make it work."

"When?"

"A week if we had to."

A week! Hunter held his breath.

"Do you know where we'd go?"

Michael's voice was muffled, as if he was moving away. Hunter only picked out random phrases. ". . . go to the bank. We need . . . quiet so he doesn't hear us."

So he doesn't hear us.

Exclamation points flared in Hunter's head. He eased forward to hear the rest.

The floor creaked.

The conversation in the kitchen came to an abrupt stop.

But he wasn't stupid. That vise grip had closed on his chest again. He'd never been welcome here, not really. Expecting anything else was downright lunacy.

Hunter walked into the kitchen easily, as if that creak in the floor was completely innocuous and he hadn't heard a word. Gabriel and Michael were at the table, and he expected them to look guilty, but they just looked tired. Three mugs of coffee sat on the table. One was untouched, but a carton of half-and-half sat there, along with a bowl of sugar. And Hunter's cell phone. The light was flashing.

At least it gave him an excuse not to look at them. He wasn't sure he could keep the feeling of betrayal off his face. Hunter dropped into a chair and glanced at the screen.

Kate.

We need to talk about last night.

That kicked his heart into action. He hit the button to clear the screen and set the phone down in favor of the coffee.

Gabriel's words on the porch were duking it out with the conversation he'd just overheard.

No offense dude, but you weigh a fucking ton.

"Hey." He looked across the table at Gabriel. "Thanks."

Gabriel half shrugged and spun his mug between his hands. "I didn't know what you wanted in it."

"No—I mean—"

Gabriel met his eyes. "I know what you meant."

"Did you fix my shoulder, too?"

Another half shrug, like it was nothing. "There was a lot of power in the fire. You were bleeding. It was easy." But then he looked away. "We had to run. I couldn't do it all the way. Hannah saw all the blood and was ready to put you on a helicopter."

Gabriel's voice was casual, but Hunter could hear the undercurrent of tension. Shadows underscored his eyes, punctuating his worry.

"What happened to the Guide?"

"Don't know. Chris and Nicky pulled the rain to stop the fires, and we thought for sure he'd find us, but . . . he didn't."

"Yet," Michael said. "He didn't find us *yet*."

Gabriel took a sip of coffee but didn't say anything.

Michael glanced over at Hunter. "You look a lot better than you did last night. You all right?"

No. He felt like his world was collapsing around him. His brain was having trouble reconciling the fact that they'd saved his life with their talk about secretly leaving town, abandoning him to this mess that they were a part of.

He looked into his coffee and nodded.

"I thought about calling your mom," Michael said. "But I was worried she'd want to come over here, and I didn't want to put her in the line of fire."

"It's fine," he said. He didn't want to see her—if she even cared to see him. His grandfather would probably call him names and demand that he pay for the damages to the carnival equipment.

But for a fraction of a second, he wished Gabriel *hadn't* used power to heal him, that this Hannah woman had put him on a medevac helicopter to shock trauma or wherever. Just so his mom would have to look at *him* for an instant, instead of wallowing in her own mess.

Then again, she'd probably ignore even that. She hadn't moved a muscle while her father was laying into him.

Michael pushed loose strands of hair back from his face. "I checked the news last night. Seven people are missing. Three are confirmed dead, but the bodies were too badly burned to identify which of the missing people are definitely dead. *Seven.* Most of those were kids. And that doesn't even count the number of people in the hospital."

The sudden guilt clogged Hunter's throat. He remembered the feeling of panic and despair on those carnival grounds. He hadn't been able to help any of them. He rubbed at his eyes.

Michael was still looking at him. "Calla is on the list of the missing."

Hunter thought of the way her body had jerked, the way she'd dropped in the middle of the flames.

She'd fallen in the middle of an inferno. She had to be one of the dead.

"At least she can't hurt anyone else," said Hunter.

"Jesus," said Gabriel. "Why do you sound *upset* about that?"

"I'm not upset."

But he was. Because he'd wanted her to stop, but he hadn't wanted her *dead.* Because he hadn't been able to stop her himself, and now more people had lost their lives. Because once again, he wasn't exactly sure where he fell on this continuum of good and evil, or even which end was *which.*

He wasn't like Calla. He knew that much.

But if he wasn't like the Guides, where did that leave his father? Where did it leave the man who'd shot Calla? The same man who'd pointed a gun at Hunter?

Hunter's first instinct had been to run.

Not to put his hands up and say, "Don't shoot. I'm one of you."

And where did it leave Kate, a girl who seemed to have as many secrets as he did himself? She'd climbed down the Ferris wheel more efficiently than he had. She'd called his name when he'd been running from the Guide—causing a hesitation that had probably saved his life. His shoulder wasn't any great distance from his heart.

She hadn't been the one with a gun. But what would happen if he told the Merricks that he suspected . . . *something* about her? About this *friend* she was texting all the time? He didn't know what to say. He couldn't even pin it down himself, so how was he going to explain it to them? He had no proof of anything, really. And they already didn't trust him.

He wasn't sure he trusted them, either, if they were going to leave him here.

His head hurt.

Seven people missing.

Seven people. All because he couldn't make himself pull a stupid trigger in the library.

All because he'd made his dad come back for him.

This line of thinking wasn't going to get him anywhere.

Hunter kept thinking of the kid who'd shown up in his kitchen that night, when Calla had come after him in his bedroom. Where had that guy gone? Why hadn't Hunter seen him around school?

He needed answers.

We need to talk about last night.

That statement could be about so many things.

Some were pleasant.

Some were not.

And there was only one way to find out which ones she wanted to talk about.

CHAPTER 17

Kate was waiting for him.

Hunter didn't spot her at first: she wore tight gray jeans and a slim-fitting olive-green tank that blended with the tree line at the edge of the carnival grounds. The sky still hung heavy with clouds, but the rain had stopped, leaving the field nothing but a soggy, charred mess. None of the carnival equipment had been removed. All the bodies sure had.

Almost everything was roped off with yellow crime scene tape.

Thank god his jeep had four-wheel drive—even so, he parked before it got too bad. He had to step through muddy tire ruts to get to her.

The place was deserted, but it felt haunted, as if the carnage from last night had left an impact in the very air.

Casper loped along beside him, happy for the adventure.

She wasn't armed, unless she had something at the small of her back, but it took everything he had not to let his eyes linger on her form. Her eyes were fierce, her shoulders thrown back, her mouth sexy as hell.

He glanced around. "What's with the cryptic meeting place?"

She ignored him. "What are you doing with the Merricks?"

Wow. As if that wasn't a loaded question.

But he could play this game, too. "You know what happened

with my grandfather. They're letting me crash there for a while."
He paused. "Why?"

"Don't play stupid."

He gave her half a smile. "I'm playing cautious."

"Why?"

"Probably the same reason you are." More sure now, he took
a step forward.

She didn't move, but he sensed the sudden tension in her body,
could feel the way her eyes tracked his movement.

He *was* out of practice. He should have noticed this when
they'd played at fighting last night.

Only now he sensed she wasn't playing at all.

"You look tense," he said easily. "I thought you wanted to
talk."

"If you're playing cautious, then you'll want to stop walking."

Well, that statement was full of threat, and definitely dictated
how this conversation was going to go.

He hesitated for a second, weighing his options. The post-
storm humidity spoke of danger, but he needed to take control
of this interaction before she did. He kept moving, knowing that
however she'd react, she was going to be fast. She wouldn't waste
energy on a strength move, not against him.

She moved half a second before he expected it—and not in
the way he expected at all.

She didn't fight, she *ran*.

He took off after her.

She was fast, launching herself through the underbrush in the
woods, heading toward the creek, barely making a sound as her
feet sprang through dead leaves. She ducked and bolted through
narrow passages, until even Casper had a hard time staying on
her trail.

And then she vanished.

Hunter drew up short, his lungs pulling for breath. His shoulder ached again, protesting all this motion.

About a hundred feet off, something skittered through a
bush.

Casper took off after it. Hunter stared. How had she gotten so far away, so—

Wham. Kate landed on him from above. It was a lot of weight all at once, and he hit the ground. Kate was on his back.

With a knife at his throat.

She had a fistful of his hair, and the blade was tight under his chin, so sharp that he could swear he was bleeding already.

"Boys are such idiots," she said.

But he wasn't listening. His hand was already hooking her wrist from the inside, using his strength to jerk her forward.

And while she was off balance, he rolled her into the dirty leaves. He straddled her waist and pinned her arms—one with his knee, one with a hand—and put the knife against *her* throat.

"Now who's the idiot?"

Her eyes lit with indignant fury.

"Don't glare at me," he said. "You're the one who left my hands free." He could still feel wetness at his neck. "That was a good trick, though. You have any more weapons hidden out here?"

Kate didn't speak, and he eased the knife away from her neck, just an inch. "I didn't come out here expecting a fight," he said.

"What were you expecting? Another chance to feel me up?"

That hurt more than it should have, but she didn't have to know that. "Why? Is that offer on the table?"

"Just kill me or let me go."

"I don't like either of those options. You're another Fifth, aren't you?"

"Oh, good. You've figured that out."

"You're working with the guy from last night?"

She kept glaring up at him, and that was answer enough. Hunter glanced around, but the trees were still. Casper was probably off chasing a rabbit or whatever. "Is he going to try to shoot me again?"

"Why did you flip sides?" she demanded.

He looked back down at her. "Who says I flipped sides?"

"You're living with the Merricks."

"Yeah, and they *hate* me."

"You should hate *them*."

For an instant, Hunter wanted to lift the knife and use it on himself. Her question narrowed his entire internal debate down to one fine point.

"They stopped those fires last night," he said quietly. "They saved my life after your *boyfriend* shot me."

"He's not my boyfriend." Her face lost some of the righteous fury. "And I know they did."

"Sounds like you care."

"About all those people? Of course I care."

That wasn't what he'd meant, but he didn't correct her. It shouldn't have made a difference, but it loosened something inside him, to hear that she couldn't disengage her conscience, either. "So what do you want, Kate? What?"

"I want your help."

"You thought you'd get it with a knife at my neck?"

"When you showed up, you were so . . . so cagey. I knew you'd figured it out. What I am." Her voice dropped. "I thought you really were on their side. I thought you'd kill me before I could explain myself."

"Guess I'm not all that predictable."

She wriggled her wrist under his hand. "Do you mind?"

He raised one eyebrow. "Just talk?"

She nodded. "Just talk."

So they sat against opposing trees, but he kept her knife, spinning it between his hands. "Maybe you should tell me the whole story. Transferred from Saint Mary's? I should have figured out *that* was a load of crap on the Ferris wheel."

She didn't blush, but her jaw was set. "I thought you'd be suspicious of someone from out of town."

"Did you know what I was, that first day?"

"I knew John Garrity had died after taking an assignment to eliminate the Merricks. The name was too close to be a coincidence."

He laughed, but not like anything was funny. "Is your mother even dead? Or was that just something to say to get close to me?"

Now she froze. "She's dead. She died on an assignment to kill a Water Elemental."

He told himself not to care. He'd fallen for this more than once already.

His father had once told him he needed to learn to cage his compassion, that others would use it against him, that it would cloud his judgment and hide what *needed* to be done.

But he couldn't help it. He heard the pain in her voice. No, he *recognized* it.

"What happened?" he said quietly.

"She was stupid. She faced him on the water."

Her eyes were hard when she said it. The derision in her voice was almost potent. "So you're here on a vendetta," he said without judgment. He couldn't really criticize—he'd come here for the same thing, once.

"No, I'm here because it's my *job*. I thought you'd understand that."

Hunter didn't have anything to say to that.

Her expression turned fierce. "I still don't understand why you'd be living with *them*. I've heard just how badass your father was."

Hunter went still. "You don't know anything about my father."

"I can imagine what he'd think about you living with a pack of Elementals he'd been sent to kill."

Hunter's hand tightened on the knife—but she was right. He had to look away.

"Did the Merricks kill him?" she asked. "Did they somehow convince you to—"

"No," he snapped, feeling his throat tighten. "No. You don't know what you're talking about."

"So tell me."

It took him a minute to make sure his voice would remain

steady. "When we came after them, the car was crushed in a rock slide. My father and uncle were killed."

He felt her eyes, and he met them, holding her there, daring her to say . . . anything. He wasn't sure what would push him over the edge.

Her voice dropped. "Michael Merrick is an Earth Elemental."

Hunter glared at her, hard. "I *know*. That was my first thought, too. I came here to finish the job."

"And you couldn't follow through."

It was so close to the truth that he flinched. He put a thumb against the edge of the blade, just a bit, letting the pain steady him. "They aren't the only Elementals in town," he said. "Their parents made a deal with the others, that they wouldn't turn them in to the Guides if the Merricks kept out of trouble and didn't use their abilities. Then the others spent *years* harassing the Merricks in an effort to make them reveal themselves."

She snorted. "Some *deal*. They used their abilities last night."

"The deal is over. When my dad couldn't . . . when he couldn't finish the job . . ." He had to swallow. "Another Guide came. He almost killed them. He caught Chris and Nick, but . . ."

Hunter stopped. She was going to misunderstand this, too.

"But what?"

He slid his thumb along the edge of her blade, harder now, feeling the sharpness, knowing it could draw blood with a little more pressure. "I helped them escape."

"Did you help them kill him, too?"

"He's not dead!" he snapped. "I still don't understand why you want my help if you think I'm nothing but a traitor."

She ignored that. "And Calla? You really did beat her up, didn't you?"

"No. I wish I had, but no. She said that so I'd have to stay away from her." He frowned. "Now that won't be a problem."

"Where does she fit in? Was she after the Merricks, too?"

"No. She wanted to bring the Guides here." He pointed at her with the knife. "Mission accomplished, huh?"

"Why?"

He punched the ground with his fist. "I *don't know* why! She kept threatening to keep starting fires if I couldn't bring more Guides here. I never expected her to blow up the whole carnival." His voice almost broke. "You think I wanted all those kids to die? I should have stopped her, Kate. I should have stopped her two weeks ago. I should have—"

He dropped her knife and pressed his fists into his eyes.

She could stab him right now and he wouldn't move a muscle to stop her.

Her hands fell on his shoulders, light and gentle and completely unexpected.

He dropped his fists to look at her, and her face was close. She knelt in the leaves in front of him, her green eyes soft and close.

"You're a mess," she said.

He snorted. "No kidding."

She leaned even closer, sliding her hands up his shoulders.

Her nearness affected him, making him want to pull her closer.

Idiot.

He caught her wrists. "Don't play with me, Kate."

"You're still bleeding."

"I'll live."

She rolled her eyes skyward, then leaned forward, her hands still trapped by his. Her breath eased against his throat, full of power, cool and hot at the same time.

He shivered before he could help it. Her full weight was on his hands. If he let go, she'd be against his chest, practically in his lap.

He pushed her back. "Stop."

She drew back, but only enough to stare into his eyes. "You have a lot of enemies."

He didn't have anything to say to that. She was right.

"Sounds exhausting," she said softly.

"You have no idea."

"I don't think I'm an enemy," she whispered.

God, he was so tired of fighting with people. He let go of her wrists. "Do what you want."

Her hands found his shoulders again, and she leaned forward. When her breath touched his skin, he closed his eyes. Power flared in the air to find the blood on his neck. He shivered.

Her voice was low, husky. "My mother used to say that the hardest part of being a Fifth was fighting the urge to help your enemies."

"My father used to say the same thing." Then he opened his eyes. "Is that why you're helping me now?"

"No." Her thumb stroked along his neck, and it didn't even sting. "I think that's why you're helping the Merricks."

"They're really helping *me*."

"Really? Did they follow you through the fire to stop Calla?"

He froze. No. They hadn't. Gabriel had pulled him out of the fire—but Hunter had gone to face Calla alone.

"Are they *helping* you," said Kate, "or are they keeping an enemy close?"

He'd be lying if he hadn't thought about this already. Hadn't Gabriel used *those exact words* the other night? Hadn't Nick demanded to see his text messages? Michael had asked him to help with his landscaping jobs. Was he being *nice*—or was he making sure he knew where Hunter was?

When Hunter and Gabriel had been fighting Calla's fires, Michael had done the same thing to Gabriel, dragging him all over town under the pretense of being *brotherly*.

Michael had talked about leaving town—in a *week*. Leaving Hunter here with nothing but a *mess* they'd all been part of.

"There are still more Elementals in town, aren't there?" said Kate.

"Yeah."

"You're in a good position to help us find them."

"Sure." Hunter made no attempt to keep the bitterness out of his voice. "I'd love to help the guy who *shot* me."

"He thought you were working with the girl who started the fires."

"Why the hell would he think that?"

"Because you were negotiating with her."

Hunter glared at her. "I wasn't *negotiating*. I was trying to get her to stop—"

"I know. I know." She paused. "And he knows. Now."

Hunter sighed and glanced away. That familiar guilt was trapping him. Did he owe the Merricks anything? Was he betraying them by even being here? All this indecision was almost painful.

Then he realized: did it matter? They'd be gone in a week.

He stared back at Kate, at the crystal blue of her eyes, which were just now beseeching him.

"How am I supposed to keep you a secret?" he asked, his voice rough.

Then, just like last night, she was in his lap before he was ready, her fingers in his hair, her lips warm against his. It was like she had power in *this*, like the feel of her lips and her skin and her breath could control him. His hands grabbed her hips, finding an inch of skin between her jeans and the tank top.

Every Elemental in town could attack him right this instant and he wouldn't care.

Everything about her kiss was so *Kate*, aggressive and gentle at the same time, like an attack you didn't know to defend yourself from until it was too late.

Power surged in the air around them, and now, alone, no secrets between them, he did nothing to hold it back. His hand slid up her side, and she didn't protest. He kissed his way down her jaw, along her neck, aware that the temperature in the woods had turned downright tropical. She smelled like something tropical, too, mangoes or papayas or something sweet and edible.

Suddenly, she was pulling at his T-shirt, and he drew back to help her.

But then her cell phone chimed.

Twice.

It hit him like a bucket of cold water.

He was already trying to disentangle himself from her—but

now she grabbed his shoulders. "Stop," she whispered. "Stop. I told you—he's not my boyfriend."

Yeah, maybe not. But that didn't mean this was . . . real.

Idiot, his subconscious was yelling. *You're an idiot.*

Kate leaned in again, touching her forehead to his. "I've wanted to kiss you since the first morning I saw you."

"All part of the plan, right?"

She flung herself off him. "You think all my text messages were part of some *plan*?" She kicked him in the leg. "You *asshole*. You think I can't separate what I'm doing here from what I think about you?"

He glared up at her. "I don't know, Kate. Maybe I can't keep up."

"Jesus, don't you trust *anybody*?"

"No, and I'm pretty sure you don't, either."

She stared back at him, her chest rising and falling as rapidly as his. She didn't say anything, and that said it all right there.

"What do your text messages say?" Hunter demanded. "Is he checking up on how things are coming along with me?"

"He doesn't even know I'm here."

"Sure."

Her breathing was fast and rapid, her cheeks flushed.

Then she reached into her pocket, jerked out her phone, and tossed it at him. "Go ahead, see for yourself."

He slid his finger across the screen, then glanced up. "Code?"

"Nine-six-seven-four."

He hit the keys and her phone opened. He pushed the icon for text messages. *Silver* was in bold letters at the top.

When you say you're going for a walk, I don't expect you to disappear for two hours.

Do not make me come looking for you, Kathryn.

"Wow," Hunter said. "He sounds charming."

Kate grabbed the phone out of his hands. "He's doing his *job*." Then she slid her fingers along the screen, texting back.

After a moment, his own phone chimed, and Hunter grabbed it from his pocket.

She'd sent him a message.

I don't want to be your enemy, Hunter.

While he was looking, another message appeared.

Silver was going to kill you last night. I stopped him.

He didn't look at her, just texted back.

Why?

Because I understand you. And I think you understand me.

He sighed. Another message appeared.

I don't want anyone to get hurt, either.

Before he could text back, she caught his hands between hers, cradling the phone. She looked up at him. "We can stop them, Hunter. We can. We can stop all of this from happening again."

He blew out a breath. "How?"

"Find out who was working with her. We'll take care of it and leave you alone."

She was using him. It was obvious. He knew it, and she knew it.

But what would his father have wanted? For Hunter to hide with the Merricks?

"I don't know who was working with her," he said.

"Can you find out?"

He kept thinking about that kid who'd been with Calla in his house. Who *was* he?

They'd probably have pictures of the missing kids on the news. He could start there. Maybe it would lead to nothing— but maybe it would lead to a whole lot of *something*.

"I only have one lead," he said. "It might not go anywhere."

"But you'll help?"

"Maybe."

"That's enough for now." She kissed him on the cheek and then was gone.

Hunter didn't check his other messages until he was in the jeep. He had a text from Gabriel.

All OK?

Hunter sat there and stared at the screen for the longest time. He thought of the gunshot, of Gabriel saving his life, of the arguments in the Merrick house, of the whispers about leaving, the quick action to shut up when they heard Hunter in the hallway. He thought of Calla. He thought of Kate, of Silver.

He thought of his father.

Then he typed back quickly.

Yep. Be back soon.

Then he clicked off the phone and started the engine.

Silver was waiting for her, sitting at the table, checking his weapons.

Kate deliberately took her time getting through the door, putting her sunglasses away, running lip gloss over her lips in front of the mirror in the front hall.

She gasped when Silver grabbed her arm and spun her around.

"Did he agree?" he said evenly.

"Let me go."

"Answer me."

"Yeah, he agreed. Now let me go, before I make you."

Silver half smiled. "Now I'm curious. Make me."

She didn't hesitate—just swung a fist into his midsection.

He blocked, of course. She was ready for it, using his momentum to throw an elbow into his groin.

She wasn't ready for his fist to smack into the side of her face. She wasn't ready for the room to go sideways.

Thank god the front hallway was carpeted.

Silver left her there. "The problem, Kathryn, is that you assume people won't want to hit that pretty face."

No, the problem was that she'd assumed Silver wouldn't hurt *her*. That he'd play, the way Hunter had at the carnival.

Stupid.

She tried to convince her joints to work. Her head was still spinning, and for an instant, she couldn't figure out which stretch of drywall was supposed to be the ceiling.

Her cheek ached. "I could stab you in your sleep," she said.

"You could try. I feel rather certain that you'd find a similar result."

Tears were burning at her eyes, and she told them to go away. Silver could probably sense the water threatening to spill over her cheeks anyway.

Hunter was supposed to be her enemy, but she couldn't ever imagine him doing *that*.

She thought of the way he'd warned his friend about those bullies at the carnival last night, the way Gabriel Merrick had gone storming across the fairgrounds to confront them.

Or how Nick Merrick had invited her to sit with him at lunch.

Silver had chastised her for letting those people off the Ferris wheel. *The ends justify the means.*

She needed to get off the floor. She fought for balance and remembered the confrontation with the Water Elemental that had led to her mother's death.

Keep that memory fresh.

But there were other memories, later ones, that threatened to cloud her judgment.

She needed to remember the moment her mother had died, everything that had gone wrong that night.

The Merricks might not have been evil, but they weren't all good, either. They couldn't be. She'd spent her life hearing about the dangers of full Elementals.

She dropped into the chair at the table, where Silver had gone back to checking his weapons. She didn't really want to be sitting here with him, but she wasn't entirely sure she could manage the walk to her bedroom.

She gingerly moved her jaw and didn't think it was broken.

Even if it were, she'd never in a million years ask Silver to use power to heal it for her.

"I'm going to see him at school tomorrow," she said. Her voice sounded strange, and every hard consonant hurt, but she ignored it. "I told him we need his help to discover the other Elementals in town. He agreed."

Silver's eyebrows went up. "Well done."

The praise took some of the sting out of the way he'd hit her in the hallway. She repeated everything Hunter had said about his father, and Calla, and the Merricks.

"And what do you think?" said Silver. "Is he working with them? Is he a threat to us?"

"I think he's confused," she said honestly. She remembered the lost look in his eyes, the true emotion when he'd talked about his father. "He doesn't know where he belongs."

"I don't like that," said Silver. "His presence in that house makes them a perfect circle. One for each element, including the Fifth? They could be unstoppable."

"He swears they're not behind the fires."

"They could be behind a lot more." Silver's eyes flicked up. "You sound as though you have feelings for this boy."

"That's insane. I resent him. He's working for the enemy."

Silver kept studying her, and she held his eyes. He finally looked away.

She could breathe again.

While she did resent Hunter for living with the Merricks, there was a tiny part of her that was intrigued, too.

And maybe a little bit jealous. Gabriel Merrick had risked his life to drag Hunter to safety.

Would Silver do the same for her?

She didn't even entertain the thought for a moment. Of

course he wouldn't. If she'd been there, wounded, Silver would have pulled out his gun and finished her off.

Kate shook herself. She needed to keep her mind on the task at hand. Hunter Garrity was just an assignment.

And she knew just how to handle an assignment.

CHAPTER 18

Hunter pulled his jeep into the Merricks' driveway and almost threw his vehicle into reverse.

His mom's car was sitting in front of the house.

It was like life kept pelting him with curveballs and he couldn't swing his bat fast enough.

Well, he sure couldn't leave her sitting in there. God only knew what the Merricks might be telling her.

He took his time getting through the front door. He didn't have a key, and part of him hoped the door would be locked just so it would take an extra couple minutes before he'd have to face her. But the door was unlocked, so he eased inside, closing the door gently behind him.

He recognized her voice immediately. She was in the kitchen, talking to Michael, it sounded like. Then another woman was speaking. He was too far away to make out the words.

He fidgeted with his keys for a second before telling himself to stop being such an idiot.

Why was she here? What if she demanded that he come home? What would he do—throw a fit and demand to stay at the Merricks'? Like that would work.

He slid down the hallway silently, but Michael was by the counter, pouring a cup of coffee.

"Hi," Michael said. "You have a visitor."

Hunter took another step, feeling his shoulders hunch. He found himself wishing for a weapon.

And what would you do with one?

Nothing, really. But he'd felt half-naked since his grandfather had confiscated them.

Half-naked ÅÇ confident.

His mother was there, at the table, next to a blond woman he vaguely recognized. Hunter couldn't look at them. He already felt like he was going to pieces; eye contact would clinch the deal.

Instead, he leaned against the door molding and jingled his keys in his pocket. "What are you doing here?"

"The fire at the school carnival was on the noon news, and after last week—I thought—I didn't know—"

Now fury poured across his shoulders, hardening them in place. She'd *just* heard about the fires? He'd been shot last night, and she hadn't known anything about the carnival until like an *hour* ago?

Even though it was something completely out of her control, he couldn't help but blame her for it.

"I'm fine," he said evenly. "You can go back home. You should have just called."

"I wasn't sure you'd answer."

Well, that was honest. He wasn't sure he would have answered, either.

A chair scraped against the floor, and he glanced up, wondering if she really *was* leaving. But it was the blond woman, young and slight and wearing the local fire station's T-shirt.

This had to be Hannah.

"We'll just give you some privacy," she said quietly. Then she moved toward Michael, took his arm, and practically dragged him out of the kitchen.

Hunter moved out of the doorway so they could pass, but he still didn't look at his mother.

"Did you go through the boxes I left you?" she asked quietly.

He shrugged. "I haven't had time."

That, at least, was the truth. He hadn't bothered to go through them before the carnival, and the last thing he'd cared about today was a box full of old pictures and his gaming system.

She was silent for a while. Then she said, "Well, go through them soon, so you can make sure you have everything you need."

He was clutching his keys so tightly, they felt like they might bend between his fingers. He wanted to snap at her to demand things like *How could you do this?!*

But he was scared of the answers. As much as he didn't want her here, he didn't want her to leave, either.

He cleared his throat and stopped clutching his keys. But then his hands wanted something to do. He settled for folding his arms across his chest. "Fine."

She didn't move. He didn't, either.

He wished he knew how to fix this.

He wanted to tell her the truth about Calla. He wanted to demand to know how she could have thought he'd *ever* do something like that.

He wanted to talk to her, to tell her everything his father had said before he died. To tell her that he felt lost, directionless, trying to figure out just who he was supposed to be now that everything he knew had been crushed under that rock slide.

He wanted to ask why she was only looking at him *now*, when he would have given anything for one minute of her attention since the day his father died. He wanted to ask how she could sit there and watch him walk out the door, how she could sit here now, motionless, and not say *anything* to him.

The longer she sat there, the more she seemed to prove his father's words, on the day before he died.

She was weak. She was ignorant. She was easily manipulated.

It made him want to rip the stupid stones off his wrist and fling them at her.

She'd been the one to give them to him, after all.

When her chair scraped the floor, he flinched but then stopped his body from making any further movement. His fingers were digging into his biceps now.

When she stopped in front of him, he didn't look.

She put her hands on his arms and looked up at him. He wanted to shove her hands off.

No, he didn't.

He finally looked at her and sandbagged all that emotion. "I'm fine."

"I don't think you are." Her eyes were heavy with feeling. "I wish you would talk to me."

How could he talk to her when she didn't understand him, not even a little bit?

"I miss him, too, Hunter," she said softly, so quietly that he almost couldn't hear her.

It was the wrong thing to say—or the last thing he wanted to hear. He slid out of her hands and turned away. "That's your problem, isn't it?"

God, he sounded like such an *asshole*. But the alternative was breaking down right here in the Merrick kitchen—and he'd had enough of that.

She let him go, and he almost called her back and apologized. He felt like he was keeping his father's dirty little secret, and it was clawing at him from the inside out. He wanted to tell her, but that would cause her more pain than anything he was doing right now.

Dad never told you the truth. About anything.

He was only using you.

She stepped past him softly, just resting a hand on his arm as she moved past. Her fingers were warm, gentle, the same hands that had tended his scrapes when he was little.

He almost put his hand over hers, not wanting her to leave.

But then she let go. "Call me if you need something. I can bring over anything else you want."

"Fine."

And just like that, she walked out of the house.

He had to stop himself from going after her. It didn't help that he knew the Merricks were in the house, had heard every word, and were probably waiting for him to come out of the kitchen.

He went out the back door and dropped into one of the porch chairs.

The air still held a chill, and the clouds overhead suited his mood. He closed his eyes and tried to let the tension drain out of his shoulders.

The solitude left him with too much room for thinking, however, and he felt worse out here. Again, he found himself wishing for a pair of wraps and a heavy bag—or an opponent and a set of mats.

When the sliding door opened, he braced himself for another lecture from Michael.

So he was surprised when a woman's voice said, "Can I join you?"

His eyes snapped open. Hannah, the girl from the kitchen. The firefighter. Michael's new girlfriend.

She was pretty, slender and casual without looking delicate. Hunter could see solid muscle in her arms, and he knew from his escapades with Gabriel that using firefighting equipment was no joke. She wasn't old, but there was nothing young about the weight in her eyes.

She'd seen a lot. He could tell.

She'd been at the carnival last night. Gabriel had said something about her wanting to put him on a helicopter to shock trauma. Had she seen Calla? Would any of the bodies be identifiable after the fire?

He didn't want to ask.

She was still looking at him, a hand on the back of the adjacent Adirondack chair.

"Sure," he said.

She dropped into the chair beside him and stared up at the same sky. Her breathing was calm and even. He had no idea what she was doing out here.

"You know," she said without looking at him, "we once got this call for a guy whose girlfriend ripped all the piercings right out of his eyebrow."

"Sick." He paused. "What did it look like?"

"Blood everywhere. He had a safety pin or something run

through four hoops, and she grabbed it and yanked it off. They all came out."

He glanced over, intrigued that her voice held the same horror and fascination that he was feeling. "Were they fighting?"

"Ah . . . no. In the 'moment,' I guess you could say." She was smiling.

He looked back at the sky. "That's a hell of a moment."

"There was another guy who'd pierced his . . . ah . . ."

"I get it."

"Yeah, *that* was ripped out during a fight. I think I learned a whole new vocabulary on that call. But that's no comparison to the guy who took a Sawzall to his—"

"Not that I'm complaining or anything," said Hunter, trying to stop *that* particular story. "But did you really come out here to tell me ambulance stories?"

"I've got some really good ones." She paused. "You okay?"

"Fine."

"Your mom was pretty upset when she got here."

"Good for her."

He was ready for a lecture, but Hannah shrugged. "I didn't want to worry her more and tell her what you looked like last night."

He wondered if that would have made a difference and decided he didn't care one way or another.

Oh, who the hell was he kidding? He cared.

"Are you going to take the EMT course with Gabriel in the spring?"

He glanced over in surprise. He hadn't even considered it.

She was looking back at him. "What's with the look? I thought you guys were best friends."

"Not really."

"You braid his hair wrong or something?"

Hunter smiled. He liked this girl. "Something like that."

"So what's with your mom? Why are you so mad at her?"

He glared back at the sky and decided maybe he didn't like this girl *that* much.

Hannah shrugged and he caught the motion out of the corner

of his eye. "I mean, she was practically hysterical when she found out you weren't here. They must have been talking about the unidentified kids on the news. Michael had to tell her about fifteen times that you *had* gotten home from the carnival, that you were fine."

Hunter scowled. He wished that didn't make him feel guilty.

They sat there in silence for a long moment.

Then Hannah said, "Look, either you're going to talk or I'm going to have to finish the story about the guy who chopped off his penis. Your call."

Hunter snorted with unexpected laughter.

Then he sobered, thinking of those *unidentified kids*. "I don't know how you can joke after—after last night—"

"Because the alternative is going crazy? If you can't fix what's wrong, you focus on what you can make right."

Hunter looked at her. "My dad used to say that."

"My dad, too. It's a good dad thing to say."

The sudden emotion grabbed Hunter around the throat, and he almost couldn't breathe through it. He hated this, how it never came on slowly but instead snuck up like a ninja to punch him right when it was least expected. He had to shift to the edge of the chair and press his fingertips into his eyes.

Hannah scooted to the edge of her chair, too, until she was close. She touched his shoulder, and there was something secure about it, something steadying. "I didn't mean to upset you."

"I'm fine."

"Michael said your dad and your uncle died in a car crash."

Now Hunter knocked her hand away, and he straightened. "I don't want to talk about it. What are you even doing out here? I don't even *know*—"

"You can't fix it," she said, her voice strong and even, as if he hadn't interrupted. "You can't."

"I know that! You don't think I know that? I can't fix *any* of it!"

"It wasn't your fault. Has anyone ever told you that? *It wasn't your fault.*"

"You don't know anything." God he was sick of the lectures. She and Michael were *perfect* for each other.

He flung himself out of the chair and stalked through the door.

Chris and Nick were in the living room with Becca. They all looked up when he passed. Becca called out to him, but he kept going—up the stairs instead of out the door.

Then he locked himself in the bathroom and tried to keep from punching the mirror.

He needed to calm down.

Breathe.

What the hell did Hannah know? Had Michael sent her out there? He was ready for a knock at the door, for someone else to want to *talk*.

It made him think of Kate, how she'd been willing to do anything *but* talk. Only her methods of diversion weren't this unpleasant.

He turned the faucet on cold and splashed water on his face, letting the water run off his chin. He looked up at the mirror to make sure it didn't look like he'd been crying.

Then he kept on looking.

What had Michael said yesterday? *There is nothing about you that would make me say you look exactly like that guy. Take a look in a mirror sometime.*

When his father had been alive, Hunter had always kept his hair short—not quite the military crew cut, but short enough to be preppy. He'd never had a single piercing.

Then the car had been crushed in the rock slide, and he'd found himself with twenty-six stitches across his hairline, leaving him with white hair to grow back in its place. He'd gone through the funeral, through the packing of their house, through his mother's withdrawal, without feeling *anything*.

Except when she reminded him how much he looked like his father.

Then he'd felt resentment.

And anger.

And guilt.

He'd gone to the grocery store one day—because his mother couldn't be bothered with basic needs—and some biker guy with three hundred and some tattoos and piercings had said, "Nice streak, kid. You need some metal and ink to go along with it."

Then he'd handed him a card for a local tattoo place.

The burn of the needle was the first new thing Hunter had really *felt* in weeks.

So he'd kept asking for more.

He stared into his eyes in the mirror.

Michael was right. Hunter looked nothing like his father anymore.

And instead of feeling good about that, it made him feel like shit.

He ducked and dried his face on the towel.

Hannah was right, too. He couldn't fix the accident. He knew that.

Could he fix this mess with his mother?

Did he want to? Did she want him to?

The upstairs was still empty, thank god. Hunter went into Nick's bedroom, where the two boxes from his grandparents' house were stacked in front of the closet.

He cracked open the first one. The photo of his father and uncle was right on top, just like yesterday. Hunter set that aside and kept going.

Yearbooks, from his high school in Pennsylvania. Old, outdated magazines—*really, Mom?* Old notebooks from school that he'd never need again. His Xbox, with the case of games.

Because he totally felt like gaming with everything else going on.

Some paperbacks he didn't remember reading, more magazines, more *crap* he'd never need. And then a brown Pendaflex folder with a rubber band wrapped around it. He could see the edges of file folders and wondered if she'd packed up his old school records, too.

The rubber band snapped when he yanked it out of the box, and two folders slipped out. He expected old report cards.

He found records, but not the school kind.

The top folder was about the Merricks. Personal information that he already knew, like their address and phone number. Grainy photos that had to be several years old, because one included their parents. Chris looked about ten.

Pages and pages about their powers, about surveillance, about potential Elemental hazards linked to the family.

His heart was pounding so hard that he couldn't believe it wasn't causing a racket all the way downstairs.

He knew the Merricks. He could read theirs later. He flipped to the next folder.

The Morgan family. Tyler, a Fire Elemental. No extreme risk. Emily, an Air Elemental, deceased. No risk. Pictures, but Hunter didn't need them. He knew their stories.

The Ramsey family. Seth, one of Becca's attackers. No extreme risk, according to the file, but obviously they were only talking about the Elemental kind.

Hunter didn't know the next family, but he wondered if the Merricks did.

In the fourth folder, as soon as he opened it, he recognized the kid in the picture.

It was the boy who'd shown up with Calla when they'd been trashing his grandfather's kitchen. Hunter felt ready to choke on his heartbeat.

Noah Dean. So he was related to Calla.

But there were no pictures of *her*, just this boy.

Well, of course. Calla had only just moved here a few years ago, to live with her aunt when her father was deployed. All these files were ages old.

Hunter checked the birthdate and quickly added. Noah was thirteen. Too young to be in high school.

No *wonder* Hunter hadn't seen him anywhere around school. He'd been next door to the high school all this time, at the middle school.

Hunter wondered if Noah was among the missing from the carnival. He'd have to check the news.

Then something else occurred to him: had his mother gone through this folder?

He stared at the pages in his hand. The rubber band on the Pendaflex had been old, or else it wouldn't have snapped so readily. But why would she have given him a stack of files and papers without going through them? His name wasn't on any of it, and it certainly wasn't packed up the way he kept his things. He'd never seen these files, so she hadn't found them in *his* room.

He quickly shoved all the papers back into the Pendaflex, trying to keep them in the order he'd found them. Then he ripped the cover off the other box.

His quilt. His sheets—again, *really, Mom?* Frigging threadbare beach towels that he didn't even consider *his*.

When he flung them to the side, something heavy clattered free.

Two of his father's best knives.

The breath left Hunter's lungs in a rush.

He pulled more towels free, more carefully this time, just in case there were other knives that might not be sheathed.

No more knives.

But between the last two towels, he found his gun, an extra magazine, and a box of bullets.

He picked up the weapon and checked the safety automatically. Just feeling the steel in his hands was as reassuring as if she'd packed his old teddy bear.

She'd packed this folder and these weapons.

I can bring over anything else you want.

His mother knew.

CHAPTER 19

Hunter wasn't sure how much he needed to keep secret.

The gun, for sure. If nothing else, it was a safety thing. He had too many of his father's lectures rattling around in his head to leave a loaded firearm lying around—especially if Hannah's kid was going to be in the house. He didn't have a lockbox, but he could lock the gun in the glove compartment of his jeep—or he'd keep it on his person.

Considering the events of the past few days, he was ready to sleep with it holstered inside his waistband.

But the folders . . . He just didn't have a history in this town, so he'd have to tell someone about them, if only to find out who the kids in other folders were. He'd only recognized Noah's face, but that wasn't enough.

He needed help. And the Merricks would probably give it to him, if he could play it straight.

They were leaving him alone this afternoon, too, which was nice—though he'd probably earned it by being such a dick that no one wanted to mess with him. When he'd grown up, it had always been three people in the house, with his uncle sometimes thrown in for variety. They lived too far from grandparents for anything more than an occasional visit. Even when he'd moved here with his mom, the dinner table had never been occupied by more than four people.

When he finally ventured downstairs, the Merrick kitchen was practically *packed.*

The four brothers. Becca and Quinn. Layne and her little brother Simon. Hannah and James.

Hunter made eleven. It brought new meaning to the phrase *odd man out.*

They had about ten buckets and boxes from KFC. Hannah's little boy appeared to be eating nothing but macaroni and potato wedges—and half of those were being fed to Casper, who was sitting under the table. The noise and energy in the room was almost enough to send Hunter back up the stairs.

But the smell was holding him *right here.* He'd never eaten lunch.

Becca appeared in front of him, taking his hand, pulling him into the kitchen. "I was worried about you," she said quietly.

"Careful," he said. "That's catching."

"Did you fall asleep?"

He'd spent the afternoon reading through the folders, but she'd given him the perfect out. "Yeah. I was knocked out."

"Well, come eat."

She dragged him toward the table, and Chris glared at the way her hand was still attached to Hunter's, so he left it there, actually using it to pull her a bit closer and speak low, under the noise in the room.

"Sorry I ignored you earlier. Long day."

Becca looked up at him. This close, he could catch her scent over the chicken, something with vanilla and almonds. "It's okay," she said. "I know you've got a lot going on."

There was true empathy in her eyes, and it softened something inside him. "Thanks for trying to help." He paused, thinking of all the warnings about trusting the Merricks. Thinking of the folders upstairs. He pushed the hair back from his face and sighed. "Maybe later I could get your opinion on something—"

A hand shoved him back, and Chris said, "Maybe later you could remember that she's not your girlfriend."

"Hey," Becca started. "It's fine."

Hunter smiled, but there was nothing friendly about it. Chris's aggression made his decision about Kate much easier to consider. "Maybe later you could remember that Becca has a mind of her own."

Chris gave him another shove, a little more violently. "I don't know what you think you're doing here—"

"Hey!" said James, his little boy voice carrying over everything else. "Use words, not hands." Then he glanced at Hannah. "Right, Mom?"

"Absolutely right," she said, completely unfazed, pulling another piece of chicken from a bucket.

But Chris backed off.

Hunter smiled more broadly. "Funny. I can think of two words right off." But Becca was already pulling Chris to the other side of the table.

"Words, not hands," said Layne. She poked Gabriel with her fork. "I think you need a T-shirt that says that."

He leaned in close. "Give me five minutes and I bet I can change your mind."

"Ugh," said Quinn, spearing a piece of chicken with her fork. "Spare us."

Michael glanced over at Hannah. "I told you you'd regret staying for dinner."

"Are you kidding? You should see dinner at the firehouse."

Hunter grabbed a paper plate and a piece of chicken, then dropped into one of the folding chairs that had been added to make enough seats. He was smashed between Nick and Simon and barely had enough room to put his plate down.

Chris was still glaring at him. "So what did you want to show Becca later?"

Becca was glaring at Chris now. "Leave him alone."

"No way," said Chris. "If it was so innocent, he can tell everyone."

Hunter pulled the skin off his chicken and fed it to Casper, well aware that everyone at the table was looking at him now.

He was spinning his wheels trying to think of something innocuous to say, but he was coming up with nothing. He was tempted to keep everything secret, to hand over the files to Kate to see what they could come up with together.

But he didn't know who all those people were, and the Merricks might.

The gun was a solid weight at the small of his back, like a heavy steel security blanket.

"I went through the things my mom packed up," he said slowly, looking at the chicken on his plate. He wasn't sure how many people at the table *knew* about Elementals, so he chose his words carefully. "She included my dad's files."

"*Files* files?" said Gabriel.

Hunter nodded.

"Anything interesting?" said Nick.

"They're old." Hunter paused. "But yeah."

"What kind of files?" said Hannah.

"Later," said Michael. He gave Hannah a crooked glance. "Maybe when the daughter of the county fire marshal isn't sitting at the table."

"Don't worry," she said. "I'll get the secrets out of you later."

"Trust me," said Michael. "You don't want these secrets."

Hunter kind of agreed with him.

Later, when Hannah and James were gone, and Quinn had driven home with Becca, Hunter brought the files downstairs and dumped them out on the table.

He'd been doubtful about Layne and Simon, but Gabriel said, "They can stay. They're good at secrets."

Hunter watched as the Merrick brothers went through their own files first.

Michael blew out a long whistle. "Your dad had a lot of information."

Layne poked Gabriel's cheek. "Did you always look surly? How old are you in that picture?"

Gabriel was staring at the grainy reproduced photograph. "Twelve? Thirteen? I don't know." He glanced up at Michael. "There's notes in here about Mom and Dad. The Guides knew what happened with Tyler's sister, and Seth's parents."

Nick looked at Hunter. "Why didn't your dad come after us *then*?"

"I don't know." He hesitated, remembering his father's caution when discussing the Merricks a few days before he died. Hunter strongly suspected that the four of them together were more intimidating than they even realized.

It reminded him of the conversation with Kate in the field, about his presence in the house making them more formidable instead of less, no matter which side he was on.

Hunter shoved the thought out of his head and pulled more files from the Pendaflex. "There are notes about Seth and Tyler, too." He slid them onto the table. "And a bunch of people I don't know."

They quickly discarded the files about Seth and Tyler. When they got to the first one Hunter didn't recognize, Nick said, "Jeff Bluster. He was a year ahead of us. His folks were friends with Tyler's. They were in on the deal."

"What happened to them?" said Hunter.

Chris shrugged. "They moved away a few years ago."

Hunter turned to the next file, on Noah Dean. "This is the kid who was with Calla when they trashed my house. She never said she had a younger brother, but maybe this is her cousin? She lives with her aunt and uncle." Hunter hesitated, then said more softly, "Lived."

Simon leaned forward and looked at the picture. He turned to Layne and signed something.

"I remember this kid, too," said Layne. "He's in eighth grade, a year behind Simon." Her younger brother signed some more, and she kept translating. "He wasn't a troublemaker. Had a lot of friends." She glanced up. "Probably still does."

"I don't know him," said Michael. "His family wasn't in on the deal—my parents probably never knew they were Elementals."

Hunter grabbed the next folder. This one and the rest were labeled POTENTIAL THREAT. "How about this girl?"

The Merricks all shook their heads, but Layne leaned over. "Alison Merryman. I know her. She's a freshman. Quiet. Sweet."

Next folder. Another seventh grader. And another one. Then an eighth grader.

Simon signed quickly. Layne leaned over. "I know him, too. He's a *jerk*." She glanced at Gabriel as Simon kept signing. "He's one of the ones who was hassling Simon at the carnival."

"He ran when I showed up," said Gabriel. "I just thought he was running from a fight."

Layne's brother looked pissed at the memory.

Hunter glanced at him. "I could help you with that," he said.

Simon's eyes widened in surprise.

Hunter shrugged. He remembered what it felt like to walk through school hallways and wonder when the next idiot was going to slam you into a locker. "If you want," he said.

Simon nodded.

"No wonder they're not getting into it with us at school," said Gabriel.

"They're all *kids*," said Nick. "They probably just figured out what they are."

That meant they weren't under heavy surveillance—yet. "Were they injured in the fire?" said Hunter. "Is there a list on one of the news websites or anything?"

Michael got his laptop and they checked. None of the names matched the list of the missing.

But Hunter noticed something else: Calla Dean was listed as missing, not one of the confirmed dead.

Did that mean something? He'd seen her fall.

Then he dismissed it. The Guide—Silver—wouldn't have left her lying in the middle of the carnival.

"Well," said Gabriel, "no one is stopping us from going over there to see."

"Going over where?" said Michael.

"The middle school."

Middle school. Nick was right—they were all kids. It was a new wrinkle.

Hunter had been ready to hand these files over to Kate, thinking it would be so easy to solve this problem, to redeem himself in his father's memory.

But they were *kids.*

He thought about Calla in the middle of the fairgrounds. She'd been too young to die, for sure, but she'd known what she was doing.

Had she organized the next group of Elementals into something they weren't ready for?

He needed to talk to these middle schoolers, to figure out which side they were on.

And he needed to do it without the Merricks.

"Let's not be stupid about this," said Michael. "There's a Guide in town. If we figured out these kids were working with Calla, then *he* will, too. We need to stay the hell away from them."

"No way," said Gabriel.

"I agree with Michael," said Hunter.

They all looked at him in surprise. He shrugged and lied through his teeth. "Well, I think we should give it a few days. Calla was obviously the ring leader. Let's see if they make another move."

Hunter glanced at Simon, a kid who was bullied mercilessly. Hunter knew what the Merricks had gone through for years. He wondered if these new Elementals were going through the same thing.

And he wondered if it would have been easy, too easy, for Calla to convince them to rebel.

CHAPTER 20

While they shared a campus, the middle school and high school had different hours. Hunter and the Merricks had to be at school early, the middle schoolers didn't start until after nine. He couldn't exactly skip class to stake out seventh and eighth graders—that would probably draw attention.

Instead, he decided to head over at the end of the day, to watch the younger students as they bolted for the buses to go home.

But that meant Hunter had seven hours of class time to kill.

Other students spent that time building locker shrines to the students who'd lost their lives. Hunter spent most of it feeling like he could have stopped the whole thing.

Or like he was betraying the Merricks somehow.

He tried to talk himself out of that feeling. He wasn't planning to feed Kate information about *them*. And what were they doing for him anyway? Letting him live in their house until they decided to pack up and leave town? Michael had made a comment this morning that he was going to figure out how much money they had to work with. There was talk about leases and walking away from the business and—Hunter had to leave the room, because it all pointed toward leaving him here to deal with this mess.

And even after reading through all the files, he had no idea where his mother stood on everything. She wasn't a Guide—unless she'd also hidden that from his father. Hunter had run all kinds of scenarios through his head, but he couldn't make any of them work at *all*. Did she approve of his father's profession? Of Hunter continuing his mission? If she didn't, she sure wouldn't have left him with weapons hidden among his things.

To say nothing of his father's old files. Did she know about the Merricks? Those files had been held together by an ancient rubber band; he didn't get the impression anyone had read through them recently.

He wanted to call her, to confront her and demand answers.

But maybe she didn't have answers. She'd hidden those things when she could have come right out and *given* them to him.

Not to mention that he'd spent *months* grieving for his father and wondering how anyone would ever understand him again. She'd known. All this time—she'd *known*.

His thoughts were spinning out, not finding traction anywhere. Hunter actually looked forward to fourth period, when he could see Kate and tell her what he'd learned, what he'd *planned*.

But Kate didn't show for fourth period, and his texts went unanswered. Now he felt like a fool, sitting around like an eager puppy expecting a bone.

As usual, he was standing at a crossroads, with no idea which direction was right.

Instead of heading to the cafeteria at lunch, he went out back, to where a few concrete picnic tables were lined up under the pine trees. The weather was still crap, with rain dripping between the branches to soak the ground and seal the chill to his body, but it was *outside*, and deserted, and he could feel the elements and think.

He lay on one of the tables and stared at the sky. The gun dug into the small of his back and the rain seemed to aim straight for his eyes.

He remembered Kate's words from yesterday. *Don't you trust anyone?*

No. He didn't. It had been his father's last lesson, and Hunter had learned it well.

A branch cracked and split somewhere to his left, and he was off the table in a heartbeat.

He landed in a crouch and surveyed the pine trees. Nothing.

His hand found the gun, but he didn't draw it—the last thing he needed was for some teacher to catch him with a firearm.

The trees were still, aside from slow drops of water rolling from leaf to leaf. The air was full of information, centering on the fact that someone hid nearby.

Yesterday, Kate had dropped out of a tree to tackle him. He glanced up, though all he found overhead was sky.

Then he *felt* motion before he saw anything, and he was moving, spinning, dropping, all before his brain registered the attack.

Everything was too fast—he couldn't even tell who'd come after him. Sheer size said it was a guy; light hair said it wasn't one of the Merricks. Then the air dropped ten degrees, turning thin and hard to breathe. Ice formed on his cheeks, stinging his eyes and stealing his vision.

Then a fist caught him in the shoulder. The left one, exactly where he'd been shot.

The sudden pain almost knocked him down. It felt like he'd been shot *again*. No, it felt like his whole arm was dislocating from his body.

His power flared without direction, pulling strength from the ground and the air, and when he swung a fist, he connected *hard*.

But he didn't stop there. Most people fought to drive an enemy away—not Hunter. He'd been taught to pull an enemy close, to cause the most damage. He blinked frost out of his eyes and threw his joints into retaliation, drawing strength from the ground, connecting, punishing.

He knew the moment when his attacker wanted to get some distance, and Hunter felt the surge of victory as he got the upper hand.

Then a fist snuck inside his guard and jabbed him right in the throat.

Hunter went down. Worse—he couldn't *breathe*. He was on all fours in the grit and pavement of the school patio, and he was going to choke to death because no one else was stupid enough to be out here in the rain.

He sensed movement, and the gun found his hand.

The movement stopped. "You're better than I thought you'd be."

He had an accent, leaving the words clipped.

Hunter coughed and it hurt like a bitch. But it meant air was working its way into his lungs, so he couldn't complain.

Get up. Get up, you wuss.

He shoved himself to his feet to face his attacker, keeping the gun pointed. At least his hand was steady.

The man was tall, younger than Hunter expected, with darker skin and ice-blue eyes. He looked military fit, with close-cropped hair and a steady stance. He also looked like he didn't take any crap—he was here to do a job, and he was going to do it.

Hunter briefly wondered if this was how he would have turned out, if his father hadn't died.

"Do us both a favor and put the gun away," said the man.

"You're Silver," Hunter said. It sounded like he was talking through a throat full of gravel. "You shot me last night."

A nod. "You're lucky I didn't kill you last night."

"You're lucky I'm not killing you right now."

"I don't think luck has anything to do with it. Put the gun away."

Hunter didn't move, and the man raised an eyebrow. "You were the proverbial sitting duck a few moments ago. Surely you realize I would have already killed you if I meant you harm."

Hunter rolled that around in his head for a moment. He couldn't sit here all day holding a gun, either. His father used to say, "Pointing a gun means nothing if you're not willing to fire it."

Could he shoot this guy?

No. He couldn't.

He slid the gun into the holster. "Where's Kate?"

"I had doubts about her ability to evaluate whether you were a threat."

Hunter rubbed at his throat. Again, he was reminded of Gabriel's comment that first night. *Keep your enemies closer.* Or the old saying, *The enemy of my enemy is my friend.* Silver had shot him, had just about kicked his ass right here in the school courtyard, but Hunter didn't get the impression that the guy was really here to fight with him.

"If you're here to stop the Elementals who are starting fires, I want the same thing," said Hunter. "I'm no threat to you."

A smile. "I'm not worried about you being a threat to *me.*"

God, this guy was cocky. Hunter bristled. "I told Kate I would help her figure out who the others are."

"I'm curious—why would you agree to turn in some, but not all?"

He had to be talking about the Merricks. "I don't have to turn in *anyone.* You know who the Merricks are. It doesn't matter anyway. They aren't the ones causing trouble."

A frown. "You know what your father was, do you not?"

Hunter frowned back at him. He wasn't sure where this conversation was going. "Yes."

"And you have no problem with the Merricks' continued existence?"

"I told you—they're not hurting anyone."

Silver leaned against the picnic table. "Did Kate tell you about her mother?"

"She told me she was killed by a Water Elemental."

The man nodded. "Did Kate mention that she went after the same Water Elemental to finish the job?"

They'd talked about vengeance, but they'd never talked about killing anyone.

Then again, he hadn't known what Kate was. Not then. "No," he said. "She didn't."

"You see, Hunter Garrity, son of John Garrity, your father was a great man. He did what needed to be done, for the good of all. I wasn't aware he had a son, so you're a bit of a mystery. I worry that you have missed the mark somewhere."

Hunter felt fury well up inside, but not at Silver. At himself. He worried about the exact same thing. "I told Kate that I would find the other Elementals."

"You talk about Elementals as if there are shades of gray. There are not. There are full Elementals, and there are Guides."

Hunter didn't say anything.

Silver studied him. "When I finish the job I've come here to do, which side will you stand on?"

"What difference does it make?" Hunter snapped.

"It makes a great deal of difference if the five of you can form a full circle. Do you understand what I'm saying to you?"

"Yeah." Silver was saying he wouldn't take the chance of Hunter helping the Merricks to fight back.

Hunter wondered if that meant Silver would kill him right now if he gave the wrong answers.

He was so sick of this debate over right and wrong. Silver's attacking him had been a relief of sorts—he could defend himself from an assault. A fight was clear-cut.

But really, wasn't this just as clear-cut?

Silver was still watching him. His voice was grave. "I knew your father. I respected him, and I was sorry to hear of his death. I would rather not kill you, but I put duty before emotion. Do you?"

Hunter looked away. Rain snuck inside the collar of his shirt to make him shiver.

"You were negotiating with Calla Dean," said Silver. "Why?"

"I didn't want her to hurt anyone else."

"Why didn't you kill her when you had the opportunity? From what I've read, she's been hurting people for a while, and many of them."

"I didn't know who else she was working with."

Silver straightened. "I don't believe that's a complete answer."

Hunter scowled. Maybe it was the repeated mentions of his father, but somehow this conversation radiated disappointment, and he felt obligated to prove himself. "I thought she was my friend at first. I thought I understood her. I wanted to find out why she was drawing the Guides here."

"You don't think she should have been put to death for the crimes she committed?"

Hunter didn't have an answer for that, either.

And wasn't that answer enough?

He kept going back to that conversation with Michael in the truck, about turning off his conscience. Was that the problem here? Had he been going about everything all wrong? Was it really so simple as needing to focus on the goal and forget how he got there?

Kate was full of rage against pure Elementals—and he got it, if they'd killed her mother. He hadn't been able to kill Michael and Gabriel a few weeks ago. He hadn't been able to kill Calla.

He hadn't been able to do the job he'd been *born to do.*

The Merricks were a family. They'd stick together. They'd do whatever they had to do to keep themselves together and safe.

And was working with Silver even a betrayal? They were *leaving.*

With a sudden flash of understanding, he wondered if this was the true reason his mother had hidden those weapons, those files. She thought he was living in enemy territory. She thought the Merricks might be a danger to him.

And they were, in a way: they'd made him a target. A bullet through his shoulder had proven that.

He'd been off track for a while now. But here, talking to Silver, a man who'd tried to kill him, he felt like he'd found the rails.

He squared his shoulders and looked up. "I'm not your enemy," he said. "Tell me what you want to know."

CHAPTER 21

Kate sat with Hunter outside the middle school. He was nursing a bottle of water, twisting it between his hands until she was reminded of Silver with his weapons.

"Nervous?" she said.

"No."

"Which one are we waiting for?"

"I'll know when I see them."

He was different this afternoon, more determined, maybe. It reminded her of the first day in the cafeteria, when she'd seen him so tightly coiled, so full of control. She wondered just what Silver had said to him.

And what it would take to make him snap again.

"Did I miss anything exciting in History?" she said.

He didn't look over. "Do you really care?"

"I care deeply about the Treaty of Versailles."

His eyes flicked her way. "Really. Describe it."

She could call his bluff since she'd read the chapter last night, thinking she'd be in school today. If Silver hadn't been so damned overbearing, she would have been. "It ended the First World War and made Germany realize they weren't the badasses they thought they were."

Hunter sniffed and looked back at the door of the school.

"Look," she said. "I don't get what your problem is."

"I don't have a problem, Kate."

"What's with the attitude?"

"No attitude." His eyes cut her way again, his gaze sharp as steel. "I'm just done being played."

"I never played you."

"Okay."

"The sarcasm really isn't attractive."

"Like I care."

His tone was a smack to the face.

But what did she expect?

She traced a fingertip over the tattoo on his forearm, something scripty and long. She recognized the symbols as Arabic or Persian or something, but she couldn't read the language. "What's this really say?" she said, making her voice provocative. "Something dirty?"

He smacked her hand away, as if she were a troublesome fly.

"So touchy," she whispered mockingly.

"You don't need to be here," he said. "I told Silver I didn't need you."

"You and Silver are besties all of a sudden?"

"Let's just say he didn't climb in my lap to get his point across."

Well, that stung. She sat in silence after that, letting the last bits of rain collect in her hair and chill her neck. She didn't want to be sitting next to him now, but getting up and leaving would let him know he'd gotten to her.

After a minute, Hunter sighed, a breath full of weight, like he was going to apologize.

But he didn't.

They sat there for the longest time, just breathing the same air, waiting for the end-of-class bell that would send students through the doors.

Maybe she was the one who owed him an apology. Or at least an explanation.

"I was never trying to play you," she said quietly.

His posture tightened, as if he was going to snap back—but then he didn't say anything. It gave her courage to continue.

"When I got here," she said, "I didn't know who you were. I was just supposed to find the Merricks and figure out how hard they'd be to kill. You were kind of like . . . a wild card."

He didn't say anything, but he was listening. She could feel it.

"That first day—you defended me in the school office, but then you had some issue with Calla, and then the fight with Gabriel Merrick—I couldn't figure you out." She paused. "I still can't."

"I can't figure you out, either," he said, his tone sharp. "I mean, you throw yourself at every guy you see—"

"I do not!"

He gave her a *look*.

She sat up straight and gave him one right back. *"What?"*

He sighed and turned his attention back to the rear door of the middle school.

Then he abruptly looked back. "What happened to your face?"

She blinked. "What?"

"You have a bruise."

Kate put a hand to her face, and he shook his head, reaching out to touch her opposite cheek. "Here," he said.

His hand was warm, and she was surprised how it almost made her breath catch, just that little bit of contact.

If she said something about it, he'd probably mock her. So she brushed his hand away. "Sparring with Silver."

He made a small sound, a disbelieving sound. *"Sparring,* huh?"

She wanted to hit him. "How did it feel when people didn't believe you about Calla?"

That got his attention. "This is nothing like that."

"Really?"

His eyes were intense now, locked on hers. "Yeah. Really."

She had a retort on the tip of her tongue, but she couldn't say anything, not with the way he was studying her.

"Did you really kiss Silver?" he asked.

"He kissed me." It was nothing to blush over, but her cheeks disagreed.

"And when you jumped me on the Ferris wheel, wasn't that an attempt to shut me up?"

"You don't have a very high opinion of me, huh?" But her cheeks still felt hot, because his words were absolutely true.

That didn't mean she hadn't enjoyed their time on the Ferris wheel.

"See, there's the difference," said Hunter. "*I never hit Calla.* The only time I ever laid a hand on her was when she was trying to kill me."

"I think you've got this all wrong."

He swung his head around to look at her. "You would, wouldn't you? I'm surprised you're not throwing yourself at me right now, just to end the conversation."

She snorted. "Like you'd know what to do if I did."

He recoiled, and she regretted it immediately. But she'd needed to sting him back for everything he'd been saying, as if the only thing she could offer this mission was a little physical distraction wrapped up with a pretty smile.

That was how Silver treated her.

And how her mother had treated her.

Hunter's shoulders were tight now, and he was peeling the label off his water bottle. He very determinedly was *not* looking at her.

Mocking him should have felt good. It didn't. It felt like crap.

"I'm sorry you don't think you can trust me," she finally said.

He didn't say anything. He probably could recite the label by heart he was studying it so hard.

"I don't trust anyone," he finally said.

That surprised her. "You trust Silver."

Hunter looked her way. "Trust isn't the right word. He's the first person I've met in a long time who brought it back to black-and-white."

And Hunter respected that. She could hear it in his voice. He might not *like* Silver, but he respected him, he respected what he was doing here.

"So you're going to turn on the Merricks."

"I'm not turning on anyone. They're not on my side."

"I watched Gabriel pull you out of the line of fire, after Silver shot you."

Hunter didn't say anything. Then he looked over. "Whose side are you on?"

"I'm just making sure you're not going to stab us in the back, too."

"I'm not stabbing anyone in the back. They know what I am. God knows they question me about it enough. They're looking out for themselves, so I need to do the same."

"What does that mean, they're looking out for themselves?"

"It means exactly what it sounds like." But he'd hesitated for a moment.

Before she could question him about it, the school bells rang and the side door was flung open. Middle schoolers came pouring out.

She couldn't believe how *young* they looked. Had she ever been this young? She'd been tiny when her mother first took her to that farm in Virginia. She'd been about this age when her bloodied face had been pressed into filthy straw. What was the worst thing these kids had ever encountered? Hangnail? Forgotten homework?

Hunter was trained on the door, watching as each kid came out. The courtyard filled with students, the gray sky dulling the bright jackets and backpacks. Girls laughed and giggled, boys yelled to each other about sports and games, and they were suddenly surrounded.

"We can't just shoot him, you know," she said.

Hunter didn't say anything, but he gave her another *look*, as if to say, *I'm not an idiot.*

She didn't like all these *looks*. They were keeping her off balance.

She didn't like being off balance.

"You act like you're so experienced all of a sudden," she scoffed. "What's your plan, then?"

He turned, put a finger to his lips, and shushed her.

Shushed her!

She wanted to cut him to his knees, but Hunter shifted on the bench, straightened a little.

Kate knew exactly who he'd spotted, because as soon as the dark-haired kid laid eyes on Hunter, he *bolted*.

Then Hunter bolted after him.

Kate swore and took up the chase.

The boy had an advantage. He'd been coming out of the door, so he was able to run along the school wall, while she and Hunter had to fight through a swarm of students to follow him.

The kid was fast, too, lean and lanky with a stride that ate up the grass and gave him early distance. They made it to the soccer fields behind the school, a long stretch of turf that offered no cover. For a terrifying moment, Kate wondered if this boy had cursed himself, because Silver was surely waiting somewhere, watching this whole episode, and he'd already proven he wasn't afraid to shoot first and ask questions later.

Then she felt *power* and knew Hunter was pulling energy from the air, from the misting rain, from the ground under their feet. For an instant, jealousy snaked through her mind—she didn't have anywhere near enough control to borrow so much at once—but then Hunter was surging forward to tackle the kid and bring him to the ground.

They rolled in the grass, but Hunter had him pinned by the time she got to them.

The boy was fighting like hell.

Her senses were wide open, and his fear assaulted Kate, his panic, his rage that they'd caught him so easily. It hit her so fiercely that she almost grabbed Hunter's arm to drag him off the boy.

She knew better. She'd learned about *that* the hard way.

"Let me go," the kid cried. "Let me go. They'll know you did this. They know—"

"Stop!" said Hunter. "I just want to talk to you—"

The boy spit in his face.

Hunter swore and ducked his head to wipe his cheek on his shoulder. "Seriously?"

"You can't stop us. There are too many, and we know where to hide."

"Don't be stupid," said Hunter. "You know what happened to Calla."

"I know Calla is going to *destroy* you."

Hunter froze. His shock was almost palpable. "What did you just say?"

The boy spit at him again. "Calla is going to kill you all."

"Calla's alive?" Kate couldn't figure out the emotion in Hunter's voice, as if relief and dismay were fighting to come out on top.

She knew one thing for sure: Silver was going to *shit a brick.* And he was probably going to blame her.

The boy was shaking, but his eyes were full of fury. "Do it. Kill me. If I disappear, you'll just make it worse for everyone."

"What does that mean?" said Hunter.

"The carnival was *nothing.* You wait. We'll show the Guides what we can really do."

"How many of you are there?" said Kate.

"Where's Calla?" demanded Hunter.

"Like I'd tell you. What's the worst you can do—kill me?"

"Break his arm," she said to Hunter.

She meant it as a threat, as something to throw a little fear into the boy. But Hunter made a movement with his wrist, sharp and quick, and then there was a snap and the kid was screaming bloody murder.

Holy crap.

Kate couldn't breathe. She must have lost time from the shock of it all, because now the kid was quiet. He'd passed out.

She wouldn't mind doing the same thing. Hunter had—he'd—it was—

Then people were yelling, just *there*, coming across the soccer field.

A teacher was grabbing Hunter's arm and dragging him away from the boy on the ground.

And another one grabbed her, too.

CHAPTER 22

Kate glared at the edge of the guidance counselor's desk and wondered if she'd get in more trouble if she just pulled the knife out of her boot and stabbed Hunter right now. What a jerk.

He was glaring at Ms. Vickers, his expression somewhat exasperated. "I didn't even hurt him."

Ms. Vickers was glaring back at him. "He said he thought you were trying to break his arm."

Hunter snorted. "It was a joke. I popped the joint. He passed out." His tone clearly said, *wuss*.

Kate couldn't blame the kid. She'd almost passed out herself. *Wuss*.

The guidance counselor was still studying Hunter. "He said it was a joke, too."

"Good. So I can go?"

"Not so fast." The woman turned toward Kate. "Where do you come into play?"

Kate wasn't sure what to say—this hadn't exactly been part of the plan. She had a phone number in her file, but it was Silver's cell phone number, and what if they asked him to come in and pick her up?

Before she could say anything, Hunter said, "She didn't have anything to do with it. She didn't realize we were just goofing off. She was trying to stop me."

His voice was lazy, almost blasé. Kate shut her mouth and tried to look innocent.

Ms. Vickers glared at Hunter across the desk. "Hunter, we've had a discussion about physical altercations twice now. If this continues, I'm going to be forced to suspend you—"

"Great." He stood and turned for the door.

"We aren't finished here."

Hunter paused. "He said it was a joke, right? So I'm not in trouble?"

Ms. Vickers's mouth tightened into a line. "Don't think I won't be watching you more carefully regarding this young man, Hunter. I'm not entirely convinced of this *joke*."

"Good for you." Then he was through the door.

Ms. Vickers swung her head around to look at Kate. "Your transcript from St. Mary's is impeccable. Were you genuinely trying to help the young man?"

Kate was sure her forged transcript read like a bestseller. She tried to get it together. "I—yes—I saw Hunter run after—"

"Fine. Go." Ms. Vickers flicked a finger toward the door. She was already dialing a phone with the other hand.

Hunter had made it to the parking lot by the time Kate caught up to him. The sun had burned off the clouds, and she felt heat prick at her neck. She grabbed Hunter by the arm.

"Are you insane?" she hissed. "I thought you really broke that kid's arm. What was the *point* of all—"

"Now he's afraid of me. I need them to be afraid of me."

She wished Hunter would just stop and *talk* to her. "Why?"

"Because Calla always had the upper hand, and that meant people got hurt. I need time to figure out what else they're planning." He shoved a key into the door of his jeep. "To figure out where she might be hiding."

"Damn it, Hunter, if you're going to work with me, then you need to *work with me*. You need to tell me what you're doing. We don't work like—"

He turned and caught her arms. She tensed to retaliate—but then she realized she didn't need to fight him off.

Because he was *kissing* her.

She lost a moment to sheer surprise. His hands were strong and gentle at the same time, sliding under her jacket to trap her waist—not that there was any danger of her going anywhere right this second. She couldn't read him at all today. First, she'd thought he hated her, then he was brutalizing that kid, and now . . . now . . .

Her back hit the side of his jeep before she even realized he'd turned her. The heat of the sunlight became a living thing, tracing power down her skin to match the sparks from his lips against hers. He was pressed against her, almost full length, his hands creeping up her sides to send heat through her body in a way that had nothing to do with sunlight or power. Silver could have had a gun trained on her right that instant, and *she wouldn't have cared.*

Hunter tasted like cinnamon and smelled like the woods, pine and bark and something very male. His mouth was so sure, and when his tongue brushed hers, a sound escaped her lips. He did it again, letting his thumbs trace over her breasts so lightly that she found herself arching into him. Suddenly she wished they were somewhere else, somewhere private, with curtains and less clothing and—

Hunter broke the kiss. Her breathing was quick, loud and desperate in the space between them.

He closed his hands on her waist again, and turned her away from his car.

Her brain was spinning its wheels, trying to find traction.

Hunter leaned close. "Just to be clear: I'd know exactly what to do if you threw yourself at me."

Then he was in his car, starting the ignition, leaving her in the parking lot, nothing more than a melted puddle of hot, bothered, and seriously pissed off.

Hunter waited at the end of the cul-de-sac and watched the two-story house from the cover of a maple tree. Someone around here was having a Friday-night party; his car blended with a dozen others without any trouble. A basketball hoop hung over the garage door of the house he watched, and someone needed to attack the yard with a lawn mower. A tricycle with pink streamers sat in the driveway, next to about sixteen different chalk-drawn rainbows. It was too dark to see the rainbows now, of course, but Hunter had watched the sun trace shadows across the lawn until darkness crept over the neighborhood, and he knew the layout of the yard so well that he could make a diorama.

The house next door had been destroyed by a fire and was now surrounded by construction fencing.

The first house Calla had burned to the ground.

According to the file, Noah Dean, that kid with the dark hair, the one with the not-broken arm, lived in the house with the rainbowed driveway.

Hunter was waiting for everyone to go to bed so he could break in and continue the interrogation.

He was waiting here, instead of somewhere else, in case Noah decided to leave.

Hunter's cell phone buzzed, and he sighed.

So far, he'd ignored five text messages.

Two from Becca.

And three from Michael.

He hadn't read any of them.

He glanced at his phone now, just out of idle curiosity. Another from Michael.

Where are you?

Hunter rolled his eyes and shoved the phone back in his pocket. Like Michael gave a crap. He probably wanted to know when Hunter was going to get his stuff out of the house so they could move on to the next city. Hunter had only one reason to go back to the Merrick house tonight: Casper.

Lights in the Dean house were slowly ticking off. Only a matter of time now.

But then the front door opened, and Hunter straightened.

Moonlight reflected on dark hair, a trash bag crinkled, and Hunter recognized his mark. He was out of the car in a heartbeat, creeping along the sidewalk.

Be a shadow, Hunter. Can you be a shadow?

It was one of the first things he'd learned from his father. He'd been six.

Noah Dean never saw him coming. Hunter had him on the ground between the houses before the kid could draw enough breath to scream.

He was fighting now, though, and his flailing foot caught a trash can.

Hunter bit back a curse and braced an arm against Noah's neck, using enough pressure that the boy whimpered and froze.

"That's better," Hunter said.

Noah's breathing was shaking. "My parents will know something is up. I was just taking out the trash."

"You and your friends have been killing people. You think I give a crap about your parents?"

"They'll call the cops—"

"Then maybe I should work faster, huh?" Hunter added another few pounds of pressure, until the boy's eyes squeezed shut.

"What?" he cried. "What do you want?"

"I want to know where Calla is hiding. What you're planning."

"I don't—I can't—" The boy choked and gasped and squirmed under Hunter's grip.

Hunter held him there for another minute, until the fear in the air was potent.

"If you think I won't hurt you," said Hunter, "you're wrong."

"Fuck you." The boy squeaked out the words. "You're just proving our point."

"And what point is that?"

"The Guides are the ones who should be destroyed." Noah squirmed again, trying to ease some of the pressure on his throat. "Your talents don't make you better than the other Elementals. They make you *worse*. Just look what you're doing *right now*."

His rage practically hit Hunter in the face.

The guilt that followed was his own. But he couldn't let this kid go. This was so much bigger than just the two of them.

"What are you planning?" said Hunter. "What's Calla planning?"

Noah choked and squirmed. "Let's just say I wouldn't want to be around here on Monday."

A door creaked around the front of the house, then a female voice called out, almost wavering. "Noah? Are you okay?"

Hunter looked down at the boy he had pinned to the ground and knew he had about three seconds to figure out what to do.

"Tell me where Calla is or I'll shoot your mother."

He must have sounded pretty convincing, because the boy's breathing shook. "Leave her alone. She doesn't know about this. My mom's not an Elemental."

Hunter had told Kate that he needed these kids to be afraid of him.

Now that Noah was, it felt horrible.

"Tell me," Hunter hissed.

"Noah?" Mrs. Dean was coming closer. She sounded worried.

Hunter drew his weapon and cocked the hammer. He added weight to Noah's throat.

"Tunnels," gasped Noah.

"Tunnels? What tunnels?"

"The—the tunnels—"

The woman's flip-flops smacked the driveway. Hunter was either going to have to shoot this woman or let Noah go.

If he couldn't shoot Calla, he sure as hell couldn't shoot an unarmed non-Elemental who was looking for her son. He let the kid go and slipped into the shadows.

The boy hadn't made it to his feet by the time his mother came around the side of the house, but he was sitting up, rubbing his throat.

She was at his side in a heartbeat, touching his face, asking if he was all right, assuring him he could take a few days off from school if that mean older boy wouldn't leave him alone. Then a hug and a promise of chocolate chip cookies.

Hunter felt his fists clench. It took a while to figure out this emotion.

Jealousy.

He had to shove thoughts of his mother out of his head.

Thoughts of Kate were quick to replace them. Not the feel of her body in the parking lot, the way she'd yielded to his kiss and practically melted under his hands. Instead, he thought of that moment in the woods, when she'd breathed power on his neck to heal the knife wound there.

The way she'd put a hand on his wrist that morning when he'd told her what happened with his grandfather.

The way she'd acted like she cared.

He wished, for just an instant, that one moment of it could be real.

CHAPTER 23

Hunter got to the top of the driveway and sighed.

Michael was waiting on the front porch.

It was almost midnight, and the brothers' car was in the driveway already, so Michael had to be waiting for him.

Casper was on the porch next to him, but the dog bolted to Hunter's side when he climbed out of the jeep. Hunter rubbed his muzzle absently, wondering how it was possible his dog could take to this new home so readily while Hunter felt more like an outsider now than ever.

He still had no idea where Calla was hiding.

He had no idea why her friends were drawing Guides here.

He had no idea what else they might be planning.

And here he had a whole weekend where he'd be trapped in the Merrick house.

Michael had a mug beside him on the step, and he was leaning back against the bannister. He didn't move when Hunter approached. "Forget something?"

Hunter frowned. "No."

"Do you remember me promising your grandfather three hundred bucks? Remember saying you'd help with jobs until it was paid off?"

Hunter flushed and looked away. He *had* forgotten.

It was starting to feel like he owed everyone a piece of himself.

He steeled his shoulders and looked back at Michael. What did the debt matter when they might not be around long enough for him to work it off?

"Sorry," he said.

His voice was flat, and Michael studied him for a minute. Hunter watched him back, looking for any indication that Michael was going to get into it.

But Michael remained still. "You want to sit down for a minute?"

"No."

"You want to tell me where you've been all night?"

Hunter offered the only thing he figured Michael wouldn't question. "I went by the house. Tried to work things out with my mom."

"You know I've got three younger brothers, right?"

Hunter frowned. "What?"

"It means I've got a pretty finely tuned bullshit detector."

Hunter turned away, his fingers forming a fist around the keys in his pocket. Michael shifted on the step, and Hunter hoped that this was *it*, that Michael would come after him, that he could rage and fight and come out on top, just once.

But the only thing that came after him was Michael's voice. "Hunter."

He kept walking.

"Hunter, come back here. Right now."

The command in Michael's tone stopped him, more effectively than a fist or a grip on the arm would have. Something about it felt reassuring and immeasurably painful at the same time, because it reminded him so much of his father.

Emotion coiled around his chest again, clouding his mind with memories he didn't want right now, memories that had him turning to face Michael, to respect authority, before realizing that nothing was stopping him from just getting in the jeep and *leaving*.

But he'd already turned, and he met Michael's eyes. He didn't move back toward the porch, however.

Michael's voice was hard. "Quit running from confrontation and sit down."

"I'm not running from you."

"No, you wouldn't run if I tried to take a swing at you. But every time I try to have a conversation, you bolt. Sit down."

Was that true? Hunter considered.

It was.

He didn't like that.

He sat down on the stoop, leaning against the post opposite Michael. "Fine. Talk."

"If you're going to stay here, you can't just disappear after school. You understand me?"

Hunter kept his voice even. "I said I was sorry about the job."

"I don't give a shit about the job! I care about the fact that you're a sixteen-year-old kid who might have a target on his back."

Hunter stared back at him until Michael looked like he wanted to reconsider taking a swing.

Then Michael sighed, a long breath that he blew out through his teeth. "Jesus, kid, I wish I could get inside your head and figure you out."

Hunter wished the same thing because maybe then Michael could explain it to *him.*

Michael was still studying him. "What happened the other night? After we went to get your stuff—I thought you'd loosen up a bit. But it's like the opposite happened."

The other night. Michael's promise to repay his grandfather.

The carnival. So much *Kate* that he almost blushed now, remembering.

The fire. Calla. The gunshot.

For an instant he wanted to tell Michael everything, just so he wouldn't have to carry it all on his own. He just wanted to crumple on these wooden boards and let all this anxiety and worry and anger and rage pour down the steps.

But the memory of his father was still too fresh, and he could only imagine how his dad would react to him breaking down. Especially with someone he was supposed to *hate*.

Buck up, Hunter. It's not anyone else's responsibility to solve your problems.

Besides, how would that go? *"Well, Michael, I'm glad you're leaving town, because I'm about ready to screw you all over. Mind if I cry on your shoulder for a sec?"*

Yeah. Sure.

He'd already lost it once, and he wouldn't do it again.

"Nothing happened," he said.

"Well, then, there's a whole lot of that *nothing* rattling around inside your skull."

"Was there a point to this conversation?"

Michael's eyes flashed, and Hunter braced for more lecturing, but the oldest Merrick simply picked up his coffee. "Can you help with a job on Sunday?"

Hunter blinked, suddenly off balance. He wasn't sure if he was relieved the grilling was over—or disappointed.

Like it mattered. "Sure."

"Don't forget this time, all right? Nick and Chris said they'd help, too, but it's a big job, and I don't want to lose the income."

He didn't want to lose the income. Probably stocking up for the big move. But what could he say? Hunter forced words past his lips. "I won't forget."

Chris's and Gabriel's doors were closed when Hunter climbed the stairs, only darkness visible under the doors, but light flooded the hallway from Nick's room. Hunter half knocked before entering.

Nick was reading a paperback, something with an old-fashioned painting on the cover. Had to be a school assignment. He looked up when Hunter came in. "Hey."

Hunter dropped his backpack next to the air mattress, beside the two plastic crates. "Hey." He paused, trying to get a read on the feeling in the room. The air told him nothing, but Nick's voice had carried the slightest edge. "Reading for school?"

"Yeah." He held up the book.

"*Heart of Darkness?*" Hunter bent to unlace his shoes. "I think I'd use Wikipedia for that one."

"Sounds about right." Nick turned back to his book.

Hunter almost wished he'd left his shoes on. "What's with the attitude?"

"I had to help Mike dig an irrigation trench because you didn't show up."

"Sounds like your problem." Hunter felt his voice gain an edge.

Now Nick looked up. "You're going to pick a fight because *you* screwed up?"

Hunter hesitated. "I'm sorry. I got caught up in something. I didn't know you'd get stuck with it."

"I have three papers due Monday. I really could have used the time."

"I said I'm sorry, all right?"

"All right."

But Hunter didn't feel like he'd been forgiven.

At least Nick shut up after that, and Hunter left him to his super exciting novel in favor of getting ready for bed in the bathroom.

Gabriel was waiting for him when he came out. He blocked the doorway.

Hunter sighed. He probably should have driven to the Target parking lot. "Can't you all just confront me at the same time?"

"Meaning?"

"Nothing. What? I'm tired." And he was. As he said the words, exhaustion climbed on his back, grabbed the coils of tension holding him together, and gripped tight.

"I want to know what's going on with you."

Hunter snorted and pushed past him. "Join the club."

Gabriel grabbed him and shoved him into the wall. His voice was low. "I heard someone from the high school went after that Noah Dean kid when school let out."

Hunter shoved back, breaking his hold. "So what?"

Gabriel wouldn't let him pass. "What are you doing, Hunter?"

Hunter glared back at him, wondering if he should tell them what Noah had said. About Calla being alive.

Then Nick appeared in his bedroom doorway. "Hey. Leave him alone."

Hunter didn't even know which one of them he was talking to.

Gabriel got closer. "What are you doing?" he said, his voice low and dangerous. "It was you, wasn't it? You went after Noah. After agreeing that we should stay away from them."

"Back off."

"Are you fucking with us again?" Gabriel shoved him harder.

The corridor was narrow, with drywall on one side and a bannister on the other, and Hunter got leverage to shove him back. "I said, *back off.*"

But Gabriel would never back off, and really, Hunter didn't want to be left alone. This was someone who'd *fight.* When Gabriel swung at him, Hunter blocked, throwing real force into it, unleashing the anger he'd been holding on to all day. That coil of tension slipped free, and Hunter threw power into his strikes until the air was ice cold and biting the inside of his chest.

But the narrow hallway worked to Gabriel's advantage, too, and he knocked Hunter's feet out from under him. Gabriel might have been stronger, but Hunter was faster and knew how to work an enemy's weight to his advantage. Hunter got leverage to roll him, throwing extra force into it.

He just hadn't considered how close to the stairs they were.

Or that Gabriel's momentum in the roll would throw Hunter *ahead* of him.

They both went down. Every step hurt like a *bitch.* The slate flooring of the foyer hurt worse, first on his shoulder, then on his head.

Especially since Gabriel landed on top of him.

Then the weight was dragged away. A relief, since Hunter needed to figure out which way was up. By the time he had it straight, Michael was glaring down at him.

Then Gabriel kicked him in the stomach. Pain exploded through the base of his rib cage, and Hunter curled in on himself, forgetting how to breathe.

God, he hadn't been hit in the stomach in . . . forever. He couldn't decide if that hurt more than his head.

Both. Both hurt.

Voices were yelling overhead, but he couldn't make sense of them through the overwhelming need to breathe. It felt like he'd been choking for half an hour. There was a good chance he was drooling on the floor.

And Gabriel was leaning over him, and his voice was fierce. "Guess you picked enemy over friend, huh, jackass?"

Hunter saw Gabriel's leg move, and just when he thought he might have to draw his weapon to avoid getting kicked again, Michael's girlfriend appeared in front of Gabriel and put a hand on his chest. "Go on," she was saying. "Take a walk. Cool off."

Hannah got Hunter into the kitchen before he was fully aware that he was off the ground and walking down the hallway. None of the Merricks followed him, so he was alone with her, following directions like *sit there* and *don't move.*

The chair came up faster than he was ready for, and he wondered how hard he'd whacked his head. He touched a hand to his temple and was surprised when it came away wet.

Blood.

Hannah was in front of him again, a folded paper towel in her hands. "Press this against your forehead. I need to get my bag from the car."

"I'm bleeding," he said, like an idiot.

"I know." Her eyes weren't too concerned, though. "Can you hold that and remain upright?"

Either he answered and didn't remember, or she left without bothering to wait for one. Whatever, she was gone, and he was sitting there, dazed and trying to make both eyes focus.

Then she was back, pulling a chair close to him and pressing gauze to his forehead instead of the paper towel. She had purple latex gloves on now, the kind doctors wore. "Hold that again," she said, grabbing his wrist to put it in place.

"What are you doing here?" he asked. For a second, his addled brain wondered if she'd been on the porch with Michael during their argument, but he couldn't make that line up.

She was digging in her bag. "I just got off work. Mike sent me a text ten minutes ago saying everyone was going to bed and we could have a quiet cup of coffee." She laughed a little, but not like it was funny.

"Sorry," he said.

She had a tiny flashlight in her hands, and she shined a light in his eyes. "It's not every day I walk in the front door of a house to see two guys fall down the stairs on top of each other."

Put that way, it sounded insanely childish. He looked away.

She tapped his chin. "No, look at me. What were you fighting about?"

"It's not important."

The light flicked to his other eye. "It rarely is." She paused. "No concussion. You're lucky you didn't break your neck. I saw him kick you. How are your ribs?"

They felt like they'd be cussing him out tomorrow. He pushed her hand away. The haze was already starting to wear off, letting the ache settle in. "I'm fine."

"I want to put some butterflies on that cut on your forehead."

Now that his thoughts were clear, he didn't want this. Gabriel was probably out in the hallway snickering, planning his next attack. Hunter pulled the gauze away from his head. "I'm *fine*."

She grabbed his hand and put the gauze back. "Shut up and take some mothering for five minutes."

It shut him up, but not because she said so.

Because a memory hit him right between the eyes.

Not his father this time, but his mother. He couldn't remember how old he was, probably ten or eleven because everything in the memory looked *bigger*. He'd come home from school with his first split lip and a cut over his eye, and he'd been more scared of how his father would react than of all the bullies in the county.

His mother had dressed his wounds and given him a Popsicle

and promised that she'd make sure his father wouldn't be hard on him.

He couldn't remember how that had turned out.

But he could remember trusting her.

Hannah was removing the backing from a butterfly bandage. "Doing all right?"

Her fingers were gentle when she pressed the adhesive strip against his forehead, and it was harder than it should've been to shake off the memory. "Yeah. Long day."

"Tell me about it." She pulled another bandage out of the box.

He'd assumed she was older than Michael, what with the kid and the job and the don't-take-any-crap attitude, but now, sitting this close to her in the dim kitchen lighting, he realized she wasn't very old at all.

"How old are you?" he asked.

"Twenty-two."

"But you have a son," he said, before realizing that made him sound like a moron.

She must have thought the same thing because she gave him a look and said, "Oh, so they're not teaching sex ed anymore?"

He felt heat color his cheeks. "No. Sorry—I shouldn't—"

"It's fine. People ask all the time. I got pregnant my junior year of high school." She shrugged. "It happens a lot. I'm lucky."

"Lucky?"

She put a third bandage across his forehead. "Yeah. My parents are great. I can work and go to school part-time, and they help with James."

"You go to school? But you have a job."

"I'd like to be a full paramedic. I'm just an EMT now." Her hands went still on his forehead, and she met his eyes. "You and Gabriel weren't fighting over a girl, were you?"

Michael came through the doorway. "Jesus, I wish it were that easy."

Hunter glared at him around Hannah's hands. "I told you I'd end up punching him in the face."

"Yeah, thanks. You left out the part about destroying the foyer in the process." Michael stroked a hand down the back of Hannah's head, then squeezed her shoulder. His expression gentled when he looked down at her. "You still want some coffee?"

She turned her head to smile up at him. Her voice softened. "That'd be great. Thanks."

Hunter watched this exchange and instantly felt like a third wheel.

But he also felt envious, similar to the way he'd felt watching Noah Dean with his mother.

He'd seen his parents like this before, this gentle consideration for each other. Hunter had always believed it, until his father had destroyed everything, dropping a bomb about using women, and every personal relationship being a means to an end.

It meant that there'd never been anything honest about his father's relationship with his mother.

But worse, Hunter didn't know what it meant about his father's relationship with *him*.

Even now, watching this casual touch between Michael and Hannah, he wanted to examine it and see what each was after.

And of course the minute he tried to decipher it, he erased the magic. Just like Kate jumping into his lap in the Ferris wheel car, it was all a carefully maneuvered ploy. Michael's hand on Hannah's hair was a mechanical touch to coerce her to stay, just like her soft voice had been a way to get a cup of—

"Hey," said Michael. "Are you listening to me?"

Hunter pressed his hands to his eyes. God, he was going to make himself crazy. "No. Sorry."

"I said I told Gabriel to knock this crap off. He said you were hassling Nick . . ."

That didn't match what Gabriel had said in the hallway, but Hunter didn't have the mental energy to figure it out now. "I wasn't hassling Nick."

Michael put up a hand. "Nick said the same thing, and then they started arguing, and I just wanted to blow my brains out because I didn't realize I was living in a juvenile detention center."

"Nice," said Hannah.

Michael looked down at him. "Do you think you can make it through the night without breaking any bones?"

"Yeah," said Hunter.

Michael glanced at her. "Is he fine?"

She looked at him. "Are you fine?"

He shoved out of the chair. "Yeah. Thanks."

Gabriel was nowhere to be found. Nick was in bed again, reading the same book. Hunter felt like he'd already done this hours ago, though it had only been about twenty minutes.

He probably should have taken a Motrin before coming up here.

"Welcome back," said Nick.

The funny thing was, his voice had lost its earlier edge. Hunter glanced at him. "Thanks."

"When Chris was ten, we pushed him down the stairs. This was twice as entertaining."

Hunter couldn't tell if he was teasing or not, and it was hurting his head to try to figure it out. "Glad to amuse you."

"It sure as hell made up for having to work tonight."

Hunter still wasn't sure how to take that. He climbed under the quilt on the air mattress and wished sleep would just take him away for a short while. After a bit, Nick clicked off the light, and Hunter's thoughts started to fade.

Unfortunately, they kept solidifying on Kate, on the feel of her breath against his skin. He kept comparing that to the image of Michael's hand on Hannah's hair in the kitchen.

"You still like that Kate girl?" said Nick out of the blue.

Hunter almost choked on his own breath. "She's all right."

"She texted me to see if anything was going on this weekend, so I invited her over. Becca will be here, and Layne and her little brother—"

Hunter looked over at him in the darkness. "You—invited *Kate* over?"

"Yeah." Nick's voice was a little challenging. "That okay?"

Hunter told his heart to quit knocking around his rib cage.

Nick had asked her over.

She was probably coming for some sort of reconnaissance or something.

But Nick had asked her. And she'd accepted.

When had this happened? Why hadn't she mentioned it?

Kate hadn't texted Hunter all evening. He checked his phone just to be sure.

No messages from her.

He didn't care.

He didn't.

He *didn't.*

Oh, who the hell was he kidding?

A pillow hit him in the head, and Hunter jumped a frigging *mile.*

He was so keyed up it was probably a miracle he didn't draw his gun.

"Easy there, Zen Master Ninja," said Nick, a wry note in his voice. "I invited her over for *you.*"

Hunter didn't move for a moment. He studied Nick's silhouette in the near dark. "For me?"

"Yeah," said Nick. "Because seriously, dude, if anyone needs to cut loose with a chick for an hour, it's *you.*"

CHAPTER 24

Hunter was hiding in the basement.

Well, not really hiding. He was showing Simon how to break some basic holds. But if he was down here, he didn't have to see Kate, and he didn't have to listen to Gabriel's minute-by-minute jabs. Much more of that, and Hunter wouldn't give a crap about his promise to Michael—he'd finish what they'd started last night.

Everyone else was out on the back porch with pizza and soda, a scene straight out of a deodorant commercial or something.

He hadn't started out hiding, but he'd heard the doorbell, the resulting footsteps overhead, and finally Nick's yell that "everyone" was here.

Hunter said he'd be up in a minute and asked Simon if he wanted to keep working.

That was an hour ago.

If he was being honest with himself, he craved the simplicity of this. Teaching something to someone who needed the skills. No ulterior motive, no elements, no betrayal. Seeing Simon gain confidence as he figured out that he wasn't powerless at all.

The basement door opened with a rattle and a creak, and Hunter held up a hand for Simon. Light footsteps came skipping down the wooden steps.

Kate? Hunter considered ducking into the alcove beside the washing machine.

Dude. Really.

It was Becca anyway, brown hair long and shining. She glanced between them. "Are you guys going to come up?"

"In a bit," Hunter started—but Simon was nodding. He mimed needing a drink, then held out a fist for Hunter to bump.

Once he was gone, Hunter hoped Becca would follow Simon, but she remained in the basement, staring up at him.

"What's up?" he said.

"You tell me."

He shrugged. "Simon asked me to help him out, so—"

"Come on. Don't do that."

This was what he'd liked about her originally. Becca didn't pull any punches—but she was gentle about it. "They don't want me up there, Becca. Not really."

"Nick said he invited Kate for you, and now you're hiding in the basement."

Hunter dropped onto the old sofa that sat against the cinderblock back wall. The basement wasn't finished, but a bunch of old furniture sat down here, and he kicked his feet up on an ottoman with torn upholstery. "I also told Nick she's a player, and I'm not interested."

Becca smiled a little ruefully. "I believe that."

Hunter frowned. "What does that mean?"

"It means I've listened to her hit on every guy on the porch. I'm surprised she's not mounting Casper."

Oh, good. Just what he wanted to hear.

Becca flopped down next to him.

"You don't have to do this," he said. "I'm fine, really. I'm just not in the mood for a party."

"I know you have a lot on your mind," she said softly. "Do you want to talk about it?"

"No."

She shifted on the sofa until she was looking at him. "Can I ask you a personal question?"

He kept his eyes on the ceiling and tried not to imagine what was going on upstairs. "Shoot."

"Have you ever been with a girl when you weren't using her for something?"

She didn't mean it as an attack, but his shoulders tightened anyway. He turned his head to look at her. "I'm sorry if I hurt you, Becca. I had—it was a lot—"

"I'm not looking for an apology, Hunter." Her eyes were kinder than he deserved—and maybe a little mischievous. "I'm just saying that you were full of confidence with me, and now you're hiding in the basement."

"I'm not *hiding*." But her comment was a little too close to what Michael had said last night, about running away.

"You know why I think you're down here?" said Becca. "Because you *like* this girl. I think you stand to lose something you might care about, and that scares the crap out of you."

Hunter refused to look away, but he didn't have much of a retort.

He had to clear his throat to speak. "How do you know that?"

"Please. I saw the look on your face when I said Kate was hitting on everyone. Don't worry, I think Quinn is about to yank her fingernails out by the roots."

Another rattle and creak, and more footfalls were coming down the wooden steps.

Honestly, was *everyone* going to check on him?

Kate.

And Nick, followed by Quinn.

But seriously, it was a miracle he was able to look past Kate. She was wearing this tight sky-blue top with inch-thin straps and a ruffle at the bottom—and the bottom ended right at the base of her rib cage. Tight black jeans sat just below her belly button, exposing a solid few inches of very toned midsection.

He couldn't have said what Nick and Quinn were wearing if someone held a gun to his head.

Kate snapped her fingers in his face. "My eyes aren't that far south, slugger."

He refused to let her make him blush. "Then you shouldn't have worn that outfit."

"I heard you were giving ass-kicking lessons down here."

Her voice was challenging, and that was a lot easier to take than anything else. He still had no idea what she was doing here. Had she texted Nick last night just to screw with him?

"Sure am," he said evenly. "Interested in an ass-kicking?"

Quinn had moved close to Nick, and just now she was murmuring something that made him laugh.

"What was that?" said Hunter.

"I said you should just go find a bedroom and get it over with."

Kate smiled and stepped closer to Hunter. "I've got time if you know what to do with it."

He wasn't sure if that was an insult or a come-on. His eyes were right on level with the button on her jeans, and it was suddenly hard to think. "Told you, I'm busy with ass-kicking."

She stepped forward until she was straddling his knees, then sat.

He tried to force his brain to think about other things, but his brain was more than content to think about the curvaceous female in his lap.

She leaned forward to whisper in his ear. "Come on, baby, teach me something I don't know."

Her voice was full of suggestion and his body wasn't complaining.

And that's exactly why he needed to shut her down.

"Sure," he said, loading his voice with just as much suggestion—but adding a touch of mockery. "Want to learn how to drive a stick?"

Quinn snorted.

Kate was just staring at him, as if trying to sort through the innuendo. Some of her easy confidence stumbled a bit.

Good. It was nice to know she could falter.

While she was off balance, he put his hands on her waist and lifted her, setting her to the side and shoving a hand into his pocket for his keys. "Come on," he said. "Try not to tear up my clutch."

He was already on the steps, but she was just staring after him. "Your clutch—? What are—"

But he was already through the door, heading for his jeep, not bothering to wait to see whether she'd follow.

Kate had half a mind to let him just leave. It would serve him right, and she sure wasn't the type to go scampering after a boy just because he snapped his fingers.

But the whole reason she'd come here was to talk to Hunter privately, and here he was giving her the perfect way to do just that.

She caught up to him beside his jeep. His dog was already in the back, flopped out on the backseat.

"Get in," Hunter said.

He barely gave her time to obey, because he was throwing the car into gear before she even had the door closed.

Her heart was skipping to some rhythm she couldn't figure out, but she pulled a stick of gum out of her bag like she was bored, then rolled it into her mouth. "Are we running from something?"

"No, I just needed to get out of there."

"Trouble in paradise?"

"Tell me, Kate, do you have absolutely no self-confidence, or are you just completely full of yourself and you don't give a shit about anyone else?"

She almost choked on the gum.

Hunter came to a stop sign at the end of the road and turned to look at her. "What are you really doing here?"

"I was invited."

"Yeah, and how'd you drum up an invitation? Did you send Nick Merrick naked pictures of yourself?"

She wanted to punch him, but some part of his words were ringing true, and that stung like crazy. "What do you care if I did?"

He turned back to the road and hit the accelerator.

"Jealous much?" she said.

His jaw was so tight she could make out the lines where muscle met bone. "If we've decided the problem is Calla and a bunch of middle schoolers, you shouldn't be hanging out with the Merricks."

"They invited me!"

"You could've said no, you know." He cut a glance her way. "Or is that foreign territory for you?"

"I'm a little sick of you acting like I'm some big slut."

"Oh, *I'm* the one acting like you're a big slut?"

She didn't give a crap that he was driving, her fist was just flying in the general direction of his face.

He caught her wrist one-handed, and he wasn't gentle about it. In a flash she saw that kid lying on the field, passing out from the pain in his arm.

She was about to pass out from the pain in her own.

Kate got ahold of his keys with her other hand, and killed the engine while they were still moving.

Then she used the fistful of keys to stab him in the crotch.

She was lucky he didn't flip the car.

They ended up on the side of the road. Casper was standing up on the backseat, one paw on the center console. Hunter's hands had a death grip on the steering wheel, and his forehead was between them.

"I think I might have to kill you," he said. "Just as soon as I can stand up straight."

Her heart found that odd syncopated rhythm again. "You deserved it."

Hunter turned his head and looked at her over his fingers. "You're right. I'm sorry. I shouldn't have said those things to you."

His apology took her by surprise more effectively than if he'd run off the road again. She couldn't remember the last time someone had *apologized* to her.

And he'd done it so simply, like it was nothing.

But beyond the apology, she couldn't get past the realization that he hadn't struck back. She could still feel tenderness in her jaw from where Silver had knocked her around, and here Hunter took a solid hit with something like . . . grace.

She cleared her throat. "Are you just apologizing because you'll never father children?"

"Probably." She made like she was going to jab him again, and he winced, then almost smiled. "Nah. I mean it."

She looked back at the road. A few houses sat down the way, but right here nothing but trees lined the roadway, and the jeep had kicked up a bunch of red and yellow leaves. The air swirled through her hair, just this side of chilly, making her want to tuck her hands under her thighs to warm her fingers.

She still couldn't figure Hunter out, and she kept her hands where she could use them.

"What were you doing over there, really?" he said.

"I wanted to ask if you've seen Silver."

That took him by surprise, and he straightened, little by little. "No. Why? Did something happen?"

"He didn't come back to the apartment last night. He texted me to say he was working on something." She didn't add the rest of Silver's commentary, how he'd told her to be a good little girl and stay out of trouble.

She couldn't decide which she hated more: his condescension or his violence.

She examined her fingernails. "I thought maybe he was *working on something* with you."

"Jealous much?"

She glared at him and wished it were something as simple as *jealousy*. "This is my job. You're the one living with the enemy. I earned this position."

"How?"

His eyes were intense, and there was no mockery in that question.

The answer was simple enough, but she faltered, trapped by his eyes.

When she didn't say anything, Hunter volunteered an explanation for her. "Silver said you avenged your mother. That you killed the Water Elemental who killed her."

She made her voice hard, until the edge almost hurt as the words passed her lips. "I did. So you see, this is *my* job. I earned it."

He looked back at the steering wheel.

She studied him, the sandy blond hair that fell forward along his cheeks, the piercings in his eyebrow and ear, the foreign tattoos. She wanted to touch them, to find out if they were warm from his skin, to let power flow between them the way it had before.

What the hell was wrong with her? Weren't they fighting?

"I haven't talked to Silver," he said. "Really, I thought I was going to be stuck here all weekend, waiting for school on Monday so I could try to question some of the other middle schoolers."

She wondered just how he would have "questioned" them. "Gonna go break some more arms?"

"I didn't break his arm." He sounded bitter. There was a long pause. "I couldn't have."

No, he didn't sound bitter.

He sounded disgusted.

She studied him in the sunlight. He looked over. "I'm not trying to take your job, Kate." Then he flung himself back in the seat and ran his hands through his hair. "God knows I don't want it."

Her lips parted, and she was aware of breathing, but she couldn't have said a word if she'd wanted to.

He didn't *want* it?

His thumbs were running over the ridges in the steering wheel again. "I don't want anyone else to get hurt, so I'll do what I have to do. But that doesn't mean I like it."

"I don't like it, either," she whispered.

He glanced over. "Then what was all the bravado about *your job*?"

"What else am I supposed to do? All I've ever heard is that full Elementals are supposed to die before they can hurt anyone. And we're supposed to be the ones to do it, because our connection to the Fifth element is what allows us the greatest connection to the spirit, to follow through and do what's *right*."

"I know," he said, almost gently. "I drank the Kool-Aid, too."

They sat there breathing the air for the longest time, until she shivered and regretted the cropped top.

Hunter put a hand out. "Keys?"

Sheepishly, she handed them to him. He started the engine and kicked on the heat—which seemed counterintuitive with the top down. But warmth rushed out of the vents, and she put her hands against them. "Thanks."

"Sure." Then he shrugged out of his pullover and handed it to her.

She took it in surprise, glad he was looking at the road as he pulled out, instead of at her. The fleece fabric was warm from his body, and it smelled like him, some faint delicious musky scent like a hint of cologne or body wash. She hugged it to her chest and inhaled.

After a minute, she looked over. "Where are we going?"

"Anywhere you want." He threw a glance her way. "I can still teach you to drive a stick if you want."

His tone was easy. Amiable. Almost desperate for some kind of normal.

Had her admission let them find some kind of truce?

She reached out a hand and clicked on the radio. "Just drive."

CHAPTER 25

"This feels kinda like that scene in *Look Who's Talking*," said Kate.

Hunter smirked. "Put your hand on my stick?" he quoted.

"Exactly."

"That was a plane, and you're not Kirstie Alley."

"Yeah, well, you're no John Travolta."

"Thank god for that."

She had no idea where they were—but she liked that. They'd driven for well over an hour, maybe two, until the highway started to wind through mountains and there were signs for falling rock. The air was cooler here, sharp and biting against her cheeks. Hunter had found an abandoned parking lot—in front of an abandoned department store—and he was teaching her to drive his car.

She'd only stalled the vehicle once before figuring out the balance between the clutch and the accelerator.

"You're better at this than I thought you'd be," Hunter said.

"Is that an insult or a compliment?"

"Lady's choice."

And now she didn't know whether to smile or smack him. Everything felt tentative. Precarious, like a small tap in either direction would have them at each other's throats again. "We're only going ten miles per hour."

"Want to try it on the highway?"

"What? No!"

"There's no one here. Give it some gas, just don't hit a light pole. See if you can figure out when it's time to switch."

She accelerated, and the car sped up, but she could feel the engine struggling in this gear, like something confined trying to break free. She hit the clutch, felt the release, and moved the stick.

The car stalled and the engine died.

Kate swore.

"Put it back in first," he said. "You tried to jump to third. Second is straight back."

"Intuitive," she said, looking at the little ball on the top of the stick.

"Well, for most people . . ."

Now she did smack him.

When she went to move the stick, his hand came over hers and stopped the motion. "Clutch first."

She did, then moved into first gear.

She didn't want to pull her hand out from under his to start the engine, but she had to.

When she put her hand on the stick shift again, however, his hand went back over hers.

"Accelerate," he said. She did, and when the engine was struggling again, he said, "Now try."

This time he helped her pull it straight back into second gear, and then, with more encouragement, she went faster and shifted into third. Wind was lifting her hair, and her heart was flying.

They came to the end of the parking lot, so she hit the brakes.

The car stalled again.

She swore again.

Hunter was laughing. "It takes practice."

Kate looked at him. "Who taught you? Your dad?"

That killed his smile. "No, actually. My uncle. The jeep used to be his. He said if I learned on a stick shift, I'd be able to drive anything."

She was quiet for a while. "Did he and your dad really die in a rock slide?"

"Yeah." He paused. "About three miles north of here. Dad had military clearance, so they kept it out of the papers. Even the funeral was pretty private."

She wondered if he'd pulled off for the driving lesson just so he wouldn't have to drive through there again. "And you still don't think the Merricks had anything to do with it?"

He looked at her. "I know they didn't. Calla all but admitted to being behind it."

Kate pulled the emergency brake and shifted on the seat to look at him. "She did? And you didn't—"

He avoided her eyes and looked back at the dashboard again. "I should have."

Her heart was thundering in her chest now. "Why didn't you?"

"I couldn't."

"Couldn't?"

"I had an opportunity—and I couldn't pull the trigger."

Kate swallowed.

Hunter looked at her. That streak of white hair fell across his eyes, catching the sunlight. "So I guess you've got one on me," he said. "How did you do it?"

She blinked.

"Your mom," he said. "When you went after the Water Elemental."

Oh. Right.

She'd given this speech before, when she'd been questioned. She'd spent an hour memorizing exactly how to answer.

"Two bullets," she said. "He'd run to the end of a pier— going for the water, I'm sure. I got him first. A shot to the hip brought him down. One to the head took him out."

Hunter didn't say anything, and her words hung in the air, sharp and dark and painful.

Then he finally exhaled, and she realized she'd been holding her breath, too.

"What did you do with the body?" he asked.

"Pushed it into the water."

"Callous."

Like before, she didn't know if that was an insult or a compliment. "It was almost morning. I needed to do something quickly."

"And how did you feel?"

She jerked her head around. "What?"

"How. Did. You. Feel?" His voice was quiet, yet deliberate.

She bit the inside of her cheek. "I don't really want to talk about this."

Hunter reached out and pushed a piece of hair back from her face, his fingers gentle against her skin as he tucked it behind her ear. "Last night I was wondering what it would be like to trust you."

Her eyes flicked up and caught his. "I've wondered the same thing." She had to take a breath. "About you."

His expression was tight, as if he were thinking, or deliberating.

Finally, he said, "I don't want any harm to come to the Merricks."

"I know," she whispered.

"I know Silver won't fix the mess with Calla and the middle schoolers and just leave town."

He was right. She couldn't even deny it.

She wet her lips. "Then why are you helping us?"

"Because I feel like I have to." He met her eyes. "You know."

He was talking about his dad. Her mom.

Yeah, she knew.

He took a deep breath and ran a hand through his hair. "They're leaving in a week. They don't know I know."

She sat up straight. "They're *leaving*?" She wondered if Silver had any idea. He couldn't possibly. He'd be bombing their house *right now*.

"I don't know where they're going," Hunter added.

"Lucky for them." This was—this was—she wasn't sure what. Good? Bad? She couldn't even nail down her emotions. Hell, she could barely catch her breath.

"I'm trusting you with this," said Hunter. A note of desperation had crept into his voice.

Like maybe he'd be on the phone to Michael Merrick in two seconds if she gave any indication of passing this information along.

Silver would kill her if he found out she knew.

But she'd seen Gabriel step into the line of fire to pull Hunter to safety. She'd seen Nick's kindness firsthand. She'd been with Silver when they watched Michael drag Hunter out of a mood and take him on a job. She'd seen them operate as a family, both with their Elemental abilities and without.

What had Silver ever offered? What had her mother?

She felt like she was running a race, right here in the driver's seat of his jeep.

"If you tell Silver," said Hunter, "it's really no different from you pulling the trigger yourself."

"No kidding," she snapped. God, she couldn't *think*.

"I don't think you want to harm them, either."

"Yeah? How do you know *that*?"

He looked at her, hard. "Because I don't think you really killed that guy on the end of some pier."

She threw her hands up. "Where do you think I did it, then?" she cried, incredulous.

"I don't think you did it at all!"

He might as well have shoved her out of the car and slammed her head against the pavement. She was sitting in an open top jeep and she couldn't breathe.

Kate flung the door open and swung her legs out. She had to walk.

She should be texting Silver about the Merricks right now. *Right now.* This was the kind of thing that would get her back on his good side.

Hunter caught her arm and swung her around.

Kate stared up at him. She should disable him somehow, steal his jeep and his phone and take off down the highway—

Then again, she'd probably only make it about half a mile.

Whatever, she'd have no trouble flagging down a ride. She'd

be back in Annapolis, Hunter would be stranded here, and the Merricks wouldn't be much more than a memory and a closed file.

Hunter caught her other arm, and his hands were gentle. She almost wished she'd given him back the pullover so she could feel his palms against bare skin.

Then he didn't say anything.

She had a thousand insults to fling at him, words to deflect his attention.

Instead, she said, "How? How did you know?"

"Because you're not callous," he said carefully.

"You're wrong. I am."

"No. You're not." He paused. "You called my name, the night Silver shot me."

She looked away.

"You did," said Hunter. "I know you did."

"He misunderstood what you were doing with Calla."

Hunter brushed it off with a wave of his hand. "You were upset when you thought I broke Noah Dean's arm."

"Because I thought it was a stupid move on school property."

Hunter smiled. "You didn't kill me the morning after the carnival."

"I was busy. Figured I had time."

Now he laughed, but he quickly sobered. His hands found her cheeks, blocking the wind, his palms warm against her face. He leaned down until his forehead was touching hers and they breathed the same air.

It felt so good to be held this way, just the two of them in a deserted parking lot on the side of a mountain, nothing around but earth and sky.

Far, far away from Elementals and death and danger and betrayal.

"I'd like to kiss you," said Hunter softly. "But I'd really like to try it without any lies between us."

For some reason, that made her eyes burn, and she worried that tears had found their way to her eyes.

His thumb stroked along her cheek, terrible confirmation.

"I don't remember how to do that," she whispered.

A smile found his lips. "How to kiss?"

She squished her eyes shut and shook her head quickly. "How to be true."

He kissed her eyelids, first the left, then the right. "Yes you do, Kate."

She let a breath ease out and was surprised to find that it shook. She'd never spoken these words to anyone, and saying them now almost burned because the weight of her failure was behind them. "I didn't kill the man who killed my mother."

She was ready for him to dig, to ask why, to turn this into an interrogation. But he hesitated, his breath warm on her temple. "Do you want to talk about it?"

"No. God, no."

Then the cord of tension snapped, and his mouth found hers.

Hunter was fierce and gentle, but there was nothing aggressive about this kiss, nothing angry. This felt like a first kiss—not just with him, but . . . but *ever*. No pretense, no games, just a boy kissing a girl because of wildfire attraction.

And here, in the middle of nowhere, there was no need to shield their abilities. His power surged and whispered against her skin. The air chilled and warmed her simultaneously, but she felt heat in his touch. The earth rejoiced that they were here, full of energy and talent and letting it ride out in streamers.

His tongue brushed her lips, teasing. Her lips parted, allowing him in, drawing at his mouth until she pulled a gasp from his throat and his hands snaked under the sweatshirt.

They'd done this before, but now was different. Somehow new and familiar at the same time. Her insides were melting away, and it was a good thing his hands were there to hold her up because she was falling against him. A hand cupped her breast, and she moaned into his mouth, arching her back when his thumb found the most sensitive bits.

Suddenly she wasn't chilly at all.

In fact, she could do with a lot less clothing.

Her hands explored under the hem of his T-shirt, stroking along the planes of his stomach, tracing the muscles of his chest. One of his hands stroked down her back and found its way beneath the waistband of her jeans, just an inch, maybe two, but just feeling his fingers on more sensitive skin had her panting into his mouth.

He dragged the sweatshirt over her head before she even knew what he was doing. Then his mouth was on her neck, his hands grabbing her thighs and lifting her, carrying her back to the car in such a way that she wanted him to quit with the gentle stuff and push her up against the side of the car, just to feel the sheer power of it.

He did exactly that. It felt even better than she expected. The radio was still on, some announcer's voice filling the afternoon air with football scores or weather reports or even the price of tea in China.

She so didn't care, because Hunter's shirt was gone and he was kissing inside the neckline of her top. He was pressed so tightly against her that she could feel everything, and it was amazing and terrifying and sensual and breathless and she couldn't think.

Her hands groped for the button to his jeans. Hunter made a low sound, an encouraging sound.

But then he broke the kiss and caught her wrist. "Wait," he said, his voice rough.

And worried. He reached past her and turned up the radio. "What did he just say?"

Kate could barely comprehend English, and she struggled to wrap her brain around this sudden shift. "What is it? What—"

"Shh." He put a finger over her lips, his attention on the radio.

Then she picked up what the announcer was saying.

"*. . . Mrs. Dean recently lost her niece Calla Dean in a school carnival fire a few days ago. She states that prior to his disappearance, Noah was a good student who had never given any* *indication of running away. He'd indicated problems with a student at the high school, and we'll update this story as further information is available. For now, local police are treating the area as a crime scene. Anyone with information should call . . ."*

Disappearance.

Noah Dean was missing.

CHAPTER 26

Hunter headed back toward Annapolis, sticking to the speed limit.

He couldn't afford attention.

A big part of his brain was crying for him to make a run for it. It wasn't like he'd gone after Noah Dean in secret. Vickers knew. Other students knew. What had that news report said? A crime scene? The cops could be *looking* for him.

And really, he shouldn't give a crap about one kid who'd caused more than his share of misery.

Hunter just couldn't shake the feeling he was somehow *responsible*.

He'd tried to find another report, but now the DJ didn't want to do much more than churn out the same crap pop songs he played every hour.

Kate was searching on her phone.

Or she was trying to.

"We're going to have to wait until we get out of the mountains," she said. "The Internet is taking forever to load."

"Should you text Silver?"

She didn't say anything, and Hunter glanced over to see her studying the face of her phone, her mouth squinched up like she was deep in thought.

"Hey," he said. "Can you text Silver and ask him what to do?"

"No."

"No?"

She looked over at him. "Have you considered that Silver might be the reason Noah is missing?"

Those coils of tension wound their way around Hunter's chest again. He felt like such an idiot—hadn't he agreed to help them yesterday? And now one kid was missing, and he felt ready to go to pieces.

Just like always, he didn't know who he was supposed to rescue and who he was supposed to destroy.

Your talents don't make you better than the other Elementals. They make you worse. Just look what you're doing right now.

He bit the inside of his lip until he tasted blood.

Then he fished his phone out of his pocket and tossed it to Kate. "Text Michael Merrick and ask if he's heard about Noah Dean."

"You want me to text *Michael Merrick* and ask for help?" Her voice was slightly incredulous.

"Not ask for—look, Kate, just do it, okay?" He ran a hand through his hair and wondered if it would be easier to drive his car straight off a cliff.

She slid her fingers across the face of the phone. "Okay. I asked if he's heard the news."

"Let's wait and see what he says."

They waited.

Ten minutes.

Fifteen.

"Text Gabriel," said Hunter.

She did.

Hunter only waited seven minutes this time.

"Try Becca."

Nothing.

Nothing.

What did that mean? Had something happened? Were they missing, too?

Or were they just partying on the back deck and no one was looking at their phone?

Either was possible. "Find Bill Chandler's name. Ask him if he's talked to Becca."

She scrolled. Texted.

"Are you sure this is the right number?" she asked after a moment.

"Yeah, I just talked to him last week."

"The text bounced back and said that line belonged to an account that has not yet been activated."

"*What?*"

"Here, I'll text Silver and ask what his status is." She paused, typing. The response must have come back immediately, because he saw her scowl out of the corner of his eye.

"What?" he said.

"I said, 'Checking in. What's your status?' He said, 'Interesting question, Kathryn. What's *your* status?'"

Now Hunter understood the scowl. "He's kind of a dick."

"Tell me about it." She was typing furiously at her phone. The wind was making a mess of her hair. She looked incredible.

Then she said. "I'm telling him I'm with you."

"Is that a good idea?"

"Honestly, I'm out of ideas. I don't know what this means, and we're in the middle of nowhere."

He didn't have anything to say to that. He'd driven her out here, and now something was happening and they were too far away to do anything about it.

He kept hearing Michael's lecture from last night, about running from confrontation.

Now it was biting him in the ass.

"Huh," said Kate.

She was killing him. "*What?*" said Hunter.

"Silver says, 'My question was rhetorical.'"

"So he knew you were with me." This wasn't getting them anywhere.

He drove, drumming his fingers on the steering wheel, thinking. He didn't have enough information. Could Noah have run away? What was the crime scene?

Did Silver have something to do with the boy's disappearance?

Then Hunter had a startling thought. Did the Merricks? Hunter's files were at the house. They could have gone after Noah Dean themselves.

Without telling Hunter?

Gabriel had kicked Hunter in the stomach last night, had laid into him with true fury.

No. They wouldn't have told him.

"Finally got Internet," said Kate. "Local news says the mom went to the grocery store, leaving Noah at home." She whistled low, through her teeth. "When she got back, he was gone and there was a pentagram on the door."

"Silver?" said Hunter, his voice grim.

"Maybe," said Kate. "He's not responding to my texts now."

Hunter froze. "Did you tell him about what happened yesterday?"

"Yes."

"So he knows Calla is still alive?"

"He said he's had no indication that her death was not final, and the word of one child is not enough to distract him from his mission."

Hunter tried to remember that moment during the carnival. He'd seen Calla fall, had seen the blood pour from her shoulder. Fire had caught at her clothes.

And then he'd run.

Focus. Keep thinking.

There hadn't been any more fires. But Noah had been so assured that Calla was still alive—but his mom, Calla's aunt, had seemed stressed when Hunter saw her. Even the news report talked about Calla's death in the carnival fire. If Calla was alive, she was hiding, or she was gone.

No, she wouldn't have left town. Not with her army of kids. But where would she be hiding? She was a popular student, captain of the girls' volleyball team. She obviously couldn't go to school, and she was way too eye-catching to move around town without being noticed.

"Where should we go?" said Kate.

Hunter blew out a long breath and ran a hand back through his hair. "Who's more likely to help us?" he said. "The Merricks or Silver?"

"I've got a better question," said Kate. "Who's less likely to *kill* us?"

The Merrick house it was.

Hunter knew something was wrong the instant he pulled into the driveway.

No SUV. No work truck. No vehicles at all.

He pulled the parking brake but didn't cut the engine.

"What's wrong?" said Kate.

"No cars."

They'd pulled off the highway to put the top back on the jeep, and just now, the interior of the car was ice cold.

He didn't think it was him this time.

The longer they waited here, the more he was going to feel like a sitting duck. His father's lessons were rattling around in his head, telling him he should have parked somewhere else and approached the house under cover.

Kate's breath was fogging on the window.

Hunter yanked the keys out of the ignition and unlocked the glove box.

Kate's eyes went wide when she saw the gun. "You've been armed this whole time?"

He gave her a look. "Tell me you're not."

"I don't have a gun."

"What do you have?"

"Maybe you can find out later." Then she turned and slid out of the jeep.

God, she was *killing* him.

Nothing was amiss in the yard, but he felt too exposed on the walk to the front door. Especially when they found it unlocked.

No, not just unlocked. Slightly *ajar.*

Hunter paused there on the front porch and opened his senses, asking the elements for information. The power to the house had been turned off: either someone had thrown the master breaker in the basement, or the power had been cut. He didn't sense any electricity. Just quiet air that carried no malice.

He had the gun in his hand anyway.

His back was to the house, so he could see as much of the yard as possible. Nothing moved.

But he couldn't shake this feeling of *wrongness*, and it seemed foolish to walk straight into a house left this way.

Casper was alert and silent by his side, waiting for a command.

"Go ahead," said Kate. Her voice was a bare breath of sound. "I'll cover you."

Well. Maybe it wasn't so bad having an ally.

He slipped through the door, all the while hearing his father's voice in his head.

Shadow shadow shadow shadow.

He wondered what his father would think of his activities in this exact moment.

The main level was unoccupied. Kate was a shadow herself, moving so silently that he could almost forget she was there— hell, Casper's nails made more sound on the tiled entryway. He'd never worked with someone like this, someone who *knew* how to move, who could fall back on training and use it to her advantage.

The kitchen was clean, no food left on the counters.

But no sign of struggle or distress, either.

Then again, the cars were gone and the power dead. The Merricks weren't here, but he had no idea whether they'd left voluntarily.

Kate pointed to the refrigerator.

Hunter eased it open.

Empty. Completely empty.

The breath left his chest in a *whoosh*.

Empty. If they'd been chased from the house, or kidnapped, or *whatever*, they wouldn't have emptied the refrigerator.

Hunter was completely unprepared for the crushing weight of disappointment and loss. It socked him in the gut and made it hard to breathe. He'd known they were planning on leaving—had actually counted on it—but he hadn't expected them truly just to ditch him here without a word.

He dropped into one of the kitchen chairs and rubbed his hands over his face.

"There's no one here," he said. "They *left*."

God, he sounded *pathetic*.

Kate dropped into the chair beside him. She didn't say anything.

She was probably thinking he was such an idiot for trusting them. Or maybe he was the one thinking that.

He wondered if they'd been planning this all along. Throw a party, distract him, get him to hook up with Kate—

Wait. It had been his idea to leave.

For god's sake, though, he'd stood outside and listened to Michael's bullshit last night, and they'd been planning to walk out on him.

He'd felt *guilty* about the fight with Gabriel. About letting Nick down.

He wanted to put his fist through this table. Casper thrust his nose into Hunter's hand, and he patted the dog absently.

"I'm sorry," Kate said quietly.

He lifted his eyes to find hers. "I knew it was coming."

She inhaled like she was going to say something—but must have thought better of it.

Instead, she reached out and put her hand over his.

And that meant more than any other way she'd touched him.

He turned his hand and caught her fingers, then squeezed.

Her phone beeped, and she jumped.

"Silver?" he said.

She glanced at the screen and shoved it back in her pocket. "No. Battery died. All that Internet searching."

Hunter straightened. "If they're gone, they're safe. Let's grab my files and get out of here."

He shoved the gun into his waistband, pulling his shirt loose to hang over it so it wouldn't be seen.

Pretty stupid, he realized later, since they walked back out the front door without any of the caution they'd used going in. He carried one box, and Kate carried the other. Their hands were occupied. Casper jogged out the door ahead of them.

Then a gun went off, the sound cracking from somewhere between the trees.

And before Hunter could even get it together to draw his own weapon, Kate went down.

CHAPTER 27

Hunter got Kate back through the door. He hollered for Casper.

His dog was barking somewhere in the yard. Hunter yelled for him again.

Another shot hit the siding on the front of the house. Hunter flinched and dragged Kate farther along the slate of the entrance hallway. They got to the rear of the foyer, to where he could see the front door, but they were partially obscured by the stairwell.

"I'm okay," she said. "I'm okay."

She was not okay. Blood was everywhere, a long streak on the floor, a spreading stain on her jeans, a lengthy smear along his forearm.

"Jesus," he whispered.

He pulled his sweatshirt off and balled it up. "Where are you hit?"

"Hip," she said, and he heard the strain in her voice. "I think it's just a flesh wound."

He couldn't tell—too much blood. He shoved the sweatshirt where most of it was. He would totally give *anything* for Hannah to walk through the door right now.

Another gunshot. Hunter jumped. Somewhere outside, Casper yelped, then whined.

Hunter struggled to position Kate more upright, to get her heart above the wound. "Casper!" he shouted. *"Hierr!"*

Then he held his breath. Kate held hers.

He heard nothing.

"Damn it!" he cried. "Casper! *Hierr!*"

Nothing.

"Casper!" His voice was breaking.

"Cops," said Kate. It sounded like she was speaking through clenched teeth. "Call the cops."

He could barely get the phone out of his pocket. His fingers were sticky with her blood and his brain wouldn't stop thinking of Casper bleeding just like this, somewhere in the yard.

The touch screen didn't want to work and his breath wouldn't stop hitching.

"Casper!" he yelled again, and he heard the desperation in his own voice. He was ready to punch a hole in the floor.

Finally, the phone gave in to his panicked swipes. He dialed 911.

The line rang forever.

Someone was out there shooting. Calla? Silver? He had no idea.

The car was at least thirty feet from the front door, and Kate couldn't walk. It wasn't like this person was firing a musket. Hunter couldn't exactly wait around for a reload so he could carry her to the jeep and back down the driveway.

And he couldn't leave Casper.

Casper.

Casper. Casper. Casper.

The dog had been licking his hands a minute ago, and now he was—

Stop.

He had to stop. He had to focus. Or none of them would make it out of this alive.

Finally an operator picked up. "Nine-one-one emergency, do you need police, fire, or ambulance?"

All the words fell out of Hunter's mouth in a rush. He sounded about twelve years old.

It wasn't until he started speaking that he realized he was crying.

"Someone's shooting at us. I need the police. I need—"

The front door started to move.

Hunter dropped the phone and had the gun in his hand.

He drew back the hammer. "Freeze or I'll shoot."

In that instant, he meant it. If that door moved half an inch, he was pulling the trigger.

The door didn't move. Nothing moved. Hunter was acutely aware of his breath echoing in the air around him, of Kate's blood, a warmth that was slowly seeping into his own jeans.

The shooter's gun went off, splintering the door and sending a round into the floor at Hunter's feet.

He swore and jerked Kate back, trying to pull her toward the kitchen and keep his gun pointed at the same time. She cried out.

Then she said, "The address. Say the address."

His phone was on the floor five feet away, but the display was lit up. The call was still live.

"Chautauga," he called. He didn't know the street number. "Blue house at the end of Chautauga Court. Just off Ritchie—"

Another shot came through the door.

It killed his phone.

Hunter fired back. It hit the upper left quadrant of the door and took out a good chunk of wood.

But he didn't hear anything. Kate was shaking against him.

Hell, he was probably shaking against her. His pulse was a thunderous rush in his ears, and his mouth had gone completely dry.

He kept the gun pointed, waiting for movement. Sound. Anything.

There.

He pulled the trigger.

The gun clicked empty.

Impossible. He'd only fired once. He pulled the trigger again. The hammer slammed into place, making a loud metallic *click*.

No spark. No kick in his hand.

No bullet flying out to stop their opponent.

The door swung wide, and Hunter gathered Kate, intending to bolt into the kitchen.

If he could even make it that far.

She felt limp in his arms, and he wondered how much blood she'd lost. It wasn't pooling on the ground, but his sweatshirt looked like it had soaked up quite a bit.

"Freeze," said a voice thick with an accent. "Or not. I can shoot you while you move just as easily."

Hunter kept his gun up, because it looked better than nothing. "I can shoot you back."

Silver raised an eyebrow. "Aren't you having some difficulty with the ignition? Funny when the spark just won't happen, isn't it?"

Hunter stared at him and didn't want to lower the weapon— was Silver saying he'd done something to prevent the gun from firing? That would take an insane amount of control, especially from this distance.

"Go to hell," rasped Kate.

"I gave you a chance, Hunter," said Silver. "One chance. And while you were allowing known Elementals to escape, I was doing a bit of research about you. Turns out your father wasn't quite the man I thought he was."

"I don't know what that means," Hunter said. He didn't care, either, but talking meant no one was dying.

"I think you know what he did. You're living proof."

"Shoot him again," Kate breathed. "Just . . . try."

Hunter cocked the hammer, but now that Silver was talking, he didn't really want him to stop.

Silver didn't look concerned. "You both know what I came here to do. You know and you chose the wrong side. You both know the penalty."

Then he drew back the hammer of his gun.

"Wait!" cried Hunter.

"No." Silver's finger pulled back on the trigger. But the shot went way off target.

Because Casper was just there, tackling Silver in a snarling hundred-pound mass of muscle and fur and teeth. Silver went down. The dog's jaws locked around his forearm, and the gun went skittering across the foyer floor.

The man was swearing, trying to get free, but Casper was a trained police dog.

Taking down a man with a gun was something he *knew how to do.*

Hunter felt giddy with relief.

"Run," whispered Kate. Her fingers were clutching Hunter's. Her lips were pale.

Then Hunter had her in his arms, and they were bolting past Silver and through the door. Sirens were screaming somewhere down the street.

He wondered if Casper could hold Silver off long enough to wait for the police—because Kate sure needed an ambulance.

But then Casper yelped, and Silver was stretching for his firearm.

Hunter all but flung Kate into the passenger seat, practically throwing himself in after her. "Casper!" he called. *"Hierr!"*

Then he had the ignition started and the car in gear.

No way he could go down the driveway; the street would be packed with cops in a second.

Thank god he had a jeep. He slammed his foot into the accelerator and the car shot forward into the backyard.

"Casper!" he called again.

The dog came galloping around the side of the house, tearing through the yard. Hunter hit the brakes and the dog leapt through the window, barely avoiding Kate.

Silver came flying around the corner next.

Hunter floored it. A gun fired. The jeep took a hit but kept moving.

Almost as an afterthought, Hunter ducked, grabbing Kate's shoulder and shoving her down. The car barreled over rocks and underbrush, and he aimed for the widest opening between the trees.

The sirens were practically on top of them; they had to be

coming up the driveway. Hunter hit the accelerator again, juggling the clutch as best he could as the car rocked and slipped over uneven ground.

He knew these woods, this path. He'd just run this trail with Gabriel a few days ago. As long as he could keep the jeep moving forward, he'd come out to the main road without anyone being able to put him at the Merrick house.

"How you doing?" he said to Kate.

"Oh, I'm swell," she murmured.

"Hospital?" he asked.

"You're crazy. He'd find us and shoot us in the waiting room."

Her words were slow and almost slurring. Hunter ran a hand through his hair. He didn't know where to go. He didn't know who would help them. Everyone he knew was a target—or had left town.

Then he remembered one person who was "off the grid."

Someone who'd refused to help.

Hunter didn't have a phone, so he couldn't call, but he knew exactly who to go to.

Becca's father.

CHAPTER 28

Bill Chandler lived in a little gray rental on the water. Hunter had only been here once, the day Bill had asked him to watch Gabriel, but he remembered the way. The clapboard siding needed a new paint job, and the gutters were coming loose along the left side of the roof, but it was secluded, private, and no one knew he was here.

Exactly what Hunter needed.

A green pickup truck sat out front, the DEPARTMENT OF NATURAL RESOURCES logo visible on the side.

Bill was home.

He opened the door when Hunter knocked. "Becca's not here," he said.

"Good. I need your help."

Bill's gaze sharpened, probably taking in the blood on Hunter's clothes. "I told you not to bring your mess to me." He started to close the door.

Hunter put a hand against the wood. "Help me or I'll tell them all where to find you." He paused, very aware that Kate could be bleeding to death in the front seat *right now*. "I'll tell them about Becca."

"Don't you threaten me, kid."

"Damn it!" snapped Hunter. He was ready to pull his gun and shoot this guy. Or himself. "Help me. Please. Just help me."

If Bill said no, he didn't know what he'd do.

He was officially in over his head.

"Fine," said Bill. He gave Hunter a once-over. "You're hurt?"

"Not me. Kate. Come on."

"I'll be right there."

Then Bill shut the door in his face.

Swearing, Hunter went back to the car. Her eyes were closed, but she made a small sound when he pulled her into his arms. Her breathing was shallow.

She was so pale.

Hunter started for the front door, but Bill reappeared and gestured for him to walk around to the back of the house. They moved past the porch and down the grassy slope to where the terrain turned to sand.

"Put her in the sand," Bill said, pointing. "Get her close to the water. I'll get some logs."

Hunter sat in the sand with her, holding her against him. He was beginning to think this was stupid, that he should have taken her to the ER anyway, but then the wind kicked up to swirl around them and the tide crawled up the shore to lick at Kate's feet. Heat from the sun poured down, warming his skin and filling the air with power.

Casper rolled in the sand beside him, basking in it.

No, this had been the right decision. Hunter felt it now.

He pulled at the power, begging for more, begging it to heal her, hoping it would be enough.

"Careful," said Bill behind him. "Don't try to force it. The elements are willing; let them work." He dropped some logs in the sand beside them, then some blankets and sleeping bags. "Get her pants off. I'll start a fire."

Hunter just stared at him.

Bill was arranging the logs into a pile and tucking dried brush between them. "Do you want me to take her pants off?" He glanced over. "We need to see how deep that wound is. She might need stitches."

Hunter had to clear his throat. "I—can you lay out a sleeping bag for her?"

"She'll do better directly on the sand. Come on, kid, you've never undressed a girl before?"

Um. No. Hunter shook himself and laid her down on the sand.

A few hours ago, she'd looked like the hottest thing he'd ever seen.

Now she was so pale, half soaked in blood. The copper scent stung his nose. That stole any hesitation he might have had. He unbuttoned her jeans and undid the zipper.

That hesitation was back. His breathing felt shallow.

God, she was practically dying in front of him, and he couldn't pull her pants off.

Then Bill was beside him. He had a knife in his hand, and he ripped her jeans straight down from the waistband before Hunter could even think to stop him.

Hunter got a good look at the torn flesh along her hip, and he lost any thoughts of seeing her naked; instead, he almost lost himself to worry.

She'd been right—the bullet had just grazed her, but it had taken a lot of skin with it.

Bill whistled through his teeth. "She's lucky. Lots of arteries in the leg, but you'd never have made it here if one of those had been hit. Let me get my suture kit."

"Your suture kit? But—you can't—"

"Did you want my help or not? There isn't much difference between stitching up a wild animal and a human being." He paused. "You can't leave it all to the elements, Hunter. It'll take days."

"Can we use power to heal her?"

"I'm assuming someone is after you?"

"Yeah."

Bill nodded. "I don't want a lot of power in the air."

So Hunter watched while Bill treated the wound, sprayed it with some kind of topical anesthetic, and then began to thread the flesh of her hip back together. For the moment, that's all his brain could focus on, the steady slip and pull of thread through skin. It should have been horrifying, but he'd been through enough horror in the last week. This was almost hypnotizing, especially with a fire crackling behind them.

"I think you've got a lot to tell me," said Bill.

Hunter shook his head. "I can't piece it all together."

"Try me."

So Hunter talked through the events of the past week, from Silver to the carnival to Calla and Noah Dean and the threats about what would happen Monday. He finished with the Merricks leaving town, how they'd packed up and deserted the house with no notice.

He had a hard time keeping the bitterness out of his voice with that one.

But Bill nodded. "Becca went with them."

"And you're okay with that?"

"Right now? Yeah, I'm okay with that." He tied off the last of the sutures. "Your girl here might not even need those by morning. Leave the stuff out here when you go. I'll burn it."

Then he turned toward the house.

"That's it?" said Hunter, dismayed. "That's all you have to say?"

"That's it. Like I said, kid: your mess."

"Jesus. No wonder Becca hates you."

Bill whirled and hit him so fast that Hunter didn't even see it coming. Suddenly, he found himself down in the sand, tasting blood in his mouth. His jaw ached like . . . well, like he'd been slugged in the jaw. Casper was standing over him, growling.

But Bill wasn't afraid of the dog, and he sure wasn't afraid of Hunter. He stared down at him. "You don't know what I've done to protect Becca. So don't talk about things you don't understand. You get me?"

Hunter made it to his knees and spit blood. "Yeah. Fine. Whatever."

"This is life or death, Hunter."

"No shit."

"Your father made the same sacrifices for you, and instead of living up to his expectations, you're right in the middle of it all. Well, you're not dragging it to my doorstep. Not if I can help it."

Hunter couldn't decide if his head was spinning or if that really didn't make any sense. He lifted his eyes to find Bill walking away. "What are you talking about?"

"I'm talking about your dad. You think it's an accident that no other Guides came after you when your father died?"

Wait.

Wait.

What?

"Come back here," said Hunter.

"Move your jeep when you can. I don't want it sitting in front of the house." Then Bill disappeared through the back door.

And Hunter heard the click of a lock.

Waiting for Kate to wake up was excruciating.

Hunter didn't want to leave her, and he had no cell phone, no way to contact anyone. He had two sleeping bags and a head full of heavy thoughts.

Every time he heard the bare snap of a twig in the woods, his gun was in his hand.

Around sundown, his stomach alerted him to the fact that he didn't have any food, either.

Kate was looking better, though. She'd regained some color, and the stitched wound appeared somewhat closed and scabbed over. Her breathing was deeper, more of a true sleep.

Now that the sun was going down, a chill crept out of the water to cling to the air. Hunter stretched out one of the sleeping bags on the sand and carefully lifted Kate onto it, then covered her with the other one.

One part of him wished she'd wake up so they could get moving.

The other part of him hoped she'd keep sleeping since they had nowhere to go.

This sucked.

He'd moved the jeep to the spot where the grass gave way to sand and then played the radio for a while, trying to catch the news, but he didn't learn anything he didn't already know. Eventually, he worried he'd run the battery down, so he turned the car off and returned to Kate's side.

When the door to the house slid open, Hunter sprang to his feet—but it was just Bill carrying two canvas bags, the kind you get at the grocery store.

"I figured you hadn't eaten in a while." Bill paused, cleared his throat. "There are some clothes in there, too. Stuff I had around here for Becca, but . . . well . . ."

"Thanks." Hunter took the bags and set them beside the blanket, though it was taking everything he had not to tear through them looking for food.

Bill reached out a hand and touched Hunter on the chin. Hunter wondered if he had a new bruise to add to the collection.

"Sorry I hit you," Bill said.

Hunter was sorry about that, too. It had hurt like a bitch and reminded him a little too thoroughly of the fight with his grandfather that had started this mess.

He didn't say anything.

"I did a lot to make sure Becca wouldn't have to deal with this kind of disaster," Bill said. "I know what she thinks of me, but I had my reason for keeping my distance." He paused. "It's just not very nice to have that thrown in my face."

Hunter wondered how much could be resolved if Bill would just say those same words to Becca.

"I'm sorry," Hunter said. He didn't entirely mean it, but he felt like he should offer something in exchange for the food and supplies.

"Did you hate your father?"

The words hit Hunter so hard that he felt like he needed to take a step back. "No," he said, his voice rough. "No, never. He— I just never knew where I stood with him."

Bill smiled a little at that: a small smile, a sad one. "Really?"

Hunter couldn't interpret that expression. "Yeah, really."

"I'd say you stood in pretty high regard. Your dad went to some lengths to keep you a secret."

"How do you know?"

"Because I knew your dad. And he never breathed a word about you."

Hunter scowled—but something about this was meshing with what Silver had said when he came after him and Kate at the Merrick house. Or what Calla Dean had said at the carnival.

Had his father kept him a secret?

But . . . why?

His head was overfull with confusion, and he couldn't take one more thing to second guess. "Maybe it means he just didn't give a crap."

"That's not how being a father works, kid." Bill gestured to the bags. "There should be enough food for tonight and tomorrow."

So Bill expected them to sleep out here, on the beach. It was October, and the night air was already growing cold. Hunter glanced at the back door and deliberated for a long moment before swallowing his pride. "Any way we can crash on your floor?"

"Not an option." Bill's voice was hard again.

Hunter was too tired to argue. "Fine. We'll sleep in the sand." At least they had blankets.

"Sometimes decisions are about picking the lesser evil."

Hunter rolled his eyes. "That's really comforting, thanks."

"Becca never understood what I was doing for her, and she hates me for it. Don't make the same mistake, okay?"

Hunter just looked back at him, wondering how making two people sleep on the beach was some kind of sacrifice for Bill Chandler.

"Think about it," said Bill.

"I'm sure I'll have plenty of time," said Hunter.

Then he turned his back, dropped to the blanket, and fished through the first bag to find the food.

Only to find he was disappointed when Bill moved away.

Especially since it took everything he had not to turn around and beg for more information.

CHAPTER 29

Hunter woke up to someone moving against him.

He didn't remember falling asleep, but now he was awake and alert. His eyes opened to meet Kate's in the near darkness.

Hers were wide. "Where are we?" she whispered.

He heard the worry in her tone. "Safe," he said. "We're on the beach behind Becca's father's house."

She shifted under the blankets to look at the sky. Night had fallen completely, and the moon and stars overhead were brilliant. The fire still burned beside them, throwing light across her face, turning her hair gold.

"How do you feel?" he asked.

She made a face. "Both better and worse than I expected. Do you have any water?"

"Yeah." He secured a bottle from one of the bags and helped her to sit up, though she didn't really need it. She didn't even wince. She drained an entire bottle of water, barely pausing for breath.

"Are you hungry?" he asked. "There's food, too."

When she nodded, he unwrapped a prepackaged peanut-butter-and-strawberry-jam sandwich. She tore into it.

He knew the feeling. He'd done the same thing to three of them earlier. So had Casper.

Halfway through the sandwich, she paused. "Did you take my pants off?"

"Bill helped."

"Oh, that's nice. Did you get a good look?"

Her voice was light, not bitchy. "Watching him put stitches in your thigh kinda stole the allure."

"Stitches?" Her hand moved under the blanket. "Wow. I slept through *that*?"

"I'm not sure I'd call it *sleeping*."

Wind tore across the water to make the flames flicker. Hunter shivered. There'd been clean jeans and a T-shirt in the bag Bill had provided, but nothing warmer than that. His fleece pullover was soaked with her blood, rolled up by the fire.

"Cold?" Kate pulled the edge of the sleeping bag back. "There's plenty of room."

If she'd said it in a dirty way, he wouldn't have taken her up on it. But because he *was* cold and her voice was casual, Hunter scooted until his legs were under the top blanket and he was sitting up beside her.

Now that they were close, however, he didn't know what to say.

Kate's hand found his under the blanket. "Thanks," she said. "For saving me."

He turned his hand and laced his fingers through hers. "What's the last thing you remember?"

"Silver pointing a gun at us." She paused. "I didn't expect to wake up." Another pause, a longer one. Her voice was heavy. "Your dog . . ."

Hunter whistled. Casper came tearing up the beach from whatever he'd been investigating.

Kate's face broke into a smile. "He's okay!"

Hunter rubbed the dog behind his ears until he started the *rawr-rawr-rawr*. "He's tough." He stroked a finger down the line of Casper's muzzle. "He's the one you should be thanking. He attacked Silver."

Kate took him up on that and started scratching Casper behind the ears herself.

The dog flopped over in the sand, looking for a belly rub. Kate obliged him.

Then she said, "So what's the plan?"

"Staying alive? I don't know." Hunter pressed his fingers into his eyes. "I don't have anywhere for us to go."

"What do we know?"

"Not much."

"Let's lay it out and make a plan."

Hunter looked at her in surprise.

"What?" she said with a spark of irritation in her eyes. "You think you're going to figure all this out on your own?"

"No—I didn't—" He stopped to figure out his words before he sounded like a moron. "I just . . . I've been on my own for a long time."

"Me, too." She stared at him, and he loved the way the fire cast shadows across her features. "We're together right now."

"Okay." He nodded. "Okay."

"Lay it out. What do we know?"

"Silver killed my phone, and I dropped the files when he shot you. I have half a tank of gas in the jeep and maybe twenty bucks in cash. I don't remember all the names of the kids who were involved with Calla, and I don't know where she's hiding. All I know is what Noah told me: that she's alive, and they're planning something for Monday."

Kate took all that in and nodded. "Do you know where she might be hiding?"

"Noah said something about tunnels. But I don't know if that means she's hiding in a tunnel somewhere, or if she's planning something to do with tunnels . . . I don't know. She's a Fire Elemental. Why start a fire in a tunnel? But if that's just where she's *hiding*, I don't get that, either. The only tunnels around here are sewer tunnels—also not conducive to fire. Gabriel spent the night in the water a few weeks ago, and he said he'd never felt more drained."

"Does Silver know any of that?" said Kate.

"Not from me." He scowled. "But he probably has my files now, so all those other kids are at risk."

"At risk? They're the ones trying to hurt people."

"Not all of them. Some of them can't be older than ten or eleven. They probably have no clue what they're getting into. And they're just trying to protect themselves." He paused. "I still don't know which is the right side, here. I could never be like Silver. But I can't sit back and watch pure Elementals hurt innocent people, either."

"Silver sees harming innocent people as a means to an end. Did your dad?"

Hunter thought back. "I don't think so." He paused. "Bill told me that my dad made sacrifices to keep me a secret. Silver said I'm living proof of what my dad did wrong. Do you know what that means?"

Kate sighed. "Maybe."

Hunter waited. More wind blew off the water to trace through his hair. The air had a definite bite to it now, and Kate rubbed at her arms.

She shifted to slide back under the blankets, then propped herself up on one shoulder, scooting back to give him room. "Get under the blankets. I'll tell you what I know."

He hesitated, then slid under, too, mirroring her position.

"When Silver and I first got here," said Kate, "he told me that John and Jay Garrity had died on a trip to destroy the Merricks. Then I met you, and your last name was Garrity, and you were new here . . . well, it was a big coincidence. Too big. When we tried to find out more about *you*, there were no listed numbers under *Garrity* in town, no homes or vehicles registered under that name, no—"

"Because I lived with my grandparents," said Hunter. "My mom's parents. And she kept her maiden name, so . . ."

"Right. So that was a mystery. Especially since you knew how to fight—but you'd obviously never been through any kind of training as a Guide. I couldn't put two-and-two together."

Hunter frowned. "I don't know what you mean."

"Hunter, when I was twelve, my mother took me to the Farm. Do you know what that means?"

"You told me about some guy teaching you how to fight."

"Yeah. There's this farm in Virginia where a guy named Roland basically beats the sensitivity out of you until you figure out how to put duty before feeling."

Hunter's eyes widened, but before he could say anything, Kate added, "*Everyone* goes there, Hunter. *Everyone*. It's mandatory."

He was trying to push images of someone beating the crap out of Kate from his mind. "My father used to tell me that he'd send me for training," he said. "He always told me *one more year*. He said I wasn't ready."

Kate's eyes were vaguely haunted, made more so by the flickering firelight. "No one is ever *ready* for that, Hunter."

Hunter bit the inside of his cheek, wanting to ask—but not wanting to.

"I think he kept you a secret," she whispered. She hesitated. "And that's a big no-no."

Like Bill had kept Becca a secret.

Hunter rolled back to stare up at the starry night and wonder what that meant.

Not for the first time, he wished his father were here right now. Not just because he'd be able to answer the thousand and one questions fighting for space in Hunter's brain. But because he'd know what to do.

His father had been all about *duty*—but then he'd kept Hunter a secret?

Hunter thought back to the day before they'd all left to go after the Merricks. His uncle had said something about its being surveillance—that was the only reason Hunter had been allowed to go.

But any time someone talked about that mission, they said that his dad was coming here to *kill* the Merricks.

Had his father's mission been reconnaissance, in advance of killing the Merricks?

Or had he never intended to kill them at all?

And what did all the folders mean?

And if he'd never meant to kill the Merricks, *what was he planning on doing?*

Too many questions. Hunter rubbed at his eyes again.

Kate put a hand on his wrist. "Will Becca's dad help us?"

Hunter snorted. "This is it. Blankets and food. He wouldn't even let us come in the house."

"Weird."

"Not weird. He's an asshole."

"We can't stay here forever."

"We can't just drive around, either. I'm worried the police are looking for me. A white jeep is pretty easy to identify." His voice turned wry. "The bullet hole in the rear quarter panel isn't exactly subtle, either."

"My mom used to say that things look better in the morning."

Hunter started to say that he didn't see how that would be possible, but Kate moved closer and laid her head on his shoulder.

It put the line of her body against his.

He kept trying to tell his own body that she was injured, that she was seeking warmth, that this had nothing to do with anything.

His body was replying, DUDE. SHE IS NOT WEARING PANTS.

"I'm glad you took me for a drive this afternoon," she said.

"You are?" he asked in surprise. "But that's why the day went to shit."

"I don't think so." She breathed against him for a long moment. "If we hadn't left, Silver might have come to the Merricks' house while everyone was still there."

Hunter froze. He hadn't considered that.

"You're a good person, Hunter," she said. "I know you care about them. I know you see it as a weakness, but it's not. You're trying to save them."

"Kate." He shifted to try to see her face. "Kate, are you crying?"

"No." But she was. She'd pressed closer to him, as if that were possible, burying her face in his chest.

He stroked a hand over her hair. "Why?" he said softly. "Why are you crying?"

She didn't answer him, and he just shifted until he was holding her more fully. She was such a creature of ... of *strength*, that he wasn't sure how to respond to this. He kissed her temple, whispering silly assurances.

Finally she stopped, and her breath was warm through his shirt.

Hunter held very still, feeling the tension in her body.

"I didn't tell you the whole truth about my mother," she finally said.

He waited, knowing this admission hung on a thin line, not wanting to upset the precarious balance of whether she'd keep talking.

"I knew she was going on an assignment," said Kate. "I wanted to go. She said I needed to keep training."

Hunter nodded and kissed her temple again. He knew a story just like this one.

His own.

"I went anyway," said Kate. "I hacked her computer ... found out what flights she was taking ... I booked different flights for myself. I found out what her mission was. I followed her everywhere. She had no idea I was there." Kate sniffed and swiped at her eyes.

"But then I saw who she was after," she continued. "It was this little restaurant owner, up at one of the fishing towns in Maine. Tiny diner, right on the water. He was using his powers to draw the best seafood. Silly, right?"

She was still crying, and Hunter wasn't sure what to say to that.

The bad parts were coming, though. He could feel it.

"I didn't even think it was a big deal," said Kate. "I mean—is that any different from having a gift that makes you a better cook? I kept waiting to see if he was hurting people at night, or if there was anything worse than that. Mom was learning his routine, so I learned it, too. She had no idea I was there."

"And what did you learn?" asked Hunter.

"I learned that he had five kids," she said. "I learned that he was a good man who gave restaurant leftovers to the homeless people in town. I kept waiting for him to do something *wrong*, and at the same time, I kept waiting for my mother to do the right thing and leave him alone."

"She didn't." Not even a question.

"No. She went after him."

"And he killed her."

Kate shook her head fiercely. "She waited until he was alone in the restaurant, and she confronted him." Now she was crying in earnest. "And you know what he said? He said he understood, and he wouldn't put up a fight if she promised to leave his family alone. Then he put his hands up and said, 'Do it.'

"He was willing to sacrifice himself for his family," she said. "Just like that. He was going to lie down and die to protect them. And my mom was going to take a father away from that family. She was going to kill a *good man* because it was her *duty*."

Hunter's brain was spinning, trying to figure out how this man had gone from being ready to sacrifice himself for his family to murdering Kate's mother.

Kate swiped at her eyes again. "She pulled out her gun and told him she appreciated his willingness to do what was right." A short, harsh laugh through the tears. "Can you believe that? *His* willingness to do what was *right*."

"How did he kill her?" said Hunter.

"He didn't," said Kate. She sat up, moving away from him, pressing her hands to her eyes, sobbing into her fingers. "I did."

"You? But—"

"I shot her. I shot her in the shoulder just to keep her from killing him. And she turned her gun on me, then fired."

Hunter knelt in front of her, wanting to touch her, not knowing how she'd take it. "Did she know it was you?"

"Maybe not when she fired the first shot. But she aimed at me again. Twice. She knew it was me. I fired back. I didn't—it was all too fast. I'd been through all that training—I just—it was me or her. She died, right there on the floor of his restaurant." Kate looked up at Hunter, tears shining on her lashes. "And if I told anyone I did it, they'd kill me. If I told anyone the Water Elemental had done it, they'd send more Guides after him and probably destroy his whole family."

"So you told them he killed her, and that you killed him." He paused. "You let him go."

She took a shuddering breath. "Yeah." Another breath, steadier this time. "Do you think I'm a horrible person?"

Hunter reached out and stroked the hair back from her face. "I think you're an amazing person who had to make a terrible choice at a terrible time."

"I'm a failure. I should have let her finish."

"No, you're *human*, and *you* did what was right."

"I don't know what's right anymore."

He'd said those exact words to Gabriel, what felt like a lifetime ago.

So he told Kate the same thing Gabriel had said to him. "Yes," he said softly. "You do."

CHAPTER 30

The blankets were warm, and the sound of the water was hypnotic, stealing tension from the air. Kate was pressed against him again, her head on his shoulder, an arm across his chest. Hunter stroked her hair absently, keeping still otherwise, sure she was asleep.

His father had been wrong. This trust felt a million times better than the walls Hunter had built around himself.

"Are you asleep?" Kate whispered, her voice barely carrying above the sound of the waves.

"No." He turned his head and brushed a kiss against her hair.

She shifted until she was braced on his chest, looking down at him. The moon overhead caught her hair and filled it with golden sparks, leaving her eyes in darkness and her features in shadow. Her voice was full of sorrow. "I've never told anyone all . . . all *that*."

He touched her face. "I'll keep your secret."

"I know you will. That's why I told you." She turned her head and kissed the inside of his wrist.

Then she lowered her head to kiss him on the lips.

It was different now, with no secrets between them, just the night sky to bear witness. Sweeter, somehow. Quieter. She tasted like strawberries and peanut butter, and the feeling of her weight on his chest was just about the greatest thing in the whole entire world.

She teased at his mouth with her tongue, sliding her hand under his shirt and tracing lines on his chest with her nails until he was sure she'd set the night on fire.

He broke the kiss, and it took just about every ounce of self-control he had. "Kate—you're hurt—"

"Please," she said, kissing along his jaw, finding his neck. She spoke into his skin. "Please. I need the distraction. Please, Hunter."

She was crying again.

"Kate," he whispered. "Kate." He brushed a thumb across her cheek, stealing the tears.

"Just kiss me," she said.

Then she didn't give him a choice. She was straddling his waist, her mouth consuming his every thought, her tongue alive in his mouth.

His hands went immediately to her waist, but that skimpy tank top barely stretched past her rib cage, and he found bare skin, soft and warm and supple.

"Take your shirt off," she said in a whispered rush—and before he could even *consider* it, she was already pulling at the hem, dragging it up his body and wrestling it over his head.

And she was sitting on his stomach, her bare legs practically wrapped around him.

He focused really hard on breathing.

Tough, since every breath made her move fractionally, and he was very conscious of every inch of warm skin resting against him.

"Kate—I don't want to hurt you—"

She leaned down close, putting her forehead against his, the way she had when they'd wrestled around behind the carnival. "So don't."

Then she pulled the tank top over her head, and she was in nothing but a bra and panties.

All the breath left his body.

He couldn't think with her straddling him like this.

Hunter caught her waist and rolled her gently, putting her back in the blankets, then caging her upper body with his arms. "You're incorrigible."

"Are you complaining?"

"Ah . . . no." He kissed her lips, her cheek, her neck. His hand stroked the safe area around her navel, the base of her ribs. When his fingers brushed the thin line of lace along her hip, she drew a quick intake of breath.

He liked that sound. A lot.

He ran his finger under the lace, tracing along the front of her body. She stretched under him, and he bent to run his mouth over her stomach, breathing in the scent of her.

Her hands were in his hair. "You're killing me," she whispered.

"In a good way?"

"Yes."

That made him pause. His hand went still on her stomach, and he rose up to look down at her. "I owe you a full truth, too."

She dragged a finger down the center of his chest in a way that made his breath shudder and his eyes fall closed.

"Maybe you can tell me later," she said.

He caught her wrist and smiled ruefully. "At school—when I kissed you in the parking lot—"

"I remember."

"I told you I'd know exactly what to do if you jumped me."

"Evidenced by what you're doing *right now*, you mean?"

That made him blush, which made her laugh.

But then she sobered. "I won't tease. What's your deep, dark truth?"

This was harder to tell her than anything else had been. It probably would have been easier if they weren't both half-naked. He wished he could stop *blushing* for god's sake. "I've never—ah—"

"Hunter Garrity."

"What?"

"Are you trying to tell me you're a virgin?"

If her voice had carried any amount of mockery, he would have denied it. But it didn't, and he didn't.

"Yes," he said.

"I figured."

"Hey!"

She didn't smile. Her cheeks appeared extra pink in the firelight now. "No—I meant . . . I am, too."

"You are?"

She nodded.

He couldn't stop staring at her. "But . . . you're so . . . so—"

"If you say *slutty*, I am going to punch you in the crotch again."

"Confident!" he said. "I was going to say *confident*."

"Look, just because I like what I look like doesn't mean I sleep around."

Now he couldn't tell if he was offending her or if she was just yanking his chain. "No one said you were sleeping around."

"Ah, I seem to recall a little comment about my inability to say *no*."

Okay, maybe he had said that. He put his cheek against hers and whispered into her ear. "I apologize. Forgive me?"

Her fingers raked through his hair again, and she shifted closer to him, pulling the blanket higher to block out the stars. "Not yet. You'll just have to make it up to me."

And Hunter realized that maybe a little distraction wasn't out of line after all.

Hunter awoke at dawn and found himself alone in the blankets. The fire was banked, the water far down the beach at low tide.

No Kate.

He sat straight up. His heart went from zero to sixty.

But then he breathed. She was in the jeep, wearing the spare jeans and bright pink T-shirt Bill had brought, fiddling with her cell phone.

Hunter rubbed a hand over his face, wishing he had access to a bar of soap and a razor. He made do with a swig of water from one of the bottles, pulled his jeans on under the blanket, and headed over to the car in bare feet.

Whatever had changed overnight had him wanting to pull her into his arms and keep her safe forever.

Especially when she looked up at him and blushed.

"Hey," he said gently. He bent down to kiss her on the neck.

"Hey." She leaned into him. He let her.

"What are you doing?"

"My phone was dead. I plugged into your charger. Is that okay?"

"Sure." He could see she had the browser open. "Anything interesting?"

"I was looking for tunnels." She glanced up. "Did you know there are two highway tunnels that lead into Baltimore?"

He took the phone and looked at the map. "Highway tunnels?"

"Well, they go under the harbor."

Hunter thought about that but couldn't make it line up in his head. "She's a Fire Elemental. What's she going to do, start a fire in the tunnel?"

"What if she had a Water Elemental working with her? Or an Earth?"

Hunter thought about it. "Collapsing a highway tunnel would definitely draw a lot of attention." Then he shook his head. "They're kids. They don't have that kind of power yet."

"But she's looking for a reaction. They're afraid. They're—"

Casper growled.

Hunter whipped his head up. The dog was staring at the woods.

Kate was completely still, but he could practically hear her heartbeat. Or maybe that was his own. The house was dark and still; the trees quiet except for the slight breeze.

Casper was still on high alert.

Hunter took her hand. "Come on."

She unplugged the phone and followed him. He brushed sand from his feet and yanked shoes on, not bothering to tie the laces.

The gun slipped into his waistband. He pulled an olive-green shirt over his head as they walked toward the opposite tree line. Casper bolted into the woods, and Hunter didn't dare raise his voice to call him back. His dog could take care of himself.

He didn't have to tell Kate to be quiet. She was simply a shadow at his side, alert and prepared.

A branch snapped somewhere off in the woods, and her back pressed against a tree.

His did, too. They'd gone in opposite directions and now stood ten feet apart, staring at each other.

Another snap, a heavy one. Malice in the air. Someone was definitely in the woods.

Kate's eyes were wide and locked on his. Their trees were too far apart to risk talking.

Then she had her cell phone in her hand, her fingers sliding across the screen.

What was she *doing*?

Then she looked up and tossed the slim black phone to him.

He read the words she'd typed.

You go northeast. I go southeast. Set 2 trails.

Like he'd split up now. He looked up and very clearly mouthed *No!*

She clearly mouthed back *Yes!*

Then she took off.

Damn her and all that independence! Hunter ran. Northeast, like she'd wanted.

Only now he did it with no caution at all. He ran full out, not bothering to hide his tracks or be stealthy. He needed *noise*, so he'd be the target.

So Kate could get away.

She was fast, like a sprinter, flying through the trees somewhere off to his right. Then he realized he could *see* her, that bright pink T-shirt flashing through the trees.

Shit.

Something cracked. That pink beacon crashed to the ground.

Hunter skidded to a stop. He said a prayer in his head, hoping she'd simply stumbled. At this distance, the pink was almost a blur, but he saw it lift from the ground. *Keep running. Keep running. Keep running.*

But he was already running toward her.

Only to skid to another stop and duck behind a tree.

Silver had an arm around Kate's neck. She was struggling against him.

An arrow protruded from one thigh, and Silver had a crossbow pressed up tight against her neck.

"Come on, Hunter," he called. "Come get your girlfriend."

"He's gone," Kate yelled, and Hunter could hear her fury from here. "He ran the other way, you *idiot.*"

"I'd say the idiotic move was turning on your cell phone, Kathryn."

Hunter peeked around the tree. He had a gun, but he didn't have a clear shot at Silver from here. He needed to think. He needed to *think.*

"Run!" she yelled. "Hunter, *run!*"

Then Silver must have done something because Kate cried out, and the sound fractured into sobs. Hunter's nails dug into the tree. He had to look. He had to look.

The pink shirt was turning red. Silver had shot her in the abdomen with the crossbow. She was crying.

Hunter made a small sound before he was aware of it.

"You can't save me, Hunter," she yelled, and her voice was weaker, breaking. "Run!"

"I can kill her slowly," Silver called. "While you watch."

Hunter couldn't believe he'd ever thought for a moment that he could have turned out like this guy.

"Or I can stop," said Silver. "We can work something out. We have similar goals, I think."

"He's lying!" said Kate. "Please—please run—he'll kill all of them, Hunter—remember sacrifice—"

She screamed.

Silver had yanked the arrow out of her thigh.

Then he stabbed her through the side of her abdomen, driving the arrow up and into her body.

Kate didn't scream, though she looked like she wanted to.

He'd pierced a lung.

Hunter was on his feet, the gun in his hand.

But an arm caught him around the neck and a hand slapped over his mouth, and suddenly Hunter was someone's prisoner, too.

CHAPTER 31

These arms were like steel. Hunter couldn't even get leverage. Especially since the ground wouldn't let go of his feet.

"Stop fighting," a voice growled in his ear. "I'm trying to help you, kid."

Michael Merrick.

Hunter stopped fighting. Michael's hand came off his mouth.

"We need to help her," Hunter said. He felt like he was choking on his words. "We need to—we need—"

"If you run out there, he'll kill you, too. Just—"

"Come on, Hunter!" yelled Silver. "You have three seconds."

Michael tightened his grip before Hunter realized he was trying to surge free. A hand was over his mouth again.

"One!" said Silver.

Hunter couldn't breathe. He couldn't see past his own rage. Michael wrestled him to the ground.

"Two!"

He had no idea what was going to happen at three, but he had to—

A gun went off.

For the longest time, Hunter couldn't hear anything but the blood rushing in his ears.

He couldn't think.

He couldn't think.

Then he realized Michael still had a death grip and was murmuring in his ear. "Keep still. Come on, Hunter. Keep still."

The leaves around them were shaking.

No, that was him, trembling, making the leaves shake.

Leaves. Foliage had grown up and around them. Hiding them from sight.

Or it would be if Hunter didn't ruin the illusion. He swallowed hard, squeezing his eyes shut tight.

He felt tears on his cheeks.

Kate was okay. She had to be okay. It had to be a ploy.

But he'd seen those arrows pierce her body.

He'd heard the gunshot.

No. They would get out of this. He could heal her. Michael could help.

Kate.

He couldn't sense her at all. He could sense Michael's fear and Silver's patience and the danger in the air, but *he couldn't feel Kate.*

"I think he's leaving," said Michael, his voice barely a whisper. "Keep still."

He didn't want to keep still. Silver was standing *right there.* Shock was filtering into fury, and Hunter wanted to shoot that motherfucker in the head. His fingers were itching for a trigger, to feel the kick and recoil and taste vengeance.

"Go ahead," called Silver, as if he felt the rage in the air and found it satisfying. "Try to shoot me."

Michael tightened his grip. "No, Hunter. *No.* You blow our cover and we are *screwed.*"

So they waited.

Silver waited.

The sun crept into the sky and fed warmth into the woods, narrowing shadows between the trees. Tension slid through the leaves and choked Hunter, until he was ready to shoot Michael, just to escape it. His shoulders began to ache from being pinned so long.

It felt like hours.

It probably *was* hours.

She was alone out there. Probably in pain.

Hang on, he thought. *Just hang on.*

Finally a cell phone rang, out there in the woods. Silver's. He answered, but his voice was too low to carry.

Hunter caught the word *terminated*.

He couldn't breathe again.

But Kate could be faking. Waiting Silver out, too. Like Casper had been waiting at the house.

The conversation was short. Silver slipped the phone into a pocket and strode out of the woods.

Michael still didn't let Hunter go.

"Wait," Michael said. "I want to wait until I feel a vehicle leaving."

Finally—*finally*—Michael released him.

Hunter swung around and hit him. As hard as he could.

Then he was scrabbling through the underbrush, stumbling once he found his feet, slipping out of his shoes in the mud. His breath was hitching again.

When he saw Kate, it was like his brain didn't want to process all of it. He saw her shoes, the borrowed jeans, again splattered with blood.

The pink shirt.

The bloodstains. The arrows. The flies, already collecting.

Then he saw her head and wished he hadn't seen any of it.

She hadn't been waiting. She hadn't been in pain.

He wanted to touch her and he didn't.

He was going to be sick.

Michael caught him and jerked him back. "Don't," he said. "You can't touch her. You can't have this traced back to you."

Hunter shoved him in the chest, throwing all his strength into it. His voice was raw and edged with pain. "You made me wait! We could have saved her."

"No, Hunter—"

He hit him again. "We could have—she's—"

"It was *too late*. He'd stabbed her through the chest. Hunter, it was too late."

"Damn you!" Another shove. "We could have—she's—she's—"

And then he was sobbing and Michael caught him, holding him tight.

"I'm sorry," Michael was saying. "I'm sorry."

Hunter let himself have about fifteen seconds of pity. Then he shoved free of Michael's hands and swiped the tears off his face.

He didn't want pity. He didn't want anything.

His fists were clenched at his sides, and he suspected he'd completely lose control if he let go.

"We need to move," Michael said quietly.

"I'm not just leaving her here."

"Hunter—"

"I'm *not* just leaving her to get eaten by insects and wild animals." His voice was shaking with fury. "Do you understand me? So either get a shovel out of your truck or I'll dig by hand."

"No shovel," said Michael.

"Fine." Hunter took a step forward.

Michael caught his arm. "I'll take care of it. Just give me a minute."

Then he knelt in the dirt and put a hand against the ground.

He was right: it only took a minute. The earth just swallowed her up, gradually at first, her body sinking into the dirt as if the ground was simply giving way. But then the hole began to fill in over her, grass and foliage growing back into place.

As if nothing had happened.

Hunter stared. He'd thought this would be better—but it was worse. He needed the action, the *physicality* of digging a hole. He needed the closure.

This was more like erasure. He dropped to his knees and touched a hand to the ground.

The last twenty-four hours had gone too fast. From mistrust to friendship to—to *what*? He felt like he'd almost caught something precious, only to have it shatter as soon as he touched it.

He knew better than anyone how life could change in the blink of an eye.

But this—this seemed too unfair. His throat tightened and made it hard to breathe again.

He had nothing to remember her. Nothing. Not even a picture. He didn't even have her texts on his cell phone.

The phone.

He fished her phone out of his pocket. What had Silver said?

I'd say the idiotic move was turning on your cell phone.

He'd been tracking her. Hunter turned it off.

But he put it back in his pocket.

She'd mentioned sacrifice. She'd done this for him, lost her life to protect him.

Well, hell if he was going to let that go to waste.

He looked up at Michael. He couldn't talk.

So he just stood up and started walking.

They sure as hell couldn't drive his jeep anywhere. But Michael didn't have the truck or their SUV—he had a rental car.

Casper was locked inside.

That was shocking enough to make Hunter stop short.

Michael shrugged. "He was in the woods. I saw him first. I didn't want him to get hurt."

Hunter nodded. He knew he should say thanks—but he wasn't ready to thank Michael for anything yet. He didn't care about this car or why Michael had it. He didn't even care where they were *going.*

But when he climbed in the car, Casper put his head on Hunter's shoulder and whined. Hunter rubbed the dog's muzzle.

Michael pulled a phone out of his pocket and dialed. When whoever answered, he spoke low. "Hey, it's Michael. Can you meet us at the hotel? Yeah, I found him."

Had to be Hannah.

Hunter's throat felt thick again.

He still couldn't believe Kate was dead.

Gone.

He was shaking again.

One girl, reduced to nothing more than a memory and a cell phone. Her mother was dead and she'd never mentioned a father—would anyone else even *miss* her?

With a start, he realized he didn't even know if *Kate Sullivan* was her real name.

And he wasn't sure how much of his reaction was shock and how much was mourning. He'd known her a week. Somehow it felt like a lifetime, so much intensity crammed into such a short span of days.

Hell, so much intensity crammed into the last twelve hours.

They'd escaped Silver at the Merrick house only to . . . what? It would have been easier if this had happened *there*.

Fate must fucking hate him.

He could still remember the smell of her hair, the way her skin felt under his fingertips.

The whole thing was senseless.

"You okay?" said Michael.

Hunter shook his head. He had to press his fists into his eyes.

"I'm sorry," Michael said. His voice was rough. "Jesus, kid. I'm sorry." He put a hand on Hunter's shoulder.

And that—*that*—was too much. Hunter smacked his hand away. "You're *sorry*? What the hell do you care, anyway? You left me here! You *left*! You fed me some line of bullshit about caring about the target on my back, and then you were gone! No one gives a shit about me until there's a mess, and then suddenly everything is my fault! I can't please anyone, and every time I try, I'm just one big fucking disappointment. Everyone is on me to pick a side. How the hell am I supposed to pick a side when everyone hates me? And the one person who *didn't* hate me was just killed in front of me."

Michael took a long breath. "I don't want to kick you when you're down, but you don't exactly make it easy to trust you, Hunter."

Great. Of course. His fault again. He looked out the window.

"Yesterday afternoon, you left suddenly, right?" said Michael. "With Kate, a stranger, someone you've been very secretive about."

Hunter didn't say anything. He didn't want to listen to any of this, but the alternative was thinking about Kate's body disappearing into the earth as if she'd never existed at all.

"And then," Michael continued, "there's a news report that Noah Dean disappeared and a pentagram is painted over his door. *This happened while you were gone.* Gabriel said you'd attacked the kid Friday, after telling us that you weren't going to do anything. What were we supposed to think?"

Hunter couldn't deny any of that—especially since he'd been in the mountains, wondering if the *Merricks* had something to do with Noah's disappearance.

"You were still going to leave," he said. "I heard your conversation with Gabriel, when you didn't want me to know."

Michael looked somewhat stunned. "My conversation with Gabriel?"

"The morning after the carnival. You were talking in the kitchen, and you specifically said, *I don't want him to hear us.*"

Michael opened his mouth. Closed it.

"Save it," said Hunter.

"No," said Michael. "I just—Jesus, if you thought we were leaving, why didn't you *say something?*"

"Because you didn't want me to know!"

"Okay, first of all, we weren't talking about you. We were talking about James."

"You—what?"

"James. Hannah's son. When I said I didn't want 'him' to overhear us, I meant the five-year-old with ears like a tape recorder. If we *were* going to leave, I wanted Hannah to hear it from me, not a rumor from her kid."

This had to be bullshit.

Right?

"Fine. If you didn't care whether I knew you were leaving, *why didn't you tell me?*"

"Because that's as far as the conversation went. The movies make it sound like it's easy to pick up and change your identity, but it's not—especially not for four people, two of whom are identical twins. They're all underage, easily identifiable—hell, I'd probably get in a shit ton of trouble with the state if they knew I'd even considered it. But no, Hunter, our plan was not to pack up the house and leave you here, with no warning at all. Is that what you've thought? All this time?"

Hunter stared out the window at the trees whipping by, and felt about six years old. His eyes were raw and his throat swollen. "Yeah," he finally said.

"God, you're as bad as my brothers."

It loosened something in Hunter's chest, this revelation. He didn't feel quite so alone. "You really weren't going to leave?"

"No. We were going to do exactly what we discussed, *together*: let the Guide deal with the middle schoolers and wait to see if that would lead to more trouble."

Hunter scowled. If he'd known that then, he probably wouldn't have talked to Silver on the quad on Friday. He wouldn't have attacked Noah Dean, and he and Kate wouldn't have been on the run.

And she might still be alive.

Sacrifice.

"But now," said Michael, "we're hiding in a hotel."

"Hiding?"

"Yeah. The Guide obviously went after that kid, and we didn't know if we were next."

Probably smart, considering that Silver did show up at the Merricks' house. "You didn't answer my calls," said Hunter.

"We didn't bring our phones because they're easy to trace. We've got two prepaid ones right now."

His voice was a bit hollow, and Hunter ran his finger along the edge of Kate's phone in his pocket. He really wanted to turn it on and read through their texts, but if it was sending out a homing beacon to Silver's phone or whatever, that was the last thing he could do.

"How did you know where I was?" he finally asked.

"Bill called Becca and told her what happened."

"Bill." Hunter snorted. "He wouldn't even let me in his house. I didn't know he cared."

"He wouldn't let you in his house? Jesus, that guy is an asshole."

"Tell me about it."

Hunter almost laughed.

Then his world came crashing back down.

He folded his arms across his stomach, trying to hold in the pain.

"Hey," said Michael.

Hunter glanced over.

"I'm sorry about what happened," Michael said quietly. "But you're not a disappointment."

Hunter took a breath, and his voice broke. "I let her die."

"Hunter, that guy was *not* messing around. She was dead before I even grabbed you."

That didn't make it better. Hunter choked on another breath. "Did you know she was a Guide? All this time?"

Hunter nodded.

Michael didn't say anything, but Hunter knew what it sounded like—that he would have turned on the Merricks.

"I didn't rat you out—I thought you were leaving. I thought I'd have to fix everything by myself."

"I let you into our home, Hunter. I said you could stay as long as you needed to."

Hunter was having a hard time hanging on to his emotions, and despair poured out of his mouth with alarming force. "I know, okay? I know." His voice almost broke again, but he saved it. "I'm sorry. I fucked up everything. This is my fault. I'm sorry."

Michael put a hand up. "Stop. I'm not—I don't want to chastise you. I'm just saying you can trust me. Us. All of us. You always could."

Hunter stared at him. He'd never trusted anyone, and his whole world had been turned upside down.

And now he probably didn't have any options. "That was then," he said. "What about now?"

Michael glanced over and put a hand on his shoulder. "Even now, kid. Even now."

Chapter 32

Michael had a hotel room in a little Residence Inn by the airport. It was more of an apartment, with a kitchenette and two bedrooms. Hunter was ready for the younger Merricks to glare at him as he came through the door.

He wasn't ready for his mother to be sitting at the table.

This was too much. He couldn't take it.

He could have handled a fight. He could have handled planning. Details. Distraction.

Something about seeing his mother there just stole all the fight from him.

He was crying before he knew it. And when her slender arms came around him, he couldn't fight her off. He just cried into her shoulder. He didn't care that the Merricks could see him; he didn't care that this was the same woman who'd watched his grandfather belt him across the face and throw him out of the house.

This was his mother.

And right now, he'd do anything for one minute of her comfort.

Especially since she was *giving* it.

She smelled like cotton and cloves and vanilla and *home*. He didn't want to let her go.

But doing this forever wouldn't solve anything.

When he finally raised his eyes from her shoulder, he was surprised to find that they were alone.

"They went to get some food," she said softly. "They'll be back in a bit."

He went to the sink and splashed cold water on his face. All of a sudden, the distance between them, packed with unspoken secrets and betrayals, felt like miles.

When he turned, she was sitting at the table.

He wanted to be sharp, like he'd been the last time she'd visited him. But now life had shifted, leaving him stronger, yes, but also more vulnerable.

"What are you doing here?" he said slowly.

"Michael called and said he'd found you."

So that had been the phone call in the car. Not Hannah.

He leaned against the counter and studied the tiles under her feet. "Were you missing me?"

"Hunter, I've been missing you since the day your father died."

He jerked his head up. "You couldn't prove it by me."

She blanched. It should have been satisfying. It wasn't.

But then she recovered. "Will you sit and talk to me?"

He sat. He crossed his arms on the table and didn't look at her. He felt weak now, for breaking down upon seeing her.

She put a hand on his arm. "That's the first time I've seen you cry since your father died."

He left her hand there. She had bracelets just like his, only hers were strung on ribbons and braided leather instead of twine. He might have made one of hers when he was little—he couldn't remember.

He didn't move away from her touch. But he made his voice hard. "I think you did enough crying for both of us."

"Is that what you thought? That I missed him too much to care about you?"

"Didn't you?"

"No! Never." Now both her hands were on his arm, and her voice was so soft. "Is that what this is about? Are you angry with me for missing him?"

"No. Yes. I don't—yes." He pushed her hands away.

"Is that why you hit that girl? Because you were angry at me?"

"Goddamn it, *I didn't hit Calla!*"

She flinched from his anger. He didn't even regret it. His breathing was fast, almost to the point that he couldn't catch it.

Then his night caught up with him again, and he put his face in his hands. "Forget it." His voice was thick now. "Just go away."

It took everything he had to keep tears from falling again.

She touched his wrist, her fingers light against his skin. "I do miss him, Hunter. I do. But I'm your mother—"

"No!" He flung her hand off. "No. A mother wouldn't have just *sat there.*"

Her eyes were wide. She didn't have to ask what he meant.

She cleared her throat, but the words still sounded strangled. "I am your mother. But this has all been difficult for me—"

"You're right," he said, sharpening his voice with sarcasm. "I'm the one being selfish. I probably should have left earlier."

She sat there looking shocked. He felt vindicated for about three seconds.

Then she started crying.

He hated her for it. *Hated* her.

And he hated himself for it, too.

"I miss him," she said, and her voice was full of tears, but anger, too. "I loved him, Hunter. Do you understand that? I loved him. He understood me. He was my best friend. And can I tell you how much it hurts me that you look at me with such *resentment* every time I express any grief? Do you have any idea?"

Hunter went absolutely still.

No. He had no idea.

"I am your mother," she continued, her voice still shaky, but strong. "I lost my husband in that car crash—thank god I didn't lose my son. But you came home from the hospital with nothing but hatred for me. Every time you looked at me, I felt it. So then I wasn't mourning one loss, but two."

"I didn't hate you," he whispered.

But she was right. He had.

"Yes," she said. "You did. And I knew you were grieving, too. I tried to understand it. I thought we could come here and start over. But it just got *worse*."

"You wouldn't even look at me!"

"Because every time I looked at you, you looked at me like I was the one who caused that accident! You're getting in fights at school, hanging out with a rougher crowd, staying out all night—do you really think it was that far a jump to think you'd hit a girl? Especially knowing how you felt about me?"

"Yes! It was!"

But no. It wasn't.

He felt so much guilt about Kate that it was impossible to think his mind could handle any more. But here it was, piling on.

He was my best friend.

"He was my best friend, too," said Hunter, and it wasn't until he spoke that he realized he was crying again.

His mother put her hand over his. He didn't deserve it, but she left it there and squeezed. "I know," she said quietly. "I know."

"And I don't hate you. I just—I just—"

She touched his face. "You just what?"

Hunter brushed her hand away. He didn't deserve her kindness. Not with what he was about to say. The words were out of his mouth before he could stop them.

"He was using you," Hunter said, almost choking on the words. "You've spent all these months crying over a man who was using you. He wasn't your best friend. He wasn't mine."

Then he couldn't hold on to the emotion anymore, after weeks—*months*—of trying to keep it at bay. He was crying in earnest.

His mother shifted closer and put her hands on his face again. "Hunter, your father was not using me. And he definitely wasn't using you."

"He was. He told me he was."

She sighed, and then her mouth set into a thin line. "Your father and I had a lot of disagreements about the things he was telling you."

He frowned and wasn't sure how to respond to that.

She continued, "He's not here to defend himself, so I won't criticize the choices he made. But I loved him, and I never doubted his love for me." Her hand went over his. "Or for you."

His throat felt tight again. "He never thought I was good enough."

"That's not true. He didn't want you to have to do the things he did. When your abilities became clear, he didn't want to send you off to have the compassion beaten out of you. He trained you himself so he could claim that he did a better job. He told you that I knew nothing so I'd be safe if anyone ever found out about you. Do you understand that? Do you know enough now?"

He felt like he understood nothing.

She squeezed his hands fiercely. "He told you to use people so you'd protect your heart, Hunter." Her voice broke again. "Because love always carries the risk of loss."

Hunter squeezed his eyes shut and thought of Kate.

"He was never disappointed in you, Hunter. Never."

"You don't know that."

She sighed and touched his cheek. He didn't want to accept her comfort—but he *so did*.

"Remember those files I gave you?"

His eyes opened. "Yes."

"Your dad set those aside before he left. He said to give them to you if he didn't make it back." She frowned. "But then he took you with him, and then the car crash—"

"Why didn't you give them to me before now?" he demanded.

"Because I didn't want you in danger!" She paused to compose herself. "And you were just so furious, and you wouldn't talk to me—you went so far as to change how you looked—"

"Because I hated looking like him! I hated the reminder every time I looked in the mirror! I hated knowing I'd failed him—"

"You didn't fail him, Hunter. You never failed him." Her eyes were shining with fresh tears. "You wouldn't talk to me. I didn't know what you'd do if I gave you those files. But then the fires happened, and the news released information about the pentagrams—I realized you were in the thick of it, firing blind. I realized I'd been wrong to keep the information from you."

Hunter rubbed his hands across his face. "It didn't help. I don't know what it all means. Did he expect me to kill all those kids on his behalf? Did he expect me to kill the Merricks if he failed?"

Her voice dropped to a whisper. "Is that what you think? That he wanted you to kill them?"

"I'm a Fifth!" he cried. "That's what we're supposed to do!"

"That's not what your father was doing, Hunter. He knew how to run a mission his way. He didn't always report the truth."

"I don't know what you're talking about."

Her eyes were fierce, level with his. "When he got the report that he was assigned to kill those boys, he wasn't heading down here for that."

"What was he doing then?"

"He was coming here to *help* them."

Everyone else was picking through a bucket of KFC, but Hunter didn't feel like eating. His mom had offered him the choice of going home versus staying here. And while things between him and her didn't feel quite so strained, the thought of facing his grandfather was too much just now.

Yet he didn't want to sit at the table with a bunch of people with mixed feelings about him, either.

But Michael had asked for trust, and Hunter owed him this much.

He still couldn't believe Kate was dead. He kept feeling that he should send her a text about his dad, just to let her know.

"You all right?" Nick was staring at him across the table.

"Yeah." He wasn't, but what else was he going to say? They

knew everything, from the drive into the mountains, to Silver preventing the gun from firing, to Kate's death.

Well, not *everything*.

Becca came around the table and put her arms around his neck from behind. "I'm sorry," she whispered.

"I'm okay, Becca. Really." He couldn't take the sympathy. He felt so guilty about all of it, and sympathy added to the weight. He refrained from pulling away. "Just . . . sit. Eat. It's fine."

When she dropped back into a chair, he felt Gabriel watching him.

He was the only Merrick who hadn't said a frigging word to Hunter since he'd walked into the hotel room.

Hunter didn't really feel like getting into it with him, either.

But he met his eyes and held them.

Go ahead, he thought. *Fuck with me. Right now. Do it.*

Gabriel didn't move.

"What's the plan?" said Chris.

Hunter cleared his throat and quit the staring match. "The last thing Noah Dean said to me was that Calla is planning something for Monday. Something big. I have no idea where she's hiding—and I can't exactly look for her while Silver is out there, waiting to shoot me."

"Monday is tomorrow," said Michael.

Tomorrow? Hunter blinked. The days had all run together.

"What about her plans?" said Becca. "Any idea what this *something big* could be?"

"Kate said . . ." He had to take a breath. "She was looking on her phone. She said there were two tunnels leading in and out of Baltimore City. They go under the harbor. She thought maybe those could be a target. But they're miles long—and I wouldn't have the first clue how to protect something like that. Not to mention I wouldn't even know where to start. I mean—"

"Why the tunnels?" said Michael.

"That's the only thing I could get out of Noah. He said 'tunnels.' I can't imagine Calla hanging out in the sewers, and I couldn't find anything about caves in Anne Arundel County—"

"There are tunnels under the school," Michael said.

Gabriel snorted. "You mean the old bomb shelter? That's a joke they play on freshmen. Like the swimming pool on the roof."

"No, it's not."

"How do you know?"

Michael gave him a look. "Gee. I don't know. How could I possibly know about *tunnels* in the *ground*—"

"What are they for?" Hunter interrupted.

"They lead to the boiler room," said Michael. "And they run the full length of both schools, connecting under the auditorium. It's pitch-black down there, full of pipes."

"Water?" said Hunter.

Michael nodded. "And gas lines."

"Holy crap," whispered Becca. "She could blow up the schools."

Hunter wanted to think that Calla didn't have it in her—but he'd seen the carnage at the carnival. He'd walked into houses that she'd personally burned. "Can the tunnels be accessed from outside the school?" said Hunter.

"No," said Michael. "There are access points in a few classrooms and at the back of the auditorium."

"How do you *know* this?" said Nick.

"Maybe I occasionally used them. You guys aren't the only ones who got crap in school, you know."

"We can't just go rushing in there," said Hunter. "If we spook those kids, they could bring the place down on top of us."

"They might not even be there now," said Michael. "Why sit in the tunnels all weekend when they can just walk in the front door with everyone else and not arouse a bit of suspicion?"

"Noah and Calla are missing," said Becca. "People would notice if they showed up for school."

"I don't know," said Chris. "If they're missing, people wouldn't be looking for them to walk in the front doors of the middle school. They might not be noticed. Especially if they didn't go to class."

"So . . . what?" said Hunter. "We risk everyone at school by waiting for class to start?"

"No," said Michael. "We'll have the schools evacuated before first period begins."

Hunter frowned. "How the hell are you going to do that?"

"Easy," said Michael. "We'll call in a bomb threat."

CHAPTER 33

Hunter couldn't believe he was at school. He felt like he'd drunk an entire pot of coffee in one swig. His nerves were *shot*.

Actually, a pot of coffee didn't sound like a bad idea.

He hadn't slept at all last night.

Every time he closed his eyes, he saw Kate.

The arrows.

The blood.

The way she sank into the earth.

Focus.

The first bell hadn't rung yet, and the hallways were packed. Kids on cell phones, checking lockers, laughing, making out, arguing. Hundreds of kids. Thousands, if you counted the middle school.

Today they *all* had a target on their backs.

Sweat was collecting under his collar. He hung close to the auditorium doors, pretending to be texting.

Really, he was just running his fingers over the blank face of Kate's phone.

The Merricks' plan was thin. There was a chance they wouldn't succeed, that Calla and her crew would blow this whole place to smithereens.

Actually, as a rescue mission, this whole plan kind of sucked. Too many variables.

Too many chances for the wrong people to escape, and for the good guys to get hurt. Again.

So Hunter had come up with his own plan.

He pressed the button to turn on the phone. He watched the little icons light up. Cell signal. WiFi.

GPS.

Then he shoved the phone in his pocket. It would only be a matter of time before Silver showed up.

The fire alarms went off, and Hunter jumped a mile. The sound slammed into his head and caused an immediate pulsing headache.

Becca had carried out her part. The bomb threat had been made.

Students immediately started bunching around the exits.

He ducked through the auditorium doors. The alarms were louder in here, echoing because of the acoustics.

Now Hunter just needed to get the Merricks out, too.

They were stationed all over the school. Hunter pulled out the disposable phone Michael had given him. He'd lied to them so many times—would they trust him now? He dashed out a quick group text to all of them.

Found Calla & kids in aud! Bolted. Heading for strip mall. Need backup!

Their replies started coming in almost instantly. They were abandoning their posts to help him. The strip mall was at least half a mile down from the school.

And completely safe.

Hunter found the trap door to the tunnels without any difficulty, a heavy plank of steel secured with nothing more than a double-end snap and a chain. A ladder led the way into darkness. Hunter's feet found one rung, then the next. The alarms caught the walls of this chamber and echoed, setting up a pulse in his head.

His pocket buzzed. Gabriel.

Don't do anything stupid. Wait for us.

If only he knew.

Hunter had expected darkness, but once he moved past the square of light from the hatch, the tunnel swallowed him up. Hunter couldn't see an inch in front of his face. His hands found pipes, concrete walls, rusted steel supports.

He opened his senses, looking for anything.

God, he'd kill for something to silence those damn alarms.

Water. Water everywhere, locked in pipes, dripping down the walls, puddling under his feet. And gas in these lines, enough explosive potential to level half the city. Sitting on the beach with Kate, he'd had access to a perfect circle of Elemental power, with the sand, the water, the fire, and the breeze. Although everything here was manufactured, this space was just as perfect.

Hunter turned a corner, and the alarms faded. The darkness somehow became more absolute, almost smothering. He could hear himself breathing. He could almost hear his own heartbeat.

His pocket buzzed again.

We're in the parking lot. Where R you?

Hunter turned the phone off.

He forced his senses farther. Water. Gas. Concrete. The air was stale down here, lacking current. He fed a little power into the water, pressing a hand to the wall where it dripped, begging for direction.

At first, nothing. Then . . . *this way.*

Another path through darkness. He must have passed below another hatch because the alarms became briefly louder before silencing. Another turn. Then another.

Then the air whispered that someone was nearby.

Hunter froze, his hand finding his gun.

This way.

He turned another corner, moving cautiously. He saw light, the very palest light, just around the next bend in the tunnel.

He kept his gun out and stepped around the edge.

And there they were. Half a dozen teenagers sitting under one lone penlight strung from the ceiling.

They froze when he appeared. Half looked like they wanted to run—and a few looked ready for a fight.

Michael had been wrong. They probably *had* been living in the tunnels all weekend. Maybe longer. Hunter could feel their hunger, the chill in their skin, their desperation.

And there, at the front of the group, was Noah.

He was one of the ones who looked ready to fight.

He was shivering. "Get out," he snapped. He rolled a lighter across his palm and put a hand on one of the pipes. "Don't make me do something you'll regret."

His voice was sharp, but he didn't sound certain.

He sounded terrified.

"Where's Calla?" Hunter said.

One of the other kids stepped forward with an ax. "She's waiting for us to do our part against the Guides."

Then he raised it to swing.

Hunter rushed forward to stop him. The kid was small, but the ax was heavy. Hunter caught his arm, driving him back. The kid tried to swing again. Hunter shoved him, hard, and the ax went clattering to the ground.

"Stop," said Hunter. "You need to get out of here. You don't know what you're up against."

"We know what to do to prove we're serious," said Noah.

"There's a Guide coming. *You need to run.*"

"Let him come," said one of the girls. "We'll bring the school down on top of him."

"Not if I take care of the problem first," said an accented voice from the darkness behind Hunter.

Followed by the click of a gun.

Hunter's training kicked in without thought. He was spinning, registering where the sound had come from, swinging a fist to send the shooter off balance. He didn't want to shoot, not here, not yet, when gas lines were so close.

But that didn't stop Silver from firing. A bullet hit a pipe, and steam exploded into the small space.

Not a gas line. Not yet.

Girls were screaming.

"Run!" yelled Hunter. "Get out of here!"

The gun fired again. A flare of light, the clang of a bullet on steel. More steam, making the near darkness even more blinding. Sneakers scuffed on concrete, and they had to be running.

"They're kids," Hunter cried. "Let them go!"

"No." Silver fired again, and Hunter darted left, hitting the pipes. He begged the steam to give him Silver's location.

Silver must have been doing the same thing, only his abilities were stronger. The gun found the edge of Hunter's jaw before Hunter even sensed motion.

Hunter froze.

"Drop your weapon."

Hunter dropped it. The dark clouds of vapor swallowed it immediately.

Silver gave him a little shove with his gun, pushing Hunter's head up. "You sent those children running. Do you honestly think they'll stop causing damage just because you told them to?"

"They're kids. They don't know what they're doing."

"They do know what they're doing. The deaths at the carnival proved that. I'm not worried about them right now. Your files will be quite helpful to track them down."

His files. The ones he'd lost when Silver tracked him to the Merrick house.

Something told him Silver wouldn't just threaten to harm those kids' parents the way he had behind Noah Dean's house.

Silver put more pressure on the weapon. "Tell me where the Merricks are hiding, and I'll give you a quick death."

"I'm going to kill *you*," Hunter said.

"Good luck," said Silver.

It wasn't a matter of luck, it was a matter of time. Hunter just had to stay alive long enough for the kids to get out of the tunnels.

Then he could blow up the school himself if that's what it took to kill this guy.

"You showed up pretty quick," he said.

"Tell me where the Merricks are hiding," Silver said again.

"Fuck you."

Silver shot him.

In the leg.

The pain was quick and immediate, and Hunter was on the ground before he even registered what had happened.

What had Bill said about arteries? Hunter's vision already felt spotty.

He rolled and looked up at Silver. "You're really an asshole."

Silver shot him in the other leg.

Hunter cried out. He couldn't help it. Pain ripped through him like a white-hot poker. It felt like the bullet had gone straight through bone.

Maybe that had really happened. He could swear he couldn't feel his feet.

He needed to find his gun. He needed to shoot Silver. Or a gas line.

Or himself, just to stop this blinding pain.

"How many more of you are there?" said Silver.

Hunter almost couldn't think to process the words. "More of me?"

"Fifths like you, living outside our notice?"

"Just me."

"I don't believe you. How did you coerce Kate to join you?"

The mention of Kate bought him a moment of clarity. "I didn't coerce her into *anything*. Kate wasn't a killer. She didn't *want* to be like you."

Hunter patted his hand along the concrete, searching for a weapon. Even the ax.

"My mistake," said Silver, "was working with children." He shot Hunter in the leg again, closer to the knee.

His vision went white for a moment, and Hunter felt like he lost a minute of time.

"Who else is like you?" Silver demanded again.

"Fuck you."

"What are you, sixteen? No wonder you couldn't save your father. No wonder you couldn't—"

"Shut up! You don't know anything! He was *nothing* like you."

"You're right," said Silver. He pointed the gun at Hunter's head. "I do what needs to be done."

He pulled the trigger.

The gun exploded. Hunter saw the flash, but that was it.

Then Silver was yelling and the smell of gas was in the air.

Then Hunter felt fire. Somewhere distant, but a raging fireball, heading this way.

The kids must have started a fire as they fled, somewhere farther down the line.

Maybe it was the blood loss, but Hunter was having a hard time figuring out what was going on.

Especially when Michael stepped out of the darkness and slammed Silver into the concrete wall with enough force to break the stones. Rock crumbled around him. Silver crumpled to the ground.

Hunter felt himself lifted by the shoulders. He opened his eyes but didn't remember closing them.

Gabriel was dragging him.

But he was looking at his brothers. "We need to do something! I can feel it building!"

Fire. He could feel *fire* building. Hunter could feel it, too, a swelling rage coming fast.

"Did they . . ." started Hunter. He had to wet his lips and really think to string a sentence together. "Did the kids make it out?"

"Yeah. They got out." Gabriel didn't sound entirely happy about that.

Hunter could feel the heat, the rage in the air around him.

Then he felt the fire, true fire, barreling through the tunnel.

His mind was trying to panic, but he could barely lift his

head. At least it let him string a sentence together. "Gabriel! We need to stop it!"

Too late. Hunter felt the fire wash over him. Heat seared his lungs and scorched his cheeks, blinding him for an instant.

But then he felt Gabriel's power in his element. His friend was trying to harness the energy, to keep it from spreading.

There was too much. He couldn't handle it all. This fire wanted to explode from these tunnels, and Gabriel couldn't hold on to it.

But then another source of power joined Gabriel's. Nick, trying to choke oxygen from the fire.

Not enough.

Chris, pulling power from the steam in the pipes, the trickles of water on the walls.

Not enough.

The fire was weakening, slowing, but not enough.

Rubble scraped against pavement, and it took Hunter too long to realize what that meant. Silver was getting to his feet.

And he was pulling power, lots of power, from the air around them. Hunter felt it building and knew Silver could kill the Merricks, right here in these tunnels, using their own power.

So he did what he'd been told never to do. He added his power to theirs.

And like a final link clicking into place, the five of them formed a perfect circle. Everything hesitated. The destructive power was right there, in Hunter's control, lighting up his vision like a power grid. Waiting for direction.

Hunter looked at Silver.

Then he shoved every ounce of power in his direction.

Hunter felt the force of energy leave his body and slam into Silver's.

And then he didn't feel anything at all.

CHAPTER 34

Hunter woke up in a hospital.

It took a moment to realize he should probably be grateful to be waking up at all.

An IV was in his hand, one of those oxygen cannulas strung around his face. Nothing really hurt, but at the same time, he had no desire to climb out of this bed, either. A dull, unsettling ache clung to his bones.

He tried to move his legs.

They worked. They hurt, but they worked.

He wasn't handcuffed to the bed, either, so that was a plus.

One of the Merrick twins was asleep in the recliner on the other side of the room. His T-shirt said *I Google Myself*.

Gabriel.

Hunter wasn't sure if that was a good thing or a bad thing.

"Hey," said Hunter.

Nothing. He tried again.

Finally, he grabbed the box of tissues on the small table beside the bed and threw it.

Gabriel sat up with a start. He grabbed the box and tossed it onto the window ledge. "Dude, you're lucky you're hurt or I'd be shoving this right up your—"

"Save it. What happened?"

"Oh Em Gee, Hunter, you are so *welcome*," Gabriel said in a lilting falsetto. "I had a *blast* saving your life."

He couldn't be too mad if he was cracking jokes.

Or maybe he was furious. Sometimes it was hard to tell with Gabriel.

"Maybe if you told me what happened, I could get around to the thanking you part."

Gabriel's face lost the mockery. "When we realized that the shopping center was a false lead, we had to make a decision: find you, or get out of the area before the school blew up." He shrugged, and mischief sparked in his eye. "So we flipped for it."

"Thank you for finding me."

"You should be thanking the coin."

Hunter didn't say anything for a long moment. Gabriel waited.

Then Hunter looked away. "I'm sorry I lied about the shopping center. I just—I didn't want anyone else to get hurt—"

"We knew you were lying."

Hunter blinked. "What?"

"We knew. How do you think we found you so fast?"

"And you still came after me?"

"I'm not sure anyone has ever told you how this whole *friendship* thing is supposed to work, but . . ." Gabriel stared at him, hard. "Yeah, you idiot. We came after you."

Hunter wasn't sure what to say to that.

So Gabriel kept talking. "It took some time to find you. And then we saw that dickhead pointing a gun at you. I tried the trick you mentioned, the one about stopping the spark before the gun could fire."

Hunter remembered the flash, the way the gun had exploded in Silver's hand. "So what happened?"

"Yeah, so I don't have enough control for all *that*, but I kinda like how it worked out anyway."

Now Hunter understood. He could read between the flippant answers. "Thank you."

"If I'd let you die, I couldn't have kicked your ass for going after Noah Dean."

Hunter propped himself up on his elbows. "Of everything, why are you still pissed about *that*?"

For the first time, Gabriel's expression showed true fury. "Because, jackass, you should have taken me *with you*."

Hunter dropped back on the pillow, wondering if he should punch Gabriel or hug him. "So that night you knocked me down the stairs—you weren't mad that I might have been screwing over your family. You were mad that I left you *behind*?"

"Hell, yes! Nicky never wants to do that stuff."

Hunter was touched. "I'm getting all misty."

"Fuck you." Then Gabriel's expression changed. "You look really different without all the piercings."

Hunter's hand flew to his face. They were all gone. "What happened?"

"You had an MRI." He glanced at the clock over the television. "Your mom will be back soon."

"She was here?"

"She's been sleeping here."

She'd been *sleeping* here? "How long have I been in the hospital?"

"Two days."

"What happened to Silver?" Hunter paused, remembering the feeling of the power driving into his enemy. "Did he die?"

Gabriel looked like he was bracing himself for Hunter's reaction. He glanced at the doorway before pulling his chair closer. "Arrested."

Hunter shoved himself upright again. "He's still alive?"

"Oh, your blast of power did a lot of damage, but not enough to kill him. We dragged him out. We needed someone to take the fall for all of it—kidnapping kids and hiding them under the school, including you. It's the only thing that covered everything: your disappearance, the shoot-out at our house—"

Hunter was incredulous. "Where do you guys fit into that?"

"Out of town. Weekend college visit for Nick. Missed the whole thing."

Hunter opened his mouth. Closed it. "Wow."

"It's helpful that Layne's dad is smoothing things over with the cops. Mike keeps saying that guy is brilliant with spin."

"What about the kids?"

"They said what we told them to say. You think they wanted to take the fall?"

"Are they all safe?"

Gabriel lifted one shoulder. "Confused." He paused. "There's no sign of Calla. We're trying to figure out exactly who's involved so we can try to keep them out of trouble."

"More Guides will come."

Gabriel nodded. "I know."

Then they fell into silence for the longest time, until Gabriel pulled his chair even closer and rested his arms on the bed rail. "How did that guy know where to find you?"

Hunter looked away from him, at the speckled tile of the hospital ceiling. "Just lucky, I guess."

Gabriel hit him on the top of his head. Hunter swung around to glare at him.

"Try again," Gabriel said.

Hunter was so sick of lying. He sighed. "I turned on her phone."

"Why? Why did you do that?"

"I didn't realize he'd get there so fast."

Gabriel waited, but Hunter didn't say anything else.

"That doesn't answer the *why*," Gabriel finally said.

"I didn't want anyone else to get hurt. I was going to kill him. And if I couldn't do it, I was going to blow up the school with him in it."

"Jesus, I could shake the crap out of you." Gabriel shoved him in the shoulder. "When you're going to do awesome stuff, *let me in on it.*"

Hunter had to look at the speckled ceiling again. "I didn't expect to survive it."

Gabriel's voice was quiet, no mockery at all now. "Why?"

Hunter was suddenly so tired. "Go away, Gabriel."

"No. *Why would you do that?*"

Hunter squeezed his eyes shut. His lashes felt wet, and he pressed his fingertips against his eyes. "Because Kate sacrificed herself for me. She was the only person who's ever trusted me."

"Dude. Hunter. No. She wasn't. She was just the only person you've ever trusted *back.*"

Hunter opened his eyes. Gabriel was right. He should have trusted the Merricks long before this.

He had a lot to make up for.

"I'm sorry I was a shitty friend," he said.

"I'm not sure 'shitty' covers it."

"I can't believe I almost killed you two weeks ago."

Gabriel rolled his eyes. "I can. You're kind of a moron."

A dark-haired nurse knocked at the door and didn't wait for a response before entering. She had a tray of food. "I'm glad to see you're awake," she said brightly. Her voice carried a touch of an accent. "Feeling hungry?"

"Not really."

"Leave it," said Gabriel. "I'm always hungry."

She set the tray on the table and plugged a stethoscope into her ears. "May I get your vital signs?"

Hunter held out his arm for the blood pressure cuff.

She tightened the Velcro, then traced a finger lightly over the tattoo above his elbow. "Ah," she said. "My favorite proverb."

"It was my dad's, too," Hunter said.

"Did he serve in Afghanistan?"

"Yes. Just six months."

"Wait a minute," said Gabriel. "Someone knows what the secret tattoo says?"

Hunter gave him a look. "It's not a secret. It's on my *arm.*"

"Enough with the suspense already. What does it say?"

"Nothing important," said Hunter.

The nurse smiled and released the pressure in the cuff. "It

says, *The first day you meet, you are friends. The next day, you are brothers.*"

Gabriel lost the smile.

Then he clapped Hunter on the shoulder.

Hunter frowned at him. "What was that for?"

"Brotherhood," he said. "Welcome to the family."

CHAPTER 35

Hunter sat in the grass and closed his eyes. The sun was warmer here, the air more crisp, as if Kate's body drew power to this spot even after her death. He could swear he smelled cinnamon and apples.

He touched his fingers to the grass and opened his eyes.

"I wish I could stare at you right now," he said.

Air swirled through the small clearing, lifting dead leaves and rustling the foliage.

He'd thought coming here would give him some kind of closure. But instead he missed her more intently. Every brush of air, every scent of earth, every sound of water hitting the distant beach reminded him of their last night together.

"I'm going to stay with the Merricks for a while," he said. "I'm still working some things out with my mom. I mean—Michael was right. She was wrong. But I was, too."

This felt stupid, talking to grass.

But he swallowed and found he couldn't stop. "I was wrong about my dad, too. I think—I think he would have liked you."

His voice broke.

"I'm sorry," he said. "I'm sorry."

The breeze kicked up fiercely, lifting his hair and drying the tears that swelled in his eyes. Then the air went calm, soothing against his skin.

And he felt her in that, too.

"I couldn't kill him for you," he said quietly, touching his fingers to the grass. "I failed again."

A hand rested on his shoulder. "You didn't fail," said Michael.

Hunter didn't say anything to that.

"You kept Silver from killing those kids."

"I didn't kill him. I should have killed him."

"Vengeance isn't a solution, Hunter. I think your dad knew that. And I think you know it, too."

He was right. Hunter wasn't ready to let go of the vengeance yet, but he was right.

Michael hesitated. "My dad used to say something that made me nuts. 'If you can't fix what went wrong—' "

"Then fix what you can make right." Hunter looked up at him. "My dad used to say that, too."

"Good advice."

Hunter looked back at the ground. The air felt peaceful.

"Thanks," he said to Michael. "For bringing me here."

"You ready to go? Or do you want more time?"

Hunter touched the grass one last time. Then he stood. "I'm ready. Let's go home."

BEYOND
THE
STORY

Spirit Playlist

"Some Nights" by fun

Anytime I write a book, there's a song that kind of kicks it off for me and gets me in the mood for that character. With *Spirit*, I didn't have a song that was talking to me. I'd listen to old music, write a chapter, scratch my head and write a little more, but I just wasn't feeling it. I asked for lots of song suggestions on Twitter, and while there were tons of great suggestions (many of which made it into this playlist), none of them really *fit* Hunter. Then I heard *Some Nights* by fun, and I knew I had Hunter's theme song. Every word fits.

"Home" by Philip Phillips

So this was the first year I didn't watch *American Idol*. (Brigid, meet deadline.) I didn't know about Philip Phillips until everyone else already did. But the instant I heard this song, I knew it would be part of the playlist for *Spirit*. I had a discussion with Alicia (my amazing editor), during which I was discussing some plot choices, and I said, "This book isn't about Hunter finding romance. It's about Hunter finding *himself*." Hunter just needed a little guidance to get there, and this song really reminds me of his relationship with Michael.

"50 Ways to Say Goodbye" by Train

This song is catchy and clever and dark and hilarious, and for some reason, it reminds me of Hunter's relationship with Kate.

"Blow Me (One Last Kiss)" by Pink

Heh. I love this song. Pink is a total badass. Or as Kristin Feliz would say, a BAMF. Totally makes me think of Kate.

"The Fighter" by Gym Class Heroes, featuring Ryan Tedder

This is totally the perfect song for gearing yourself up for something difficult. Fits the book and totally fits my life. Love it.

"Cupid Shuffle" by Cupid

This song has nothing to do with the book. But for some reason, I downloaded it, and I couldn't stop listening to it while writing *Spirit*. Look, they're not all going to be cool songs, okay? (But come on. You want to do the dance now, don't you? *Down down, do your dance . . .*)

"Give Your Heart a Break" by Demi Lovato

I just loved this song the first time I heard it. It's so unusual to hear a song sung by a woman promising not to hurt a *guy*. It's a ballad (sort of), and I loved the turnabout. Perfectly fit Hunter and Kate's story.

"Don't You Worry Child" by Swedish House Mafia

I didn't hear this song until *Spirit* was in edits, but I found myself with a lot of necessary revisions, and this song totally fit the mood. Fast, driving beat, and absolutely perfect lyrics for Hunter.

"Shake It Out" by Florence + the Machine

Usually I listen to songs by Florence + the Machine and I have no idea what they're about. I just listen and like them. This song is no different, but the song moves me and made me think about Kate differently, letting me soften her edges. So in that way, I'd say this is Kate's song.

"My Oh My" by Tristan Prettyman

Oh, this song has Kate and Hunter written all over it. Kate knows who she is and what she wants, and then she meets Hunter, and ends up questioning everything she thought she knew. (And Tristan Prettyman has an awesome voice!)

Read on for a bonus novella in the Elemental series, *Breathless*.

CHAPTER 1

Nick Merrick sat on his bed and ran his thumb along the edge of the sealed envelope.

He didn't want to open it.

He probably didn't need to. It was thin, and thin letters from universities typically meant one thing: rejection.

It wasn't his first-choice school anyway. He'd applied at University of Maryland because they had a solid physics program and it was an in-state school. If they rejected him, he didn't really care.

Much.

He'd thought applying early at a few local schools would be a safe bet, just to get himself into the rhythm of it, seeing what kind of feedback he'd get.

Apparently it meant he'd get used to rejection right off the bat.

The worst part was the twinge of guilt in his stomach.

Not because he might *have to* go out of state.

The guilt was because he *wanted* to. Sort of.

A new town would mean anonymity. No one would know about his powers.

No one would know him as Gabriel Merrick's twin brother, half of a unit.

A new town meant he could just be Nick.

Whatever that meant. Sometimes he worried that he'd get his wish, that he'd end up in some strange town, surrounded by new people, and he'd realize that there was nothing there, that his entire being was based on his brothers' expectations of him.

Well, it wasn't like he didn't have options. A local school would have meant he could still stay home and help Michael with the business. If he couldn't go to Maryland, he could go to the community college down the road. Nothing wrong with that.

Except . . . he didn't *want* to go to the community college.

The colored balls in the Galileo thermometer on his desk started to shift, and Nick glanced up. He was changing the temperature. His blinds rattled against the window frame, too, as a gusty breeze tore through his room.

This was stupid. He should just open the envelope.

If only his powers gave him X-ray vision.

Not like he really needed it. He could imagine how the letter would begin.

Dear Nicholas, We regret to inform you that you're a selfish bastard—

Yeah, right. Nick swore and shoved the letter between two textbooks on the desk. He could read it later.

Michael had asked him to reconcile a stack of invoices anyway. Better to let numbers steal his attention, especially since his oldest brother would be pissed if he got home and found a stack of paperwork still waiting for him.

The kitchen was empty, but he'd passed his youngest brother in the living room, along with his girlfriend. Chris and Becca were watching a movie, but from the glimpse Nick had gotten, there wasn't a whole lot of *watching* going on. Not like Nick needed a glimpse: the air was more than happy to whisper about their activities.

Gabriel was out, doing something with Layne, and Michael would be on a job for another hour, at least.

Quiet.

Nick tore into a foil package of Pop-Tarts and fired up the

laptop. With a toaster pastry between his teeth, he began to sort through the pile of carbon credit card slips, invoices, and canceled checks.

Michael was great about documenting what he was doing and how much it cost.

He wasn't so great about making sure he was actually *paid* for it.

Nick had been doing most of the bookkeeping since he was thirteen. Now he could do it in his sleep.

His brain kept drifting to that letter, sandwiched between those textbooks on his desk.

At least he'd been the one to get the mail today, so no one else knew. God, that would have been a disaster. Hell, Gabriel probably would have put him in a headlock until he tore the envelope open.

Aw. Poor Nicky. They don't want you.

Gabriel wouldn't be upset. He didn't want his twin to go.

That was another big part of the guilt.

He caught himself entering line items twice, and he pulled his hands off the keys to rub at his eyes. School was closed this week, thanks to the recent fire in the library, but he should probably be using the extra time to study. There was no money for college, so grades were everything right now.

His cell phone buzzed against the table, making him jump. The air had turned sharp and cold while he'd been going through these invoices, and he tried to make himself relax, knowing the air would do the same if he could mentally get himself to a better place.

He ran a thumb along the screen to wake it. A text message.

Quinn. His girlfriend.

Sort of.

Really, his relationship with Quinn was just one more thing that belonged on a list of all that made him feel insecure, uncertain, and guilty.

Any way you can pick me up at the Y?

Nick glanced at the clock. Gabriel had the car and Michael had the truck. Michael would be home first, but not for another twenty minutes. He typed back quickly.

Not for a while. You OK?

Fought with Mom again.

Nick winced. He texted back.

I can get you. 30 mins OK?

Sure. I'll be in studio.

The *studio* was really just a room at the back of the Y, with half a mirrored wall and a barre bolted awkwardly into the patches of drywall. But Quinn's parents wouldn't pay for dance lessons, and Quinn had been kicked off the school dance team.

Unlike Nick, she knew exactly who, what, and where she wanted to be.

She just couldn't get there.

He hadn't met her parents yet, but apparently her mother had been put on this earth with the sole purpose of torturing Quinn, and her dad had nothing better to do than stare at the television—when he wasn't running his mouth about how amazing Quinn's older brother was. Quinn had a younger brother, too. He stayed out of the line of fire by hiding behind headphones and video game controllers.

Tensions had been running high in Quinn's house before a fire had burned the place down—part of a string of arson attacks started by another Elemental in town. But now her family was living in temporary housing, a cramped three-bedroom condo closer to Annapolis.

And Nick thought he had problems.

He didn't hear the front door open, but the air told him when Michael was home.

It also told him that Chris and Becca were struggling to right themselves in the living room.

Nick smiled and entered the last invoice into the computer, then set aside the three where payments were missing.

Michael looked beat when he walked into the kitchen, and Nick was glad he'd gotten the paperwork done.

His brother grabbed a bottle of water from the refrigerator and dropped into a chair. "Thanks for taking care of that."

Nick always did, but he shrugged. "It's nothing."

"You think you could help me with a job tomorrow, since school is out?"

Nick had been planning to spend the day doing more college applications, tweaking entrance essays, and taking a few more SAT practice tests.

But Michael looked exhausted, and Nick could put that stuff off for a few hours. "Sure," he said. Then he paused, thinking of Quinn. "You think you could let me borrow the truck for an hour?"

Michael had to be tired, because he took another drink of water, then tossed the keys on the table.

Nick's eyebrows went up.

Michael shrugged, then shoved out of the chair, heading for the doorway. "I know you won't do anything irresponsible."

Nick never did.

And sometimes he wondered if that was part of the problem.

Quinn Briscoe stretched her left leg against the barre in the empty room, then folded her upper body as low as she could. She didn't do ballet, not really, but she'd taken enough classes as a kid that she always started and finished with a classical warm-up—just because that was the most thorough routine she knew, and it hadn't let her down yet.

Her thighs were screaming, and she told them to go to hell.

Really, she wished she'd worn sweatpants instead of these stretchy booty shorts. Then she wouldn't have to look at how massive her legs were.

Besides, it was probably cold outside.

The shorts hadn't been her choice. They were part of the cheerleading uniform at Old Mill, and she'd had her first practice this afternoon. Apparently athletes didn't get the week off from school, just a modified schedule.

For five minutes, Quinn had allowed herself to be excited about the cheer squad. It wasn't her type of thing, not really, but she'd been kicked off the dance team for being mouthy—and too fat, she was sure, given the teacher's comments about *body type*—and cheerleading seemed like the next best thing.

Then Taylor Morrisey, squad captain, started calling her "Crisco," a mockery of her last name.

The other girls had started doing the same.

Quinn had flipped off Taylor and stormed out of there—only to go home to find out that Jake, her older brother, was home from college for a few days.

That wasn't the problem. Quinn accepted his existence, just like she did the rest of her family.

But her mother had told Jake he could sleep in Quinn's bed, and Quinn could make do on the floor.

And instead of refusing out of chivalry or kindness or whatever boys were *supposed* to do, Jake had smirked at her and said, "Yeah, isn't that where dogs usually sleep?"

Quinn had lost it. Moreover, her mom had taken Jake's side. Of course perfect, scholarship-winning, Duke-basketball-playing Jake couldn't sleep on the couch.

Of course their argument had devolved into a screaming match.

Of course Quinn had walked out. Again.

And she was getting sick of crashing at Becca's, watching her best friend's perfect relationship with her mom and her perfect relationship with Chris Merrick.

Quinn switched legs and stretched farther. R&B music pulsed into her head through the earbuds connected to her iPod, completely at odds with the classical routine, but she thrived on the rage in the lyrics.

The music caught her, and she spun off the barre, flying across the floor in a complicated routine of leaps and turns. Each step let her spring higher, until it felt like the air became a part of the dance and carried her along.

Then the song ended, and she was staring at herself in the smudgy mirror, her chest rising and falling from the exertion.

God, her thighs looked massive.

She scowled and turned away so she wouldn't have to look at herself.

Only to find Nick Merrick standing in the doorway.

Quinn stopped short and yanked the earbuds free, feeling heat crawl up her neck. She wasn't shy about boys, but her rage-inspired dancing felt like it should be private.

No, indulging her own insecurities felt like it should be private.

"How long have you been there?" she demanded.

"A minute or so," he said equably. "I wasn't exactly timing myself."

Nick was quite possibly the only guy she'd ever met who seemed completely unaffected by her attitude.

Years of putting up with his twin probably had something to do with it.

But it was enough to make her want to be nicer. She coiled up the headphones in her palm and turned for her bag. "Sorry. You took me by surprise."

"You seemed into it. I didn't want to interrupt." He paused, then came closer. "I was wishing I could hear the music."

Quinn straightened and found him right in front of her. She sucked in her stomach and shook her ponytail back over her shoulder.

Nick and his twin brother were two of the hottest guys in school, and at first she'd been sure Nick was only interested because she had a bit of a reputation for being easy—not that she did anything to erase that viewpoint. She liked boys, and she knew how to get their attention, heavy thighs and all.

But Nick had surprised her by being a gentleman. They'd kissed, a few times—and he had one hell of a mouth—but they hadn't done much more than that. And even at his house, in his room, where there wasn't anyone to stop him from doing *anything,* Nick proved to be a pretty good sounding board for her problems instead of trying to shut her up and get in her pants.

Then again, Nick's twin brother made no secrets of how he felt about her. She hated Gabriel Merrick almost as much as she hated Jake. Maybe Nick wasn't doing anything with her because he figured he could do better.

Even Gabriel had mocked her choice to be a cheerleader.

He'd said she belonged on the bottom of the pyramid with the *sturdy girls*.

"Hey. *Hey*." Nick's hands closed over hers, and she realized she was kneeling, fighting with the zipper on her bag, and she'd already started a tear in the nylon stitching.

His blue eyes were close, intent on her face. She had to be flushed; it felt like it was a thousand degrees in here.

"What happened?" he said carefully.

She squished her eyes shut and thought about her day. Jake. Her mom. Cheerleading.

She opened her eyes and caught her body in the edge of the mirror, the way the shorts were cutting into her stomach, creating a little roll there.

Crisco.

She wanted to punch the glass, to watch cracks form a disjointed spiderweb across her reflection. Her hand formed a fist.

But she didn't swing it. Something worse happened.

She started crying.

CHAPTER 2

Nick knew what was expected when girls started crying: a hug, a minute or two of listening, a minute or two to offer some soothing words, and a wry smile followed by the suggestion that they find some chocolate. Or ice cream. Or both.

Much like the accounting, he could do it in his sleep.

But Quinn didn't even let him get to the hug. She jerked her hands away from him and swiped the dampness from her eyes, then stood. "God. Next time I start to do that, smack me or something."

"Sure. Sounds perfectly socially acceptable." He paused. "You okay?"

She pulled her ponytail free and started to retie it. "I hate when they make me do that."

"Who?"

"Everyone."

"I was shooting for a more specific list of people."

She turned away from him. "I don't think the cheerleading thing is going to work out."

"Did something happen?"

"Your brother was right."

Sometimes she jumped between topics until Nick couldn't keep track of what she was talking about. It probably made most people nuts, but it was one of the things he liked best about her—nothing was expected. "Which brother?"

She gave him a look. "Gabriel. I am too fat to be a cheer-leader."

Sometimes his twin could be a real ass. "Quinn—you're not fat."

"You're right. I'm sure they were calling me Crisco because I make great cookies."

Damn. He let out a breath. "But you're *not*—"

"I really don't want to talk about this."

"You want to talk about what happened with your mom?"

"Hell, no." She jammed the iPod into the side pocket of her bag.

When she straightened, he caught her waist and tossed her into the air. She gasped, but he caught her and held her up, his hands braced on her rib cage. "I couldn't do this with a fat girl."

And okay, he probably could. Landscaping wasn't light work, and he was used to slinging bags of pea gravel and limestone. Quinn was no feather, but his biceps weren't screaming at him, either.

Quinn glared down at him. "Put me down before you lose your hands in the rolls."

"Oh, stop it. You're not fat. You're solid." She was, too. Her calves sported clear definition, and he could feel the strength in her abdominal muscles.

"That's what every girl wants to hear, Nick. That she's *solid*." She wiggled. "Put me down."

He lifted her higher, until his arms were straight. "I will when you quit with the pity party."

"Or when I knee you in the face."

A knock sounded at the door frame. "You guys mind if I work in here?"

Nick glanced over. A young man stood there, in knee-length cutoff sweatpants and a red T-shirt. He looked vaguely familiar, like maybe Nick had seen him around school or something. Brown eyes, dark, unkempt hair that was just this side of too long on top, caramel skin. An easy smile with a shadow of *un-*

ease behind it. Then again, maybe that was just the scar on his upper lip, the drawn skin making the smile a little crooked and dark at the same time.

"Come on in," said Quinn. "We were just goofing off."

Oh. Right. Quinn.

Nick set her down.

Quinn obviously knew the guy, because she gave him a one-armed hug. "I haven't seen you around here lately."

He shrugged. "Work, school, dance. The holy trinity. You know." Then his eyes flicked to Nick. "New partner?"

"Not the way you mean," Quinn said. "He's not a dancer. Adam, this is Nick."

Adam. The name fit him like a chord strummed on a guitar.

Nick couldn't stop staring at him.

But Adam didn't seem to notice. He just ducked his head through the shoulder strap and dropped his bag by the mirror. It should have been a throwaway motion, but instead there was a lyrical quality to his movement, like music flowed in his head. "I thought you might have been working on lifts," he said.

"Nah," said Nick. "Just a reality check."

Quinn elbowed him in the ribs. "What are you working on?"

Adam pulled an iPod and a little player with speakers out of his bag. "An audition piece. There's an opening at the dance school downtown."

Quinn clapped. "Can we watch?"

Adam glanced at Nick. "I don't want to bore your friend."

"I wouldn't be bored," Nick said quickly. Then he checked himself. What was with the sudden enthusiasm? He shrugged. "I watch Quinn all the time."

A slow smile found Adam's mouth. "Sure, then. Find a place to sit."

Nick sat against the wall at the back of the studio, and Quinn sat beside him, a good six inches of space between them. She pulled her sweatshirt into her lap and ripped the cap off a bottle of water. Nick had initially expected her to be one of those clingy girls who wanted to drape on his shoulder—but she never did.

Another reason he liked her.

Adam hit a button on the iPod, and music swelled through the small studio. Nick knew the song, one of those new lyrical R&B collaborations. The rhythm pulsed through his body and caught his heartbeat, the way music always did. It probably had something to do with the way sound waves traveled through the air—it always felt like he could hear with his whole body.

But the air liked Adam, too, liked the way he leaped across the floor and defied gravity, each movement timed perfectly with the beat.

Nick had never wanted to be a dancer, but right now, he felt a flash of envy. And admiration. And—and something—

"What do you think?" Quinn whispered.

"He's good. Great. The dance. It's great." God, what was *wrong* with him? He rubbed at the back of his neck and pretended to stare at the floor. "It's fine."

"He's super talented. He's been trying to get in that school for two years, but he needs a scholarship."

Nick heard longing in her voice and turned to look at her. "Do you wish you could go there?"

She kept her eyes on Adam and shrugged one shoulder. "I could never get in."

"Have you tried?"

Quinn cut angry eyes his way. "I'd need a scholarship, too, Nick, and they're not exactly writing checks to everyone who walks through the door."

He'd grown up countering his brothers' anger—and Quinn had nothing on that. He didn't look away. *"Have you tried?"*

She sat there glaring at him, and Nick just looked back.

The music cut off suddenly, and they both jerked to attention.

Adam was fiddling with the music player. "It's driving me crazy," he said, almost to himself. "It's missing something, but I can't figure out what."

"A partner," said Nick without thinking.

Adam's hands went still on the iPod, and he looked over.

Nick shrugged a little, wondering at what point his brain had decided to disengage from his mouth. "Sorry. Just thinking out loud."

Adam smiled again, that slow smile that pulled a little crooked because of the scar. His dark eyes shined in the overhead lights, and his voice was just a touch suggestive. "You volunteering?"

The breath rushed out of Nick's chest.

Shit. Now he was blushing.

If Gabriel were here, there would be *no end* to the mockery.

Well, that shut it down, whatever it was. Flustered, Nick shoved Quinn in the shoulder. "No," he growled. "Quinn is."

"What?" said Quinn, sounding like she wondered when Nick had lost his mind. "I'm not good enough to dance with him."

"Sure you are," said Adam. He walked across the studio and stuck out a hand to Quinn.

But his eyes were on Nick. Nick wasn't even looking at him, but he could *feel* it.

He just wasn't entirely sure how he felt *about* it.

Nick nodded at the floor, then looked at Quinn. "Stop doubting yourself. Give it a try."

She let Adam pull her to her feet, and Nick was glad they were moving away. Adam's presence left him doubly off balance somehow, like trying to walk a narrow beam during an earthquake.

Adam and Quinn were talking now, going through the choreography or the music or whatever. Nick had no idea. His brain could barely process the conversation.

No, his thoughts kept replaying the moment two minutes ago.

You volunteering?

He wasn't offended. He wasn't shocked. He was—

Nick shut that thought down before it could finish. His life was already complicated enough. He and his brothers were marked for death. They were ostracized by the Elemental community. Nick knew exactly what was expected of him: good grades, hard work, and the occasional girlfriend. He knew how to handle all three, could do it blindfolded.

But that stray thought had weaseled its way into the back of his head, lodging there so firmly that he couldn't ignore it.

For the tiniest fraction of a second, when Adam had looked down at him, asking about volunteering, Nick had wondered what would have happened if he'd said *yes.*

Quinn threw her body into the music, trying to match Adam's complicated choreography. He was a couple years older, but she'd known him since she was a kid, when their parents dumped them in the same ballet and tap combo class. She'd recognized his talent even then, the boy in scuffed dance shoes and frayed sweatpants who moved like a slave to the rhythm. They lived at opposite ends of the same neighborhood, so they'd gone to different elementary and middle schools—but when she was a freshman in high school, they'd caught up to each other. He'd been a junior, lean and agile and always smiling. With his dark eyes and dark hair—not to mention his talent—she'd crushed on him for *weeks,* following him around like a puppy dog.

He'd been totally sweet about it—until the day she cranked up her nerve and declared her feelings for him.

He'd kissed her on the forehead and told her he wasn't into girls. Then, presumably to soften the blow, he'd confessed that he was personally crushing on the football team's starting center.

Unfortunately, the wrong guys had overheard him. Quinn never knew who did it, but someone had punched Adam in the back of his head when he was standing at his locker. Perfectly timed, Adam's head had snapped forward, right into the metal plate that stuck out to hold a combination lock.

She'd heard that it had taken fourteen stitches to close the gash on his lip.

She hadn't heard it from Adam—he never came back to school. She'd tried to reach out on Facebook, but his Wall was full of epithets.

And the next day, his account was deleted altogether.

Quinn kind of lost track of him until last year, when he'd shown up at the Y, saying his basement apartment was just too confining. He'd gotten his GED instead of returning to high school, and now, at nineteen, he was working two jobs while taking here-and-there classes at the local community college.

But he could still dance like no one she'd ever seen.

Quinn missed a cue and almost ended up with her face planted in the wood floor. Adam caught her, and she struggled to right herself.

"See?" she snapped. "I can't keep up with you."

"No," he said, putting a hand on her waist to set her straight. "I actually think your friend was right. It was missing a partner."

"Do you know anyone who can do it with you?"

Adam gave her half a smile. "I thought *you* were."

Her eyes flared. "No! This is your audition piece. I'm sure you know someone—"

"I do know someone. I'm looking at her."

"Oh, I get it, you think having someone do a face plant on stage will make you look better?"

Now he grinned. He was insanely adorable and she was instantly reminded of why she'd had a crush on him in the first place. "Afraid?"

"I—just—you—"

"Yes," Nick called from behind her. "She is."

Quinn scowled. "I'd mess it up for you."

"I've auditioned three times and gotten nowhere. I don't think you could *mess it up* for me." He paused, and his eyes went serious. "There's a different energy to it now. Can't you feel it?"

Actually, she could. Despite nearly smashing her face in, up to that point, the music had seemed to carry her, like her movement and the song had combined to form something more potent than just a hastily thrown-together dance in a dusty backroom studio at the Y.

She bit the inside of her cheek, trying not to imagine how massive and ungainly she looked next to Adam. "When is your audition?"

"Next month. Four weeks."

"Four weeks?" she exclaimed. "Are you *kidding* me?"

"Come on, that's nothing."

"Yes, but—but—"

"Don't let her out of it," Nick said.

Quinn swung her head around. "Maybe we can cut the commentary?"

Nick met her eyes from across the room, and held them. "Sure, if you say yes."

"But I don't—"

"Jesus, Quinn," Nick snapped. "What else do you have to do?"

And that was one of the things she liked about Nick. He put up with her whining until she was almost sick of herself, and then he called her on her bullshit.

At least it would get her out of the house and away from her mother. And Jake.

And away from those idiot cheerleaders.

And maybe, somewhere deep down inside, she really wanted to see if she could do this.

She looked back at Adam. "All right. Let's work it out."

They sketched out a routine, modifying his original piece to incorporate a partner, putting together some moves that she could work on alone.

The whole time, Nick sat without complaint, even when she asked if he needed to go. He'd shrugged and said he was enjoying the music. She'd had other guys come to the studio before, but they usually sighed and started shuffling around after a half hour.

Nick watched. It was both flattering and unnerving.

They danced until her muscles ached and the director was walking around, turning off lights and threatening to lock them inside.

Then they were walking outside, stepping into the cold night air, their breath just starting to fog.

Yes, she was definitely regretting the little booty shorts. Quinn shivered.

Nick had keys in his hand, and he hit the clicker. The lights on his brother's red work truck flashed. "Get in," he said. "I'll put the heat on."

Oh, wow. She had to grab the handle over the door to even get into this thing.

Adam was standing there, watching her.

No. He was watching *Nick*. Nick, who was pointedly not looking back at him.

"So, tomorrow morning?" said Adam.

"Sure," she said, even though he wasn't even looking at her. "Nine?"

"You coming, too?" he said to Nick.

Nick shrugged and looked at the sky. "Can't. I told my brother I'd help with a job."

"So can I get your number then?"

Nick sucked in a breath, looking thrown, like Adam had socked him in the stomach.

Quinn stifled a giggle at his reaction. If Nick Merrick was into guys, half the female population at Old Mill would be sobbing. "Adam, he's not gay."

For the first time all night, Adam lost the smile.

Nick ran a hand through his hair, looking completely unnerved. "Sorry, man—I just—"

"Nah." Adam shook it off, and a shadow of his smile reappeared. "It's cool. My bad." He gave Quinn a wave and said, "I'll see you tomorrow."

Nick was quiet when they headed out on the road.

"Sorry," she said, trying to warm her hands by the vents. The truck cab was freezing, and the engine didn't seem to want to blow warm air. "He didn't mean anything by it."

Nick's voice was somewhat hollow. "It's okay."

"He's not usually that bold. I can't believe he asked for your number."

Nick didn't say anything. Quinn wondered if he really *was* pissed.

That made her frown. "It's not catching, you know," she said.

He glanced over, and his voice was mild. "Quinn, I'm not upset about it."

She chewed on that for a minute and wondered whether to push or to leave it.

Before she could make a decision, Nick reached out and touched her cheek. "I think you sell yourself short. You're an amazing dancer."

His hand was warm, and she leaned into the contact. "Thanks heaps, but you don't know what you're talking about."

He laughed. "I guess. But I couldn't see any great disparity between you and him."

"*Disparity*. God, sometimes it's a wonder you and Gabriel are twin brothers."

Nick sobered. "Why?"

"You're like a walking SAT prep book. I guarantee if you went home, Gabriel wouldn't even know the meaning of the word. On the outside, you're absolutely identical, but on the inside, it's like you're polar opposites."

He sighed and ran his hand through his hair again. "Trust me, I know exactly what you mean."

CHAPTER 3

Nick threw the truck into park in the lot in front of Quinn's condo building.

He made no move to kill the engine.

She made no move to get out.

In fact, she was staring out the windshield, clutching her sweatshirt to her chest again. The moonlight traced silver along the lines of her face, leaving her eyes in shadow. Her jaw was tight.

"Do you want me to drive you to Becca's instead?" he said.

She shook her head and glanced over. "Can I crash with you again?"

Nick kept his eyes on the steering wheel and didn't say anything. He'd let her spend the night *once*, after Gabriel had cut her self-esteem to shreds by making a bunch of cracks about her weight. Quinn had been so full of rage and self-hatred that Nick had been worried she'd go home and find a set of razor blades or something.

He'd never let a girl spend the night before.

He'd never wanted to.

He didn't want to now.

Besides, if Michael found her there, he'd make damn sure she left, and he'd probably make it as humiliating as possible, just to be sure Nick wouldn't try to sneak a girl in again.

But maybe sharing his bed with Quinn again was exactly what he *should* do, just to shake loose all the indecisions rattling around inside his head.

And she obviously didn't want to go home.

"Please?" she whispered.

Nick let a breath out through his teeth. His thoughts felt stuck on a spinning roulette wheel, bouncing along, never settling where he expected, leaving him half-hoping it would keep spinning—and half-hoping it would stop.

Quinn read too much into his hesitation. She crawled across the cab to climb into his lap, until she was pinned between him and the steering wheel. Her hands traced their way up his chest, and she whispered against his lips. "Need convincing?"

Maybe he did.

Nick kissed her, tasting her lips, teasing her mouth with his tongue. Her waist fit between his hands perfectly, and in the close confines of the truck cab, he was very aware of every motion of her body. She was warm and smelled like sugar cookies, and it was . . . pleasant.

It was always pleasant.

Not just with Quinn—with any girl. Not great, not electrifying, not earth-moving.

Pleasant.

When he was younger, he'd thought maybe it was a maturity thing. Gabriel had barely been thirteen when he started talking about boobs and porn and whatever else he ran on at the mouth about. And of course he'd shared everything with Nick.

Nick hadn't really cared. He'd *pretended* to care, because their parents were gone and he was so desperately terrified of losing anyone else, especially his twin, so he'd done everything he could to live up to his brothers' expectations of him. He'd gone along with it, thinking that hormones would catch up at some point, that one day he'd wake up imagining cheerleaders soaping up in the shower or something.

He never did.

His imagination was perfectly content to feed him other

ideas, however. Ideas that Nick shoved out of his head practically upon thinking them.

Ideas that would definitely drive a wedge between him and his brothers, if they knew.

So he kept dating girls, still hoping that one day he'd wake up with new ideas.

Sometimes he could get into it, could seek out bare skin with his hands and mouth, could let them half undress him and explore his body in the darkness. Like now, with everything cloaked in shadow and a tongue stroking his, a strong body pressing into him, fingers in his hair.

Nick made a small sound in his throat. Like this, he could pretend he was with—

Stop.

No, he couldn't. He couldn't pretend anything. He couldn't even let himself *think* it. He shoved those thoughts from his brain and told that roulette wheel to keep fucking spinning and settle somewhere else.

Quinn must have felt the change in his body, the sudden tension, because she drew back. The inside of the truck was stifling hot. "What's wrong?" she whispered.

Everything. "Nothing. It's just—nothing." He paused, trying to breathe. Him! Fighting for air! And words. He choked on half of them. "Just—you don't need to sleep with me if you want me to help you, Quinn."

She went still. "You think I'm trying to sleep with you so I can get a place to stay?"

He gave her a look. Her hand was still on the button to his jeans, for god's sake. "Aren't you?"

She shoved herself off him and grabbed her bag.

Nick caught her arm. "Hey," he said gently. "I'm sorry. I didn't mean— I'll help you because I'm your friend."

Friend. It was the wrong thing to say, and he knew it instantly. She was still poised to shove the truck door open, but she looked at him over her shoulder. Her eyes were so striking, even bluer than his were. "Why don't you want to sleep with me?"

He raised an eyebrow. "Right now? Because we're in a parking lot."

"No," she said quietly. "I mean, why don't you want to sleep with me *ever*?"

Nick drew back and let go of her arm. He gave her his easy smile. "Maybe I'm a gentleman."

Quinn didn't smile back. "I know I'm not as hot as the girls you usually date, Nick." She paused. "Are you just taking a break or something? Using me as a filler girlfriend so you have time to let the chafing heal?"

"Wow." He dragged the word into three syllables.

"Or is this like a favor for Becca? Did Chris tell you to give me a little attention—"

"Are we seriously having this conversation?"

"No. Forget it—no." Then she was out of the truck.

He was behind her in a heartbeat, trailing her up the steps. "Quinn. Stop. I don't—"

"Go away, Nick."

She was crying; the air told him that much. Crying because he hadn't tried to have sex with her in the cab of his brother's truck.

Irony was like a devil on his shoulder, thinking this was a grand ol' knee slapper.

He stopped her on the top landing. Her face was flushed and damp, her blond hair wild and full of moonlight. She looked like an angel of vengeance, ready to kick his ass.

"Let me go," she snapped.

"I know this isn't all about me," he said carefully.

That made fresh tears well, and she pressed fingers to her eyes. "You're right. It's about like fourteen different people. So why don't you go away and let me deal with it?"

"Quinn." He moved closer and spoke low. "Quinn. Please talk to me."

She swiped the tears free and looked up at him. "Why do you even give a crap, Nick?"

Because she was a hot mess, every emotion on her sleeve, and he admired that—no, he *envied* that. Because he could feel her intensity when she danced, and he craved that kind of passion in his life. Because she was trapped by circumstance, and so was he.

Because, until tonight, she'd never expected anything from him, and that was damn refreshing.

He studied her face, her eyes that had turned so furious. Every breath that came out of her lungs whispered to him about her tension, her fluttering heartbeat, her anger.

"No one *wants* me," she said fiercely.

"Quinn—that's not true."

She got right up close to him, putting her chest against his. "It's not? Do *you* want me, Nick?"

If it had been any other girl, or any other tone, he could have played along. He probably could have thrown her up against the wall and kissed her silly. But it felt like she was throwing all her cards on the table. Lying to Quinn now would be like the worst kind of cruelty.

It didn't matter anyway. She'd read his hesitation, or maybe she'd just read the look in his eyes. She turned away.

Shit.

"Quinn. Quinn, stop—"

She whirled. Her hand flew.

She didn't slap him. She *punched* him. Hard.

Before he could get it together, she was shoving her key into the door at the top of the steps and then slamming it in his face.

And Nick stood there staring at the wood, wishing he could call her back.

And what would he say? *It's not you. It's me.*

Yeah. Right.

But at least in this case it was true. It had nothing to do with not wanting Quinn.

And everything to do with not wanting *any* girl.

Quinn just wanted to go to her room, throw her bag down, and crawl into bed.

Unfortunately, Jake was in there.

And he was entertaining. The door was locked. Quinn could hear female giggling and smell pot.

In her *room*.

Tears bit at her eyes. It was almost enough to make her turn on her heel and go after Nick.

On the opposite side of the hallway, her parents' bedroom door clicked open. Her mother stood there in rumpled pajamas. She looked about as happy as Quinn felt, that is, not at all.

She'd also obviously been drinking. That scent, sickly sweet, was battling with the marijuana wafting under Quinn's door.

"Do you know what time it is?" her mother hissed.

"I don't know why you're whispering," Quinn said, sniffing back the tears. "Jake's obviously not sleeping."

"Well, at least he has the decency to be quiet about it."

"I'm standing in the hallway! You're the one who came out here to talk to me."

Her mother threw her hands up. "I'm not starting this again."

"Whatever." Quinn turned away. "I guess I'll just make up my bed on the couch." She tossed a glare over her shoulder. "You know he's smoking pot in there."

Her mother's lips pursed. "Your brother is home from college. I'm not an idiot, Quinn."

It wasn't worth getting her mom riled up when she was lit, but Quinn was already fired up from the argument in the stairway, and she just couldn't keep the rage confined in her chest. "You're the one allowing illegal activity in your home."

"Oh, and I'm sure you were out late working the soup kitchen? Maybe you could cut the attitude."

Her mother's voice was devolving into mockery—with a bite. Her voice always gained this cruel edge, as if, when drunk, her sole mission in life was to eliminate any shred of dignity Quinn might be able to cling to.

Quinn wished she had somewhere she could storm off to. At least their house had a basement and a backyard; this itty-bitty condo wasn't doing anyone any favors. "I wasn't breaking the law," she said.

"Oh, who knows what you're doing anymore, Quinn?"

"I was dancing!"

Her mother rolled her eyes, like that was *worse* than illegal activity.

"You won't let me take lessons," Quinn snapped. "You should be happy I'm going somewhere free."

"Why would I throw money at something like *that*? You've already gotten yourself kicked off the dance team at school. You mouth off to everyone. You're ungrateful and nasty and no one can stand you."

"Well, you're just a *bitch*."

Her mother's eyes took on a furious gleam, until Quinn wondered if she'd come after her. Sometimes she did. Quinn would hit back. Her father usually dragged them apart.

But her mother just pointed. Her voice was a hoarse yell. "Get out of this house."

"Where do you want me to go? I can't walk to Becca's now."

"Maybe you should have thought of that before you decided to act like such a spoiled little drama queen!"

Her mother was yelling full out, now. Those stupid tears were still biting at Quinn's eyes. She didn't know how the woman could do this every time, just say a few slurred words and cut Quinn to her knees. Effortlessly.

Then her bedroom door swung open and Jake came out. He was shirtless and barefoot, loose drawstring pants hanging from his hips.

He walked right between Quinn and their mother, ignoring the clear cord of tension connecting them. He grabbed a box of Ho Hos from the cabinet and then a bag of popcorn, too.

When he was walking back, he smacked Quinn on the ass. "I'd offer you some, little sis, but I know you're working on that."

Quinn grabbed the food and tore it out of his hands. "Fuck you, Jake!" she screamed, as the bag tore and popcorn went everywhere. "God, I *hate* you."

"Get out!" her mother screamed. "Get out of here!"

Quinn couldn't move fast enough. She slammed the door behind her so hard that the little old man on the second floor opened his front door to peer out curiously.

She didn't even spare him a glance, just swiped tears from her eyes and kept running.

She had her phone, a sweatshirt, and about ten dollars.

It was freezing outside.

God, she hated everyone.

With nowhere else to go, she ducked into the 7-Eleven at the end of the street, the one that shared a building with a rundown old liquor store. There was no one in the convenience store except the bored cashier, but the Pakistani guy must have been used to half-hysterical girls coming in late at night because he barely gave her a glance.

I'd offer you some, but I know you're working on that.

What an asshole.

But the worst part was, she couldn't stop thinking about those Ho Hos. How there was a box, right there on the shelf in front of her. How she just wanted to shove them all in her mouth and feel better.

Well, what else did she have to do?

Quinn took the box to the counter and paid. She'd eaten two before she made it out the door.

The chocolate, the filling, the sugar rush—Quinn felt better and worse immediately. Cold air caught the tears on her cheeks and set her face to stinging.

"Hey, baby. Time for a chocolate fix?"

Quinn paused before she could shove the third one into her mouth. Two guys sat straddling motorcycles in front of the bar. She didn't recognize them, but they weren't very old. Probably not high school, but not much beyond that. Dark clothes, heavy boots, cool gazes.

The one with dark hair and calculating eyes took a drink from an honest-to-god flask, then gave her a clear up-and-down. His gaze barely went north of her neck. "I like your shorts, cutie. Cold night, huh?"

She should be afraid. She knew she should. But it was so nice to have someone look at her with a shred of desire that she didn't care. It wasn't like anyone would give a crap if she disappeared anyway.

She licked the chocolate off her fingers. "I'm all right."

He laughed, low and masculine and genuinely amused. "I'll say."

She sauntered over to them and glanced at the flask. "Care to share?"

He seemed startled—but then he handed it over. She took a sip. The liquid burned her tongue and then her throat. She had no idea what it was, and she didn't care.

The other one, with lighter hair and brown eyes, leaned forward against the handlebars on his bike. Despite his rough appearance, his eyes were kind—and he was actually looking at *her*, not just her assets. "What are you doing out here?"

"Same thing you are," she said. "Just looking to have some fun."

The dark one laughed. "We can help you with that." He patted the seat behind him. "Want a ride?"

His voice promised something more than just a ride on the back of his motorcycle.

Reason smacked Quinn across the face, and she hesitated.

Then the light-haired one shook his head. "No way. If she comes along, she's riding with me."

And because his eyes were kinder, because Quinn had nowhere to go and no one to call, she swung her leg over the back of his motorcycle and scooched up real close to him. He didn't smell like liquor at all—and she would know—but instead some mixture of leather and sweat and a faint whiff of an intoxicating cologne.

She didn't even know his name, but she didn't care. He was warm, and she wrapped her arms around his chest.

He glanced over his shoulder. "You sure are friendly."

No. Lonely.

"You complaining?" she said.

"Not at all." He started the ignition on his bike and revved the engine. The vibration rolled through her body and she held on, thriving on the adrenaline.

They went to Sandy Point, driving around the barriers and down to the beach. Clear trespassing. They didn't care, and she sure didn't give a crap. She learned her driver's name was Matt, he was twenty, and just like her brother, he was home from college for a few days.

She didn't like thinking of Jake, or of Nick for that matter, so when they asked if she had a boyfriend, she said no and took another long drink from their flask. A fleece blanket appeared from a compartment on Matt's bike, and she lay back to look at the stars while her head spun from the liquor.

This was probably the stupidest thing she'd ever done.

But hey, she wasn't lonely now, and they weren't trying to get in her pants or anything. And what if they did want her for sex? At least someone wanted her for *something*.

Dancing with Adam, the warmth and security and self-confidence, all felt a bazillion miles away.

A new bottle appeared. She recognized the label and held a hand out.

"You have any salt?" she joked.

They chuckled. The tequila burned like swallowing fire, and every breath cooled her lips. The stars danced. She forgot her name and laughed at nothing, snuggling into Matt when he tried to wrestle the bottle out of her hands.

And finally, the stars and darkness overtook her, and she passed out there on the sand.

CHAPTER 4

Nick lay in bed and stared at the ceiling, wondering when sleep would get around to stealing his thoughts. It was close to midnight, and the house had been still and quiet when he came in. Everyone else had to be asleep.

He had a headache, probably from when Quinn had decked him.

Or maybe it was just from wrestling with his thoughts all evening.

He'd tried to text Quinn, but she'd ignored it.

Nick sighed and picked up the paperback on his bedside table—but then he read the same sentence sixteen times.

All his brain wanted to think about was Adam. The lines of his body, the strength in his dancing, the way the music swept through the room and seemed to be part of the movement.

So can I get your number?

Nick hit himself in the head with the spine of his novel and blew out a long breath. These thoughts couldn't go anywhere. Too complicated. Too dangerous. *Quinn*, he thought. *Think about Quinn.*

So he thought about Quinn.

Dancing with Adam.

The phone rang downstairs, and Nick jumped like he'd been caught doing something inappropriate.

The house phone only rang with business calls, but no one was calling about landscaping at midnight. Probably a wrong number. Nick swung his legs out of bed to go answer it before it woke up his brothers.

The phone was on its fourth ring by the time he made it into the darkened kitchen. Nick fumbled for the right button and answered out of habit: "Merrick Landscaping."

A bare hesitation on the other end of the line. "Is this Nick?"

He froze. He recognized the voice, and it sent his heart racing. "Yeah?"

"This is Adam. Quinn's friend. We met—"

"I know. Yeah. I mean—" He needed to get it together. His heart wouldn't stop pounding, and Nick couldn't figure out whether it was from panic or excitement. "I remember. How'd you get this number?"

"It was on the side of your truck." Another pause. "Look, I've never made a call quite like this one . . ."

Nick held his breath and wondered how he wanted that statement to end.

". . . but some guy named Matt just called me and said Quinn was passed out on the beach."

Wait. "What? Quinn's *where?*"

"Sandy Point. He said he picked her up outside a bar, and she—"

"Outside a bar?" Nick's thoughts took a nosedive. He had to fight to keep his voice down. God, he should have snuck her in the house. "Is she okay? Who's this Matt guy?"

"I don't know. He said she's okay, just drunk, and he didn't want to try to put her on his motorcycle, but he didn't want to leave her alone, and there was another guy yelling in the background—"

"His *motorcycle?*" What the hell had Quinn gotten herself involved in?

"I don't know." Adam's voice was tense with worry. He paused. "I don't have a car."

Oh. So that's why he'd called.

"I'll go get her," Nick said. "Thanks for letting me know."

Another hesitation. "If she needs a place to crash, you can bring her here."

Guilt was jabbing Nick with a pitchfork. He should have brought her *here*. But Adam's voice implied that he was no stranger to Quinn's problems at home, either. "Your folks won't mind?"

"I have an apartment. Give me your cell. I'll text you the address."

When Nick hung up, Gabriel was in the kitchen doorway. He was wearing sweatpants and an old T-shirt, and his hair stuck up in tufts. "What's going on?"

"Quinn's drunk on the beach and needs someone to pick her up." He glanced at the silent stairwell. "Cover for me, okay?"

"Sure." Gabriel ran a hand through his hair, then rubbed at his eyes. "Let me put some clothes on. I can come with you."

Nick opened his mouth to accept—then reconsidered. Gabriel and Quinn were like oil and vinegar. If she was already in a bad place, adding Gabriel to the mix would just make things worse.

Hell, Gabriel would probably pick a fight on the beach.

And honestly, Nick didn't want him to meet Adam.

What the hell was he thinking? He shook it off.

"No," he said, "I'm just going to run her over to her dance friend's house."

His twin was watching him. "You sure, Nicky?"

"Yeah." His phone chimed. Nick glanced at it.

An unknown number, with an address. Then a second text.

You want me to go with you to get her?

Nick stared at that line a minute longer than he needed to.

Then he glanced up at Gabriel. "Don't worry. Quinn's friend is going to help."

The air in the truck cab stung Nick's cheeks and turned his breath to fog.

He needed to chill the hell out.

Adam was sitting in the passenger seat, his hands over the vents. "Cold tonight."

"Yeah."

"Thanks for driving."

Nick shrugged and found his mouth didn't want to form words. He reached over and kicked up the heat a few more notches.

"Hey," Adam said softly.

Nick almost didn't want to glance over.

But Adam continued. "I didn't mean to make you uncomfortable. Earlier. You know."

Nick wasn't sure what the safe answer to that was. He ran a hand through his hair, feeling it stand up in tufts the way Gabriel's had back in the kitchen.

What had Quinn said? *Identical on the outside, polar opposites on the inside.*

"It's cool." Even his voice sounded strangled.

But Adam took that at face value, turning his head to look out at the night. They drove in complete silence until Nick realized he was going to have to turn on the radio or talk.

Music didn't seem like a good idea.

"Do you think she's all right?" Nick said. "Did that guy seem—"

Adam didn't look away from the window. His voice was resigned. "He said she'd been ranting about some guy named Nick all night, and then she drank half a bottle of tequila and passed out in the sand. He said my number was the first one in her contacts."

Shit.

Adam glanced over. "You two have a fight?"

There was absolutely no way Nick could break it down, right here and now. So he just shrugged noncommittally.

Adam bristled. "Look, if you have a problem with me—"

"I don't." They came to a stop light, and Nick looked at him. The street lights shined through the windshield and caught the caramel highlights in Adam's skin, painting embers in his hair.

Nick rubbed his eyes and looked back at the road. "I don't

have a problem with you at all." He paused. "Quinn and I—we had a misunderstanding. I was trying to help her, but she slammed the door in my face."

"How long have you been seeing each other?"

"Couple weeks."

"I'd ask if it was serious, but I think I already know."

Nick frowned. "What does that mean?"

"If a girl's slamming a door on you two weeks in, it doesn't exactly bode well for the rest of the relationship."

"Yeah, I guess." Nick sighed. Unfortunately, Quinn and drama seemed to go hand in hand.

The cab was starting to warm up. He reached for the controls to dial back the air—at exactly the same time Adam stretched out an arm to do the same thing. Their fingers brushed.

Nick jumped like he'd been stung.

Then he half-wished he'd left his hand there, just to experience the feeling for one millisecond longer. The touch had been light, brief, but long enough that Nick could imagine the softness of Adam's skin, the gentle strength of his fingers.

He had to lock his hands on the steering wheel.

Adam managed to turn the heat down, but he was studying Nick now.

Talk. Say something. Anything.

"How did you and Quinn meet?" Nick said quickly.

"We met when we were kids. In dance class."

"You're really talented."

The words were out before he could stop them. Nick winced. What was he, some teen groupie?

"Thank you." Nick could swear Adam was hiding a smile now. "My parents tried to put me in martial arts, but I hated it. Apparently, I was a hyperactive pain in the ass, so dance seemed like the next best thing."

"Quinn said you're trying to get a scholarship. You think you have a shot?"

Adam shrugged. "Maybe, maybe not. If I miss this time, I'll try again. A little failure never hurt anybody. I know what I want to do with my life."

Nick thought of that envelope smashed between textbooks on his desk. The one he was too afraid to open.

"What about you?" said Adam.

"I'm a senior. I'm throwing some college apps out there, seeing what happens."

"What do your parents think?"

Nick was used to the question, but it still hit him like a punch, every time. He hated having to rehash it for strangers—but at least they were driving and he could keep his eyes on the road. "My parents died when I was twelve," he said. "I live with my three brothers."

Adam was silent for a moment. "I'm sorry."

"It's fine. Really."

Another moment of silence, until Nick was sure Adam was going to press for more information.

But then he didn't. "So—what do your *brothers* think?"

Nick snorted. "Mixed bag." He glanced over when they came to a traffic light, and it was a mistake. Because the windows were dark and the cab was warming up, and he wanted to keep on looking.

He quickly jerked his eyes back to the road ahead and focused on talking. "My older brother says he's all for it—but I don't know if that's true or not. He runs my parents' landscaping company . . . well, you saw the side of the truck. We all help him, but even still, he barely has time to eat. Losing one of us . . ." Nick just shrugged and didn't complete the thought.

"What about your other brothers?"

"What's with the twenty questions?"

Adam looked out the window. "I thought we were having a conversation."

Yeah—if a conversation was like stumbling along a dark hallway, wondering what your hands would find if you reached out.

Then again, they weren't talking about anything serious. He'd had more personal discussions with the cafeteria ladies.

Nick flexed his fingers on the steering wheel again and wished he'd brought Gabriel along instead.

No. He didn't.

"I'm not going to jump you, if that's what you're worried about," Adam said, a shred of humor in his voice—but a shred of sadness hid there, too. "I promise, I have some self-control."

"I'm not worried about it."

"You look like a strong guy. You could probably fight me off."

Nick cut him a withering glance, but his brain was all too willing to suggest images of what Adam was suggesting.

Stop it, stop it, stop it.

If the thought of college was enough to drive a wedge between him and his brothers, thoughts like these would hammer it home. He'd been fighting with this for *years*, and here one drive in the truck was about to undo him.

Nick drew a ragged breath. He wished for some traffic or something to steal his attention, but the highway was mostly deserted this late at night. He wished for different thoughts. Silence swelled in the cab of the truck again, taunting Nick to look at his passenger.

He didn't. But he had to talk or he was going to make himself crazy. So he picked up the earlier conversations. "I think my younger brother—Chris—is waiting to see what happens if I leave. He might be thinking about college, too, but he won't say anything until he's sure about it."

"The cautious type."

Nick smiled. "Gabriel and I call him the brooding type."

"Gabriel. Number three?"

That killed the smile. "Yeah. My twin brother. He says he doesn't care if I go away to school, but I know he does."

"Identical twin?"

"Yeah."

"Niiiiice."

Nick cut him another look, and Adam smiled. "Sorry."

A street sign announced the park entrance, and Nick hit the turn signal. The gates were closed and padlocked, so he parked on the side of the road. He'd been here before with his brothers, dozens of times. He could find the path to the beach blindfolded. Good thing, too, since there were no lights overhead.

Wind was coming in from the water, just this side of too cold. Nick didn't mind the sharpness against his cheeks, knowing his element would steal the warmth left over from his conversation with Adam. He asked the air for information, trying to determine if there was any sense of danger here.

But the wind only seemed willing to carry the scents of the night: the richness of the pine trees lining the road, the heavy scent of the distant sea, and whatever cologne Adam was wearing, something musky and warm, like oranges and cloves. Somehow it was stronger out here than it had been in the truck, and once his brain identified it, Nick wanted to get closer, to bask in the scent and bury his face in it.

No girl had ever affected him this strongly.

No guy had, either, but this was the first time he'd been alone with a boy he felt attracted to, and it was like his senses were trying to latch on to the opportunity.

A boy who thought Nick felt threatened by his presence.

Nick wondered what would have happened if he'd lost the defensive looks in the truck. If he'd sat in the cab for two minutes. If he'd—

Quinn, he thought. *Focus on Quinn.*

Right. His girlfriend. Who needed rescuing—both from boys and herself, apparently.

She wasn't far. The wind brought him the scent of a campfire, and he followed that. Adam followed him, silent but very present.

And there was Quinn, passed out on a fleece blanket between two guys. She was still fully clothed, but tension hovered in the air, making Nick pause to size up the situation. Big guys. Drunk guys who stopped laughing when they caught sight of Nick and Adam.

Now Nick regretted not bringing Gabriel.

Wuss.

"Thanks for the call," said Adam, his voice easy, as if they hadn't walked into a tense situation. "We can take Quinn home."

The one guy, the darker haired one, sneered. "We didn't call for a couple of fags."

Nick froze. It wasn't like he hadn't heard the word around school—usually as a joke in the locker room—but it hit him very differently when it was directed at him. When he'd been walking along having . . . *thoughts.*

Adam didn't hesitate, he just walked over and started picking Quinn up. "I'm sure Quinn didn't, either, but apparently you two showed up."

Both men were on their feet. The dark-haired one went after Adam.

Nick was quick. He caught the guy's arm, but he didn't fight him. "Hey." Wind whipped around him, responding to his emotion. But he was used to placating his twin, and he kept his voice easy. "Chill out. We're just here to take her home."

The guy swung around and punched him in the face.

Nick hit the sand before he realized he was falling.

Damn, it hurt. It hurt about a bazillion times more than when Quinn had done the same thing. He hadn't even been *expecting* it. At least when he tried to stop his twin from fighting, Gabriel listened.

Nick found his footing in the sand. Now he was *pissed,* and the air enjoyed that, pulling sand into tiny tornadoes at his feet. The wind turned ice cold, coming off the water like it was blowing from a glacier.

The other guy, the one with lighter hair, had grabbed his friend. Adam had Quinn, and he looked like he was wrestling with whether to put her down and help. He'd moved back, toward their motorcycles and the tree line.

"Go," Nick said to him. "Get her to the truck."

Adam glanced between him and the guys on the beach. "I'm not sure that's the best idea."

Nick wasn't sure, either. He wasn't a fighter, not really. And what was he going to do? Suffocate them? Freeze them to death? Blast them with sand?

"It's all right," said the light-haired guy. He still had a death grip on his friend, but his words had a hint of slur. "Take her home. I just wanted to make sure she was okay."

"Yeah," said Nick. "Looks like it." But he glanced at Adam

and took a step toward the trail. Adam met his eyes, and they shared a moment of silent agreement.

Adam didn't want to fight, either.

And that was refreshing.

The dark-haired guy swore. "I'm going to kill those—"

"Run," said Nick.

Adam ran. Nick was right behind him.

And then they were tearing through the darkness, leaping into the truck.

And then they were gone.

CHAPTER 5

Nick had to fight to keep the truck near the speed limit. He kept checking the rearview mirror, looking for motorcycles or any sign of danger.

"They can't follow us," Adam said. "At least, I don't think they can."

Nick didn't look away from the road. Quinn was a heavy weight against him, buckled into the middle bench seat. He had a pretty good sense that she was drooling on his shoulder.

"How do you know?"

"I disabled their bikes. Maybe."

Nick looked over. "How did you do that?"

Adam shrugged, and it looked like he was trying to hide a smile. "Yanked some wires. I don't know."

Nick smiled. "Smart."

Adam snorted, and his voice turned a bit self-deprecating. "Yeah, not too bad for a 'couple of fags,' huh?" Before Nick could say anything to that, Adam looked over again. "Sorry to drag you into that. The guy sounded okay on the phone."

"I'm just glad Quinn wasn't hurt." Though she smelled like a frigging distillery.

"Are *you* okay?"

Nick shrugged. He could already feel swelling starting on his jaw, and blood was a bitter taste on the side of his tongue. "It's not the first time I've been hit, and it probably won't be the last. I'll be all right." Gabriel would probably shit a brick when he got home, though.

"He was going to hit *me*," said Adam, and there was something like wonder in his voice.

"I'm happy to hit you if you feel like you're missing out on the full experience."

"No, just—" Adam hesitated. "Thanks."

Nick shrugged again, uncomfortable. He wasn't used to being the *rescuer*. "I wasn't trying to fight him. I thought I could talk him down."

"Still. No one's ever done that for me."

Nick didn't know what to say to that. Then Adam's cell phone chimed, and that was enough to distract him from the conversation.

"Wow," said Adam. "It's from that guy on the beach. He said he's sorry his friend got out of control."

"I'm surprised he's not begging us not to press charges."

Adam looked at him. Nick could feel the weight of his eyes in the darkness. "Do you want to?"

Nick shook his head. The last thing he needed to do was draw attention to his family. To say nothing of dragging Quinn into it. She had enough problems.

Adam's cell phone chimed again, and he read off the screen. "He says he has a little sister, and he took care of her, so he wanted to look after Quinn. He says neither of them hurt her." A pause, another chime, and Adam guffawed. "He asked if we'd give her his number."

Nick snorted. "I'm surprised he can text coherently, as hammered as they were."

"I think there's a fair bit of autocorrect going on. Every time he tries to say her name, it says Quinine."

Nick laughed outright at that.

But then he sobered when he glanced over and found Adam staring at him.

Nick knew that look. It was how girls sometimes looked at him, with cartoon hearts practically exploding from their eyes.

It was unnerving.

With girls, he could smile back. Flirt. A glance here, a touch there, a teasing word. It cost him nothing, and it was what everyone *expected*.

Right now, it left him breathless and uncertain. Because what everyone *expected* was in direct contradiction with what he *wanted*.

He locked his hands on the steering wheel and his eyes on the road. "You'll have to tell me where you live again."

Adam must have noticed the sharpness in his voice, because he gave the return directions flatly, reciting his address by rote. The hearts were gone from his eyes, and he was studying the windshield with almost as much focus as Nick.

Nick didn't like that.

He dulled the edge in his tone. "You sure you don't mind her sleeping it off at your place?"

"Nah," said Adam quietly. "It's nothing."

Adam lived in a basement apartment at one of the aging brick complexes on the edge of Annapolis. The apartment was small, practically an efficiency. One bedroom, one bathroom, and a kitchen–living room–dining room combo. All beige carpet, white walls with dark photography prints everywhere, and minimal furniture. A tiny two-seater kitchen table was tucked into the corner by the oven, and there was a couch and an end table, but no television. Just piles of books everywhere. Cluttered, but neat and orderly.

The air was peaceful here, and Nick took a long breath for what felt like the first time all evening.

"You can put her on the bed," Adam whispered, though they'd been speaking normally in the car and she hadn't stirred.

Nick shouldered through the doorway and eased Quinn onto the bed, pulling a black and blue–checked quilt over her sleeping form. Her breathing still felt regular, and the air whispered nothing of danger, so he felt pretty sure she was fine.

Then he straightened and realized he was in Adam's room. Alone.

It felt quiet and intimate and smelled like oranges and cloves, and Nick didn't want to leave.

But what was he going to do? Sit here?

God, he felt so selfish. Quinn was lying here, practically unconscious. He should have just taken her to his house initially.

But then Adam wouldn't have called.

He reached for the normal mental barriers to tell himself to shut up, but here, in someone else's space, it was a lot harder to lie to himself.

He needed to leave.

Adam stuck his head through the doorway. "I started some coffee. How do you take it?"

This would be the perfect opportunity to decline, to get out and go home.

"Just cream," he said.

When he was sitting at the little table in the kitchen, his hands wrapped around a mug, he fought for something to say.

But all he could think about was the way Adam's hands had poured cream into the mugs, or the graceful way he moved about the kitchen, or the shape of his mouth or the brown of his eyes or the—

Adam sat down and Nick jerked his eyes back to his mug. He took a quick gulp.

"How's the coffee?" Adam's voice was amused. And close.

This table was too damn small.

"It's great. Thanks." Nick still couldn't look at him. His cheeks felt warm, and he hoped that was just the steam from the coffee. He doubted it.

Adam was silent for a long minute. A weighted minute.

Then he said, his voice completely sober, "When I was seventeen, Quinn told me she had a crush on me. I told her I had a crush on the starting center of the football team. A few days later, someone slammed my face into the corner of my locker. I never saw who did it. But he broke my nose and two teeth. I had to have reconstructive surgery. I didn't go back to school."

Nick was looking at him now. "Holy shit."

Adam shrugged. "It wasn't that long ago. I'm surprised you didn't hear about it."

Nick frowned. "I think—I think I did. I remember something . . ." He shook his head. It was one of those high school dramas, the complete focus of hallway gossip for like five minutes, then gone.

Unless you were the center of the drama, like Adam.

Nick wasn't entirely sure what to say. That he understood? He'd gotten in enough fights because of being an Elemental that he could relate—but saying so didn't seem right.

He had to clear his throat. "I'm surprised you provoked those guys on the beach."

Adam shrugged. "I'm not going to live in fear because of who I am. If that idiot who hit me thought he could scare me straight, it didn't work."

The words made Nick's throat swell. He had to look back at his mug. It hammered home his exact position. Being an Elemental, struggling to find his place among his brothers, hiding who he was with Quinn and every other girl. Funny how the first place he'd found some shred of peace was in a stranger's apartment, drinking coffee while his girlfriend slept off a bender.

"You're going to have one hell of a bruise," Adam said.

"Yeah, well."

Adam touched his face, and Nick froze. His fingers were warm, gentle, and Nick wanted to freeze *time*.

Then Adam said, "I'm an idiot. I should have gotten you some ice."

And his fingers were gone, and Nick was sitting there practically breathless with wanting him back.

One touch, and he was going to pieces. He wanted to slam his forehead on the table.

Adam came back with ice wrapped in a towel, and Nick was so scattered that he almost said that water was Chris's thing, and it would probably help more to just leave it uncovered.

But then the towel was against his bruised cheek, and Adam's other hand was on his neck to stabilize it, and even though Nick knew he should be taking over the holding of the towel, he didn't want to move for fear of disrupting this moment.

It was nothing short of a miracle that the heat off his face wasn't instantly melting all the ice.

Adam's thumb tapped against his neck. "Your heart is racing."

No kidding.

Nick turned his head away and took the ice-filled towel. He set it on the table and had to look into his coffee mug again.

"Sorry," said Adam. "I know there's no point in pushing your buttons. You're just adorable when you blush like that." Then he was grinning. "Or like that."

"Yeah, this is fantastic." Even his voice was gravelly and uncertain.

Adam picked up the towel and held it out. "I'll stop. You hold the—"

Nick shifted forward and kissed him.

He hadn't given it a moment's consideration—and if he had, he probably wouldn't have done it at all. But now he couldn't imagine stopping.

Kissing a girl was nothing like this. The basic mechanics, sure. But kissing Adam, there was a strength behind it, a raw masculinity despite his lyrical movement and gentle fingers. Nick was distantly aware of the ice hitting the floor.

Then Adam was kissing him back, drawing at Nick's tongue with his own. He had a hand behind Nick's neck, stroking the hair there, and Nick wished he could freeze this exact moment.

Oh, and the next moment, when Adam bit at Nick's lip.

And the moment after that, when Nick stroked a hand up Adam's neck, finding the first start of stubble across his jaw.

It was like every thought he'd ever blocked, every fantasy he'd ever refused to acknowledge, was blasting through his brain all at once with the force of a hurricane. Everything he knew was with a girl. Like reciting a learned lesson, something he could do because he had to.

This—this was new. And exciting. And primal and raw and *right*.

And insanely hot. He wished there weren't so many damn clothes in the way.

They were going to be on the floor in a minute.

"Easy. Easy," said Adam.

Nick felt like he was coming up for air.

Hell, he was practically *panting*.

He looked into Adam's brown eyes, which were just now searching his.

"Well," said Adam, a slight smile on his lips. "That was unexpected."

Unexpected. Somehow the best and worst word to use. All of a sudden, the emotion of the evening caught up with him, and Nick felt the inexplicable urge to put his head on Adam's shoulder and cry.

But then a girl cleared her throat from behind him.

"You can say that again," said Quinn.

CHAPTER 6

Quinn wondered just how many times life was going to jerk her around today.

She'd have to storm past Nick and Adam to get to the front door, but a sliding glass door led out of the living room. An alcoholic buzz still made her thoughts swim, but she managed to get the lock thrown. She stumbled onto the tiny concrete patio. Cold air bit at her cheeks before Nick caught up to her.

"Stop," he said. "Quinn, stop, please—"

She swung around and hit him. Rage-filled strikes that slammed into his chest and made her head ache and vision whirl.

She was vaguely aware she was crying, and she had no idea how many times she hit him before he caught her arms and forced her still.

Quinn looked up at him. Her body felt like she was still moving. The stars spun overhead. Her stomach rolled.

"Quinn," he whispered.

"Nick," she said back.

And then she threw up on his feet.

He deserved it, but that didn't make it any less humiliating. She expected him to shove her away in disgust, or to drop her there in her own puke, because she could barely hold herself upright.

But he kicked off his shoes and picked her up.

"I want you to leave me alone," she said, even as her head lolled onto his shoulder against her will.

"No offense," he said as he carried her back into the apartment, "but I'm pretty sure you're as screwed up about *what you want* as I am."

He cleaned her up and put her back in Adam's bed. Then he wrapped the quilt around her and lay down beside her.

Adam brought her Tylenol and a glass of water, then left them alone.

Quinn stared through the darkness at the ceiling. It wasn't spinning now. Every breath seemed to clear her head.

Stupid tears were still leaking out of her eyes, and she angrily swiped them away.

"I'm sorry," said Nick.

"So you're gay?"

He was silent for a moment, and his voice was careful. "I don't know."

"No offense," she said, mocking his earlier tone, "but I'm pretty sure that's the kind of thing you'd *know* by now."

He rolled up on one shoulder to look down at her—but he didn't say anything.

And then she recognized the uncertainty in his eyes, the mixture of worry and fear and panic and need. She struggled with acceptance every day—she'd never considered that someone like Nick Merrick would be struggling with the same thing. He'd seemed like such a *rock*, such a steady, put-together guy, and she'd latched on to him, hoping to find some security.

He was really just as screwed up as she was.

That chased the anger away. "Do your brothers know?" she said quietly.

"I don't know if there's anything to *know*, Quinn."

Well, that sounded like a heaping load of self-denial. She didn't look away from him and chose her words carefully. "Do they have any idea you might have entertained the thought of kissing another boy?"

His voice was resigned. "No."

"Not even Gabriel?"

"No. Jesus, *no*."

She stretched her hand out from under the blanket and found his. "It's okay," she said. "I won't tell anyone."

He rolled back to stare at the same ceiling, but he kept hold of her hand. "I should have just taken you back to my house tonight."

"No, I'm glad this happened." Then she winced. "I mean, not the puking part. But I thought you were just stringing me along."

"Quinn." He squeezed her hand. "I kind of *was*."

She moved closer and put her head on his shoulder. "But now I understand why."

Nick sighed, but he didn't say anything.

"I should have known you were too good to be true," she said.

"What does that mean?"

"It means my luck sucks," she said. "It was nice dating a guy who treated me like a friend instead of a blow-up doll."

"You were the one trying to unzip my pants in the truck!"

"Yeah, well, I thought you weren't interested. I didn't realize that your divining rod just pointed in a different direction."

"You're killing me," he said. But it sounded like he was smiling.

Quinn sighed. "So I'm back on the market. You should have left me on the beach with those guys."

His voice sharpened right up. "Quinn, that was insane. You know that, right? After what happened with Becca—you can't— you just—"

"I had nowhere to go!" she cried. "My mother threw me out again—"

"Next time, call me. Or Becca. This was *crazy*. Anything could have happened."

"Becca was with Chris. And you—you weren't—"

"I wasn't what?" He pushed her off him so he could look down at her. His voice was fierce. "I wasn't your friend? I wasn't concerned? Jesus, Quinn, just because I don't want to sleep with you doesn't mean I don't *care* about you."

She stared at him. No one had ever lectured her like that.

She kind of liked it.

Nick ran a hand through his hair. "God, you're crazy. Do you think people will only like you because you put out?"

"I don't just *think* that," she snapped. "It's true."

"It's not," he said softly. "I promise you. It's not." He paused. "You said it was nice dating a guy who was a friend. Why don't you slow down a bit and take a break from all the . . . ah, *extracurriculars?*"

Quinn smiled. "You and your vocabulary."

"I'm serious," he said. "Why don't you put all that passion into your dancing?"

"So you want me to hump Adam on stage? I'm not sure that's the kind of audition he's looking for."

"Quinn."

She squeezed her eyes shut. She was losing Becca to Chris. It was okay, and she *got* it, but now she was going to lose Nick, too. It was almost enough to force tears between her lashes again.

She opened her eyes and looked down at him. Her voice was choked. "Could we keep dating?" When Nick frowned, she rushed on. "Not like for reals. Just—just for a little while?"

"Why?"

Because she didn't trust herself not to jump on another motorcycle the next time her mom was a raging bitch or a cheerleader called her fat or there wasn't any chocolate in the house. Because Nick was still someone steady to lean on, someone who wouldn't use her. Somehow this revelation made him safer, and for the first time, she wanted to cling to a boy especially because he *didn't* want to put his Tab A into her Slot B.

Not like she could say that. "It would help you, right? Keep a secret?" When he didn't say anything, she studied his eyes. "Or . . . are you going to come out . . . ?"

He sat up quickly and rubbed at his face. "No. *No.* I don't know."

She spoke carefully. "It would buy us both some time."

His hands dropped. "So . . . a secret. Why would you do that for me?"

Quinn hugged him and spoke into his shoulder. "Because you're *my* friend, too." She paused, and a smile found its way into her voice. "You know, if I'm dancing with Adam, my *boyfriend* would have to come along to a lot of my rehearsals."

He laughed again, more softly this time. But then he hesitated. "Do you really think I could?"

Nick finally climbed into bed at five in the morning. He was going to be a zombie on those landscaping jobs today.

Quinn was safely asleep at Becca's, with a stern warning to call him if she felt any need to go anywhere else.

And Adam . . .

"Hey. You're up. Everything okay with Quinn?"

Nick jumped a mile. He was lucky he didn't pee his pants. Gabriel was there in the doorway, wearing running shoes and a hoody.

"Yeah," Nick said. "Long night."

"Anything interesting happen?"

Ha.

For a heartbeat of time, Nick considered telling him everything. Then he shook his head. "Nah," he said. "I'm going back to sleep for a few hours."

"Sure you don't want to go for a run?"

Maybe Gabriel sensed the energy in the room, because Nick was actually considering it. Being out in the crisp air, letting oxygen fill his lungs and charge him with power.

But then he thought of those jobs later this morning.

He thought of the secrets he was keeping from his twin.

He thought of that envelope on his desk, with the letter he didn't want to open. Or that kiss, when he'd been swept into the maelstrom of emotion and touch and tongues and—

His phone buzzed on the nightstand, and Nick glanced at the lit-up display. His heart skipped a beat when he recognized Adam's number.

Then he realized Gabriel was still waiting.

"Not today," Nick said. "You go on without me."

When his brother was gone, Nick unlocked the screen to read Adam's message.

When you're sure of what you want, I'll be right here.